THE CONTAINED

BOOK 2 OF THE NECROPOLIS TRILOGY

SEAN DEVILLE

SEVERED PRESS

THE CONTAINED

WWW.SEVEREDPRESS.COM

ISBN: 978-1-925597-33-2

"They're coming to get you, Barbara"
– Johnny, *Night of the Living Dead*

Important Characters

British Government

Arnold Craver – Head of the Centre for the Protection of National Infrastructure (MI5)
Bill Dodson – Prime Minister's Private Secretary
'Davina' – Interrogator MI6
Sir Nicholas Marston – Chief of the Defence Staff
Sir Michael Young – Head of MI5
Sir Stuart Watkins – Head of MI6
Snow – MI6 Agent

British Military

Arthur Mansfield (General) – Commander, Operation Hadrian
Bull (Sergeant) – Royal Marines
Craig O'Sullivan (Sergeant) – SAS
David Croft (Major) – Investigating Officer for the Centre for the Protection of National Infrastructure
Lewis Hudson (Captain) – SAS
Lucy Savage (Captain) – Head of Biomedical Science, Porton Down Research Centre
Mark Grainger (Captain) – Grenadier Guards
Vorne (Sergeant) – Grenadier Guards

US Government/Law enforcement

Ben Silver – White House Chief of Staff
Damian Rodney – President of the United States
Fiona Carter – SAC FBI
General Roberts – Head of the Joint Chiefs of Staff
Jason Tucker – Head of FBI
Keith Johnson – CIA Director
Madeleine Cozens – Head of Homeland Security
Mitch Carter – FBI SWAT
Philip Bradstone (General) – NATO Supreme Allied Commander Europe
Wynona Cooke – Assistant Director FBI

The Sons of the Resurrection Cult

James Jones – The Chief Cleric
Abraham (Conrad Schmidt) – Cult Leader
Fabrice Chevalier – Warrior of Truth

Civilians

Alexei – Russian Mob
Brian – Police Officer
Gavin Hemsworth
Jack Nathan
Owen Patterson
Rachel – Undead
Rasheed Khan
Simone Holden
Stan – Police Officer
Victor Durand – Scientist

The Washin

Friday, September 18th, 2015

Great Britain Quarantined

The world woke up this morning, still reeling from the horrific events of two days ago, when the world watched a once proud and great country brought to its knees by what is now believed to have been a Bio-weapon terrorist attack. News is coming out that a religious death cult is being held responsible for the outbreak that saw Great Britain quarantined and abandoned. The YouTube video presently circulating across the internet that claims to be from the perpetrators of the attack has still not been verified by the authorities. With over a billion views to date, its claims have left the worlds governments in turmoil. Although multiple government sources will neither confirm or deny this, rumors continue to circulate across the internet that the cult released a pathogen that resulted in an outbreak that has resulted in mans worst nightmare coming true. Zombies, it now seems, are real. Millions are now believed dead, and the United Nations Security Council are still in emergency session.

Rer
foll
imp

The
that
rela
the
beh
of a
exp
in I
its
beh
con
or v

It n
tota
thir
dec

TOP SECRET

THIS IS A COVER SHEET

FOR CLASSIFIED INFORMATION

ALL INDIVIDUALS HANDLING THIS INFORMATION ARE REQUIRED TO PROTECT IT FROM UNAUTHORISED DISCLOSURE IN THE INTEREST OF NATIONAL SECURITY OF THE UNITED STATES.

HANDLING, STORAGE, REPRODUCTION, AND DISPOSITION OF THE ATTACHED DOCUMENT WILL BE IN ACCORDANCE WITH APPLICABLE EXECUTIVE ORDER(S), STATUTE(S) AND AGENCY IMPLEMENTING REGULATIONS.

UNLAWFUL VIEWING, REPRODUCTION, OR TRANSPORT IS A FEDERAL OFFENCE UNDER 18 U.S. Code § 798 AND CARRIES A TERM OF A MINIMUM OF LIFE IMPRISONMENT.

(This cover sheet is unclassified)

TOP SECRET

703-101
NSN 75690-01-21207904

NSN 75690-01-21207904

The Office of The Secretary of Defence

A confidential report to the President of the United States

11.17.2015
To: The President of the United States of America
From: Carl McGruber, Secretary of Defence

Mr. President,

Through liaison with the Director of the CIA and the Joint Chiefs of Staff, we have collated the information regarding the events in the United Kingdom and have concluded that the terrorist threat to this country is real. It is our recommendation that we take no action at this time to suppress the biological threat on the UK mainland, and instead concentrate on finding the culprits and countering the potential threat that we believe our country now faces.

Our present understanding of how the contagion works is this. Although initially spread through contaminated milk in coffee shops, the pathogen is now spread by bites and by direct exposure to bodily fluids. From analysis of the information forwarded to us by the remnants of the UK Government and MI6, who are still holding out in their London headquarters, we know that someone exposed to the virus, even via skin contact, will turn within, on average, ten minutes. They will then become violent, with immense strength and stamina, similar to someone on PCP. They will be immune to most painful stimuli and can sustain injuries that would kill most humans. If they are killed by anything other than brain trauma, they will resurrect as—what you will know from popular horror fiction—the undead. Of the samples captured by MI6 agents on the ground, we have been told that the undead display no vital functions. They have no heartbeat, no blood pressure, and show only the faintest of brain readings on MRI or EEG. Although dead, the isolated virus seems to kill all other pathogens in the body, slowing decomposition considerably. The reanimated can move although they cannot perform fine motor functions. It is understood that they can, however, climb and open doors. It has been shown that they can ultimately only be stopped by destroying the brain stem. This explains why the UK forces had such difficulty killing anyone infected.

The NSA were able to salvage much of the data from their UK counterparts at GCHQ upon the facility's evacuation. That combined with the MI6 interrogation of the captured terrorists has led us to believe that, whilst the laboratory used to make the virus was on the UK mainland and the chief scientist behind the virus was still at that lab on its destruction, the main perpetrator of this atrocity is still at large. We have as yet no knowledge of how the lab was funded or whether further samples of the virus have been smuggled out of the country. We have been advised that we will be kept appraised of any developments brought forth from the data seized at the laboratory, but we have not, as of yet, been given access to it. Due to the biological hazard presented by this contagion, the Joint Chiefs rejected the initial proposal to send our own Special Forces to aid the operation to seize the laboratory.

Regarding the threat made via the hacked National Emergency Broadcast Network, that was later uploaded to YouTube. Despite our attempts to suppress it, the video has reached almost one and a half billion views. The original upload was done through a host of proxy servers, and it is impossible to determine even which country it originated in, never mind who created the video. We believe, however, the video is authentic, and that the threat posed to our nation is possibly the worst since the Cuban Missile Crisis. We advise that all Federal and State law enforcement agencies be put on high alert and that operation Clean Sweep be implemented immediately. We have confirmation from the Justice Department that Clean Sweep is legal under executive order and that FEMA can have the detention camps ready for detainees by the end of the day. The first stage of Clean Sweep should see half a million radicals, terrorist suspects, and undesirables taken off the streets within 48 hours. The NSA will begin blocking alternative media sites, and the main news broadcasters and print news have confirmed they will push the narrative we give them. All it requires is your approval, Mr. President.

Regarding the quarantine of the UK mainland, this is now complete. There is a twenty-five-mile naval exclusion zone, and all civilian air traffic is banned from going anywhere near the UK in a one-hundred-mile radius. NATO assets will still be able to do aerial operations within the exclusion zone. This has obviously impacted European air travel, but no country has yet objected. Any vessel or aircraft trying to breach this quarantine will receive one warning, before being either shot down or sunk. We have confirmation from NATO and the Russian Republic that they will aid in this quarantine. The Russians have assured us that they will not use this crisis to further their territorial demands, but we have seen evidence that they are moving troops to their borders. The official line on this from the Kremlin is that they are securing their borders, which at this time is deemed to be an acceptable explanation. The only other fear at present is if infected individuals try and swim the UK channel, or if reanimated corpses fall into the ocean and get swept away.

We will brief you further as and when developments arise. We do not at this stage recommend declaring martial law, and do not advise suspending the Constitution at this time. However, that may well be a necessity in the future.

Carl McGruber,
Secretary of Defence

COSMIC TOP SECRET

Supreme Headquarters Allied Powers Europe

Confidential Report Regarding the Quarantine of the UK mainland

(This cover sheet is classified)

17.11.2015

Progress report on Operation Hadrian

Ref AC/324- D(2016)0007
To: General Philip Bradstone, Supreme Allied Commander Europe
(SACEUR)

General Bradstone,

As you are aware, the evacuation of military assets from the UK
mainland has been of limited success. Whilst many of the active front
line troops and assets have been retrieved, much of the administration
and logistical support could not be salvaged in time. The unquarantined
assets available to NATO are outlined in Appendix A. As you can see,
the majority of the Royal Navy's surface fleet has been salvaged, as well
as around 70% of RAF aircraft. However, much of the British Army's
heavy equipment could not be removed from the mainland in time, and
over 50,000 front line troops from the Army, Marines, and Parachute
Regiment were left behind.

It was decided early on to abandon attempts to contain the virus, as the
contagion was too widely dispersed and too virulent to have any chance
of stopping its spread. Upon assuming command of all military and
civilian forces on the assassination of the Prime Minister and much of
his cabinet, I made the decision to abandon the areas of infection, and
those assets I could not evacuate to Ireland have been ordered moved to
Cornwall, which so far seems to have been spared from the infection.
The town of Newquay will be our centre of operations for Operation
Hadrian. Cornwall will be where we will have our designated safe zone.
Martial law has been implemented, and civilians are being conscripted
into work details based on specific skill sets. There is a heavy flow of
refugees into the area, and these people will be allocated to the work
zones after medical checks. At some point, however, we will have to
deploy military assets to turn further refugees away so we can start
bridge demolition and set up the defensive kill zone. This is regrettable,
but it is essential we maintain a foothold on the island. Consideration
may have to be taken on reducing the threat of the infected by heavy
carpet bombing of the areas approaching this safe zone. This will
regrettably see the deaths of thousands, but better that than see them
converted into the undead army.

We estimate we have three days before the first of the infected arrive. Satellite imagery shows the bulk of the infected are still in the major cities, although they are spreading rapidly. We cannot abandon the island completely; we must at least try and attempt to salvage something, even if just to give those left behind some semblance of hope. General Arthur Mansfield, who lost his immediate family in the Birmingham outbreak, has volunteered to command the air and ground forces. Under his guidance, construction has already begun on the defensive walls around the new safe zones. The plan is to construct the walls with the associated fire zones from Padstow in the north to the town of Par in the south. This is a twenty-one-mile-long stretch of land, and there is no guarantee we will achieve this task, but we are fortunate that there are four regiments of the Royal Engineers Corps that were airlifted to the area. This followed the assessment of the virus by Captain Savage (Head of Biomedical Science, Porton Down Research Centre) and Major David Croft (Investigating Officer for the Centre for the Protection of National Infrastructure) during the initial outbreak.

I have two pressing concerns regarding the safety of mainland Europe and Ireland. Firstly, we saw first-hand in London that the infected can swim, and I know you are coordinating with the countries on the southern aspect of the English Channel to secure their coastlines. My second concern is the nuclear power stations. We need to prepare for the inevitability that at least one of these will go into meltdown. It is hoped that their remote location will mean the bulk of the infected will stay away from them, choosing instead to concentrate on the population centres. That being said, we have taken steps to fortify these facilities as best we can, in the hope that they can be somehow decommissioned. It is, however, a problem that is not going to go away, and will present challenges for years to come.

Regards,

General Nicholas Marston
Chief of the UK Defence Staff and Commander of remaining UK forces

THE CONTAINED

17.31PM, 16th September 2015, The London Eye, London, UK

Rachel. She had been called Rachel. The memory was fleeting, like mist on the wind, and then it was gone, the ghosts of the last synapses as they finally died. All she was now was primeval hunger, a hunger for something that would never satiate her, never satisfy the burning that churned within her core. The hunger for human flesh that she could never digest, and within hours, would probably not even be able to swallow. But the hunger was there, and it would not be denied. It roared at her, consumed her. She lifted her head up and sniffed the air, the smell of burning still strong. But even with the buildings around her still aflame from the napalm strikes, she could almost taste her prey on the wind, and her mouth salivated. Flesh, juicy, soft human flesh. She wanted it, she craved it, and she let out a low moan of what could have once been desperation. The smell of humanity was all around her, and she turned slowly, her balance unsteady from the damage that had been inflicted inside her by the virus and by the ravages of humanity's assault.

She was dead, and yet she wasn't. If doctors had connected her up to their machines, all they would find would be a slight spark in the brain stem. Everything else was dead. Her heart no longer beat its life-giving rhythm. Her lungs no longer yearned for the air—and that was probably for the best because they were presently filled with water from when the explosion had flung her body into the Thames. Her kidneys no longer filtered the blood, because no blood was sent to them. And yet despite all that, she moved. She moved and she craved.

She saw the motion with her one remaining good eye and lurched drunkenly towards it. Not human, infected. They were too fast for her, scuttling away, aware of the danger she represented to them, quick enough to avoid her grasp. She was beyond the new species now, no longer linked to their hive mind. Occasionally, words would float through her liquefying brain, but they meant nothing to her; just sounds, their meaning lost. The infected were now just something else for her to eat, but first, she had to catch them. Deep down, they knew to avoid her, knew to avoid all her kind, even as their numbers slowly swelled. Rachel had died, her right arm being blown clean off, her abdomen pierced by steel rebar. Her face was now a mass of scars and burns, and she was a moving, broken specimen. But still she walked, for nothing meant more than the call of the flesh. To feel its texture between her teeth, to feel it and taste it as she swallowed, only to instantly need to consume more. That was now all she was.

Then she smelt something else. She looked behind her, almost falling as she turned. Approaching her was another lumbering monstrosity. No limbs missing, but half the scalp gone and the suit burnt and charred to mere rags. They looked at each other briefly, recognition that they were the same registering somewhere in their diseased, dead minds. Awkwardly, they moved together, drawn by some invisible force. Close now, they could smell each other, could feel the connection, the need to stay together, to find more of their kind. To join, to hunt, to feed, to consume. To kill. And kill and kill.

17.42PM, 16th September 2015, Watford Islamic Mosque, Watford, UK

Asr was over, the prayers finished, but many of the true faithful stayed in what they saw as the safety of the mosque. They had all seen the news, and many worshippers had stayed away, either in their homes or fleeing to the illusion of safety. But dozens had still come and Dr. Mohammad Khan circulated amongst them, offering reassurance that their fates were always down to the will of Allah, and that Allah was just and protected those who believed. Some, he was able to reassure; most looked at him with helplessness and despair. Many of the women huddled together, their children clinging to them, eyes full of the terror for what they had seen on their news hours before. The men tried to comfort them, but their hearts were just as heavy, despair and anguish filling the building like thick smoke. Hell was coming, and there was nothing anybody could do about it. Despite his best efforts, Dr. Khan knew his words did little to help. Heck, half of what he was saying he didn't believe himself.

The mosque doors were locked and the windows were secure, and he was sure that this was as safe a place as any for the faithful. He himself had overseen its fortification last year, ever since the day some apparent white supremacist maniac had smashed all the windows and desecrated the insides by hurling in rinds of uncooked bacon and defecating in the middle of the floor. The police had known who the culprit was, but the lack of proof had prevented any meaningful action. Now, the windows were grilled, and the doors reinforced with steel. It would take a sustained effort to breach this holy inner sanctum. But that moment wasn't here yet. They still had time, time to prepare, time for others to join them in their refuge.

There was a banging on the main door. This he had been expecting, and Mohammad opened it to allow his son to enter. As Imam of the mosque, it was his duty to look after those who came asking for shelter, and his son often helped. Although lately, that help had occurred less and less, his son distracted by other things. He was helping now though, perhaps more than he ever had in his twenty-year history, because what his son now did carried incredible risk.

"I have the supplies, Father," Rasheed said. He had four bags laden with food in his hands, and the two men with him were carrying more supplies up from the large white transit van parked on the street. Rasheed looked stressed, his cheeks flushed.

"You have done well, son," Mohammed said. Rasheed had volunteered to go out for essentials, and this was his third run, the supplies acquired from the nearby Wholesale warehouse. The place had been locked up tight, but there were no guards there now, and the fact that Rasheed had worked there meant he had the key. With the building empty, Rasheed could come and go as he pleased, at least initially. Mohammed noticed blood above his son's right eye and grabbed his head, examining the wound with concerned eyes. Rasheed squirmed away, shaking off the fatherly concern. He was a man now, not a child. "What happened?" his father demanded.

"People are desperate, now more than ever. Several infidels tried to take what is ours." Rasheed looked at the two men he was with; one of them smiled. "We educated them in the ways of Allah." All three of them deposited their loads on the floor, the two friends quickly going back outside for the next run.

"You should not talk this way," Mohammad admonished. "They are still God's children. Violence is not the way of Islam. You know this. The Holy Koran teaches…"

"The Koran teaches a lot of things, Father. But now is not the time for a lecture," Rasheed admonished. His father, taken aback at his son's tone, made to respond, but Rasheed stopped him with a raised palm. "We have food that needs unloading, and we haven't much time." Rasheed made to follow his two friends who were already back outside, but his father grabbed him.

"What do you mean we don't have much time?"

"When we were leaving the warehouse carpark, we saw the infected, thousands of them. They descended like a swarm, running faster than men should run. We barely got past them before they blocked the road.

3

Please, Father, I must unload this stuff." Rasheed pulled away and made for the door, but turned, his face full of fear. "Father, there were so many of them." He paused and said the truth that was in his heart. "I'm afraid, Father. I've never been this afraid before."

"So am I, son. There is no shame in it. Allah gives us fear for a reason. Accept it as the gift it is meant to be." Rasheed nodded and went outside. The father watched his son run back down to the van. How his mother would be proud of him were she still alive here today. But he knew she would also be worried, worried by his insistence to veer away from the peaceful path, to listen to the radical preachers who distorted and manipulated the words of the true faith for their own ends. To accept the cancer within Islam as the cure. But none of that really mattered now. All that mattered in this moment was living, surviving in this makeshift fortress.

17.53PM, 16th September 2015, GCHQ, Cheltenham, UK

Sir Paul Crispin looked at the interior of his office for the last time. He had decided to stay, overseeing the collection of as much data as possible, holding on 'til the last minute. They still needed the information that the UK's surveillance hub could provide. But there were already reports of infected in Worcester, less than 26 miles away to the north, and most of his personnel had been shipped out. So now they were leaving whilst they still could. Some of the senior staff had been lucky, leaving by helicopter before the quarantine had been imposed. Others had just disappeared from their posts, their cars no longer in the massive car park that surrounded this immense government building. But not Sir Paul—he had stayed to the last along with others who shared his commitment, and whilst he could understand the desire of some to flee in the face of such horrors, he had nothing but contempt for those who abandoned ship in this darkest of hours. They were everything wrong with modern day Britain. To many, honour and duty were forgotten concepts it seemed.

"Sir, your ride is here," the voice said behind him. Crispin turned and looked at his secretary Sandra. He could tell she had been crying.

"You didn't have to stay you know," Crispin said, "but I'm glad you did."

"Where would I have gone? My parents live in Central London, and all my friends work here. My place is here; you showed me that." Crispin turned finally and gave her a respectful smile. She could teach some of his peers a thing or two about the obligation working here carried.

"I'm going to miss this place. Always knew this time would come…but never like this." He stepped forward and picked up a bag that was in the middle of the floor, trinkets and mementos from his office. The remnants of decades of service, decades of sacrifice.

"Is everyone else away?"

"We will be the last to leave, Sir Paul," she said, stepping aside so he could pass her.

"You know you never had to call me sir, don't you?" Crispin enquired.

"I know," Sandra said. "But everyone here respects you too much not to, including me." Crispin put a hand on her shoulder, noticed that she was close to tears. She was still in her twenties, and yet she was the best employee he had ever worked with.

"Come here," he said, dropping the bag and embracing her in a fatherly hug that she accepted gladly. Her tears came again, in a flood, in a torrent of anguish that had been building behind a dam of resolute defiance. He held her, felt his own tears threaten, but held them back. Now was not the time. Now was never the time.

17.58PM, 16th September 2015, Glasgow, UK

So this was the end of days. He had awoken on the street, homeless and alone, only to find the whole world had gone mad. Through a hangover-induced haze, he had seen the infected rip into the terrified commuters, overcoming the police, felling adults and children alike. He had seen horrors that would shock the average man. But they did not shock Jock. When you lose an arm and lie screaming from the pain in a burning Land Rover for what seems like an eternity, the terrors of the infected and the undead didn't hold that much power over you. His own mind held infinitely more abominations than those that roamed his beloved streets.

What had surprised him was his desire for self-preservation. Jock had been slowly trying to kill himself with alcohol for years now; he freely admitted this to himself in his more lucid moments. The alcohol calmed the flashbacks and quietened the voices that came to him, but also offered the promise of eventual blissful release. And yet, when faced with the plague, he had run, had hid, had survived. Scurrying through back streets and shortcuts that only a homeless person would know, he had removed himself from his normal begging ground, to an area thinned of human population. Several times, he had come across groups of infected, only to avoid them by stealth and luck. Eventually, he had found himself outside an abandoned off-licence, its doors smashed open. The calmness of the street and the fact that his heart felt like it was doing everything it could to escape his rib cage had compelled him to seek refuge. Holding a piece of metal pipe in his one good arm, his other meagre possessions long since abandoned, he had explored the establishment's interior and, finding it empty, had brought down the security shutters using the switch he found behind the counter. Momentarily safe from the dangers outside, he had marvelled at the array of alcohol available to him, an Aladdin's cave of ethanol and oblivion. Well, if the end had come, it was only fitting that he should go out in style. He had no illusion that he could survive much longer out on the infested streets of Glasgow.

He was now into his third bottle of red wine. Sat in the corner farthest away from the front entrance, Jock sang softly to himself, remembering fallen comrades, true friends who he would never see the likes of again. That was the problem with war—you made a bond with dozens of people that could rarely be achieved in civilian life. When you fought beside them, when you saved their lives and they saved yours, you got to know and respect people to such a degree that you would die and kill for them. That wasn't the problem, because as he freely admitted to himself, he loved war. Up to a point. The problem was when those people were taken from you by bullets, by bombs, and by fire, the resulting chasm in one's life couldn't be filled, and whilst Jock didn't know if others felt the same way, he found himself resenting the very people he had lost. He had found something that made him whole, made him complete, only for that completeness to be rocked by the death of those around him. And he had lost so many, and then almost joined their ranks. Then the truth of war descended on him with a greater force than the ordinance that had blown his Land Rover clean off the road. Returning from a foreign land, broken and ruined, he was abandoned by the people who had sent him to those hot, godless countries in the first place.

He finished the last drops in the bottle and flung it across the off-licence interior, hearing it crash into the far wall. He instantly regretted the action, because within seconds, he heard a shuffling outside on the street. This was followed almost instantly by something slamming into the barriers which, whilst sturdy, rocked and swayed at the assault. Jock stood gingerly, dizziness and drunkenness hitting him in waves. From his now elevated position, he could see over the alcohol-lined shelves, could see multiple figures through the slats and the holes in the steel shutters. He stepped forward, using the wall to balance him.

"Fuck," he said under his breath.

"*Feeeeed,*" multiple mouths hissed at him from outside. They knew he was here. How long before the barrier was breached? Could it hold out against their strength and determination? He had seen the strength these creatures possessed, had seen one rip a child's arm clean off. Did he even care? Jock didn't actually think he did. There was something almost appealing in the thought of becoming one of them. No more pain, no more nightmares, no more rejection by society. His drunken and diseased mind began to play out some bizarre utopian fantasy, and Jock walked over to the counter, almost stumbling twice, his shoes crunching on broken glass from the previous ransacking the off-licence had experienced. His good hand latched onto a bottle of vodka on the way, and he now opened the screw top with his teeth, the mobility of his teeth giving a mild discomfort that he ignored. Spitting the lid away, he downed a mouthful, safe in the knowledge that his liver was well accustomed to such excessive ethanol consumption.

"You want me, do you fuckers?" Jock shouted, his words slurred. Should he let them in? They would get him eventually if he didn't drink himself to death first. But what was best? A slow death by alcohol poisoning or becoming them, joining them, helping them overthrow a society that had used him and cast him on the shit heap. There was a renewed excitement from outside in reaction to his voice, and Jock found himself smiling.

"So you do want me? Well fuck, why not." Taking a final swig of vodka, he walked around the counter and cast the bottle aside. What was the point in carrying on? He had nothing to live for, hadn't for years now. The flight mechanism had saved him when the infection had first appeared this morning, but now on reflection, he saw the futility of it all. His hand now free, his other lost in a war that nobody seemed to this day to understand, he pressed the button to raise the shutters. As the metal ascended, the infected poured in, their smell preceding them.

"Shit, this is going to hurt," he heard a voice say in his head and then they were upon him. And hurt it did, more than when he lost his arm to friendly fire. And yet he didn't scream, didn't fight, and welcomed the end. And as the infection took hold, as his mind died to be taken over by the collective, he finally knew peace, a peace he had yearned and craved for. As his human mind was swallowed up by the virus, he said two final words before his brain became nothing more than an operating system to propel his body.

"Thank you."

17.52PM, 16th September 2015, MI6 Building, London, UK

The pain came in waves now, building slowly, then rapidly, no rhythm to it to enable him to steel himself. It was more than he could endure, more than he could comprehend, and any thought other than the pain was stripped from his mind. It was all he was, and it seemed all he would ever be.

When he had been arrested at the heliport, he had not envisioned anything like this. Oh, he knew he would be interrogated, knew he would be treated harshly, but he had the faith in his God to protect him from that. And he's had faith in the British justice system. It never occurred to him that one of the oldest legal systems on the planet would just be abandoned. And he certainly hadn't expected torture. Whilst he was one of those responsible for spreading the plague across London, the one who had contaminated the milk in various coffee houses that hundreds of people had gone on to drink, nothing in his worst nightmares had prepared him for the reaction of the agents of Satan. The woman, the one who called herself Davina, had hooked him up to her torture devices and had left him here to suffer such torment as to make the devil himself sit up and take notice.

A fresh wave of electricity travelled down the fine copper needles that were imbedded in various parts of his flesh, and he bit down on his gag hard, the scream stifled by its presence and by exhaustion. How long would this go on for? Where was his God now? He knew that The Lord Our God was all about suffering and atonement…but this? Was this what he truly deserved? Had he not fulfilled God's plan? Had he not done exactly as he was asked? Then why this? Why leave him to such a fate?

The pain increased, as unbelievable as that was, and he squirmed as best he could in his restraints. Fabrice didn't know how long he had been here, didn't know what time it was. Time was now meaningless to him. It meant nothing, because there was no end to it, only the now and the memory of how bad the pain really could be. Nobody came to oversee him, nobody came to examine or feed him, the saline drip still half full, dripping life-sustaining fluid into his body. Then the pain stopped, and a wave of relief washed over him. He blinked his eyes, his vision blurred, his mind still reeling. But this had happened before. The computer software running the torture sequence was devious and relentless. Fabrice braced himself for the inevitable, for the pain to begin again, but the seconds ticked past. And still the pain didn't start again, and despite his best judgement, he allowed a glimmer of hope to form in his mind. Was it over? Had the machine he was connected to somehow broken?

He began to count in his head what he thought were seconds, and as the count passed 500, his hope blossomed. Thank God.

But then the pain hit him with such intensity, every muscle in his body contracted, and he bit down with such force that he actually felt three of his teeth break. His vision whited out, and he begged for unconsciousness, but of course, that never came. It wasn't just saline that was being fed into him, but a constant drip of neuro stimulants that heightened his sensations but also kept him from blacking out. Designed specifically for Davina at her request by the Black Ops research guys at the CIA, this was only the third time she had ever used it. Fabrice nearly died at that moment, not physically, but mentally, and he almost ceased to be a human being. He became the pain, was one with it. Soon, his mind would simply snap, and there would be nobody even there to witness it.

17.58PM, 16th September, Nursing Home, Northern London, UK

"My arm, I can't feel my arm."

Archie looked through the smoke at the source of the tortured voice, flinching from the explosions all around him, and looked at his fallen mate who writhed in the sand, a bleeding and charred stump where his right arm had once been.

"Medic," he heard himself cry, but his voice was drowned out by the incessant rattle of machine gun fire and the explosions of mortar shells all around. Archie shouted again, and he wrenched himself from sleep to find himself dazed and drenched in sweat. He looked up at the ceiling confused and frightened, and for several minutes, he didn't know where he was.

Archie had been put in the home a year ago when his dementia had become too dangerous to live on his own. His family couldn't look after him; they had their own lives to lead, and besides, his growing aggression had made it dangerous to have him around young children for prolonged periods. The staff at the nursing home knew how to handle him, and the medication the doctors prescribed helped. But as the dementia progressed, the nightmares came more frequently, and it was always the same dream, watching his best friend die on Sword Beach during the D-Day landings. Mercifully, the dream always ended before the bullet that had finally ended his pal's life had blown open his left eye socket.

Sitting up, he found he was fully dressed, and so he decided it was time to go to work. He was obviously late, and if he wasn't careful, that bastard of a boss would give him the sack. His mind swam in an illusion of a reality that no longer existed, and, wandering from his small room, he walked the corridor and down a flight of stairs into the common room. The room smelt, and he witnessed several people crying. Who were they, and what were they doing in his house?

"Get out, all of you," he slurred, his speech still not recovered from the mini stroke he'd suffered two months previously, and he staggered around the room almost drunkenly, ineffectively trying to push and pull people around. His efforts were resisted easily, and he fell on his backside, tears welling in his eyes. He didn't understand what was going on. Why didn't he understand?

There were no staff left in the home, having all fled to leave the old and the decrepit to their ultimate fate. So the residents who still had their wits about them were doing what they could to help the rest who age had stricken useless. Now just a burden on society, they had been dumped here in this substandard, council-run facility where their daily needs were barely met. And now they didn't even have that.

"Come on, Archie, get up off their floor," a gentle voice said, and he felt weak hands cajoling him.

"Mildred, where's Mildred?" he said pathetically.

"She's not here, Archie," the voice answered. "Stand up so we can get you off the carpet. It's filthy down there." He looked at the person trying to help him, a sweet old lady who had been here over five years, and reluctantly let her help him. He recognised her somewhat, and for a moment, she looked like an angel. She helped him over to the side of the room's entrance where he sat down on a chair that smelt of stale urine, next to a man who was drooling on himself. The angel smiled at him one last time and then disappeared to help some of the others. The room was filled with confusion and sobs. And then it was filled with terror.

Archie looked to his left and saw a lone man standing in the doorway to the common room. He was naked from the waist up, his torso smeared with blood. What was most obvious about him, though, was the very real fact that his left arm was missing.

"Arnold?" Archie whispered, remembering the figure from his dream. In his demented mind, the present became combined with the past, and even though his old friend had been in uniform and looked nothing like the demon before him, the two figures merged as one in his mind.

"Medic," Archie cried and stood shambolically, staggering over to the figure, who just watched him with an almost curious look. "It's alright, mate, I've got you." Archie put his hands on the naked flesh, which is when the figure struck him across the face with the back of its one good hand. Archie fell, something cracking in his shoulder as he landed. Pain and dismay washed over him, and he watched in disbelief as half a dozen blood-soaked figures joined the first. These six didn't wait and look; they stormed into the room and infected everything they could. All Archie could do was lie there and weep at the carnage as his body rapidly succumbed to the infection.

18.01PM, 16th September 2015, Hounslow, London, UK

This was his city now, his country. There was no need for fear, no need for doubt or regret. He owned it, he owned it all. Every shop, every house, every car, and every street was his to do with as he wished. Hours ago, these streets had been filled with the dead and the dying. Now they were barren, cleared of all life by the infected who even now were off spreading the contagion they carried to fresh victims. The contagion that he was immune to, the contagion that had altered him, improved him. Even now, he could feel it within his body, changing him, enhancing him. Owen Patterson stopped in the middle of the street and looked again at the stumps where his severed fingers had once been. Whilst those fingers weren't growing back, the flesh was already knitting together, healing the wounds. The phantom pain still lingered, but even that was diminishing, becoming nothing but a mere distraction. Owen smiled, relishing the gifts he had been given. He felt almost superhuman. The price of two fingers was more than enough for what he had been given. Being bitten, it seemed, had been a blessing. It would only occur to him later, much later, that perhaps it was in fact a curse.

Owen turned around, looking at the assorted creations of humanity, the Heckler and Koch machine gun he had liberated from the abandoned Armed Response vehicle held firm in his undamaged hand. Another gift, another grace that life had bestowed upon him. Oh, this was sweet, this was just perfect. But he couldn't stand in the middle of the street feeling pleased with himself. He had shit to do, places to go, and people to see. There were plans that he needed to make, and the sooner the better. And first off, he had to see if his gang were still alive. There was one thing better than being king of the city...having minions to lord over and do your bidding. If they were still alive, if they weren't running bloodied and infected with the other crazies, Owen knew where they would be. And so that's where he was heading now, with a bag full of guns and alcohol he had acquired from an off-licence moments earlier. He hadn't stolen it, for how could he steal what was already his? This whole city was his property now, and he was going to damned well make sure anyone left over from the virus understood that. They would fucking do his bidding or he would inflict such agony on them, such damage that they would wish they had surrendered themselves to the infected.

Owen turned the corner into the next street and saw a small crowd bent over something in the middle of the road. They were obviously infected, and he walked purposefully towards them, no longer afraid by their strength and the threat they posed to mere mortal men. He knew they were not a danger to him, not anymore. One of the infected sensed him and its head darted to look as he approached. It began to stand, hissing at him, but as he got closer, it seemed to cower back down, and then turned away from him to continue with its meal. The five infected had hunted down a Labrador, and were presently consuming the contents of its rib cage, hands clawing at the flesh that they then ripped out and consumed. Owen stopped next to the group, and watched them feed on the animal. He saw that its eyes were already gone, saw that its tongue no longer lolled out of its mouth, a mouth whose lower jaw had been ripped clean off. One of the infected bled from an arm riddled with teeth marks, but the injury didn't seem to bother it.

He watched them a moment longer, fascinated by their lack of interest in him. His curiosity grew and he lifted a foot and gently kicked one of the infected in the back. It shifted in position, but ignored him. So the next kick had more force, and the infected went sprawling over the dog's carcass, sending the others scattering. He watched as they turned towards him, hissing out words that could just be recognised as human speech.

"Must feeeeeed."

"Leave usss, let us feeeeed."

Owen was surprised that most of what he heard wasn't from their lips. It was in his head. There had been a faint murmuring in his mind ever since he woke up, like the sound of distant traffic. Only now, up close, did he understand what it was. He could hear them, could hear their thoughts.

"I can hear you," Owen said. "I can hear you, in here," he said, tapping his temple with his damaged hand. And then he said the next thing not with his mouth, but with his mind. *"Can you hear me?"*

"Yesss," the distorted voices said. *"Yes, we heeaar."*

"Fucking awesome!" Owen shouted in delight. "This is so cool."

18.03PM, 16th September 2015, St Pancras Railway Station, London, UK

He had been in here over eight hours now, and the battery on his phone had long since died. Watching live video of the death of London tended to do that. He had sat and watched in shocked horror as the events of the morning unfolded, unable to leave his makeshift prison. Prison was probably a better word to use than refuge, despite the door in front of him being the only reason he was still alive. Several times, he had tried to open that door, but every time, a noise from outside had caused panic to slam the door shut again, and then the pounding had followed. And the voices, the disjointed, incomprehensible voices. Occasionally, an arm would sweep into the gap under the door, the fingers reaching, flexing, trying to get purchase on him. And once, hands had appeared at the top of the door, and a devastated face had appeared, the eyes staring at him insanely. But although there was space to do so, it had not climbed over the door, and had instead retreated. So here he was, in a space not big enough to spread his arms out wide, his only companion the toilet upon whose lid he now sat.

It had happened so quickly. So intent on getting to the lavatory, he had missed many of the signs that the world was going to oblivion. Reaching the toilet stall, he had lowered his pants, sat down, and almost sighed with pleasure as the pressure was released. Mid movement, something had banged hard on the door to his toilet cubicle.

"Hey, it's occupied," he had shouted. Seriously, the people in this city were a nightmare. The sooner he moved back up north the better. Reaching for the paper, there was another bang on the door, and he rolled his eyes in disdain. Disdain quickly turned to bewilderment, which turned to fear. And all because of the blood that began to seep under the door. It wasn't a lot, but it was unmistakeable against the stark white clinical surroundings.

"What the fuck...?" he said softly. There was a scream, and then the sound of gunshots. And then his whole world literally went to shit.

Now, he listened at the door and could hear nothing. His previous attempts to pull himself up and look over the top of the stall had been in vain...he just didn't have the upper body strength to raise himself up enough to see what needed to be seen, so the truth of the world out of his vision was unknown to him. But he had to get out of here. It wouldn't be long before thirst drove him to drink from the toilet bowl, and he didn't think he could do that. Not now, but what about in a day, two days? The first time he had opened the door, nervously, tentatively, he had pulled it inwards to see the source of the blood, a body lying faceless below the hand basins. Faceless because the face was just a mass of red and gore. Another body lay near it, again obviously dead, its throat ripped out. Then a howl swept in from the entrance to the gent's toilets followed by a crazy-eyed, blood-soaked lunatic that rushed right at him. If he'd hesitated for just one second, he wouldn't have been able to get the door closed in time. Thank God they opened inwards, and he was relieved to discover it made an effective barrier against a world now infested by devils. The hinges and the lock held against a barrage of fists and feet that must have lasted a good minute.

The noises from the slaughter in the train station carried on for a good thirty minutes after that. But it took him a whole hour before he even touched the cubicle door again. Gently rapping his knuckle on it twice, the pounding began again. Christ, had that thing been waiting out there for him all that time?

But now he was hungry and thirsty, and he needed to do something. He couldn't end his days sat on a fucking public toilet. And then there was the smell; it was already unbearable, and he was finding it difficult to breath. So he stood, determination and desperation spurring him on.

"Come on, you can do this," he said, not really believing a word he had just said. He wasn't a brave man. He knocked on the door three times and stepped back. The door didn't erupt, and he heard nothing from outside. He hit the door harder this time, and again there was no response. Taking a deep breath, he opened the portal enough for him to cautiously look out. The two bodies he had originally seen were no longer there. The only thing that marked their existence was the sea of red that coated the floor.

"Hello?" he said at a half-shout, ready to slam the door shut. But nothing came. No demons swarmed him, no ghouls sounded off in the distance. Carefully, he took a step out into the main toilet area, avoiding the blood where he could. To the left, he could see a foot and half a leg poking out from behind the corner, and he made his way over to it, knowing it was the only way out. The closer he got, the more of the leg he could see, until it stopped just below the knee. The rest of the leg's owner was nowhere to be seen, and he felt bile rise up his throat.

"Jesus." He'd known it was bad, had watched the BBC footage of the police being overwhelmed outside this very station. Before his battery had run out of juice, he'd watched a CNN report about the assassination of the Prime Minister and the evacuation of London. He was trapped in a city home to millions of infected maniacs who all possessed the strength of the damned.

The corridor outside the toilets was clear, the main pedestrian area of the train station littered with debris and several motionless bodies. The only sounds he heard came from himself, and he moved out of the toilets and up the wall, hugging it, ready to turn and flee should the need arise. At some point, that option would be off the table, and was it really an option, even now? Coming to the end of the corridor, he looked down the length of what had been the station's shopping area, and the mezzanine floor that led to the northbound trains seemed deserted. In the distance, he thought he heard a siren, but the sound was fleeting, maybe even imagined. There was nobody here, and he moved further out into the space, his eyes spotting the discarded machine gun that lay like a treasure in a pool of blood.

He almost didn't hear it, the movement was so stealthy. In fact, in his last moments, he realised his mistake from a kind of sixth sense. Turning around, he saw the creature that had dropped from the floor above. It must have vaulted over the glass barrier and had landed with almost cat-like grace. It stood, staring at him with deep, red eyes and a jaw hanging halfway off. Another sound, behind him now, and he turned his head to see another of the beasts standing from finishing its drop.

"No," he said weakly. They had been waiting for him, waiting for his own body's needs to force him out into the open. He looked down at the gun, so far away, so useless, and then both infected rushed him. They didn't kill him. The collective only killed as a last resort now. They needed numbers; they needed soldiers. It was still not the time to feed for most of them. It was the time to spread, to grow stronger. His scream filled the station, and the hope of the half dozen non-infected humans still trapped within the building died with those terrified sounds.

18.04PM, 16th September 2015, London Southend Airport, Southend on Sea, UK

"It's time to go, sir." Captain Grainger looked up at his colour sergeant and nodded. He stood, his back aching from sitting on the cold tarmac for too long.

"Are all the men away?" Grainger asked.

"Yes, sir. We will be on the last flight out."

"And the civilians?" Colour Sergeant Vorne looked at his commanding officer with a disapproving frown.

"They aren't your responsibility, sir, not anymore." Vorne impatiently looked at his watch. "It's time to leave," he said again. Grainger nodded. Tasked with defending Whitehall and Parliament, he had failed in his mission. But then it had been a mission against impossible odds. This virus, this contagion was like a bulldozer, rolling over everything in its path. Unstoppable, unfathomable. He had saved his men, or more rightly, they had saved themselves. But he hadn't been able to save the seat of British Government, which even now was probably still burning from the air strikes that had been dropped on it. Thousands of years of history and empire wiped out in a matter of hours. His land, his country was being overrun. Picking up his gear, he followed his sergeant to the plane fifty metres away.

"You did well today, Sergeant," Grainger said. Vorne didn't turn around, but he thought he saw the man stiffen slightly. "These men owe you a lot."

"Thank you, sir." Vorne didn't say anymore, just accepted his commanding officer's praise. Grainger suspected it made him feel uncomfortable. The sergeant did what he did because it was his job, because it was his duty. Vorne didn't need medals and glory. The only thing that mattered to him was keeping his men alive.

After escaping by boat and travelling east down the Thames, they had been dropped off at the coastal resort of Southend on Sea. The decision had been made to forsake the cities, to leave millions of people to fend for themselves, to abandon the majority to the indestructible plague that would descend upon all of them. Being just a captain, Grainger didn't have any say in such decisions, but the feeling of hopelessness bit into him. He had seen first-hand that fighting against this infestation was an impossible task, and yet part of him still wanted to try. But only a part of him—the more sensible part saw the futility in it all. There just weren't enough guns, enough men, enough bullets. This was an enemy that couldn't be fought at close range, that swarmed in incredible numbers, that came back even when they were dead. He couldn't risk his men on such a suicide mission. Even worse than the thought of them dying was the thought of them becoming one of the enemy, turning on their brothers.

He didn't want to be there when one of them became infected, knowing his standing orders would mean him having to put a bullet into that soldier's brain. He didn't think he could do it. These men looked up to him, trusted him. How the hell could he be expected to shoot them in cold blood, knowing that he would be judged in the eyes of every other private and corporal under his command? Vorne wouldn't judge, of course. Hell, if it came to that, Vorne would probably be the one carefully prying the revolver out of his hand and doing the deed for him.

They reached the plane. Despite earlier being at the heart of the battle, Grainger had volunteered his men to hold the airport until the main bulk of the evacuated forces were in the air. He knew his men wouldn't like it, but it was their job, and thankfully, they were now leaving before the infection had reached them. Several of the men had deserted in the subsequent hours, but most of them remained. Grainger found himself surprised by how few men had abandoned his ranks. He had expected a lot more, and he felt that he owed a lot to those that had chosen to remain. He was their leader now, not because of the bars on his uniform, but because they knew that leadership was their best chance of staying alive.

"How long is the flight to Newquay?" Grainger asked. He sounded tired, beaten.

"Just over an hour. Come on, sir," Vorne said, falling behind his captain slightly, pushing him forward with a gentle hand. "There's still plenty for us to do."

18.07PM, 16th September, 2015, Over the English Channel

Keith looked out of the cockpit of his light aircraft, the blood in his veins already ice. He had taken off forty minutes before, his flight from the UK mainland delayed because, by some bizarre twist of fate, he had somehow missed the news that billions of other people had seen. It wasn't until the mid-afternoon that he learnt of the infection, of the plague sweeping the country. He had watched with growing disbelief as the TV played out horrific scenes from what could have been a cliché horror movie, and he knew he only had one option open to him…to flee.

Being a pilot with his own plane, he knew that this was his only chance. But it had taken time to get the plane ready, to get to the airport, to gather the essentials. And now he feared he was too late, knew that the warning given to him by people left at the airport was in fact true. There was no escaping the island, not for him, as evidenced by the fighter jet that flew to the left of him.

"To the pilot of the light aircraft, I say again you are attempting to break NATO quarantine. You must turn around or I will be forced to shoot you down. This is your final warning." The voice that spoke to him over the radio had a French accent. How could they? He wasn't infected, hadn't even been anywhere near the infected areas. Keith wanted to live, and although he tried to fool himself that this was all an elaborate bluff, he knew that the threat was real. But there was no going back. He had witnessed the televised scenes of London, of Manchester, had seen the hordes descending on the soldiers and the police, no defence against the virus that ripped its way across the country. No, fuck them, he wasn't going to turn round. He could see the French coast; he wasn't turning back now. Keeping the jet in the periphery of his vision, he kept on his flight plan, and after several seconds breathed a sigh of relief when the jet banked away.

"I'm going to make it," he muttered to himself. But he didn't. In the space of a second, the plane he was in rocked violently and the cabin exploded with light and shrapnel. His scream lasted all of half a second before the explosive depleted uranium round shattered his skull, sending his brain into a mist of pink, bloodied matter. The plane exploded in mid-air, the burning debris falling into the sea below.

18.09PM, 16th September 2015, MI6 Building, London, UK

Snow looked out of the window of the MI6 Building and followed the progress of a small group of bedraggled infected that joined the larger group outside the building's barrier wall. He had expected there to be more of them, for the presence of humanity to act like a beacon to these monsters, but their overall numbers were strangely limited. He heard a muffled rifle shot and saw one of the infected fall backwards, its head exploding. Another shot felled a second. Snipers on the roof, constantly whittling down the numbers, their bodies strewn all around, some ordaining the fences around the building with their still corpses. Still except one, its body writhing as it dangled, its clothing stuck on one of the railing spikes. Why didn't someone shoot it to put it out of its misery?

Snow had noticed, in his thirty-minute observation, that whenever one of the infected was shot, another just stepped into its place, and a constant trickle of reinforcements kept the numbers about the same. It was like they were coordinating, surrounding the building with just enough bodies so as to keep those inside trapped. And it was working; there was no leaving the building now for most of the people trapped inside. Even most of the secret exits through the tunnels on the other side of the river were reportedly off limits now. The infected seemed to know things, seemed able to anticipate and coordinate.

Could they think strategically? His bosses seemed to think so, seemed to think that they somehow communicated rather than acting randomly. Stripped of their humanity, they seemed to work on a more primal level, hunting in packs, killing those that posed a threat, converting the weak and the vulnerable. And when they needed to, the infected could attack in large numbers, overwhelming any defensive force not protected by high concrete walls. Snow turned his gaze up from the street and inspected the London skyline. Smoke rose from multiple locations, and he could see that the iconic Parliament building was still on fire, the tower that housed the iconic clock no longer visible. Never again would Big Ben chime. Never again would the seat of Western civilisation see democracy again.

His thoughts turned back to the infected. They had once had lives. Cleaners, lawyers, soldiers, mothers. Now, they were a ravenous horde who killed without mercy, who were even now relentlessly pushing outwards from the cities. And there was nothing to stop them. The only weapon they had now was to try and understand them, to somehow find a cure to this devastation. That's why there were scientists on the lower levels. And that's why he was here, sent to fetch a trio of biologists from Cambridge and make them an offer. Wait here for the infected to arrive and end your days in fear, or come to the heart of it and help find the cure. The international quarantine meant there was no escape from this decaying island, so really what else was there for them to do? Of course, the cream of the scientific crop had been spirited away in Operation Noah, so these weren't the best and the brightest. And whilst those rescued in Operation Noah would undoubtedly be working on the cure, there was no way they could work on the actual virus itself. It was too dangerous to be let off the UK mainland, even if held in the most secure biohazard facility. That's why they needed a research hub in the heart of the infection, and where better than the blast-proof fortress that was the MI6 Building?

Of the three scientists he had rescued, there was one he really didn't like. Snow was a man quick to make judgements, and his gut was usually right. This man just seemed off on so many levels, Snow's mind firing off alarm bells whenever he was in the man's presence. Fifteen years doing this job had given him a level of intuition that was seldom wrong, and Snow's nose told him that this particular fellow was dangerous. Snow had almost refused him a place on the helicopter, but he wasn't the one making the orders here. He was merely a foot soldier in what was now a war for the survival of the human race. Snow had met some cold customers in his time, but Dr. Victor Durand might as well have been made of stone. It was quite clear to him that Durand was a merciless, self-serving bastard, and he was undoubtedly a sociopath. Right now, the scientist was most likely taking great delight prodding and poking the specimens they had captured. No, that Snow had captured. Truth be told, he would rather be in a room with a dozen infected than with Durand, unless he was in there with strict instructions to do the man damage. Every time he saw the biologist, Snow had a pressing urge to punch the man in the face. He'd had every intention of telling all this to his superiors on his return to the MI6 Building, but on arrival, most of those superiors were conspicuous by their absence, having been evacuated or fled in panic. This had naturally left a power vacuum.

There were five specimens downstairs. Specimens? Were they already dehumanising these poor souls? The three infected had been a bitch to catch, and even with the protective NBC suits they wore, he had lost one of his men. One of the infected had just leapt on his back and ripped off his gas mask. Snow had ended up shooting them both, and all because some mad scientists wanted to experiment. Yes, the orders came from on high, but none of the top brass were here anymore. Most of them were in Ireland or Brussels. Even that psychotic bitch Davina had made it out whilst he found himself stuck here playing nursemaid. His own fault really; he'd been in the MI6 Building when the emergency recall had been broadcast and had been shipped out to grab the scientists that somebody, somewhere deemed important.

By the time he was safely in quarantine, the lockdown of the UK mainland was in place. Sorry, old chap, I'm afraid you're here for the duration. Bad show and all that. Still, stiff upper lip, eh? Oh, and as you're here, it would be awfully decent if you could run a few errands for us. Earn your keep, as it were. The implication was obvious. Work or leave. And so within thirty minutes of returning from Cambridge, some fucking madman had sent him back out there again. He's had to kill three people to make that mission, and he was only sure that two of those had been infected.

The other two specimens had been easier to catch, slower, more cumbersome, but they had been more unnerving. Because they were dead. There was no denying it. At least the infected were alive, unbelievably strong and insane, yes, but alive. The zombies didn't writhe and buck like the infected, but even with the Kevlar hoods tied over their heads, they had constantly tried to bite his team, the sound of their jaws snapping shut almost a melody. Snow believed it was a mistake to bring the viral carriers into the secure facility, but the scientists and the pen pushers insisted they needed to research the virus, to find out what made it tick. As if finding a cure now would make any difference. There were millions infected by now, and by the end of the week, the whole of the country would be overrun. And that probably included this facility. There was always a way in, no matter how secure the facility. If it wasn't a flaw in the perimeter, then it was a flaw in the humanity that the perimeter protected.

Every second, another voice was added to the great order of the collected mind. Like the hum of traffic in the distance, it was always there, no matter the distance. There was no leader, just the wisdom of millions working together with one overriding goal: to spread the infection to as many people as possible as fast as possible. With the army now gone from London, the main threat to their existence was from the air, and the howls rose up as their brothers and sisters were consumed by the fire and the bullets and the explosions. But they were too many, too well spread, and the enemy too few to even make a dent in their numbers.

Hundreds gathered outside the MI6 Building, not really knowing why, but somehow knowing the threat it posed, the memories of those abducted and dragged inside there for all to see. They had scaled the fences, blocked the exits, but they could not get inside. Those who tried to climb the walls fell to the snipers' bullets. Those who tried to smash the windows merely broke bones and tore flesh on the bomb-proof glass. How to get inside? How? Tell us how.

But there was another threat, one that they ignored as the virus told them to ignore it. As the dead amongst them mounted, many of those not killed by headshots returned. Anew, improved, no longer part of the collective, they feasted on the living and the infected alike. And as enhanced as they were, the infected could only survive so much damage from their cousins, and slowly, the number of zombies around the fortress began to grow. A competing army of brothers and sisters, the resurrection of the forsaken.

18.12PM, 16th September 2015, Shepherd's Bush, London, UK

The banging on the main door to the apartments had stopped about thirty minutes ago. If the door had been wood, it would have shattered within minutes, she was certain. But it was reinforced, designed to stop home invasion. Steel in a steel frame. She had heard the ground floor windows being shattered, but suspected the bars on the exterior had stopped everything but the wind from entering. But then she wasn't on the ground floor, and she looked out of her top-floor window to the street below. There was little in the way of movement, humanity having either fled or been converted hours ago. The road was a mass of abandoned cars, debris, and motionless human forms. A car burned in the middle of the road, and crows pecked at the body of what had once been an elderly lady. Could the virus be passed on to birds? Why the hell was she worrying about that for fuck's sake? She had her own problems to deal with.

And she had watched it all. She had woken late to find the world had gone insane. If she had done what her parents had demanded, gone out and got herself a proper job, a nine-to-five existence, she would have been out there now, probably one of them. But she hadn't been out there and she was safe. Of course, she was also trapped. She knew that, there was no denying it, especially with the constant reminders that were displayed through her window. Even as she thought that, three infected ran across the road from a side street. In the distance, she heard a scream rise on the wind. In the distance, she heard an explosion, and a fresh plume of smoke rose into the sky.

She had enough food for several days, and the taps still ran. But how long would that go on for? How long before lack of provisions forced her out into the streets? There was a shop right next to the ground floor entrance to the terraced flats she lived in, but getting the food it contained and surviving that journey would be fraught with risk. And how many millions of others were like her, trapped, afraid, and knowing deep down that it was over? There were plenty of convenience stores spread across the city, but how many could people safely get to? What if the infected lay in wait, using human weakness as a trap? Why did they need to break down her door when eventually she would be forced to venture to them?

But there was something she was missing. It was there in her mind, glaring at her, but she couldn't focus on it, couldn't see what was right in front of her. On the street below, one of the three infected broke off and crossed the road again. It leapt up onto a wall and began to scale one of the buildings, using the drainpipe and the inconsistencies in the brickwork. It got halfway up the building before the drainpipe broke loose, sending the infected crashing to the ground. It writhed and churned where it fell, one leg at an odd angle. Despite that, it got up, hobbling off after its kind, still intent on killing, on maiming, on biting. How many had successfully made such climbs? Were they all that agile, like monkeys she had seen at the zoo when she was a child? Could they get to her? Could one of them get through the very window she looked out of? What about…?

The fire escape. That was what was in her head screaming at her. What if they came up the fire escape? She rushed from her living room to the corridor that led to the back of the apartment. It was lit by the natural daylight that fell through a window at the end of the corridor. That was her way out in case of fire, her only chance to avoid being burned alive. Out the window, down onto a flat roof below it, then down a metal staircase to the safety of the back alley behind her building. Safety? Well, it wasn't safe now, nothing was. She reached the window, checked that it was locked, and knew the lock wouldn't be enough.

Because windows were made of glass, and glass was no barrier to these things.

There was another scream, this time from the flat in the terrace next door. She didn't know who lived there, had never met them. All she knew was that she rarely heard a peep from them, which in London was the definition of the perfect neighbour. Not so now as another scream, this one filled with utter terror, rippled through the air. There was a smash, and looking out of the window, she saw something fall onto the flat roof. She didn't know what it was, but it was quickly followed by the body of a man. He landed face down on the bitumen laid surface, arms outstretched as if to break his fall. There was blood all down the back of the white T-shirt he wore, which was ripped at the neck. A knife protruded from just below his right shoulder, the handle sticking out at an odd angle. Something inside told her to step back, to hide, but she was too transfixed. And that's when the head turned, the blood-red eyes locking onto hers. He laid there for several seconds, staring deep into her soul, her hand coming up to her face to stifle a gasp. He had seen her and he was infected; the signs were unmistakeable.

Then he was up. As dread took over, she backed away from the window only to see the infected's head and shoulders appear at the window. It pawed at the glass, trying to lift the window up, its eyes flicking to try and find some way to gain access. It howled, and with incredible force, head-butted the window. A red smear appeared on the site of impact, but the double glazing held. Please, God, let it hold. He head-butted the window a second time, and the glass crazed, but didn't break. Dazed, the infected stepped back and disappeared from sight. By this time, she had retreated back to the living room, a good five metres away from the window. If it couldn't see her anymore, would it go away? Then the glass shattered inwards, and a projectile landed at her feet, bouncing on the fake wooden floor. She looked at it stunned, saw that it was some sort of rock, perhaps a paperweight. Then the face was back at the window, the hands ripping at the jagged glass, pulling what was left of it out of the frame, opening up the way to get in, impervious to the cuts and the slashes it was inflicting upon itself. Then a voice as inhuman as the very sound of Satan filled her ears, full of need and hate and desire.

"*FEEEEEEEEEEEEEEEEEEEEEEEEEED!*"

She was the one screaming then.

18.22PM, 16th September 2015, Watford Islamic Mosque, Watford, UK

Stood at the top window, Rasheed saw them first. One, then two, then dozens. They moved quickly, together, spreading out across the street. Within a minute, there were hundreds, filling the very road itself. Some broke off to investigate the buildings nearby, and there were the sounds of breaking glass. The sheer weight of numbers pressed them against cars and hedges, and several car alarms began to blare, the noise bringing a roar from the massed infected. They moved like insects, he thought. Rasheed backed away from the window and ran down the stairs.

"Father, the infected are here." There were the sounds of panic from the several dozen people present, and a baby began to cry in distress, its mother vainly trying to stop the sound that might as well have been a beacon.

"Everyone towards the centre of the room. Away from the windows," Mohammed said. The child still cried, too young to understand anything other than its very own primal nature.

"Ayesha, you must quiet the child," someone said, and the mother wrapped the child closer, trying to bathe it in her love, but all she had in her heart was terror.

There was a growing noise outside as the horde made its way up the street towards the mosque. Thousands of voices reduced to a primal hum of insane desire. There was the sound of gunfire, then a second shot. *Who had a gun around here?* thought Rasheed. And what was the point against such numbers? Unless…unless it was someone ending their own life. Rasheed ran back upstairs. He did not hear his father call after him. He had to see, he had to know what they were up against. Ignoring his two friends who stood away from the window, he carefully crouched and moved to where he had previously been watching, and peeked out careful so as not to let those outside see. This was what he had witnessed outside the warehouse; this was the wave of infection that he had hoped would somehow pass them by. Only this time, he could watch it from on high, not from the cabin of a van in which he was fleeing.

It hadn't passed them by. It was here, a tsunami of death and decay that was falling on them relentlessly. Rasheed stared out of the window and saw thousands. They ripped everything apart, smashing entry into every building, dragging people out into the street where dozens would attack to bite and claw and eat. They were eating the people; he could see it happening with his own eyes. How could this be? This was surely the work of Dajjal, the Antichrist. And that meant only one thing. The apocalypse was here.

18.27PM, 16th September 2015, Sheffield City Centre, UK

Kevin looked out of his flat window and watched the city burn. The sky above the rooftops was painted with smoke from a dozen fires that would continue to burn until there was nothing flammable left remaining. The riots had started about two hours ago, and were now proceeding unchecked, growing in a brazen frenzy of drunken destruction. Gangs of youths ran rampant in the street below, no longer looting, now merely acting on some primal rage. Kevin felt the siren's call, felt the urge to join in the wanton destruction. But he would not join in, his leg set in plaster, preventing the free movement that would be required. He would become a target rather than a perpetrator. So instead, he drank beer and watched his fellow humans rip their own city apart.

The BBC were still broadcasting on the emergency channel, and he had this playing in the background. Through it, he knew most of what the government wanted him to know.

"Stock up on provisions."
"Stay in your homes."
"Follow the orders of law enforcement."

Law enforcement? There was no law enforcement. Hell, there probably wasn't even a government left anymore. That had to be a joke. His flat overlooked the main shopping area of Sheffield's heart, and he hadn't seen a copper in hours. No police and the impending slaughter that was probably only a day away had sent many mad with a lust for destruction. Kevin wondered if there would even be a city left by the time the infected arrived. The radio had told him that they were spreading out from Manchester and Leeds, both cities merely an hour away by car. How fast could an infected run? How quickly before they could get here?

He was trapped. Unable to drive, unable to catch a lift with those who had chosen to flee. It was in crisis that you realised who your true friends were. At first, he had cursed them, but now that he had time to think about it, where would they go? The radio had mentioned the safe zone being set up in Cornwall, but there was no chance to get there. The radio told him everything he needed to know, and everything he didn't want to know. It told him of the clogged motorways, the fact martial law was in force, and the fact that the country had been quarantined. There was a crash as one of the last windows in the streets below was shattered, this

25

time by a child's casual use of a brick. As he watched, a car sped down the street, people scattering at its approach. There were at least four people in the car, and one hung out one of the back windows, jeering at the pedestrians. It looked to Kevin like the car was deliberately trying to run people over. And then it was gone, turning a corner, the noise of its engine fading into the overall throng of the city.

Kevin shuffled away from the window. Four floors up, his observations had gone unnoticed. For now, he was safe, so long as one of those silly fuckers didn't set fire to his building. Hobbling, he made his way over to the refrigerator and pulled out another can of beer. He had twenty-four cans left in the fridge, and he intended to drink them all before death enveloped his city. His city? No, that wasn't right. He'd only lived here for four years. Travelling here from Australia to go to university and then on to a job now seemed like a fucking idiotic idea. Coming here had been more about escaping than an education. His mother had been against it, but what the hell did she know? Turned out that she knew a lot more than he did.

"Fuck."

18.30PM, 16th September 2015, MI6 Building, London, UK

"Starting the second incision." Victor Durand watched through the shatterproof glass window into what had once been a secure interrogation room. Now it was a makeshift surgical laboratory, the centrepiece to which was a metal mortuary table. Strapped to it was one of the infected captured earlier in the day, and the naked form thrashed as best it could, the restraints stopping virtually all motion. Its mouth was covered to stop it spitting, or worse vomiting the virus everywhere. They had tried sedating the subjects, but the sedatives had no effect on the infected, their metabolisms seemingly burning up whatever chemical concoction that was pumped into them. And they didn't have the facilities to do general anaesthesia. So be it, the experiment would be done with them awake. No matter, they were no longer human.

In the room were three other scientists, dressed in hazmat suits, one of them brandishing a scalpel as he began to remove a slice of skin tissue from the bound figure. The creature didn't seem to react to the pain; it just continued trying even more violently to break her bonds. The scientist carried on regardless. With tweezers, he extracted the slice of skin, mindful of the blood and the fact that one slip with the scalpel would doom him. One of the other scientists, stood behind him, zoomed onto the wound with the digital video camera she held, the image projected on the screen by which Victor stood. He watched the magnified image, saw the bleeding stop almost instantly. He pressed the intercom button situated next the window.

"I want to see how they react to various toxins, see if we can find anything they are vulnerable to that makes them react." He released the button. Part of him wanted to be in there himself, doing the wet-fingered work. But he was too important to risk like that. That was the excuse he gave himself. Besides, he didn't have the surgical skills needed to do this work; the largest living thing he had ever experimented on being a plump laboratory rat. No, let his minions do all the leg work, let them take all the risks. Although nobody was officially in charge, he had quickly accepted the role of senior scientist. He had the credentials and the personality, and everyone had just sort of accepted him in the role. So now, he got to boss people around.

The third scientist moved a wheeled trolley over to the end of the table by the infected's legs. On the trolley were various marked vials with glass pipettes. He picked up one of the loaded pipettes and hovered it over the infected shin.

"Applying three drops of hydrofluoric acid." The liquid hit the skin, and instantly, it began to eat into the flesh. The infected hardly reacted. "As before, they seem generally unbothered by pain stimuli." Victor watched as the scientist tried other chemicals, all with similar results. This fascinated him. All living things reacted to damaging stimuli, but these things hardly seemed to care. Stepping away from the window, he walked out of the observation room.

He had already reached the conclusion that the infected were a new species. They had human form, but their brain chemistry was vastly different, some parts of the brain actually showing atrophy as those aspects that defined humanity died off. The reptilian parts, however, those grew. The virus seemed to reshape the very structures of the brain, which would explain why the infected were not responsive to threats or reason. And the remodelling happened quickly, faster than should be biologically possible. Another mystery to add to the list for him to solve.

There were other things about them that had been witnessed. They would sacrifice themselves gladly if it meant the greater good of their collective was met. That was the other thing he had concluded, that they shared an almost telepathic link with each other, forming what amounted to a hive mind. Only there was no queen for this hive; it was just a collective consciousness that, although losing fear and reason and guilt and remorse, somehow seemed to retain the ability to coordinate strategically. He had read the field reports from across the country, read how the infected had used stealth as well as their vast numbers to overwhelm defensive positions. Their very weight of numbers had caused the grenadier guards to abandon Parliament, a building that lay in ruins from the napalm that was dropped along the roads and the streets around the historic buildings.

But what about the undead? It was a term he might as well use for those infected who had been killed and who had resurrected. Why let decades of horror literature go to waste? How the undead came back, he still could not explain, although the lack of decomposition seemed to be due to the virulence of the virus killing all other organisms in the body. That was the next thing he needed to test. He needed to kill an infected under controlled conditions and find out why and how they defied the clutches of the Grim Reaper. And if he was going to do that, he would need more specimens. Lots more. Coming to the end of the corridor he was walking along, he stopped by a vending machine and picked out a can of Coke. The front had been broken open, and there was no need for money anymore because there was no longer an economy. Whilst the building's stores had been rationed, nobody had thought to gather up the dubious nutrition from similar machines scattered around the building. How long before the supplies ran out? he wondered. How long before they had to start raiding the city just to feed themselves? No matter, he thought, breaking open the tab on the can. The drink was still cool, and he downed half of it, relishing the sugar and the caffeine hit. Really, considering the precarious position he found himself in, he knew he should be worried. But he wasn't. So far, with the scientific discoveries he was unearthing and the lack of ethical insight into his actions, he knew this was the best day of his fucking life. The only thing that would make it better was when those in charge finally relented on his earlier request that had been shot down in flames. They said no now, but he knew, in his heart, that it was only a matter of time before they let him start the essential experiments. The ones where he infected live human subjects with the virus under controlled conditions.

Wouldn't that be a sight to see?

18.37PM, 16th September 2015, M1, South of Leeds, UK

"Come on, honey, you have to keep moving."

"But Daddy, I'm tired and my feet hurt."

"I know, petal, but there are bad people coming, and we have to get away from them."

James, leaning against the side of a stationary white van, watched the father and his daughter as they walked past, the pained, panicked look in the father's eyes so familiar to him now. He had seen it dozens of times today, perhaps hundreds. People used to the normality of existence transported to a world where the rules no longer applied. And, of course, one of those faces with that look had been his own, as witnessed in the rearview mirror of his car when he had finally decided to abandon it.

There was no way traffic was going anywhere on this motorway. All the lanes were blocked, some of the cars still running, their owners deserting them in blind panic. All around him people walked on foot, and James had stopped to rest, his aged frame not up to the task his mind was demanding of it. He was sixty for Christ's sake; he shouldn't be walking miles in shoes that were designed more for decoration than hiking. The heels throbbed from the blisters that had undoubtedly burst, and his thighs ached from the exertion his muscles were unused to.

He had been healthy, back in the day. Shit, he'd run marathons. But then wealth and the good life and running a successful multi-million-pound business had stopped all that. So here he was, on a road to nowhere, fleeing demons he still didn't really believe existed. But the news had been clear, and the screaming people he had seen running past his place of business had convinced him it was time to leave. Being situated right near the motorway had allowed him to get out of Leeds city centre, but it hadn't been long before his expensive Aston Martin had become blocked by the cars and buses of people with the same intention. And now he was on foot, part of the exodus trying to get somewhere safe. His wealth, all his hard work, now amounted to nothing.

James didn't know what attracted his attention, but he looked back up the motorway, past the crowds of people. Something didn't look right, didn't feel right. He stood up to full height, pushing himself off the van. What was this? No. No, it couldn't be. People were running, running in his direction, those people closer to him steadily joining in the race. If there were infected coming, staying on the road was a fool's errand, and he painfully made his way around the van to the hard shoulder. There was a steep grassy incline, and he pulled himself up it, his heart protesting further at this most unwanted of exercise. Breathing heavily, light headed and almost dizzy with the exertion, he looked back up the motorway from his new vantage point. And there they were. About two hundred metres up from his position the panic was unmistakeable, the people trying to flee from something that was faster and stronger than they were.

To get away from the carnage, he had to descend the bank on the other side, which led to a small single lane road. He started to gingerly climb his way down, his feet now in agony. And in his panic, he didn't see the hole in the Earth. Probably the opening to a rabbit warren, or maybe just a random dip in the ground, but the effect was lethal. His foot fell into it, twisting him sideways, something in his leg cracking. James came crashing to the ground, his overweight form hitting the ground hard, his head jarred violently by the impact. The pain from his leg followed seconds later, and he bit down on his tongue hard, his mind filling with agony and despair. Stars floated in his vision, and blackness swept in from the sides as he passed out. Just as darkness descended on his mind, he thought he heard a scream. He wasn't conscious long enough to realise the scream had come from his own lips and that a dozen creatures with red eyes had heard it on the wind. When James regained consciousness, he no longer knew his name and the pain in his leg was of no consequence to him, nor the throbbing where his left ear had been. All that mattered to him now was to feed, to kill, and to spread the disease that was now coursing through his system.

18.40PM, 16th September 2015, Her Majesty's Prison, Belmarsh, UK

Only in the dead of night had he heard the prison this quiet before. On a normal day, he would be down in the mess hall eating what the authorities called food, but there was no evening meal served today. No, Chris was still locked in his cell, the TV and the window his only entertainment. He had some books and magazines, but they couldn't tell him what he needed to know. For that, he had been glued to the BBC News 24 channel, which he was amazed was still broadcasting. He knew it was bad, had witnessed the infected from the window in his cell, had seen them maraud through the streets around the prison, but that had been hours ago. The streets were deserted now, anything human either in hiding or consumed by the viral wave that was washing over the country.

Chris didn't think it possible for him to feel relieved to be in prison. But he was relieved now. He knew it was a temporary respite, because although he was safe from the infected, there were other problems building up that would become a pressing concern before long. Firstly, he was locked in a room with no food, and he doubted very much if there was anyone left from the prison staff to provide such. The last screw he had heard had been over four hours ago, and he had witnessed several of them leaving the prison by the main gate.

Then there was the water and the electricity. It was only a matter of time before both were no longer available. So whilst he was unlikely to fall victim to whatever plague this was, he still faced a rather unpleasant fate of starvation or death by thirst.

"...still indications that the government has a chance of getting control of the infection sweeping the country. The official line is that you should stay in your homes and await further instructions, but..." The woman on the screen bowed her head, tears obviously welling up inside her. "I can't do this anymore," she said, not looking at the camera. "This is all bullshit." Even in his situation, Chris was shocked. It was the end of the world, and he was still surprised to hear a middle-class woman swear on the country's news network. The woman presenter looked back up at the camera. She shook her head, obviously at something that was being said to her over her earpiece. "Dominic, they need to know the truth," she said to someone off camera. "Goddamnit, these are people's lives we are talking about. But..." That was when the broadcast cut out and the BBC News 24 logo came on the screen. A little message scrolled across the bottom of the screen stating that the broadcast would resume shortly.

"Fuck," Chris said, and he stood up from his bed. This was the only channel he had; all the other permitted channels were off the air. So he was left with the window, and he took the two steps that were required for him to look out on the world, not that there was a great deal to see. Even though it was basically in the heart of London, the area surrounding was pretty secluded. However, there was plenty to see now. The main road running up to the front of the prison was no longer deserted. There were hundreds of infected running down the road. He stood there watching them, mesmerised by their numbers. He had sometimes dreamed of a mass prison break, the population rising up and overpowering the wardens, storming out into the surrounding lands, rejoicing in the freedom they would fleetingly enjoy. But he'd never once imagined anyone breaking into prison, especially not in these numbers. But it was okay, he was safe. The walls needed ladders to climb, and the numerous gates and doors would stop the virus getting to him. Surely that was the case.

"This is BBC broadcasting from the emergency broadcast bunker at Wood Norton. This is the latest information from NATO command." Chris turned away from the window and moved back to his bunk. He suddenly didn't want to know what was happening out there anymore. He looked at the TV, noticing the different presenter. Obviously, the powers that be couldn't have the fucking truth be told, even when the truth was all that was left in the world.

"We can again advise that citizens should avoid the cities of London, Manchester, Birmingham, Leeds, Glasgow, and Nottingham, which are centres of the viral outbreak. Those in the south and southwest of the country are advised to vacate your position and relocate to Cornwall where a safe zone is being set up. For those of you in other parts of the country, either stay in your homes or organise into groups for mutual defence…"

Mutual defence? What a crock of shite. There was no defending against this. If the fucking army couldn't defend Parliament, what hope had a disarmed and fattened population? Chris found himself wondering what had happened to his ex-wife, whether she had become one of the deadly mob or had somehow escaped. He hoped the former; he hoped she was wandering the streets, craving flesh like the vampire she had always been.

Over the sound of the TV, he heard something and he used the remote to mute the broadcast. At first, he heard nothing, but then the sound came again. Was that a scream? Then the noise grew, as his fellow prisoners reacted to something. He moved to the cell door, putting his ear to it, only to jump back when something slammed hard against the other side of it. He moved back further when the panel in the door slid open, and the demonic face looked in at him. Shit, they were inside. How did they get inside? The door slammed again, and the face pushed right up into the hole in the door, all teeth and bloodied eyes and spittle.

"*Feeeeeeed!*" the thing roared, and Chris thought he recognised the face. As distorted and rage-filled as it was, it was a face he had seen every day for months. It was one of his cell block screws.

"Fuck off!" Chris shouted. His back was now right up against the far wall of the cell, and the face looked at him with hunger. It was then that he heard a sound he had heard every day since his arrival, a sound he had until today both loved and loathed. As he stood there, looking into the face of Satan, the door to his cell unlocked, swinging open to display a monster transformed. The figure in the door didn't move at first, but after a few seconds, it backed away, walking out of sight. For the briefest of moments, Chris found he could fool himself into believing the bastard of a warden had come back to rescue them, to let them out of their cells and give them a fighting chance. He even took a hesitant step forward, but seconds later, the door frame was filled again, this time by a complete stranger, face gouged, one eye dangling by its optic nerve, teeth bared in a hideous snarl, its lower lip all but missing. The apparition took a step into the cell, limping from an obviously damaged leg. The once-white T-shirt that would have mesmerised him in the outside world due to the marvellous pair of breasts it covered, now mesmerised him because of the scarlet-red gore that stained it.

"Stay away from me, you fuck," Chris commanded, but it didn't stay away. No, it did quite the opposite.

18.48PM, 16th September 2015, Hayton Vale, Devon, UK

Major David Croft. A meaningless title now. Was there even a British Army left for him to be a major of? There certainly wasn't a country. He stood and watched the smoke rise from the ruined farmhouse, the result of multiple explosions that had destroyed the secret laboratory that lay beneath it, the laboratory that had been used to create the deadliest pathogen ever unleashed on mankind. The madman who created it, dead by his own hand, now lay entombed with the decaying corpses of his creations. And all Croft could think about was the fact that he had failed in his mission. They hadn't secured the scientist that had created the plague sweeping across the British mainland, and they hadn't secured his research. The only thing they had been able to salvage was a USB stick containing the information on the organisation that had funded the whole thing. Good for revenge, but not much use when you wanted to try and save an island of over sixty-five million people. At least this time, the men he had commanded had come out of it alive. Perhaps commanded was the wrong word; despite his rank, nobody took orders from him here. The SAS had their own way of doing things.

He felt someone stir behind him, and turned to see Captain Savage looking at the ruins.

"It needs a name," Savage said. She wasn't looking at Croft. She looked like she was lost in thought.

"What does?"

"The virus, it needs a name. Something that's going to kill millions of people should be called something."

"What did you have in mind?" Croft asked. He could tell she had already thought of something, already made a decision about what this man-made monstrosity should be called.

"Necropolis. We should call it the Necropolis virus," Savage said.

"Catchy," Croft retorted. He didn't smile. There could be no humour in a situation like this. He had failed in his mission to capture the scientist who had created the virus, and had been told mere minutes ago by the Chief of the Defence Staff that he was now trapped on an island which, by the end of the week, would be almost entirely populated by ravenous, blood-thirsty maniacs intent on ripping his throat out. Oh, and zombies, don't forget the zombies.

"What's catchy?" Captain Hudson of the SAS walked towards him, his face solemn.

"Captain Savage has decided to name the virus Necropolis," Croft said.

"Hmm," Hudson nodded. "Seems appropriate."

"What's the word on your men?" Croft asked, nodding to the group about ten metres away.

"I gave them the choice to go off on their own, and some of them took it. Less than I expected, but more than I would have liked. We're heading back to the helicopter, and then I have orders to go to Newquay. Looks like the Top Brass had the same idea as you, Croft. Hereford will already have been evacuated by now." Hudson turned to his female counterpart. "I presume you will want to stick with us, Captain," Hudson said addressing the only female in the group.

"Fucking right I'm staying with you," Savage said. That drew a smile from the SAS captain.

"Why, Captain Savage, if I'm not mistaken, I think that's the first time I've heard you swear," Croft teased.

"Well, get used to it. There's likely going to be more where that came from."

It could smell them. It wanted their meat, wanted to dig its teeth deep into the muscle and the skin, to feast on the juicy innards. The virus demanded it, the virus commanded it. But it was a primitive beast, and that worked against the virus. Because it still had cunning, and it still had a desire for self-preservation, and that won over the desire to feed and to spread implanted in it by the weaker strain of the virus. It had seen what the men had done to its brothers and sisters. It had seen the damage their loud sticks had caused, the throats and the organs and the legs blown apart by devices outside of nature. It wanted to feed, yes, but it also wanted to live. So it growled softly deep in its throat, a growl that was matched by the three others of its kind that stood behind it. Hidden from sight in the forest, they had already decided they would stalk their new prey, and take it if the opportunity arose.

Their creator was dead, buried deep within the ground below them. They didn't know this, didn't even remember how they had been brought into this world. They now survived purely on instinct and primal drive. But there was something else there, something familiar. It cocked its head as it heard a sound inside its mind, tried to understand what the sound meant. He had heard it in the time before. It meant something to him then, but it danced about on the edge of its comprehension. The infected Doberman shook its head, as if to try and rid itself of cobwebs, saliva spraying in an arc. Those sounds meant something; those sounds almost made it feel like it had to do something. But the virus had destroyed all memory of the time before, the time before the injections, the torture and the transformation. So it ignored the sound, which its former self would have recognised as voices. Voices on the ether, telling it to feed, to kill and to spread. But it would do none of those right now, for it had other more important things in mind. Right now, it and its kind would stalk and they would hunt. And if the opportunity arose, only then would they kill. The three mutated dogs turned and ran off into the woods, knowing that their smell would keep them close to the creatures on two legs.

18.49PM, 16th September 2016, Newquay airport, Cornwall, UK

ATTENTION

YOU ARE NOW UNDER NATO MILITARY QUARANTINE
UPON ARRIVAL REPORT TO ADMINISTRATION
YOU WILL BE ASSIGNED DUTIES AND ARE EXPECTED TO
COMPLY

MARTIAL LAW IS IN EFFECT

That had been the large sign that had greeted her when she had left the plane. It had been on disembarking from the plane that they had all been told that there was no escape from the UK, that the whole country had been quarantined indefinitely. No flights in, no flights out. She was trapped on an island with an infected horde of maniacs getting closer and closer every hour. The news hadn't gone down well with the people around her, many of whom were civilians who had been expecting some kind of dramatic rescue. That didn't happen, and now they were stuck.

But for the time being, she was safe, for several days at least it seemed. Her evacuation plane had landed thirty minutes earlier, and now she sat outside on a grass verge, watching thousands of people mill about in an airport that wasn't designed for the numbers. Dr. Simone Holden, Consultant in Accident and Emergency, felt the trauma of the day's events finally hit her. She couldn't control it. She had no energy left, no will to resist. She could do open heart massage on dying children, could stick a needle in a patient's spine, but this? She couldn't deal with this. She couldn't even cry. She was just spent, so she sat, arms around her knees, and slowly rocked to a spectral beat.

The image of the fences on the M1 falling as her bus drove away from the thousands trying to flee the infected were etched in her mind. It was all she seemed able to think about, and she stared into space, almost visualising the events on the runway tarmac. It was perhaps ironic that only last night she had been drowning her sorrows in gin. How inadequate and meaningless she had thought her life had been. A boring relationship, an unfulfilling career, and a burnt-out mind. But how wrong she had been—that was paradise compared to this. She would give everything, everything to have that back now. How had she even had the audacity to complain about her life? It was the life billions only dreamt of, and now it was nothing.

Someone suddenly sat down beside her, but she didn't turn to look who it was. She saw the person was offering her something and finally relented, seeing a cup of coffee in a dented Styrofoam cup held in a shaking hand.

"Your hand's shaking," Holden said, accepting the gift.

"Yep," Brian said. Brian, the man who, with his partner, had rescued her from the hospital she had found herself trapped in. The man who had all but dragged her to the M1 out through North London. The man who had boarded the evacuation bus with only three rounds of ammunition left for his machine gun. The man who had risked his life for her even though he didn't know her before today.

"Thanks," she said taking a sip. The coffee, despite being awful, was somehow the best thing she had ever tasted. "What do we do now?"

"I have no idea. Me and Stan are due to be given our orders in about twenty minutes. We'll learn what the situation is then." Holden looked at him intently. "What?"

"I don't even know your last name," Holden said, a tear forming at last. "How can I not know your last name?" Brian put a comforting arm around her, and she felt something, electricity, something she hadn't felt for a long time. He gave her a quick hug, almost fatherly.

"Because I didn't tell you." He let go of her and put out his right hand for her to shake, and she swapped the hands holding the cup so she could. "Hi Doc, I'm Brian Moss." She laughed at that, didn't even know she had that emotion still in her. She shook it, held his hand a moment too long. They looked at each other, both knowing where this was probably heading. She let go of his hand.

"Will we get out of this do you think?"

"I don't know, Simone, I really don't." That was the first time he had called her Simone. She hoped it wasn't going to be the last. He stood, his good deed seemingly over. "I'll come and get you after the debriefing, let you know what the score is." Looking down at her, he forced a smile, hesitated holding her gaze, and then walked off with purpose. Holden watched him walk, saw the confident gait, the strength in the man. She had always gone for the academic types, those who could challenge her mind. But here was a man who didn't hide behind books and words. This was a man who could challenge her soul. Holden shook her head in confusion. A moment ago, she was being ripped apart with despair, and now she was contemplating romance. She took another sip of her coffee and looked back after him. No, not romance.

Stan stood on the tarmac with several hundred other people. A collection of police and military, they waited to be told what was going to happen next. He turned his head as another plane landed, its wheels bouncing off the runway as the pilot brought the aircraft to the ground. But why were they here? Why weren't they in another country?

He lingered at the back of the queue, not talking to anyone. He had nothing to say, nothing he wanted anyone to hear. Stan had left his life behind on a frantic trek across a disease-ridden city, only to end up in the back end of the country. It was a place he knew well from his younger days—he had spent several summers surfing the waves of Newquay—but he doubted he'd be doing any surfing in the foreseeable future. Stan looked around again and saw Brian rushing over to him.

"Did you find her?" Stan asked.

"Yeah, she'll live," Brian said absently. "Not missed anything then?"

"No, some bigwig is supposed to be addressing us shortly." Stan reached into his top pocket and extracted a pack of cigarettes.

"Mate, you quit like a year ago," Brian admonished. Stan just shrugged and took out a cigarette, putting the rest of the packet back in his pocket.

"I think dying of lung cancer is the least of my worries right now." Putting the fag in his mouth, Stan took a lighter from another packet and lit the end. He inhaled deeply. "Fuck I've missed these." There was a murmur in the crowd, and the military members who were mostly all together suddenly stood to attention.

"Looks like the action's starting," Brian said.

"At ease," a voice at the front of the crowd said.

"Why are we standing at the back?" Brian asked. Stan just shrugged, and Brian strained to see who was speaking. A head appeared above the crowd as the person addressing everyone obviously stood on something.

"Some of you know me. For those who don't, my name is General Arthur Mansfield. I have been given the delightful task of salvaging what's left of this country. That means I'm in charge, the civilian authorities having now been placed under complete military control. So for you people not in the armed forces," he paused to look out across the crowd, "that means you work for me now." The non-military members of the crowd shuffled and mumbled to each other. That was not something many of them wanted to hear. "You answer to me, and I answer to General Marston, the Chief of the Defence Staff. And he, well he answers to God, NATO, and the President of the United States.

"The situation is this. This country has been overrun by an infection that spreads rapidly throughout the population. Many of you have seen the results of this, have fled from areas where the very people who lived there turned against you, attacked you. These infected individuals are not your families anymore; they are not your friends. You are no longer tasked with protecting them. You are tasked with protecting those who have survived the plague's ravages. You are here because we need you, and because of that, we expect you to do your duty. You were all registered on your arrival, and you will all be given assignments based on your skills and your experience. Please check with Colonel Tucker in the airport's departure lounge for your detail." A helicopter passed overhead, large, bulky, transporting God only knew what. "Any questions?" The general looked around, mainly at the civilians. He didn't expect the military personnel to do anything but stand there and soak it in. Nobody said anything, which was how he liked it. This was the fourth such speech he had made today, and he was getting tired of it. "That is all."

"Shit," Stan mumbled under his breath. "I've just been conscripted. Fuck this for a game of soldiers."

"It is what it is, Stan. We just have to get on with it. At least we're alive. At least we're being fed." Brian put a reassuring hand on his friend's shoulder. "We'll get through this. We always do." In front of them, a fellow police officer turned. He was a senior rank, an Inspector, and his uniform was ripped at the shoulder showing the white shirt underneath.

"Hi, Stewart," the stranger said, offering a hand and a name. The two friends shook in turn and introduced themselves, Brian shaking last. Stewart held Brian's hand a fraction too long before releasing it. He turned to Stan. "Where did you get out from?"

"London," Stan said. "We were near Euston Station when it all went south."

"Holy shit, and you made it out?" Stewart was looking at them almost in awe.

"It would seem so. You?" Brian asked.

"Hell, I work in Newquay. I was dragged up here mid-afternoon. They've had me moving boxes around since then." There was a shout from behind Stewart, obviously an attempt to grab his attention. "Listen, I've got to go. Come to the mess tent around eight tonight. I'll introduce you to some of the lads."

"Eight o'clock it is then," Brian said. Stewart nodded to them, turned, and ran off to the person who had shouted at him.

"Seems like a nice guy," Stan said

"We'll see," Brian answered. "I have a feeling nice will get you killed in this Brave New World."

18.55, 16th September 2015, Hounslow, London, UK

Owen had taken a detour, and his initial optimism was starting to falter. The growing doubt had been brought on by his present state. He was now ravenously hungry, and that had brought on the true realisation of the situation to him. Food. What about the food? This was now a cause of growing pessimism. *How long would there be food? How long would the power stay on?* he wondered. That was something he hadn't considered. With no society to keep it going, it wouldn't be long before basic utilities and sanitation began to fail. And what happened when the food started to spoil? Even canned goods had a finite shelf life. And why was he so fucking hungry? It was actually painful.

Needing sustenance badly, he decided to stop at the local mini supermarket. The road was strewn with the debris of chaos, but humanity seemed to have deserted this part of the city for good. Likely, there were still some hopeless souls hiding behind their curtains, hoping their flimsy doors would keep the infected at bay, but none of them made themselves known to him.

On seeing the shop, he had half-expected to find it ransacked, but it was anything but. The windows were smashed, but as he peered inside, he saw that the lights were on and most of the shelves were relatively untouched. The infection had hit too quickly for anyone to do anything but flee. It looked like he basically had the place to himself, apart from the occasional infected that scuttled about on the periphery of his vision. Owen wondered why they didn't bother him. He didn't need a medical degree to realise he was somehow immune to the infection, and that being exposed to the virus made him somehow connected to those who weren't immune. Owen knew he would have to investigate the possibilities of this discovery. But right now, he needed food. And lots of it.

His stomach growled at him again, and the automatic shop door opened as he approached. Slinging the machine gun over his shoulder where the bag with the rest of his arsenal resided, he picked up a shopping basket and began to help himself to the spoils. He scooped rather than placed food into the basket, a pork pie unwrapped with his teeth and consumed in two bites. A second followed in short order.

Halfway down the second aisle, his basket half full of an unhealthy assortment of mainly crisps and canned goods, Owen heard a noise. It sounded like it was off in the back, away from the public area of the store. He knew he had nothing to fear from the infected, but humans were a different kettle of fish. He, more than anyone, knew the depths man would stoop to, and Owen did not want to become a display in irony. Surviving the most infectious disease ever unleashed, only to have his skull caved in by some half-manic shop owner was not how he wanted to go out. Putting the basket down, he readied his machine gun.

"Hello?" Nobody responded, but there was more noise. "Get your fucking arse out here where I can see you," Owen demanded loudly. He heard a door open, and a low moan floated to him from the unseen. What the fuck was this? Looking behind himself briefly, Owen backed up, taking several steps, his basket abandoned, a discarded packet of noodles scuttling across the floor as his foot hit it. He readied his machine gun and saw that his hands were shaking. Why the fuck were his hands shaking?

"Look, I don't want any trouble. But if you start anything, I will fucking shoot you. Know that, okay?" No response, except the shuffling of feet. And then it appeared. IT was definitely an adequate description because what Owen saw clearly shouldn't have been moving about. Appearing around the end of the shelves, the old man meandered drunkenly into Owen's shopping aisle. The man was missing his left arm below the elbow and the skin of his scalp flapped low over his eye where it had been peeled away from the skull. The once immaculate white shirt was now a completely different colour. Owen felt the gun drop, disbelief taking him in the moment.

"What the...?" The creature, because that was what it now was, looked in his general direction, only the eyes were black as pitch. Did it even see him? It took a step towards him, a second, its jaw opening and closing, as if testing that the muscles still worked. This wasn't one of the infected; it didn't have their energy, their vitality. No, this was something else. And what was worse, he couldn't hear it in his mind. The emotion he thought he didn't need to feel anymore crept in, worming its way into his thoughts. Panic, he could taste it.

Owen knew he had to act and he lined up a shot and pulled the trigger, felt the impact in his shoulder. The round took the beast in its chest and it almost fell. But it didn't fall, steadied itself, and took another step. Closer now, Owen could smell the stench coming off it.

"Shit," Owen cursed; the noise of the shot had been painful in his ears. He hadn't expected that, hadn't learnt the lesson from when he had shot Gary hours before with Gary's uncle's shotgun. But he had to fire again, and he did. This time, the shot missed, and a bottle shattered on one of the far-off shelves. The monster was nearly on him now, close enough that Owen could read the name tag on its shirt. This guy had worked here? He composed himself, stepped back, inhaled a deep breath, and lined the shot up again. This one took the zombie just over the left eye. Its head was flung back and the rest of the body went with it, falling onto the basket Owen had just discarded. The body twitched for a few seconds, and then it was still.

"Fucking zombies," Owen muttered to himself. He stood for a moment, his ears ringing. *What if there were more?* his brain said. What if they are waiting for you in the back? What if they swarm on you and eat you? And then he heard it, the whisper.

"There, food there?" There were infected outside, attracted by the noise.

"Go away you fucks," Owen yelled in his mind. The infected weren't a threat, but Owen now knew they weren't the only things on the street. A coldness filled his spine. What happens when the infected started to die in large numbers? Is this what they become? Is this what he'd inherited, a city of walking fucking corpses? Maybe this wasn't his city after all.

"FUCK!" Owen roared.

18.56, 16th September 2015, Oxford, UK

Luke sat watching the TV set. He didn't really see what was being displayed, didn't really hear the presenters talking about the day's events. His mind was elsewhere, shocked into submission by what he had done not thirty minutes before. The shotgun still rested across his legs, and the smell of gunpowder was still powerful in the air.

He had watched with horror as the country fell apart. Being self-employed, he had the luxury of working from home, and today, he had been redesigning the architectural plans for his latest project, when his Facebook messenger notifications had pinged. It was his wife, Angela.

> My God have you seen the news

> Been busy. What's up?

> Just turn on BBC news, you won't believe it

He had initially pulled up the streaming site on his computer, but he soon transferred to the fifty-inch plasma in the living room. That had been at ten in the morning, and he had watched transfixed as the true enormity of what was happening became clear. The only time he had pulled himself away from the TV, his project completely forgotten, was to go to the toilet and to look in on their four-month-old daughter who was sleeping quietly in the other room. He had chosen to be the house husband, his wife feeling she couldn't damage her prospects with too much time off at this important stage of her career. The child had not been planned. She was loved, just not planned.

By eleven-thirty, it was evident that the shit had hit the fan, and his phone buzzed with another social media message.

> I'm scared honey. I'm coming home

She arrived an hour later. By then, the world had been told of the brutal murder of the prime minister and most of his cabinet. The live feeds from the infected cities had ceased, and the various news channels were now resorting to playing uploaded videos from YouTube. By the time his wife had returned, Luke had abandoned the TV, had already drunk enough gin to get himself drunk, and was completely entranced by the horrors viewable on the internet's various upload channels. By mid-afternoon, the true unadulterated horror of their situation was undeniable. They had rung round relatives and friends, but most of the numbers they dialled didn't answer.

By six o'clock, Luke did what he believed any loving husband would have done. If he had been sober, things might have been different. But he wasn't, and leaving his wife sobbing in the kitchen, their daughter cradled in her arms, he had gone into the spare room, opened up the gun safe and taken out the shotgun. Loading it with cartridges, he had staggered down the stairs, and without giving anyone a chance to think, he had walked into the kitchen and fired the first barrel directly into the sleeping form of his daughter. His wife was flung onto the ground by the blast, and the second shot exploded her head, cutting off her scream.

There was a noise outside, and he rose from his chair and walked over to the window. Outside, the neighbours to the right were loading up their car. Where did they hope to go? The country was fucked. Luke opened up the gun, the spent cartridges still inside, and he loaded new ones from his trouser pocket that he had stuffed full earlier. For the third time that day, the fleeing neighbour heard a loud bang from the house next door. He looked briefly at the house owned by the people he didn't know, and then finished securing the cases to the roof rack of his car. He briefly considered going round to see if everything was all right, but he quickly abandoned the idea. He had to leave, and he had to leave now.

18.57PM, 16th September 2016, Docklands, London, UK

This morning when he had woken up, he had technically been worth four hundred and seventy-two million pounds. Now? Now he was worth only what he could carry. Alexei had awoken early, as he always did, and had followed the routine he always followed. Thirty minutes of yoga followed by a full upper-body workout in his own personal gym. He had cooked himself a protein-heavy breakfast, necessary to maintain the muscular bulk that helped make him such a dominating presence. Barely surviving as a starving runt on the streets of Moscow, he had long ago vowed to be the one who handed out the beatings rather than the one who cowered at the end of another's boot. This was a promise he had followed through on, in spades.

That had been thirty years ago. He had turned the hardship into an inner resolve that he had used to first escape the madness of the streets. Crime had been the only way, running errands for a local crime family. Alexei had showed them utter devotion, and when the tasks became more numerous, more dangerous, he had done what was asked of him without question. By the age of seventeen, he had gained the reputation as a ruthless enforcer. By the age of nineteen, he had become a trusted lieutenant. But that wasn't enough for him, and when he was offered a chance to be involved in an expansion into European operations, he had jumped at the chance. The collapse of Communism was very good for business.

Now, he ran the whole London operation for his bosses. He would never betray them, because they had taken him off the street and given him the life he now enjoyed. And his bosses knew that, knew that no bribe or threat would ever be big enough to sway him. Unfortunately, today, none of that did him any good. Alexei sat on the balcony of his luxury penthouse apartment and watched Canary Wharf burn.

He was into his third Cuban cigar, half a bottle of 1982 Chateau Lafite Rothschild on the table beside him, the glass he was drinking it from presently empty. The HSBC tower had caught fire about an hour ago, and the flames were now two-thirds of the way up the immense structure. Alexei had no idea how the fire had started, but with no fire service left in London, it was only a matter of time before the whole building went. It was beautiful, and would be a beacon well into the night.

Part of his morning routine was to venture down to the small café on the ground floor. Although he was effectively a crime boss, he was all but a legitimate businessman now. Whilst he still oversaw the drug trafficking and the people smuggling, he had quickly come to the conclusion that there was money to be made from property and had carefully amassed a sizeable portfolio. Whilst it was all in his own name, all the profits he gave to his overlords, which was why he was a multi-millionaire only in technical terms. Alexei was nothing more than a custodian, but he wouldn't have it any other way. He showed them everything, gave them everything, and in return, they were generous, knowing that even a man of his integrity and dedication might one day be tempted by such immense wealth. Alexie thanked them, but kept his life free of trinkets and the trappings of money. Except for wine, wine was his second passion.

If he was honest, the money made him feel uncomfortable. He didn't feel, deep down, that he was worth it. Even now, he still slept on a blanket on the floor. It was who he was. He could spot a deal, could crush a competitor in a business proposition, but he was still a dog. He came from the streets, and he secretly believed he would end up back on the streets. That was why he was still able to kill anyone and anything without remorse. He held no rules in this regard.

That morning, sitting outside the café, enjoying his second cup of coffee, he had felt the change in the air. One of the things that had helped him survive on the cold streets of the Russian capital had been a nose that smelt out trouble. He could almost taste it. He looked at his Rolex, a gift from his patrons, and saw that the time had been nine-thirty in the morning. The café was on the border of an ornate plaza, the central water feature an archaic attempt to instil a feeling of grandeur in those who ventured past it. On the other side of the fountain, he saw someone stumble and collapse to the ground. Several Good Samaritans had zeroed in to help the stricken man, but they had quickly scattered when the vomiting had started. Alexie could hear it, the sound almost echoing across the structures around him. The whole plaza, at that moment, seemed to stop still in time. Alexie's spine tingled.

He had stood and walked into the café, noticing a second person collapse. There were three customers which he ignored, and he moved to the back, walking through a door into a private office. Nobody stopped him. Even if he had no right to be there, everyone was suddenly mesmerised by the scream that punched into their reality. He had every right to be here, but right now, he knew it was time to be elsewhere

In the back office sat a man twenty years his senior. Also Russian, the man was another cog in the mafia structure that Alexei controlled, his lined face a testament to a lifetime of serious smoking and alcohol consumption. He was also the closest thing that Alexie had to a friend in this whole fucking city. Friends were a liability in his line of work.

"Ivan," he said calmly, "I want you to close the café." Ivan looked at him and raised an eyebrow, surprised to hear Alexie speak Russian. Another scream, louder than the first, forced its way into the confines of the office. Ivan merely nodded and stood with difficulty.

"These old bones are failing me, my friend."

"That's because you try and drink yourself to death every night."

"And yet here I still am," the old man said with a smile.

"Bring everything and come with me." With that Alexie left the office.

Alexei was many things. He may have had to drag himself out of the gutter, he may have killed over thirty-seven people, and he may have been completely devoid of humour. One thing he was not, however, was stupid. He had an amazing gift for self-preservation, and that gift kicked into play on the morning of September the sixteenth. As his penthouse apartment had been raided by Special Branch on more than one occasion, he did not keep anything illegal there. Standing outside the cafe, he watched the humanity around him fall to pieces. He had always believed that the social fabric of Western society would collapse in on itself, but never like this. Never so quickly. He observed those who had fallen now attacking people. There were only three so far, but his senses told him something big, something game changing was happening here. Whilst some stood and stared out of bewilderment, he calculated what he was seeing. And he didn't like it.

Ivan and another, younger man from the café joined him, Ivan carrying a large bag. Putting the bag on the ground, Ivan took out three handguns and handed them round. Alexei looked at him, his eyes lighting up. It had been almost a year since he had held a weapon, and he missed the feel of it in his hand. He wasn't so precious as to require a specific gun like some gangsters. He didn't need gold-coated barrels and jewel-encrusted handles. So long as the gun was able to put a bullet in the desired target, then he was happy.

"Come," Alexei said. He walked off with purpose back towards the building that housed his penthouse, the other two men following him. That had been how his morning had begun. Now, nearly seven hours later, he sat and watched the flames. Ivan joined him on the balcony, a half-empty bottle of vodka in hand. The old man stood at the railing.

"So this is how it ends," Ivan said. He sounded almost bored.

"I don't think so," said Alexei. "We still have options. I am confident we will see Mother Russia again." Ivan turned to him and shook his head sadly.

"I always took you for a pessimist; I considered it one of your strengths. But the NATO dogs have quarantined the country. We are trapped here with these…these infected. Surely, it is better to just accept that and enjoy what life we have left." Ivan took another swig from his bottle, staggering slightly. There was a slight slur to his speech, the vodka definitely starting to have an effect on him. To be fair, though, he had started before lunchtime.

"Ivan, you forget, I spent seven years smuggling people into this country. And I know exactly how to smuggle them out."

18.58PM, 16th September 2016, Hayton Vale, Devon, UK

It had not taken them long to get back to the farmhouse on foot, and Croft looked longingly at the helicopter that would shortly be taking them all away from here. Gavin Henderson watched them nervously from the door of his farmhouse, a cup of something hot in his hand. *Christ, I could do with some of that*, thought Croft, but there really was no time. He watched as Hudson walked over to the helicopter, the pilot standing patiently outside. He didn't hear the conversation, but saw the pilot nod and get into the cockpit. The SAS who had decided to remain with their commanding officer walked past him towards their transport.

"You leaving now?" Gavin asked.

"Yes," said Croft. "You should come with us. It won't be safe here for long."

"No," Gavin said. "Nowhere will be safe, not from what I've seen on the news." The BBC was the only UK broadcaster still transmitting, and that was a very limited service. Gavin had spent the last few hours glued to CNN, which came over his satellite dish. The world only had one story to tell today.

"What will you do? You'll be all alone?" Savage asked. Not for the first time. Croft had noticed that she was staying close by his side. Croft didn't mind. Was it attraction or just survival instincts? he wondered. Probably the latter—the last thing people should be thinking about at the end of the world was bloody sex. Still, Croft felt something inside that he thought had died years ago. He liked this woman, he liked the possibility that she represented. And he had a strong suspicion that the feeling was mutual.

"The only man I ever loved is probably dead," Gavin said virtually emotionless. "There's nothing left for me now, and if it's the end, I want it to be somewhere I know. If I'm going to die, it's going to be here with my memories on my own land." With that, he turned and went back into his house, closing the door behind him.

"I can't decide if he's brave or just fucking foolish," Savage said, staring at where he had been standing.

"He's given up, I've seen it before," Croft said. "By nightfall, he will likely have eaten his shotgun." Savage looked at him, shocked.

"Then we have to help him, take him with us," Savage demanded. Croft looked at her. She was a doctor, so he understood where she was coming from, but he knew she still didn't understand the true reality of the situation.

"No, we don't," he said coldly. "I know it sounds harsh, and I'm sorry for that. That being said, the reality is the only people who will survive are those who choose to fight. Even then, most of us will likely die anyway. Those who give up that fight need to be allowed that choice. We have to respect that because we no longer have the luxury of carrying people who can't help themselves." Croft put a hand on her shoulder and gave it a squeeze. "Do you understand what I'm saying?" She nodded reluctantly. He looked her deep in the eyes, saw the tears forming, knew that she was holding it together, but only just. That's all any of them could hope for now, to hold it together and somehow get through this. "Come on, time to go," he said releasing her. She didn't follow him, not right away, but stood a moment, watching the closed door, hoping that Gavin would come out. Millions had already perished, and she was nearly in tears about one man who she didn't even know. Nothing made sense anymore.

Gavin watched through the kitchen window as the helicopter took off, the sky beginning to darken as the sun started its descent. Within moments, the helicopter was out of sight, the sound of its departure disappearing as it flew quickly away. He paused a moment lost in thought, then stepped back from the window and sat down at the kitchen table, his hand finding the shotgun that rested there. He had cleaned it three times today. All his preparations, all his readiness had come to nothing. He had failed to heed the most basic of warnings that had been given to him when he had been infected by the survivalist bug. At the end of days, do you really want to be left in the world that's gone to shit? Do you really want to be alive when everyone around you is either dead or dying? A world without electricity, without medicine, without basic sanitation or law. Because that was what you were signing up for. Do you want to be alone in that world? Do you want to be the one to witness the world around you burn?

It would have been different if he could have shared the end with someone. At least they could have put up a fight together, been there for each other. He would have had something to live for then, something worth surviving for. But now, but now everyone was probably dead. The landline still worked, but nobody answered when he rang them, and oh how he had tried. His lover, his family, all likely consumed by the plague. And every hour of every day would bring the plague ever closer to what was supposed to be his safe haven. The barriers wouldn't keep them out. Likelihood was they would find him and end him. He patted the shotgun, the decision already made. Now, all he needed was to act on that decision.

"Not yet." Standing, he walked purposely out of the kitchen into the downstairs landing, grabbing his coat from a hook on the wall. The keys were in a dish, and he plucked them up and walked out the front door. That dish had been made for him by his niece, that sweet, innocent child who he knew would never see a dawn again through human eyes. If she wasn't dead, she would be one of them, he was certain of it. Terrible images came to him of her feasting on his brother's carcass, and he found tears forming in his eyes. It was too much, he couldn't take this. Passing through, the door swung closed behind him. This time tomorrow, he would be dead; he had already made that choice. He had no desire to join the ranks of the infected. Best end it before that horror arrived.

He had chosen to release all the animals before he released himself from this world, and he made his way over to the chicken coop. They were unusually quiet, and as he came upon their enclosure, he saw why. Blood and feathers were scattered across the grass, a large hole ripped into the chicken wire to gain entry. What the hell had done that, and why hadn't he heard them? It must have happened when the helicopter was taking off.

"What the fuck?" Something had forced its way in and slaughtered everything. He looked around, worried that whatever did this might still be around. What the hell could break through chicken wire like that? Part of him told him to go back for the shotgun, but that part was silenced when he heard the pained squeal of one of his pigs. The pig pen was around the side of the main farmhouse, and he ran as more pigs joined in the chorus of distress.

He saw them as soon as he rounded the house, but he didn't know what he saw. They looked like dogs, Dobermans, but their bodies glistened as if skinned alive. And they were big, bigger than they should have been, their muscles distorted and grotesque. But the basic shape of what they once were was still visible. There were three of them, and two were chewing through the wire fence of the pig pen, wooden support struts simply snapping as mutant jaws closed on them. Then things got infinitely worse. One of the creatures turned its head and looked at him, its body turning to face him head on. It growled, deep in its throat. It sounded like no dog he had ever heard.

"Oh shit," Gavin said, looking around frantically. There was a splintering sound as another wooden post broke, and then the whole fence collapsed, two of the beasts leaping into the pigs' home. The pigs and piglets scattered, but the dogs were too fast, and two of the smaller pigs were wrenched from the ground, teeth biting into their necks, killing them almost instantly. The third dog took a step towards Gavin, and he moved to his right, the back door to his house a metre away. One of the larger pigs bolted through the break in the fence, and it rushed past the third dog, distracting it momentarily. Gavin took that as his chance, and he ran, hitting the door, flinging it open, slamming it shut behind him just as something monumental crashed into it. The wood of the door splintered, but Gavin didn't turn to look. He made his way through rooms, heading for the kitchen. He heard something shatter, a window. Entering the kitchen, he turned to close the door behind him, saw the hellhound close on his heels and threw the door shut in its face. There was the sound of a collision and the door juddered. But it held, thank God it held. Minutes ago, he had already made up his mind to take his own life, but now he was running, trying to survive.

Something hit the door again, and again, and the frame splintered. This was just an internal door, held shut only by a thumb latch. The shotgun. Gavin grabbed it, knew it was loaded, checked anyway. He heard a pig run past outside below the window, and then that same window exploded inwards as something huge and black flung itself through. The thing landed clumsily, rolling several times, sliding on the tiled floor. It ended up in the corner by the fridge, and Gavin brought the shotgun up, fired at it almost point-blank range. The dog's head exploded, black blood erupting all across the wall and the whiteness of the refrigerator. There was a crack, and Gavin turned to see the door breaking open. The third dog, the biggest of the three, was roaring forward at him. He barely had time to get the shotgun levelled in time and he hit the trigger just as it launched itself. The shot hit it in the abdomen, sending the dog backwards, its innards exploding. Gavin felt cold wetness land on his face, and he wiped the death away from his eyes with his sleeve. The dog landed twitching but useless, and, with shaking hands, Gavin opened the breach, ejecting the spent rounds. He fumbled for the open box of shells on the kitchen table, heard the bark from somewhere outside the property, and knew the last dog was coming.

One moment, it could sense its brothers, and the next, they were gone. The infected dog took a deep swallow of the pig meat it had just bitten off and turned from the dying animal it was feeding off. The pig lay panting, its legs kicking feebly as it quickly bled out from the neck wound that had brought it down. The dog sniffed and licked its bloodied maw then barked. There was no bark in response. The man, they had gone after the man, and men had sticks that killed. Giving the pig a final nudge with its snout, the dog turned and stealthily moved towards the house.

It couldn't sense its brothers, but it could smell them. It knew right then that it was now alone, and it whimpered softly to itself. A normal dog would have run off into the forest, but this wasn't a normal dog, and the other smell was so enticing, so inviting. The man, the prime meat, the thing it had been created to kill was in there. No pig could even compare to that. The dog made its way to the shattered back door and stepped hesitantly inside. Both scents were stronger now. The smell of death and the smell of man. It had to feed on the man, had to now that its brothers were dead. Something within it made that unavoidable. So it grew bolder, its nails clicking on the tiles as it worked its way through the human construction. It heard something crack shut, heard some other human sounds, and came upon the kitchen. There stood the man over the bodies of its brothers. One of them still twitched, the virus trying in vain to repair the wounds. It looked at the writhing form and then back at the man, saw it was pointing something. Then there was a roar, and the dog felt something hard and hot hit it clean in the face. In its dying seconds, the dog heard the man walk over to its twitching brother and there was another explosion. And then it was dead.

Gavin stood for several moments, numbed by what had just happened. Christ, he hadn't seen this coming. He had always thought it would be an economic crisis or a war that would see the end of things. Even a flu pandemic, but not this new reality. Not a zombie apocalypse. How the hell was he even supposed to believe in the natural order of things when monsters now stalked the Earth? All that sacrifice, all that anguish and rejection just so he could find himself trapped here, and now with nothing but his own tortured mind as company.

There had only been three dogs; he was sure there had only been three. Listening, he heard nothing but the natural sounds of nature and his own ragged breathing. He put the shotgun down, saw his hands shaking, felt nausea rise up his throat. Within seconds, he was on his knees, vomit streaming out between his teeth, shock hitting him like a brick wall. He felt it pour up and out through his nose, felt the burn at the back of his throat as the acid ejected itself from his body. He threw up again, tears streaming down his face, and he let out a roar of anguish.

"FUUUUUCK!"

The nausea subsided, his body shaking. It took a minute to compose himself, and he pulled himself up onto unsteady feet. His vision blurred momentarily, and blackness began to creep into his eyes, but he inhaled deeply and willed it away. Shaking his head, he staggered over to the sink and put his head under the cold tap, the water blissfully flowing over his scalp and face. Then he saw it. Blood, why was there blood in the water? He washed his face with his hands, saw more blood. Shit, he was covered in it. He pulled his T-shirt away from his body, saw the red stains and the small lumps of flesh that had adhered to the cloth. He yanked it off and threw it away in disgust.

"No, must get clean," he said to himself. Using the dispenser by the sink, he squirted copious amounts of anti-bacterial hand wash into his hands and smeared it over his head and scalp. He lathered it and turned both taps on full. It was a big kitchen sink, and he again easily put his head under the tap, trying in vain to wash the carnage away, ignoring the fact that the water was now getting too hot to be comfortable. Hadn't they said on the news that you could catch the infection from bodily fluids? The soldiers had come and then the soldiers had left and then hell had followed. The dogs had to be infected—it was the only thing that made sense.

"No, no, no, not like this," Gavin pleaded. Grabbing a towel, he dried his hair and his face. Had he done enough? Had he got to it in time? His face and scalp itched. Was that from the cleaning, or was it the virus worming its way into his body? Panic won, and he dashed from the kitchen down the corridor and into the downstairs lavatory where a mirror met him. Leaning on the sink, he pushed his face up close, tried to find any canine remnants on his face or in his blonde hair. He didn't see anything, and looking at himself in the mirror, he said a single word.

"Shit." And that was when he saw it, the black spec on one of his front teeth. The blood was in his mouth. That was when the cramps started, doubling him over. Collapsing into a foetal position, he felt his innards flip, and fire exploded in his head. His right arm shot out in spasm, smashing against the toilet porcelain, and he thought he heard something break. But the pain in the rest of his body was so great he couldn't tell. Gavin vomited again, this time not due to adrenaline overload, but because the virus wanted out, wanted to spread. He tried to crawl, he really did, although where to he had no notion. With herculean effort, he got halfway out of the lavatory before his body just gave out. There was a tearing sensation deep within his abdomen and his bowels erupted. Right then was when Gavin almost died. But he didn't. As the hours progressed, he would wish he had eaten that shotgun after all.

17.01, 16th September 2015, Plymouth City Airport, UK

Captain John Gallagher stepped out of the maintenance shed and looked out across the once-abandoned airport. Well, abandoned apart from hundreds of soldiers and the over one hundred and fifty Challenger 2 battle tanks that were parked on its asphalt surface, some of their engines still running. It had taken several hours to make ready the tanks from their base in Tidworth and wait for their crews, some of whom never turned up. In formation, it took several more hours to traverse the civilian-laden streets and roads to get to this point. Much of their journey had been over fields and through deserted villages. Deserted of pedestrians, not of fear. When faced with an obstacle, the choice was often made to go over rather than around, walls, fences, and cars crushed underneath as the tanks retreated away from where the infected would be heading to. Now, they were idle as they were refuelled with their precious life-blood.

There were more than just tanks, of course. There were dozens of Scimitars and Warriors, all waiting for the re-fuel trucks to deliver the vital diesel, without which they were effectively useless. He didn't like the fact that they had fled, abandoning the country east of them, but those were their orders. And in hindsight, he could understand them. The infection was spread across the country. Even several squadrons of one of the world's most powerful battle tanks would have been useless against that threat. No, the plan was to centralise the remaining forces in one place, project the power where it could be projected. He understood the logic, just didn't like the feeling of defeat that came with it.

He wasn't in charge here. There were people much more qualified for that. He hadn't even seen combat, still a virgin when it came to facing an enemy on the field. But his men seemed to think he was competent, which was usually a good indication. They didn't give him any grief at least, and he knew some of his peers didn't have that luxury. On the drive over, seeing the carnage the armoured convoy created, he wondered just how long morale and discipline could be maintained. These men had abandoned families and friends. They had abandoned dozens of vehicles due to there not being anyone qualified to drive them. Desertion, reprehensible in war, was probably understandable in the present situation.

With the obvious exception of the infected, his biggest fear was the diesel supply. Would NATO be willing to re-supply them given the quarantine? Probably not. The nearest refinery in Plymouth had been sucked dry, the tankers travelling under armoured convoy. Even now, according to the rumours, there were teams of conscripted civilians siphoning diesel out of every car they encountered, and every petrol station was being drained. Armoured vehicles were to be the main ground weapon in the coming battles. And they needed sustenance. The beasts needed feeding.

19.04, 16th September, 2015, The Irish Sea

The small fishing boat had left Liverpool under the cover of darkness. The five people on board were hoping they could evade the quarantine and escape to the relative safety of Ireland. Normally, the boat's captain wouldn't have wanted to come out in this kind of weather with children on board, the sea very choppy and the winds picking up, but he felt he had no choice for his family.

He had not been the only one leaving the Liverpool docks, and some of those other boats still showed on his radar, spread out to give everyone as big a chance as possible. Surely, the quarantine couldn't catch everyone. I mean, how many Navy vessels were out there? Should he encounter one, he would just turn back and try again from a different direction. The captain didn't quite understand the realities of what the quarantine meant, despite the very obvious warning that had been broadcast across the BBC emergency channel. That was just scaremongering, and this was still England. People still had rights.

It was several seconds before he noticed the new radar contact. In fact, there were two of them, both to the west of his position. That meant he had already been seen, the Navy's radar much stronger than his own out of date model. Should he turn back, or try and bluff it? Would they really turn him away? Was there a chance that, on proving there was no infection on board, they would give him free passage? He thought about asking his wife who was below with the children, but he didn't want to leave the wheel, not in these squally seas. A particularly large wave suddenly hit his boat, and he fought for control of the boat. When he next looked at his radar, he noticed that some of the refugee boats to the north had disappeared from the screen.

"What the hell?" he asked himself. No other thoughts went through his mind because the RGM-84 Harpoon anti-ship missile ploughed into his vessel at nearly five hundred miles an hour, detonating on contact. The explosion ripped through the wheel house, and seconds later, the fuel tank went up also. There were no survivors, and even if there had been, they wouldn't have lasted long in the cold waters of the Irish Sea. The defensive line had been set, and nobody, absolutely nobody, was getting past it.

19.12, 16th September 2015, Hounslow, London, UK

It was getting dark by the time he reached his destination. Owen had seen dozens of infected, and they had all ignored him, which was good. However, the zombies were different, two of them chasing after him on their drunken uncoordinated legs. Both had been easy to outrun, and they had diverted from him to attack a group of infected who were feeding on a dog's carcass. Owen had stopped to watch, amazed that the infected did nothing to counter the attacks that were rained down upon them, the zombies acting freely. What happened when the zombies outnumbered the infected? Which was the greater threat to humanity?

Walking up stone steps, the multi-storey housing estate was as quiet as a tomb. The only sounds he heard were his own feet and his own laboured breath. He stopped at the fourth landing, taking a moment to fill his lungs. There was the faint smell of burning, and Owen found himself wondering how the rest of the city was fairing. The fact that he had been able to pick up a whole arsenal of weapons that had been abandoned in the middle of some street suggested to him the city wasn't doing very well. There was a loud curse from down below, and he stepped up to the barrier and looked down into a concrete courtyard. A lone man was being chased by seven infected, all converging from different directions. These things could think; they could coordinate. The man tripped, as so often happens when panic takes over, and they were on him in a second. Owen heard his pathetic plight and watched as all seven of his assailants took turns to bite chunks from the man, each one then running off, probably still chewing their latest meal. The man lay moaning and bleeding, undoubtedly turning rapidly into the very thing that had attacked him. Poor bastard, to be so weak when the world presented so much opportunity.

The entertainment over, Owen turned and walked up the passageway that fronted a dozen flats. He stopped at the fifth one and looked at the door for a moment. There were sounds coming from inside, faint but distinctly human. Evidence that people were home. He slammed his fist on the door three times, not loud enough to wake the dead, but almost.

"*Food, hear food*," the whisper came in his mind, and he felt the all-seeing eyes of the infected turn to where he was.

"No food here," he shouted back in his thoughts. "Fuck off." He felt their attention withdraw. That was interesting—the infected were definitely drawn to sounds. Owen, noticing that nobody was answering the door, slammed his fist on it again, only this time, he bent down and opened the letter box.

"Open the door, you fucking wankers. It's freezing out here." Looking through the slot, he saw a face appear at the end of the apartment corridor.

"Owen?" an almost whispered voice answered.

"No, it's the fucking Easter Bunny. Are you going to let me in or what?" A figure came into view and shuffled over to the door.

"Jesus, Owen, keep the noise down." Owen heard a lock unlatch and saw the door open a fraction, the chain still present. Scared eyes scanned him through the opening. Owen held up one of the rucksacks.

"I've brought beer."

Owen sat in the armchair of the apartment's living room. There were three people with him, and two of them were looking at him with a mixture of fear and awe. The other, a woman in her mid-fifties, was looking at him with obvious contempt. The beer he drank was warm, from his own supplies. The owner of this apartment didn't have any in.

"Steve, I can't believe you're making me drink warm beer."

"I'm sorry, Owen, but Mum doesn't let me keep any in the flat." Steve turned to look at the older woman who was glaring at him.

"Mrs. Bentley, that's not very nice of you."

"You, I want you out of here. Why the fuck did you let him in, Steve?"

"He's my friend, Mum," Steve protested.

"Your friend? He's a bastard, and I want him out of here." She was shaking now, Owen could see that. Normally, he would have been enraged at such disrespect, but he actually found the whole thing amusing.

"What?" Owen questioned in mock protest. "You'd throw me back out there with those maniacs?" Owen tipped back the beer, finishing it off, and then threw the empty can behind the chair he was seated on. Steve's mum visibly flinched at the atrocity. "That's not very Christian of you."

"Fuck you!" she shouted.

"Mum, don't, you might make him angry," a weak voice said. This was the final person in the room, Steve's sister. Truth be told, she was the reason Owen had come here. He had a notion in his head, a thought that needed expanding, testing. He wanted to try something, and who better than Steve's well-fit sixteen-year-old sister?

"Don't worry, Claire," Owen said standing. "I'm not angry. Your mum has every right to express her displeasure. This is her home after all."

"You're damn right this is my home," Vera Bentley stated. Owen nodded. He knelt down and opened the rucksack full of supplies which was at his feet. Extracting a six pack of lager, he stood back up and held them out to Claire.

"Claire, be a dear and put these in the fridge." She hesitated, looking at her mother for guidance. Before the matriarch of the house could object, he said, "I promise I'll be gone before half those beers are drunk. I just came here to talk to Steve, and as it's the end of the world, I think it's only right to have a few drinks. Wouldn't you agree?" With that, he used his other hand to pull back his coat from his waist. The action was subtle, but it exposed the handgun that was tucked down the front of his pants. Mrs. Bentley saw the gun, and she went pale. This put a different complexion on things. She knew Owen's reputation, but she never thought he would have a gun. Owen looked at her and raised a questioning eyebrow.

"Do as he says, Claire, and then go to your room." Claire nervously took the cans from his grasp, unnerved by the intense gaze he held her in.

"Do as your mum says, love. I only want to talk to Steve." She retreated from the room followed by her mother, who closed the door after her. Owen watched them go and then knelt back down to the rucksack. He withdrew an unopened bottle of Jack Daniels whiskey, and kneeling down held it up to Steve. "Get that down your neck, lad." It was then that Steve noticed the bandaged hand.

"What happened to your hand, Owen?"

"I got bit, didn't I? One of those fuckers tore my fingers clean off." Steve's eyes went wide, and he almost fell over the sofa backing up away from his friend. "What the hell's wrong with you?"

"You've been bitten, that means you're infected, man. You need to get out of here. Why the hell did you come here?"

"Why did I come here? I thought we were friends?" Owen pretended that his feelings were hurt. He looked at the cowering minion before him and almost laughed in his face. "This," he said raising his damaged hand, "this happened hours ago. You don't need to worry." But Steve was worrying, and he backed up further. "Oh enough of this shit," Owen said, pulling the pistol from his waist. "Sit the fuck down and have a drink with me, you dumb fuck." Steve didn't move; he just kept moving his gaze between the gun and Owen's face.

"This is my family, Owen. You shouldn't be here," Steve pleaded. Owen flipped the safety off the gun.

"I said sit down. You are going to have a drink with me, or I am going to put a bullet in you. What's it going to be?" Owen had come here for a specific reason, but another thought occurred to him. There it was, bright as day, something that had clicked in his head from one of the few school lessons he hadn't played truant from. It was the story of Typhoid Mary, how she hadn't showed the symptoms of the disease, but had been instead a carrier, spreading it to all and sundry. Owen suddenly wondered if he was the same, but with a disease far more deadly. For some reason, he had the urge to find out, to do a little experiment, to, as the scientists were want to say, "test the hypothesis". And he didn't like Steve, not really. Felt he was a clinger on when really he was just a mummy's boy. What kind of fucking man allowed a woman to say there couldn't be alcohol in the house for fuck's sake? That was not the makings of an alpha male. Owen took a step forward and used the gun to point at one of the room's chairs. "I'm going to count to three, Steve. One."

"Owen, please."

"Two."

"Okay, okay, shit," Steve whimpered and sat down in the offered chair.

"Now, isn't that better? Here." The other hand still held the whiskey, and he moved close enough for Steve to grab it off him, which he did reluctantly. Breaking the seal in the lid, Steve unscrewed it and paused. He looked at Owen with pleading eyes. "Drink, you fuckwit." Steve did as he was told, putting the bottle up to his lips and taking a small sip. The taste was foul, and Owen laughed at the guy's obvious discomfort. "That's a sip. I said drink." Owen moved forward and put the gun right up against the man's temple, pushing him back into the seat he was now cowering on. Steve brought the bottle up to his lips again with shaking hands, and this time took a big gulp. It burned his throat worse than the first time, and he coughed violently. Owen withdrew the gun and smiled. "Better. You know sooner or later, you are going to have to realise you've got a set of balls in those trousers. You're a man; it's time to start acting like it." With his free hand, he grabbed the bottle off Steve.

"How can people drink that?" Steve moaned, tears still streaming from his eyes from the violence of the coughing. Christ, he had almost thrown up.

"Very easily, son." Owen took a large mouthful from the bottle and swallowed it down. "Ahhh, that hits the spot." He took another hit, loving the power he held more than the actual alcohol. Finished, he held the bottle back out. "Your turn."

"Please, Owen, I'll throw up." There were real tears now, tears of humiliation, of fear and maybe even a little bit of anger. Owen moved quickly, swatting Steve on the side of the head with the gun. Not hard, almost playful, but enough to get a reaction. "Fuck," Steve swore, and that was when Owen got right in his face, the gun finding itself jabbing Steve painfully in the groin.

"I said, IT'S YOUR FUCKING TURN!" Owen shouted.

"Jesus, okay." Steve took the bottle and drank again, little knowing that Owen had deliberately licked the inside of the bottle rim at the end of his last drink. Steve drank, his reaction not as severe this time, his body beginning to accept the abuse that was being forced on it. *Now we see*, thought Owen and he ruffled Steve's hair.

"Good boy." Owen moved away and sat back down in the chair he had so recently vacated. "You know for a moment there I thought you were going to be a fucking pussy."

19.21, 16th September 2015, Hullavington Airport off Junction 17, M4 motorway, UK

Jack Nathan sat outside in the evening air with the other civilians, a chill breeze moving a copse of trees rhythmically off into the distance. He could almost believe that the trees themselves were breathing. There weren't that many, no military here, and Jack suspected that many of them had once been important people. He also suspected they weren't important anymore. A week ago, he would have been intimidated to be amongst them, cowed by their affluence and self-importance. Being a black teenager from a working class home, he never felt comfortable being around the middle class, those with wealth, and as the only black face out of uniform, he was wary, hunting for those knowing looks he had seen so often in his short life. But there were no looks today, as if the colour of his skin no longer mattered. But then, of course, it never did in the first place. All he saw was frightened people, who didn't have a clue how to survive in this new world.

Most of the civilians had been here when he arrived, and none of them spoke to him. He suspected the fact that he had jumped off the back of a military truck and had been treated warmly by the other soldiers had something to do with that. Oh, and the fact he had a machine gun might have contributed somewhat to that as well. No, now the only looks he saw were respect, tinged with a modicum of fear. That was something he could live with quite easily.

"I think it's only fair you have one of these, lad." That was what the soldier he had been sat next to in the back of the army truck had said, opening a crate and handing him what he knew to be an SA80. The soldier had patiently shown him how to load and unload, how to make the gun safe and how to use the thing.

"Is this allowed?" Jack had asked. "I mean, you won't get into trouble for this, will you?" The soldier had looked at him, smiled, and clamped him on the back of the neck with a huge hand that matched the colour of his own skin.

"These stripes say it's allowed," the soldier had said pointing to the sergeant's stripes on his army fatigues. "We need as many good men as we can get. You're old enough to fuck, so you're old enough to fight." Jack had sat in awe at what he was now allowed to hold, and despite the trauma he had been through, he couldn't help but smile. His dad had been wrong. Army grunts weren't all that bad after all.

"Thanks, Sergeant," Jack had said.

"Bull," the other soldier sharing the back of the truck had said. "Call him Bull."

All around him military personnel were loading up helicopters. He had been doing his part, but had needed to take a break as there was a big difference in lugging crates around compared to his previous employment of flipping burgers. Now he sat, just taking in the reality of everything around him. The military were in charge now, the handful of police officers he saw following orders from the officers who, Jack noted, didn't actually seem to be doing anything themselves. Well, as his dad had always said, lions led by donkeys. That had probably been his dad's favourite saying from his days in the Royal Marines.

Jack felt someone approach behind him and he turned to see the hulking figure of Bull. If the civilians had been intimidated by Jack, the presence of this mountain of a man left them in awe.

"Time to go, Jack," the man said. Jack stood, his machine gun hanging over his shoulder almost casually. One of the seated civilians stood, grabbing the sergeant's attention.

"Sergeant, is there any word on when we will be leaving?" The elderly man sounded posh, a professor of something or other. He had crazy professor hair that really needed the attention of a good barber. For a moment, the man reminded Jack of the vagrant who was always trying to steal food from the back of the bins of the restaurant. But, of course, the vagrant hadn't been wearing a suit and sporting a Rolex.

"Non-combat civilians go with the last transports," Bull said matter-of-factly. He had no time for such people now. The civilians weren't in charge anymore, and the sooner they realised that the better. Most of them in this world were now nothing more than dead weight. If Bull had his way, he would leave them to the infected.

"But when will that be?" a woman said. Her voice was tinged with desperation. Jack looked at her. Middle-aged, well-dressed, overweight, and totally unprepared for the horror the country had become.

"Lady, you'd have to ask my captain for that information. I just work for a living. Come on, Jack, helicopter's waiting for you." The burly soldier didn't hide his irritation. Bull turned and walked away, Jack following.

"Can I ask you something?" Jack asked as they walked.

"Of course you can, lad."

"Why did you let me on the truck back at Windsor? There were so many people there you could have helped, why just me?" Bull stopped, appraising Jack with deep blue eyes, eyes that had seen things that human souls shouldn't see.

"Because you remind me of my son. There's something in you that I've seen in him so many times." Jack paused, looking at the man, seeing the pain beneath the tough exterior.

"I'm sorry. Your son didn't make it, did he?"

"No, lad," Bull said, turning his head to look off into the distance. "No, he didn't."

19.22, 16th September 2015, M40 out of London, UK

Occasionally, he would raise his head up and take brief glimpses out of the windows, but that was all that his courage would allow. He had woken up thirty minutes ago, amazed that he had fallen asleep. He had seen it, had seen it all. How the hell does anyone sleep after that? Still in shock, he lay down across the seats of his articulated lorry so that nobody passing on the street could see him. Because the only people left out there were going to be infected.

The traffic had jammed up within minutes of him joining the M40. There were just too many people trying to flee, and all it took was for one car to break down, one car to crash into another, and then the whole thing would just collapse. And collapse is exactly what happened. He didn't know why the traffic stopped moving; he just knew it did. That had been at 1PM, and by 2PM, people were starting to abandon their cars. Bret couldn't do that. He wouldn't get far on foot, not with his arthritis. And what was even more annoying was the empty eastbound lane. At around three in the afternoon, a military column had barrelled past him, heading west. If he could have crossed over into that side of the motorway, he would have, but the barrier made that impossible for him. The occasional car passed on that side after that, but then nothing. It was like a thirsty man stuck on a raft at sea.

So all he could do was grow impatient, fear bringing him closer and closer to the point of desperation. Eventually, he snapped, and putting his truck in gear, he began to move forward, blowing his horn loudly. Some cars tried to move, others didn't, not until his bumper met them, and then they moved. All the time, Radio 4 rang out the death knoll of a dying civilisation.

"It is advised you stay in your homes and wait for the situation to be brought under control." Fuck that. He'd seen the images on CNN. He'd seen the burning of Parliament and devastation of the Victoria embankment all recorded by an overzealous news helicopter. There was no coming back from that. Zombies, man, who would have even believed?

Of course, his escape plan was a fool's errand; he knew it. Up ahead there were other trucks, and there was no way he was going to get past them. And then something flew past in the corner of his vision. All around him, people were moving, then there was a scream, and then they were running. Out on the grassy embankment where most of the people had ventured to travel by foot, he saw a woman brought down with lightning speed by something that had leaped down from the embankment at the side of the motorway. Then another figure leapt. Then the voice came to him. Hide, you have to hide. Switching off the engine, he lay down out of sight. So he didn't see any of the remaining slaughter. But he heard it, he heard it all. He only checked that the doors to his cabin were locked about a thousand times. And then, inexplicably, he had fallen asleep.

Raising his head up again, he saw nothing, heard nothing. No, that wasn't right. He could hear something. What was that, in the distance, getting closer? Helicopters, was that helicopters? Hope filled him, and he craned his neck as he looked out of the available windows. There, up to the right, flying low. This was it, his only chance. Unlocking the passenger door, he pulled himself out of the cabin, his body complaining at the motion, parts of him having seized up from being in such an awkward position for so long. Standing on shaky feet, he watched as the helicopters got closer, and a vision appeared in his head of them rescuing him. Waving his arms, he begged them to see him, to save him. There were three copters, surely one of them had a winch. Ripping the white shirt from his body, he waved that as well as his arms. He almost called out, but what was the point? They couldn't hear him.

But the helicopters passed over him. There was no rescue today, and as they moved off into the distance, he realised how vulnerable he now was. Shit, he was out in the open. Out here with them, and he did a full three-sixty. Nothing, there was nothing out here with him. It was as he was putting his shirt back on that the severed hand landed at his feet. He looked at it, saw three of the fingers were missing, saw the bite marks and the wedding ring still attached to one of the half-severed fingers. And then he looked up and behind him. Sat crouched on the roof of his lorry was an abomination. Satanic eyes stared at him, and then the voice rose up from the very bowels of hell.

"*Feeeeeeeeeeeeeed!*"

19.25, 16th September 2015, Hounslow, London, UK

Owen stood over the squirming body. Thirty seconds ago, Steve had projectile vomited all across the room and had collapsed into a heap clutching his stomach, howling in agony. This was excellent, thought Owen, this was bloody outstanding.

"Fuck me, I'm the Angel of Death." So wrapped up in his plan, Owen had all but forgotten the voices that floated in the ether of his consciousness. But now with Steve slowly turning, another voice was added, the voice of Steve. Weak now, but growing stronger with each passing second. He nudged Steve with his foot, heard a faint human whimper, but telepathically, he was witness to the ravaging of the Sapien mind as the virus began to take over. He moved over to the living room door and opened it.

"Mrs. Bentley," he shouted, "Steve needs you. There's something wrong." There was movement from upstairs, and then feet could be heard, and a harassed figure came rushing down the stairs.

"What have you done, you bastard?" she roared at him as she pushed past through the doorway.

"I think he just drank too much." She ignored him and fell to her knees by her son."Steve. What's wrong? Talk to me." Vera gently grabbed his shoulders and tried to get him to look at her. A lifetime of mothering allowed her to almost ignore the smell of vomit.

"I can see now why you don't keep drink in the house, Mrs. Bentley." Vera turned her head towards him.

"You shut your mouth, Owen Patterson." She tried to exert some kind of authority, but deep down, she knew she no longer had any. All the rules no longer applied. There were no more courts, or police, or laws. Men like Owen now owned this land, and they had let him into their home. Steve, why did you let him in? Because if he hadn't, Owen probably would have forced his way in anyway. Tears were in her eyes. Looking at Owen, she didn't see the once loving face turn towards her, the blood-red eyes glaring at her with desperate hunger. But Owen saw them, and he stepped back to watch the drama unfold. Noticing where Owen was looking, Vera turned back to her son, only for him to grab her head with vice-like hands. She started screaming just as he bit off her nose.

"Her ear, Steve, take her ear." Owen said this out loud, and was pleasantly surprised when the now fully infected Steve did exactly what he was commanded. The woman writhed and slapped, but could not escape the grip her former son now had on her hair. With one hand he held her whilst with the other, he slowly peeled the ear away from her skull. She screamed afresh, only to black out from the trauma. Steve released her and popped the ear into his mouth, where along with the torn nose he began to chew.

"Well done, Steve. Well done indeed." The infected didn't seem to react to the praise. In a loud voice, Owen said, "Bring her." Steve hesitated for several seconds, his head twitching from side to side. But then he grabbed the unconscious body of his mother and hoisted her over his shoulder. Owen led the way out of the living room, and Steve followed him to the front door which Owen opened. "Out you go, pet." He grabbed Steve by the back of the head and whispered in his ear. "What do you need to do, Steve?"

"Feeeeed. Spreeaaad," Steve replied softly.

"That's right, Steve. Off you go." Steve passed through the door, still holding his mother, her head clashing with the door frame as she was carried out. Owen winced. "Don't eat your mum now, will you?" Gently guiding the infected man out through the door with his mind, he closed it after them and put the latch in place. Turning, he looked up the staircase to see Claire staring right at him.

"Well sweetness, it looks like it's just the two of us." Claire ran. Owen followed.

19.26PM, 16th September 2015, Watford Islamic Mosque, Watford, UK

The infected had found them. Mohammed had hoped that they would just pass by the Mosque, but they hadn't. Because the child had started to cry. Less than a year old, perhaps it sensed the tension in its mother, or perhaps it sensed the futility of its existence, somehow knowing that it would never grow up to think, to have conscious thoughts, to do anything but react and eat and shit. But whatever the reason, the baby had cried loudly and uncontrollably, and nothing the mother had done had been able to stop it. And Mohammed had said the words, had soiled his own soul with his panic and his foolishness.

"Will you shut that fucking child up?" The occupants of the room looked at him aghast, astonished that such words had come from his mouth. Mohammed had stood there, knuckles white, ashamed and guilty in the face of God, and the mother, clutching the child, had fled from the room to where the female toilets were, the now screams of the child almost echoing inside the building. He wanted to go after her, to repent, to say it was the moment. But it wasn't. Deep inside, he felt it, demanded that the child be silent, because it had now endangered all of them.

And then the crying stopped. A stillness fell across those gathered, the only noise from the carnage in the streets outside. Mohammed looked around those assembled and saw looks of approval as well as looks of disappointment. They looked to him for leadership, for spiritual guidance, and he had shown them he was just as flawed as the rest of them. Then there was a new noise, as his son came running down the stairs.

"Father, they are here," Rasheed had said. Moments later, the main door rocked in its frame as a dozen infected charged into it. "They know we are here now."

"Yes, son," was all he could say. People moved away from the windows, retreating into the centre of the room. Some fled up the steps to the first floor, thinking that somehow that was safer.

"What do we do?" someone asked.

"The only thing we can do," Mohammed said. "We pray." And with those words, the mother and her baby were forgotten. It would not be for over an hour that someone needing the restroom would find her, huddled in the corner of the lavatory, a lifeless bundle in her arms, her face wracked with sobs, her mind infested with madness. In her panic, in her fear of the infected and the danger her baby was putting everyone in, she had smothered her own child. There she sat, clutching the corpse, rocking ever so slightly as she mumbled incoherently. And still the infected pounded at the doors, unable to get in, but determined to try relentlessly.

19.27PM, 16th September 2015, Hounslow, London, UK

Owen didn't need a gun for this. He needed a knife, and he visited the living room briefly to acquire one out of his bag. He looked at it, turning it back and forth, its polished surface catching the light. He realised he had never actually stabbed anyone before, and didn't intend to use it for that today. No, this was purely for intimidation. Whilst he could use the gun for that, the gun represented death. The knife represented pain and the threat of pain.

Claire was a tasty little number, and he was looking forward to what he was about to do. Yesterday, these thoughts probably wouldn't have been flying around his head. He had certainly had the urge to rape someone before, but never was that urge as strong as it was right now. There was no defying it. But that was because he was different now, better. It was like his conscience had been burned off, leaving him pure and able to follow through on what his heart really wanted. And although he didn't know why, what he wanted to do was to fuck someone who was infected. Owen wanted to see just how far his powers over them went. And who better than Steve's gorgeous little sister? Stepping out of the living room, he began to ascend the stairs.

"Claire? Where you at, girl? Daddy's got something for you." He felt himself chuckle, the thought that he was actually bordering on insanity entering his head for a second. He clutched the knife tightly, the knuckles going white with the effort. This was the best he had ever felt, power coursing through him, and he wanted to share the love, so to speak. This was who he was, who he was meant to be; it was so clear to him now. Reaching the top of the stairs, he looked around. There were four doors, two of them closed. Likely, the girl was in one of the closed rooms.

"Claire, don't make me come and find you. It'll be much worse for you if you do." Was that a whimper? He tried the first closed door, and it opened easily to an empty room with a double bed. *Well, there's the stage for tonight's play*, thought Owen. Grabbing the second door, he found it locked.

"Seriously, girl?" Owen tested the door. It wouldn't take much, and it didn't. Two kicks broke the lock, and he found himself looking at the snivelling girl in the apartment's bathroom. She screamed and cowered away from him. He stood in the doorway shaking his head.

"Leave me alone. Just leave me the fuck alone," she implored. Owen laughed mockingly.

"I think we both know that that's not going to happen." He pointed the knife at her, a hunting knife with a serrated edge. "We can do this the easy way or the hard way. If you make me do it the hard way, I will make you sorry you were ever born."

"What the fuck do you want?"

"Come on girl, what does every man want when faced with such a sweet little cunt?" Owen took a step into the room, his arm moving the knife in an up and down motion. "I'm going to fuck you, girl, and if you make me happy, if you please me, you might actually make it out alive."

"Please don't hurt me." She held her arms across her breasts, her pyjamas the only thing between him and her naked body. She had no weapons, nothing to fight off this maniac. Because that was what he was, she could see it in his eyes, had seen it ever since he entered the apartment. She'd met him twice before, but he had never been like this. He'd never had the madness that was now clearly visible in his face for all to see.

"Now that's up to you, sweetness. You do as I say, and I'll not hurt a single hair on that pretty little head. But if you test me, if you piss me off, well..." Owen stepped over to her, getting right into her space. He was experienced enough to stand slightly side on so that she wouldn't be tempted to plant a knee into his crotch. That would never do, but he suspected she didn't have the fire in her. This one would be a beggar, a pleader, and from experience, he knew how to manipulate her with the minimum of effort. After all, he had done this before.

He grabbed her by an ear with his corrupted hand and brought the knife up close to her face. "Very sharp this, love," he said, running the point down her cheek, just hard enough to leave a faint mark. She whimpered, her eyes almost exploding out of her head. "Sharp enough to slice bits off you." Claire tried to look away, but he forced her to look into his eyes. "Bitch, you look at me when I'm laying down knowledge."

"I'm sorry, I'm sorry." Tears welled in her eyes, and he could see the humiliation having the desired effect.

"Have you had cock before?"

"W...what?" She couldn't believe the question.

"Cock, have you ever had a cock inside you? Don't lie to me, because I'll know." She hesitated then nodded, more tears now flowing freely.

"Good. Then let's see what you've learnt." Saying that, he grabbed her by the hair and pulled her out of the bathroom.

19.28PM GMT, 16th September 2015, PINDAR, London, UK

The tall male infected leaned against the reinforced metal door, sniffing the air. There was a memory here. This seemed familiar to him, seemed to represent something important, something vital. Seventeen infected watched him, curious eyes following his actions, and out on the street, several dozen more waited eagerly, unaware that security cameras watched their every move. This was the main entrance hall to the Ministry of Defence. Once guarded by soldiers and armed police, it now lay deserted except for the children of the infected and the technology that kept those children at bay.

The tall infected reached into his suit pocket and pulled out an expensive leather wallet, and he opened it clumsily. Picking out a single plastic card, he let the wallet fall to the ground, and he brought the card up to his face and examined it. What was this? Why did he carry it, why was it so important? If he could still read, he would have been able to remember his name, for it was written in bold letters under a photograph of himself on the card. Brian Pilcher, Assistant Head of Operations. He had been on his way to work, stood minding his own business, one of several waiting to cross the road in busy rush hour traffic. All had seemed right with the world until the man standing in the centre of his little group had suddenly vomited all over those around him. Brian felt his leg go wet as the virus-laden soup soaked through his trousers. He had cursed his dismay at the man, stepping back in disgust, but safe in the knowledge that he had the foresight to have a spare pair of trousers in his office. Pilcher never got to wear them. Ten minutes later, he had collapsed in the centre of Trafalgar Square, the virus changing him, deleting him, improving him.

As a former employee of the Ministry of Defence, he had used this card to access the secret bunker below where he stood almost every day for the last seven years. With no armed security guards to stop him and his kind, all that stood between the infected and the secure PINDAR bunker was one door that the infected had been unable to break, breaking bones and bruising flesh in the process. But they didn't need to break it, because the people down below had not had the common sense to cut off the door's power supply, had not envisaged what was about to happen next. In their collective memory, the image of Brian and his keycard access floated to the surface, and Brian felt himself compelled to drag himself here, where he now stood awaiting the instructions from the Hive.

His hand moved, and he waved the card across a panel by the side of the door. It beeped, and a green light flashed, Brian and several of the other infected recoiling in surprise. Then the door opened, and he looked back at his brothers and sisters for a moment, almost mesmerised by the action. They waited for him. He had been appointed the leader and the voices urged him on. Moving forward slowly, he looked into a deserted lobby where three doors awaited him. Two of the infected behind him rushed past, and then those outside swarmed into the building, a cry escaping their throats as the blood lust and the need overcame them. Brian clutched the card, as if it was now part of him, its edges digging into the flesh of his palm. The card bent slightly, and he moved with the pack, his fogged memories guiding them to their target. As one, they moved, choosing the door that led to the staircase. With a roar, they descended into one of the country's most secure military facilities.

19.35PM GMT, 16th September 2015, NATO Headquarters, Belgium

General Marston sat, clearly in pain, but determined not to succumb to the painkillers the doctors had kept trying to force down his neck. He needed a clear head, and opiate-based prescription medication wasn't going to allow for that. The bullet had passed right through, hadn't hit anything vital, and had left him with one of the least severe injuries of his military career. Still, it hurt like buggery, and he wasn't a young man anymore. This wound would always come back to haunt him in the cold winter months and bring with it memories of the man who had performed the ultimate betrayal of his country. Marston would never forget watching his prime minister be killed right in front of him by the man who was supposed to be his ultimate protector.

He was not alone—dozens of people milled about in the conference room. The meeting would start shortly, the various members of NATO represented here to decide what to do about the growing threat posed to Europe and the world by the United Kingdom. The American contingent had already made it clear that nukes were off the table at present due to the threats made by the anonymous YouTube video, an opinion endorsed by the French. Although not members of NATO, it had only seemed prudent to invite the French to the meeting because, being directly across the English Channel, they were now on the front line of the containment.

It was that very English Channel that the French Government didn't want radioactive fallout drifting across if at all possible.

Marston was a man without a country. He still controlled a sizeable military force, but how long could the soldiers on the mainland hold out? They were being reinforced by parachute drops, but how long would the various military leaders in this room keep approving that? At least there were no politicians in the room; these were all military men, and Marston knew most of them by reputation. But some were more military than others. There were so many things they had to consider, and the itinerary for the meeting lay on the conference table before him, extending to several sheets. He looked at the listed items to be discussed on the first page and knew that this meeting would go on for many hours. He never thought he would be in a room considering these things about his own country. There were ten items on the front page of the dossier everyone had been handed when they entered, Marston having ripped away the cover sheets.

1) The threat posed by infected individuals swimming the English Channel
2) The threat posed by the UK's nuclear reactors. Can they be decommissioned?
3) Increased build-up of troops on the Russian border
4) Should essential personnel be evacuated from Ireland?
5) How to control the mass migration of people from Northern Europe
6) Should NATO endorse the use of nuclear weapons on the UK mainland?
7) The feasibility of Operation Hadrian
8) Extending the boundary of the No Fly Zone
9) The threat posed by terrorists obtaining a sample of the virus
10) How to prevent the spread of the virus should an outbreak occur in a European city

There were dozens more items to discuss, many of them distasteful, but necessary. The hoops he, as Chief of the Defence Staff, had needed to jump through just to authorise a simple drone strike on terrorist positions in far-flung hell holes had driven him up the wall, and here they all were, about to calmly discuss the possibility of slaughtering millions of people—his people, the people he was sworn to protect. A wave of nausea swept over him, and he picked up a glass of iced water and drank it down greedily. Was it the wound or the thought of what they might need to do to keep the rest of the world safe that made him feel sick?

"General?" Marston turned his chair around to the owner of the voice. He didn't know her by name, but knew her to be one of the communication officers.

"Yes, Lieutenant?"

"We just got word from London. PINDAR has fallen."

19.37PM, 16th September 2015, Hounslow, London, UK

Owen looked down at the naked girl. She was already starting to turn, her body thrashing from where it was bound to the bed. The smell from where she had soiled herself was quite disgusting, and he was rather glad he had cum quickly before all that nastiness had happened. He had forced her onto the bed, tied her down to the very helpful bedposts, and had his way with her. And he hadn't been gentle about it, her breasts bleeding from several bite wounds he had inflicted. He wanted to ensure the virus was passed to her, at least that was what he told himself. Truth was, it was just another mark of the sickness that was his growing psychosis.

She had screamed, but at no time had she fought back. *Silly cunt,* he thought, *did she somehow think she was going to make it out of this unscathed?* Just as he climaxed, he had bitten down hard into the lobe of her ear, almost severing it. Then the excitement had passed and he had climbed off her, leaving her whimpering and broken. He didn't care, that's what he told himself, his mind revelling in the power rather than accepting responsibility for the trauma he had just caused to another life. And with that done, he had sat in the corner of the room to witness the transformation.

Ten minutes, the same as her brother. Owen didn't bother to dress, because he knew he was far from done here. Even though he had already cum, his penis was painfully erect, the implications of what lay before him maddeningly erotic to him. When she finally turned, he would untie her and he would wash her. And then he would see what real fun he could have. And yet there was a faint sense of unease. Deep inside something screamed at him, just as it had screamed with the other he had raped before. That time he had been drunk, and had felt uneasy for days afterwards. But he wasn't drunk now. The voice was his conscience, and every step down the road of depravity, the voice got weaker. Now, it was no more noticeable than the sound of traffic on a warm summer's night. He was no longer the owner of the voice; it was merely a remnant of who he had used to be. But still it persisted, trying to save him from the path he was heading down. It was a futile attempt.

"Looking good there, Claire," he said mockingly. Something attracted his attention, and he turned his head to listen. Leaving the bedroom, he walked naked along the hallway and down the stairs. Outside, he could hear the infected breaking into another flat, and he smiled.

"They grow up so quickly," he muttered to himself. Opening the front door, he looked out at the chaos. Four doors down, a woman was being dragged out of her home by three infected. They hauled her off her feet and threw her against the barrier, which prevented her body from falling to the concrete concourse below. Owen stepped out and looked at them. One of the infected spared him a glance, but it was fleeting, like a serf looking at the Noble Lord as he rode past. Crossing his arms, Owen watched the show. The infected clearly still weren't intent on killing, just converting, and he felt their craving for flesh which they were being denied. How could he see into their minds?

"Hey, you three," he shouted. Two of them turned to look at him.

"Help me," the woman said weakly, a hand grasping the air. The three infected held her down, their strength too much for her.

"Fuck off, bitch, I'm not talking to you," Owen said. "My pets need feeding, I think they've earnt it. Go on, boys, have your fill." The three infected looked at him, confusion in their faces, then they looked at each other, and Owen could almost see the delight settle over them. "Yes, I command you to feed. Fill your bellies, my friends."

"No, please," the woman cried. So far unbitten, she shrieked as the first infected clenched its teeth into her thigh, ripping a chunk of muscle and skin off. It looked at its two brothers as it slowly chewed the flesh, and Owen felt the delight it felt ripple through him. It was faint, but the sensation was there and he liked it. He wanted more of it. The other two paused only briefly before ripping into the woman who flailed at them with middle-aged arms devoid of strength or muscle tone. Owen shivered with pleasure.

"Take your time though, lads. And remember where the juiciest bits are to be found." With that, he projected an image into their minds and walked back into the flat. He didn't bother to close the door; there was no need for security anymore. Behind him, the three infected began to fight with each other, wanting to be the first to get to the meat between their victim's legs.

19.59PM, 16th September 2016, Newquay Airport, Cornwall, UK

General Mansfield stood, hand firmly holding his hat in place as the transport helicopter descended. Although he was in charge, he knew that there were still some people around who had authority to tell him what to do. There was Sir Nicholas Marston, now sat safely in Brussels, issuing orders to the beleaguered forces left on the UK mainland, and then there was the man who would shortly step off the helicopter. The Chief of the Defence Forces was clear in this regard—Major David Croft was to be consulted on all matters involving the infected. It had been the major and his team that had uncovered the source of the infection, and the possible identity of the people responsible. It was Croft who had suspected a plot within the heart of government whilst those who employed him saw nothing.

"Just so we are clear, Nicholas," Mansfield had said, "I have the final say in deployment and defence." The satellite phone he held had felt clammy in his hands, the voice on the other end sometimes distorted.

"I wouldn't expect otherwise, Arthur," Marston had said. "I don't know anyone better to do what needs to be done. You have full authority under NATO command to do as you see fit. My advice, however, is to listen to this man; he's a valuable asset."

That conversation had been thirty minutes ago, and he had waited apprehensively for the arrival of Croft and the SAS team. Now they were here. Mansfield's adjutant bowed down and moved forward as the helicopter touched down, the general staying well away from the rotors. The side door opened and hardened men stepped out, all in full combat gear. One by one, they moved away from the helicopter, not a single one giving the general a salute. Fucking SAS, law unto themselves sometimes.

He was surprised to see a woman climb out of the helicopter, followed by a man who Mansfield instantly knew to be Croft. He had the look, the look of a man who had faced a thousand demons, the thousand-yard stare scanning the world around him. The SAS soldiers had a similar look, but not as intense as Croft, who was directed by the adjutant to where Mansfield stood. Besides, Croft looked exactly like his picture. Croft looked at the general, paused, and shouted something to one of the soldiers he had shared his ride with. The soldier responded, looked briefly at the general, and then walked off towards the mess tent. Croft came over, followed by the woman.

Brian stood outside the mess tent watching the helicopter unload its cargo. *Must be important guests if the general himself is out here to meet them,* Brian thought to himself. Stan walked through the tent flaps, a sandwich half-eaten in his hand.

"Are you fucking eating again?" Brian asked.

"Hey, it's hungry work this, you know. I've got to keep up my strength." Stan pointed at the helicopter with his food-laden hand. "Who are the VIPs?" he asked.

"I don't know," Brian said, his attention drawn to Captain Hudson who moved towards their position, "but I wouldn't be surprised if they are SAS."

"Yes, that guy looks a bit handy," Stan said. "Good to know those guys are helping out." Stan took another bite, looked at what remained, and then just shrugged and stuffed the rest of the sandwich in his mouth. Brian looked at him with mock disdain.

"What happened to you thinking about becoming a vegetarian anyway?" Brian asked. His partner held up a finger, chewing rapidly so as to swallow his mouthful. He finally achieved the task and patted his chest as if the food had gotten temporarily stuck.

"I said I was thinking about it. I didn't say it would ever happen. We'll likely be dead in a week anyway, so what's the point?"

Brian turned his attention back to the new arrivals, Hudson passing the two men with a nod of acknowledgment. The policeman watched as Croft walked over to the general and the two shook hands.

"No salutes, must be an important fellow."

"Yeah?" Stan asked. He clapped his friend on the shoulder. "Come on, mate, you've not eaten all day. Why don't you get some food inside you?"

"Is there any left?" Brian said mockingly.

Croft, the general, his adjutant, and Savage walked slowly away from the helicopter. They headed towards a concrete building about seventy metres away, the Union Jack flying proudly from a flagpole that had been erected on its flat roof. A flag for a country that no longer existed.

"So you have the identity of the person responsible for all this?" Mansfield asked.

"Yes and no," Croft answered cryptically. "The files we recovered from the laboratory Captain Hudson raided outline much of the details of how the virus was created, how it was paid for. We have passed all that to NATO command, and it is hoped that they can dig out who started all this. There is a paper trail to follow, but who knows where that is going to lead." Croft held the computer tablet that had been used to transmit the information found on the USB stick to Brussels. He'd had a good look at it on the ride over from the now decimated laboratory, and had found the information quite revealing. James Jones, the scientist responsible for this tragedy, had not known the actual identity of the man who funded him, it seemed. "What we know is this is a religious death cult led by an individual known only as Brother Abraham. The shipping manifests, receipts, and the various shell companies Jones was able to provide suggest to me that the group behind all this is based in America, so that's probably where the leader is to be found."

"America?" Mansfield was surprised. "Our Yank friends aren't going to like that."

"No, they aren't," Croft agreed. They wouldn't like it at all. The embarrassment would be immense, especially with some of the documents Croft had seen. Jones had put a lot of data together, some of it being documents with a certain smell to them. It was actually Savage who had first seen them, paging through the various PDF files and word documents. Right there, in all their glory, were documents implicating the United States Government. The other thing of note was that the British Government came out even worse, the head of MI5, the man responsible for protecting the country, a traitor of the worst kind.

Savage didn't say anything during the walk, just followed behind the men, her mind reeling from the revelation of it all. She still hadn't come to terms with the fact that it was all over. Her career, her friends, the country she loved so much. Country had come before personal gain, and where had that gotten her? She was trapped, and right now, she felt like a fifth wheel.

She had been the only one to step off the helicopter who had saluted the general, unlike Croft who really wasn't military anymore. She was still a soldier, and soldiers usually didn't speak to generals unless they were spoken to first, especially generals with this man's reputation. The man she had saluted had barely looked at her, and when he had, there had been just the faintest hint of derision. This confirmed the arrogant disregard that the grapevine spoke about with regards to Mansfield. The general, apparently, didn't agree with women in uniform, an outdated and obsolete notion that at any other time would have amused Savage. It didn't amuse her now, and when the time was right, she would likely voice these concerns, hopefully safe in the knowledge that Croft would back her to the hilt should the need arise. This wasn't where she needed to be. She may have been a soldier, but she was also a scientist, and a damn good one. What she needed to be doing was working on a cure. That was the sole purpose of her life now, and the sooner she started on that, then the better it would be for everyone.

20.13PM, 16th September 2015, Trafalgar Square, London, UK

Meat. She needed meat. Propelled purely on instinct, Rachel lurched forwards after an infected that had come too close, but it dodged away from her and ran off, probably in search of meat itself. Two predators after a dwindling resource. She wasn't alone now, and she moved with those who had gathered around her, the undead group she was at the head of now numbering four dozen. That was not to say she led the group; the zombies moved wherever their reflexes took them, wherever the chance for meat occurred. Their numbers were building though, and they seemed to move together like a shoal of uncoordinated decaying fish.

Another two undead appeared across the square, and the two groups slowly combined, the scent of humans and infected sending them into a frenzy of desire, the hunger all they knew. There were humans here, in the structures all around them, prime targets for the relentlessness of the undead. Although they were no longer aware of it, Rachel and her kind had the advantage. They didn't actually need to feed to stay alive, despite the gnawing ache within them. They didn't need to drink, and they didn't even need to breathe, though one or two still seemed to go through the motions, their lungs expanding uselessly.

Rachel felt the crowd turn, and they moved towards one of the buildings. One of them had seen something, smelt something, and a noise rose amongst them as they surged forward, Rachel almost falling due to her uncoordinated manner. The presence of other bodies held her up, and she regained her dubious balance. If she had fallen, the others would have likely just trampled her underfoot, no longer caring about the wellbeing of themselves or those around them.

She didn't really see anymore, the optic nerve in her remaining eye decaying, the muscles that controlled it losing their coordination. She just felt where she needed to go, as did all the other undead around her. That was how she found herself climbing a short flight of steps, her body colliding with a wooden door, random fists around her and from behind her flailing at the object blocking their entry. There food was in there, and they would find a way inside.

20.15PM, 16th September 2015, Hounslow, London, UK

"It's all clear, you can come out." Owen stood in the middle of the street and shouted the words at the top of his lungs. He shouted again.

He looked around at the windows, looking for curtains twitching, for terrified faces glaring out at him, but he saw nothing. Nothing appeared from the row of shops to his left and he shook his head in disappointment. Surely, there were still people left, people for him to ruin. He remembered a line from a TV programme he once watched, "Everybody is mine to torment." Owen couldn't have put it better himself. The world was indeed his oyster.

Claire stood behind him, still naked, a dog collar around her neck and a chain running from it to Owen's good hand. The chain and collar he had found on the carcass of an Alsatian. Dogs, it seemed, were prime targets for the infected, and Owen wondered if they too could carry the virus. This one wouldn't have been able to…it hadn't possessed any legs.

The bag of guns he held slung over his other shoulder. He kept a pistol stuck down the back of his trousers, just in case some of the others arrived. The others, the undead. They were slow and cumbersome and infrequent at present, but he knew their numbers would grow as those carrying the infection died, either from their injuries or starvation. Could the infected starve? There was so much about them he didn't know.

Claire swayed slightly back and forth, her head twitching sharply this way and that as if following the flight of something around her head. Owen sensed she was hunting, seeking the meat she craved, the whispers of her brothers and sisters roaring through her head. He wanted more like her. He wanted a whole army to do his bidding, and he would seek them out and make them his playthings, his minions. And who better than his old chums at the Hounslow Police Station? Of course, there was no guarantee that there would be anyone left there, but it was only down the road. With a yank of the chain, Owen started walking again.

"Come, bitch," he ordered. She didn't hesitate, falling in behind him, her head still undergoing the violent ticking motions. He had seen that movement before, he remembered. It was not unheard of for his small gang to harass the homeless, catching them alone at night, roughing them up a bit, sometimes maiming them. But there was one they never messed with, the man who talked to himself, the man with the beard and the smell you could detect at twenty paces. His head had twitched like that, and everybody knew not to fool with him. Because quite frankly, the man was insane, and the insane were unpredictable. And cowards like Owen avoided the unpredictable. They liked the odds to be heavily in their favour.

Owen felt the leash go taut and he turned to see Claire moving off towards one of the shopfront windows.

"You smell something, don't you, bitch?" he said. She turned her head, eyes wide, and then looked back at where her body was pointing. "Go on then, have your fun." Owen let go of the leash, and she was off, leaping over a parked car, her feet crunching over broken glass. Within seconds, she had disappeared through the smashed shopfront of a mini supermarket. He waited, placing the gun bag on the floor. He heard noise from within the building and withdrew the gun from his belt, ready for whatever came out.

A man appeared, panicked and out of breath. He ran out onto the pavement, almost falling on his ass, his overweight form not used to strenuous activity. Claire did not follow, and there was a scream from inside. In one hand, the man held a cricket bat, dented and blood-stained. Shit, thought Owen. He pointed the gun at the new arrival, who so far hadn't really seen him.

"Hey," Owen shouted. The man turned towards him. "You better not have damaged my property."

"What?" There was another scream, this one most likely a child, and the man recoiled from the sound, moving away from the shattered window. Owen fired a shot that went above the man's head, and the newcomer almost jumped out of his skin.

"I said you better not have damaged my property."

"Please, we have to go. There's one of them in there. My wife…"

"You take one step, and I will put a bullet through your leg and leave you for the infected. The noise will surely draw dozens of them." He took a step towards the man, a vicious idea forming in his warped and sick mind. "Claire, get your fucking sweet backside out here, girl!" Owen shouted. He heard her in his mind before he saw her, and she appeared in the doorway, blood dripping from her mouth. Damn, he would have to clean her up again. If she had been wearing clothes, they would have been ruined, which was pretty much why he had left her naked. Owen suspected his pet would see a lot of work over the next few days.

"Oh Jesus," the man said, backing up. Owen fired, the shot missing on purpose, the bullet shattering the windscreen of the car Claire had previously jumped over. "Fuck," the terrified man said, and he dropped the cricket bat so he could hold his hands up as if to form some kind of shield. A voice called out a name from within the shop. It was weak, petrified.

"John? Is your name John?"

"Please," John said. "My wife, my daughter."

"Forget about them, John," Owen said. "In ten minutes, they won't even know who you are. Claire here has seen to that, haven't you,

Claire?" John looked at the horrific form of Claire, and she hissed at him, clawing the air with her fake nails, an invisible force holding her back. "But you can still be with them, John. So I have a deal for you. I can either put a bullet through your stomach and leave you here to bleed out." Owen lowered the gun. "Or you can be with your family. You can spend your last ten minutes together, in each other's arms. Think how precious those last ten minutes will be, John. Think of your daughter, think of how she needs you now."

"What do you—?"

"Clock's ticking, John. So what's it going to be? A bullet or let Claire here give you a kiss." John looked at the infected, who now took a step closer. She was no longer hissing, and she almost seemed to smile. He looked back at Owen.

"You're fucking insane."

"Oh, I know," Owen said, smiling broadly. "Claire, plenty of tongue now, babe." Owen lowered the gun and watched with fascination as the infected pounced.

20.22PM, 16th September 2015, Watford Islamic Mosque, Watford, UK

The pounding and the shrieking was maddening. Mohammed tried to keep the reality out with prayer, but the truth of their situation would not be denied. They were all doomed, there was no escaping it. Stood over his flock, who mostly sat on the floor and wept quietly, he turned full circle, seeing the faces at every window, distorted by the privacy glass. Many of the windows were now smeared red as displayed by the failing light outside. The windows were holding, but for how long would that continue? Surely, it was only a matter of time before this holy place was desecrated. It was a mistake to have stayed here, but where could they have run to? If only that child had kept quiet, maybe they would have had a chance.

And where was his son? Why was he not here? Probably on the upper level with his friends, watching the streets outside from the upstairs windows perhaps. Or perhaps not. He should be down here with the rest of them, ready to comfort those whose faith was being tested. But, of course, that was not his son, that was not the boy he had raised to be a good Muslim. Despite the fact that the infected already knew they were here, Mohammed felt reluctant to shout his son's name out loud. Quiet still seemed like the best course of action because there was always the hope that the demons outside would be distracted by some other event, filtering away after an easier prize. Surely, there was always hope, so, stepping around a sleeping old lady who was curled up on the floor at his feet, he made his way over to the stairs and ascended them on arthritic knees.

Rasheed was a good son; he respected his family and his elders. But that respect only went so far, the boy having developed beliefs that went counter to what Mohammed preached. Mohammed believed in forgiveness and peace, whereas Rasheed felt that Western society was corrupted and anti-Islam. He tried to tell his son that society was only anti-Islam when those who followed the faith struck out against the majority, and that the more atrocities the radicals perpetrated the more likely they would awaken a sleeping giant of hate and bigotry. Mohammed knew his history, knew what Western governments were capable of, knew the atrocities they could unleash on the minorities in their midst if the wolf of hate was fed and nurtured. Rasheed would have none of it. They kill our Brothers and Sisters for oil, for profit he would say, bowing to the whims of the evil Zionists. They don't deserve the peace and tranquillity they crave whilst allowing their fetid leaders to bomb and maim and bribe those in other countries. Mohammed had tried to teach his son reason, and whilst his son had listened respectively, every sermon seemed to push the boy further into the arms of the radicals. In all honesty, Mohammed was surprised his son was even here.

The smell at the top was unmistakeable, and he saw the haze hanging over the three men. Smoking such substances in the house of Allah was Haram, and Mohammed felt anger rise within him. But he could also understand the need his young boy felt to partake in such substances. This was the end of times, and perhaps understanding was the better tactic to take here.

"Father," Rasheed said, acknowledging his father. The boy took another hit of the roach and passed it on to one of his friends. The friend took it gladly, but hesitated looking at the elder Imam. Mohammed just shrugged, and a smile of relief formed on the friend's face. The friend inhaled deeply.

"Is now the best time to be smoking such poison, Rasheed?"

"If not now, then when, Father?"

"You know what I mean. You know my feelings on such drugs." Mohammed had tried to raise his son as a good Muslim. But as the boy grew older, his own interpretation of the word of Allah began to take a different path, his mind warped by those he encountered who believed in hate and violence. Mohammed could not understand why his son chose this path, could not understand why he rejected the more moderate teachings, why the call of Jihad was so strong to him. How could one reject the truth that Islam was a religion of peace, of tolerance? Instead,

Rasheed had succumbed to the allure of the more radical road, the road of the extremist, and as the years rolled by, Mohammed was powerless as he watched the son he loved thoroughly reject the values of the country he was born in.

"Indeed Father, but if it was good enough for the warriors of Suleiman, then I see no problem with it. After all, does the Holy Koran not say…?"

"Do not quote scripture to me," Mohammed admonished. "I am not here for an argument." It was an argument he knew he was unlikely to win either. Technically, there was nothing in the Holy Koran that forbade hashish.

"Forgive me, Father. I meant no disrespect." And yet you smoke that vile shit in my mosque, thought Mohammed. No, now was not the time for this. Now was the time for family to be together. Mohammed looked at the three men, sat on the floor so as to be able to pass the joint between them. Neither of them had stood up when he had arrived. The young had no respect anymore. Especially the radicals like those his son acquainted himself with, believers in violence and the open rejection of British values. They gathered together and learnt a hatred that should never have been allowed in Islam, manipulated by those who used the naivety and inexperience of the young for their own ends. Of course, none of that mattered now. Despite clinging to hope, deep down he knew that very shortly he would be sitting at the right hand of the Prophet.

A noise from outside, over and above the normal din, attracted his attention, and Mohammed walked over to the window. Carefully, he looked out at the road below, and what he saw turned his blood to ice.

"Oh no," Mohammed said.

Bob, his name had been Bob. He remembered that but didn't really understand what it meant. He stood looking at the black panel van, its engine purring from where it had been abandoned. It seemed alive, and something in Bob's mind told him what he needed to do, told him things that until a moment ago he didn't even think he knew. Stepping up to the open door, he stuck his head inside and inhaled deeply. The smell was faint, but it was there. Flesh had been in here, but it had been several hours ago, long since fled. So now, he would use this thing to get more meat.

The prey used these things to move about, to flee and to fight, and he fleetingly was aware of hundreds of images of his fellow infected being run over by these metal beasts. Memories of his former self came to him, sat in similar things, and he slumped down into the driver's seat, the confined space now alien to him. Alien, but at the same time familiar. It felt right to sit here, like this was where he was meant to be. Clumsily, he grabbed the seatbelt and pulled it across himself, as he had done so many times before, but he didn't engage it. A million minds told him what he had to do through a fog of sound and decaying thoughts, and he put the van into gear.

The van moved forward slowly, almost at a walking pace, towards the throng of infected, who parted almost rhythmically to let their brother pass. Bob pressed down harder on the gas pedal, the van accelerating, and he saw the road ahead being cleared of vehicles and debris. They were making him a path, a channel so he could drive this thing right at the stronghold of the enemy, of the meat. With strength they hadn't possessed in their former lives, the infected worked together to move cars out of his way, giving him a clear run at the building where the flesh held out. The van got faster, and Bob almost lost control, hitting the curb as his viral-ridden brain struggled to find the coordination the vehicle demanded. He might have driven such a vehicle for much of his adult life, but now he was left with instinct, much of the muscle memory having been stripped away.

The door to the mosque grew bigger, and seconds later, the van hit the main doors at forty miles an hour. Reinforced as they were, they didn't stand a chance. Neither did Bob. Without his seatbelt engaged, he was thrown forward into the steering wheel, his forehead hitting the inside of the windshield with a force great enough to break through at the point of impact. There was no airbag. Four ribs broke, and as he rebounded, he felt something give in his neck. Even with the virus inside him, he felt consciousness give way, the thoughts of the collective slipping from his mind. As he struggled with life, the infected took their opportunity, scrambling through the breach as best they could. With the van halfway into the building, the only real way was through the van, and they flung open the back for entry, clawing forward, scrambling over the body of their fallen comrade. Someone opened the driver's door, and Bob felt himself pushed out, falling to the floor. Feet scrambled over him, breaking more bones, smashing his already-damaged skull into the plush, carpeted floor. Then a foot landed on his neck and the weakened vertebrae gave way. When he reanimated, he was a dead cripple, biting feebly at the air, everything below the neck useless. He was not to join the feast and would be left to end his days as a slowly decaying skull on a useless body.

The sound would have been ear-splitting downstairs, and Mohammed rushed from the window as quickly as his legs would allow. His son stood quickly, following his elder. At the top of the stairs, Mohammed descended one, two steps and then stopped. Looking down, he could see his fellow worshippers beginning to rise, some shouting. People ran. Then came the screams. Within seconds, he witnesses unfamiliar bodies move amongst them and he retreated back up the steps. They were inside; the infected were here. Terror filled his heart, and then refilled it afresh when the first of the infected appeared at the bottom of the stairs. It had once been a middle-aged businessman, and it still wore the attire of a wage slave. But today, it wore a new fashion, the blood from the wounds that had been inflicted upon its face painting a drying landscape on his tan suit. Half its lower lip was missing, and one eye socket empty, the other eye blood red.

"*Feeeeeeeeeeeeeeeeed,*" it demanded.

The infected did not rush, but ascended slowly, ignoring the carnage that was ensuing behind it. It even used the bannister, as if its balance was somehow compromised. Its head twitched rhythmically, and it stumbled slightly, only to easily regain its footing. Never once did it take its eye off of Mohammed. A second infected joined him, a third. There were twenty steps in all, and before he had taken another breath, the three devils were already halfway up. Mohammed staggered backwards, suddenly propelled by his son who positioned himself at the top of the stairs in between his father and the threat. And then he saw it, saw the hand move to the back of the jeans, saw the gun drawn.

"Where did you get a—?" Mohammed started, but his question was cut off by an almighty sound as Rasheed fired down into the infected. Amazingly, the first round missed, panic and a lack of familiarity taking its toll on Rasheed's aim. The second round didn't miss, hitting the businessman to the left of the forehead, the force propelling the body back down the stairs, the two other infected easily avoiding their fallen comrade on the wide staircase. Four more infected appeared at the bottom of the steps, and Mohammed's world became the sounds of shots and the roar of the damned.

"WHORES!" Rasheed shouted, firing shot after shot. Most weren't fatal wounds, however, not to those who carried the virus. Normal men would have been felled by the trauma of the shock, but those who came at him were far from normal. As he pulled the trigger for the last time, the gun now empty, hands clawed at him, pulling him down onto the staircase, teeth and nails ripping into his skin. Mohammed witnessed it all, tears in his eyes, his heart broken, and he staggered backwards, tripping over himself. As the infected poured forth from the stairs, as they overwhelmed him and the two remaining men, Mohammed felt his faith slip. Then it was his life.

20.30PM, 16th September 2015, MI6 Building, London, UK

The phone conversation had really not gone as planned. He had hoped with the news that they were the last real resistance in the country's capital, he would be given carte blanche to find a cure for this disease. But his request to begin live human trials had been denied yet again. It irritated him to no end. Why couldn't those in power just accept that this was a time for desperate measures? It would be days before he could get the test subjects he needed, and he suspected that, the way things were going, they wouldn't have days. How long could this fortress hold out against the growing zombie and infected hordes?

But perhaps there was another way. Had he not overheard something about prisoners in the basement? Was not one of the men responsible for unleashing the apocalypse in captivity here? Surely, nobody would mind if such a villain was used to further scientific progress. He had been told not to go ahead with the proposed experiments, but there was no real oversight here, no effective power structure, not now. Most of the senior staff were in another country, and those remaining would surely follow his suggestions if he made the right kind of noises. He had already witnessed the look of despair and defeat in so many of their faces. What if he came to them with the idea for a cure? Yes, he would do that, he decided. They needed him—it was why he was here. It was why he had been pulled out of his office where the half-finished cup of Earl Grey would still likely be sat cold on his antique oak desk.

Durand pushed himself away from the table in the office he had been allocated and stood. The cells were seven floors below, but he didn't have access to that level. Of course, it wouldn't be hard to persuade someone who did to move the prisoners up a floor to where the infected were housed. Yes, he would do this because this needed to be done. He didn't care if the "scientific opinion" of NATO disagreed with him. They weren't here. They weren't risking their lives stuck in a city of the undead. He had been promised he would be evacuated, promised his life would be saved. But they had evacuated him to the extraction point too late. So fuck them, fuck them all.

Fabrice didn't hear the door open, didn't see the individuals walk over to his table, didn't hear their voices as they commented on Davina's handy work. But he felt the pain stop and whimpered with the knowledge that it would only start again. The world without pain descended on him, and in his disorientation, a part of him almost wished for the pain to return.

"Do we just pull these things out or what?" a voice said.

"Yeah, they are basically acupuncture needles, so they should just come straight out with a tug." A hand grabbed his arm, and he felt one of the needles be extracted from his flesh. Yesterday, the pain from that would have made him cry out, but now it was nothing, almost meaningless.

"Fuck me, this guy's a mess."

"Well wait 'til Doctor Frankenstein gets through with him." More needles were removed, and then Fabrice felt his restraints relaxed. Fabrice moaned and tried to flex his arms which were totally cramped up. Through blurred vision, he saw a third person enter, pushing a wheelchair. A hand slapped him hard on the face. Slapped him again. He almost welcomed it.

"You're not going to give me any trouble now, are you, cunt?" Fabrice looked at the man who had spoken to him, tried to focus. For some reason, he had forgotten how to breathe. He couldn't speak, the words not forming properly. No, he shook his head weakly, he wouldn't give them any trouble. He wasn't capable, hadn't been for several hours.

"Good boy." The voice sounded Irish. He felt rough hands lifting him up off the table. A thought occurred to him that he should feel embarrassed being naked in front of them, but it was fleeting. Fabrice had other concerns. Although the needles had been removed, spasms still shot through his body, and he jerked violently, causing those carrying him to curse. Someone smacked him hard across the head.

"I told you to fucking behave." He tried to say sorry, even made a sound resembling the word. Then he was dumped into the wheelchair, and the restraints were re-applied and a hood was forced over his head. Why couldn't they just leave him alone?

The light in his torture chamber had been dim. When the hood was removed, he was almost blinded by the fluorescents overhead. He had no idea where he was, and had no idea how long it had been since he had been rescued. He wasn't really sure rescued was the right word, but it was the only one he could come up with at the moment. The pain was mostly gone, that was all that mattered. Still groggy, and still suffering the after effects of Davina's manipulations, his eyes tried to witness what was around him, but the light was so bright it was as if he had never used them before.

A tremor rippled through his right arm, and he clenched his teeth only to find more pain from the fractured molars. No man was supposed to endure this kind of torment. Surely, this was reserved for those who went against God's will. Wasn't that what hell was for, after all? Perhaps that was where he was. Had he died and done something to displease his maker?

"Mr. Chevalier, a pleasure to finally meet you." He had been able to see the body, but it had taken several seconds for his eyes to acclimatise, and now he saw the face. Still holding the hood, a tall, thin, gangly man in a hazmat suit stood before him. The gaunt face smiled behind the Perspex visor, but Fabrice knew instantly not to trust that smile. With his attire and his skeletal features, the man looked like a fucking mad scientist.

"The pleasure's all yours," Fabrice managed.

"Oh no, sir, you do yourself an injustice. It is an honour to meet you, the man that helped destroy a country." Durand threw the hood aside and looked down at his captive. "And I want to thank you for providing me the opportunity of a lifetime."

"Why don't you just let me die?"

"What?" Durand said taking a step back. "Where would be the fun in that?" He reached to his left and dragged over a metal chair, placing it a metre from where Fabrice sat shackled into his wheelchair. Durand sat. "And you should thank me, I have saved you from days of torment, against express orders, you understand. I'm taking quite the risk." Another man, also wearing a hazmat suit, appeared from behind Fabrice and handed Durand a small metal case. Without a word, the man left by a door behind the good doctor. The door hissed on opening and closing.

"Whatever you have planned for me, my God will return to me a thousand fold."

"Yes," Durand said tapping the case, "yes, I'm sure he will. But you call your God HE. How do you know that he even has a sex?"

"What?"

"You call your God he, but surely God doesn't have a gender. He's not some old bloke with a beard living in a cloud. Surely, your God is the infinite everything. Perhaps IT would be a better way of describing it." Durand loved religious fanatics. He loved to use their own beliefs against them, could taunt them for hours if they would let him.

"Fuck off," Fabrice said defiantly. "He's all there ever was and all there ever will be. You can mock him all you want, but you will suffer for it in the next life."

"Well, let's hope not." Durand opened the case and looked inside. "I have a gift for you, a gift that will take away all the pain. It will take away all the worry and make you the strongest you have ever been." Fabrice watched as Durand extracted something from the case. "Isn't karma a bitch," Durand said, putting the case aside and standing.

"What is that?" Fabrice demanded. Fear sparked the remnants of his adrenaline and he began to struggle in his bonds.

"This? This is the blood of an infected individual." Carefully, Durand opened the vial. Fabrice felt strong hands grab his head from behind. Despite his resistance, his head was jerked back so that he was forced to look at the ceiling.

"Don't," Fabrice now begged. "Not this, please not like this."

"What, you infect London and then blanch at the prospect of joining your God's army? Shame on you, you should be honoured. I'm almost offended. But this is science, and there is no room for personal feeling in science. We know the virus isn't airborne, but we also know direct skin contact is all that is required for the infection to take hold." Durand opened the test tube he was holding. He had considered injection as a means to transfer the virus, but there was too much risk of a needle-stick injury. "But we haven't as yet seen such transmission happen under laboratory conditions." Durand stepped over to his bound captive. "That's why you're here." With that, Durand poured the contents of the tube into Fabrice's naked lap. "Now, we shall see how much your God truly loves you."

20.42PM, 16th September 2015, Hounslow, London, UK

John had chosen to be with his family, and now he followed obediently behind Owen with what had been his wife. The child Owen had sent on her way—he had no need for her. Even now, the seven year old would be hunting the streets for fresh meat, competing with the undead and the other unconstrained infected. What disappointed Owen the most was how few people he was encountering, and how few infected. It seemed the latter had all moved on, so he decided to go to a place where during the day there were tens of thousands of people. At the end of the road, he turned right, still dragging Claire by the leash, his eyes flitting briefly over the sign stating that this was the way to Heathrow Airport. The police station had been a nonstarter, flames pouring from heat-shattered windows, the structure beyond destroyed. Part of Owen had been delighted, but another part was filled with regrets that his original big plan had been foiled. It was then that he decided to head for the country's biggest airport.

John's wife had been surprisingly attractive considering the balding, pot-bellied fool she had been married to. Owen had stood over the trio as they had turned, still fascinated by the process, taunting them as they lost their humanity, every minute threatening to kill the child, just for the fun of it. Whilst this was going on, he willed Claire to clean herself up, and she had disappeared back into the shop, only to return minutes later without any blood visible on her skin, a half-empty bottle of mouthwash gripped in her demonic-like hand. The trio hardly noticed her transformation, and then it no longer mattered because the vomiting and the defecation started. Owen had needed to step back from the utter stench of the display. That bit he was never going to get used to, he had to admit that to himself. And then it was done, all three of them rising from the ground, ready to begin the hunt. But only one had been given such a luxury. The parents he decided to keep for himself.

The idea came to him like ideas do. He would build an army of infected, to loot and pillage as he saw fit. He would need soldiers to keep the true zombies at bay, so he would pick the strongest and the fittest males he could find. But what he wanted most were women, a harem of willing sex slaves ready to follow his every command. Claire and John's wife were only the first. There would be many, many more. He could see it, could see the expanse of his lust in his mind. But right now, he needed numbers, and he was excited to discover how many he could actually control. Would it be a few dozen, hundreds? What if he could control thousands?

Both of the other infected were now naked, Owen ordering them to shed their soiled clothing. That would be the uniform of his army, human skin. He turned another corner, nearing a dual carriageway, the airport perimeter now visible. He knew this place, had been here earlier today. This was where that bastard Clive had threatened him with a gun. Did he mean to come this way? Was his subconscious leading him to achieve some kind of revenge? Two minutes' travel up the road, and he found himself looking at the corpse of the former fast food restaurant manager, the bastard who had threatened him with a gun. The body was hours old and buzzed with flies. So it looked like revenge wouldn't be required after all. But hell, it didn't stop him having a little fun in the bargain.

"You two, feed." Without a moment's hesitation, his newest recruits ran past him and began to rip the clothes off the cadaver. Claire whimpered, and Owen could feel the craving gnawing away inside her.

"Oh no, Claire, you have something more important to eat," he said, unbuckling his pants. Her telepathic instructions clear, Claire fell to her knees before him and set her mouth to work.

"John, make sure to get the best bit," Owen said out loud. Telepathy was all well and good, but Owen liked the sound of his own voice, liked the commanding tone he could project in a world empty of humanity. The creature formally known as John pulled his head away from the abdomen, chewing rhythmically, and looked at his master. The creature swallowed and then frantically began to pull and rip at the dead man's trousers.

"That's right, John. Make sure you eat those nice juicy balls." This was surely more fun than any man was ever meant to experience, and he looked up into the cloudless sky and roared at the top of his lungs. "King of the world, Ma, king of the fucking world."

Owen had briefly considered going back home to check on his mother. But he had quickly abandoned that idea. There was nothing for him there. He loathed the woman, not because she didn't love him, but because she had stood by helpless and let him become what he was. If she'd done what a mother should have done, maybe his soul wouldn't have been ripped to shreds.

He also hated her for marrying that wanker who had briefly called himself a father. He wasn't around now, and Owen hoped he was dead in a ditch somewhere, the infected feasting on his face. No, he wouldn't go home because there was only one end result from that. Deep down, under the lies and the excuses, he knew he would end up killing her. And that would truly be the end of him. The remnants of his conscience still believed there was still some way to come back from the murderer he had become, some small chance of salvation. So he stayed away. Besides, his mother was probably incoherent now, collapsed on the sofa with half a bottle of gin inside her. What was the point of killing someone if they were too drunk to really truly experience such a gift?

20.47PM, 16th September 2016, Newquay Airport, Cornwall, UK

"I think the calculations need adjusting," Savage said. Stood in the hastily erected command tent on the edge of Newquay Airport, she looked at the three men before her. There were other people in the room, but it was these three men she needed to convince. Separating them was a large table ordained with a map of the Southwest of England.

"I have been assured that the calculations are accurate," General Mansfield said defensively. This was the latest from NATO—surely, the predictions of the spread of the infection would be more accurate than the hunch of a mere captain. Savage looked at Croft, who gazed back at her thoughtfully. The general's aide seemed to be taking notes of everything that was being said.

"I'm going to have to agree with the captain," Croft said. "I think three days is way too optimistic. We need to plan for the infected to arrive any day now." He turned to the general and placed his hand on the table. "You have to hold this," Croft said, moving the map. "You have to be ready for them, and if you're not going to be ready, then you have to slow them down."

"NATO will be helping with that. We have been promised considerable air support. Whatever isn't enforcing the blockade will be able to come to our aid. We have our own attack helicopters, of course, but they will only be able to run so many sorties. Fuel isn't a problem, ordinance is." The general looked at Savage with a hint of disapproval, but then nodded his head in acceptance. "Alright, we will plan for first engagement within twenty-four hours. This means, of course, we will have to start the scorched earth now, and anything east of this line," the general drew his finger over a red line that was drawn on the map, "will have to be sacrificed."

"There's no other way, General," Croft said solemnly.

"They said you were a cold son of a bitch, Croft," the general said. There was no malice in the remark; if anything, there was only respect. "I see why General Marston speaks so highly of you." Croft just nodded. He had learnt to ignore compliments, especially when they sounded like insults,

"What are your defensive plans?" Croft asked, changing the subject.

"Quite simple, really. Walls, lots of walls. We are starting with the airport first, as well as ten main outposts east of here along a defensive line. We were lucky in that there was a large stockpile of Hesco Bastion walls in Plymouth waiting for export. That's already being laid out around our present position. I've got teams emptying everything from timber merchants to DIY stores. Every tree from here to Dartmoor is being felled. In an ideal world, I'd build a fucking wall right across the peninsula, but I don't have enough time, enough materials, and I don't have enough men to defend it. But we can hold key areas, with defensive outposts between them. Tomorrow, I'm relocating my headquarters to one of the large hotels in Newquay."

"So that's Operation Hadrian. Sounds like a solid plan," Croft said agreeably. The general was about to say something further, but his attention was drawn as the flap to the tent opened, someone entering. Both Croft and the general turned to see who it was. Savage was already looking in that direction, and she was the first to see the weary soldier enter the tent.

"Captain Grainger reporting as ordered, sir." Grainger stood at attention as soon as he saw his superior officer.

"At ease, Captain, good to have you with us. Croft, you probably owe this chap your life. It was his lads that held Westminster Bridge long enough for you to get away." Croft took a step over to the captain and stuck out his hand. The captain shook it.

"Thanks for that," Croft said. The captain had a firm handshake, and a confident air about him.

"Just following orders, sir," Grainger said.

"So, Captain, now that you're here, why don't you give us your first-hand knowledge of how to combat the infected?"

Having moved from the map table, they were now sat on camping chairs around an empty upturned crate, the ground beneath them grass, uncovered and uneven. Three glasses of scotch lay on the crate, Savage holding hers almost lovingly. She barely touched it. She was too fascinated by what the captain was telling them. Croft had almost emptied his, the other two glasses hardly touched. The aid stood taking further notes, the general bustle of the command tent almost forgotten.

"I've seen infected take a fifty-calibre round to the torso and still keep on coming. I've seen them lose limbs, and I've seen them on fire. The only way you stop these things is killing the brain. Headshots seem to take them down alright."

"Because otherwise they come back," Savage stated.

"Yes, I've seen that too," said Grainger.

"And you say you think they communicate." This was what fascinated Savage the most. As a scientist, this was what she lived for.

"Oh for sure," Grainger recounted. "They can work individually and in large groups. In large numbers, you will run out of bullets before you get even close to stopping them. If it wasn't for that Spectre Gunship coming to my rescue, I would likely have been overrun."

"We've had reports from the satellite feeds of them using vehicles," Croft added.

"I didn't see that, Major, but it doesn't surprise me. They know when to hide, when to retreat, and when to swarm."

"Some of the science boffins think they communicate telepathically," Mansfield added.

"As mad as it sounds, that wouldn't surprise me either, sir." Telepathy, thought Croft. Shit, this just kept getting better and better.

"How are your lads, by the way? Ready for more duty?" The general looked at this subordinate as he leant forward to pick up his glass. The captain looked at his but decided against it. He had a feeling if he started, he wouldn't be able to stop.

"Duty is all they have left, sir. Just point us to where you need us."

20.58PM GMT, 16th September 2015, NATO Headquarters, Belgium

"God damn you, Croft." General Marston looked at the telephone handset he had just finished speaking into and carefully placed it back onto its cradle. Goddamn you to hell. He had not been speaking to Croft, but to General Mansfield. He knew whose idea this was though. Marston closed his eyes, felt the angina surge in his chest, or was it just indigestion caused by the unpleasantness of what they now needed to do? Three days he had been assured, had been promised. Three days he could have delayed the inevitable, but not anymore.

Of course, Croft was right. Croft was always right; that's why he had been given the job. And to be fair, he wasn't even the first to have come up with the idea, he had just confirmed what was slowly growing within the bowels of NATO itself. Croft could make the decisions that lesser men would hesitate to, and he could make them quickly. For Operation Hadrian to work, they needed to create a buffer to the east of the defensive line, a buffer to provide time for what needed to be done. Because that was the new worry here: time. Nobody knew how quickly a 27-mile-long array of defensive positions would take to build. Oh, such things had been done before—hell at the battle of Alesia, the Romans had surrounded the besieged city with two walls over twenty miles long in total, and had managed it in a matter of weeks. They didn't have weeks though. They had days at best, and the Romans had not had to defend against this kind of enemy. The Gauls had grown tired in battle and had retreated several times, something the infected would never do. But it was essential for the walls to be built, because the defensive line was hope, and hope was the only thing that would keep what was left of humanity alive on the British mainland.

But what Croft was recommending…could he order that? Could he tell the Supreme Commander of NATO that they needed to bomb UK cities and towns and villages that had been overrun, and even worse, that had not yet been hit by the infection? It would kill tens of thousands of people fleeing the infection, and trap millions more. And then after the bombing would come, the seeding of the land, the laying down of thousands of deadly anti-personnel mines, scattering the ground with death that would kill infected and unwary refugees alike. Could he really give that recommendation?

Of course he could; there was no other way. There were already B-52s on route from the United States, dispatched by a president who, unlike previous incumbents, actually seemed to know what he was doing. So, in a matter of hours, he would have his delivery system. He would have the means to rain an apocalypse on infected and innocents alike. Most of the country was already sacrificed to the infection, millions just waiting for the virus to claim them. An unstoppable army the likes of which the world had never seen before. What were a few thousand more deaths? What were a few million when the whole world was at risk? They had to maintain a foothold on that green and pleasant land. They just had to.

But that was only the first of Croft's recommendations. The power of the infected came from their numbers. Thousands they could defend against, millions they couldn't. So why not cut off the head of the snake? Why not strike at the very pool from which the infected took their recruits? Nobody wanted nukes raining down on the UK mainland. Not only was there the danger of the radiation that would drift over mainland Europe, there was also the promise made by the terrorists themselves. Nukes were out of the question in the short term. But there were other means to go along with the high-level carpet bombing of the cities and numerous choke points caused by humanity's flight. Dropped on the unsuspected and the innocent, to some it would almost be a blessing.

Ultimately, nukes would have to be used; it was the only definitive way. It was hoped that the information acquired from the raid on the laboratory would lead to the head of the terrorist snake. Once that head was removed, and once the threat promised by the terrorists was neutralised, then perhaps the nukes would indeed fly. But until then, there was Croft's final suggestion. What about that other weapon of mass destruction, the one that wasn't presently in NATO's arsenal? For that, they would need the help of the Russians. Marston picked up the phone again. He punched in the numbers and waited for the person to answer on the other end. Someone answered.

"Hello, General Marston here. Please put me through to General Bradstone." Would his superiors go for it? Would NATO high command be willing to kill millions of people, people they were supposed to protect?

21.12PM, 16th September 2015, Heathrow Airport, London, UK

Owen Paterson was not disappointed. There were infected here, there were infected here in abundance. Approaching the airport by the southeast, he found part of the perimeter fence down, but he resisted the temptation to lead his group of infected onto the runway. He had seen smoke from the airport about ten minutes earlier, and now he saw what it was from. A shattered plane, probably a 747, lay scattered across the runway, its fuselage in several pieces. Owen could clearly see that it hadn't crashed. It had blown up on the runway. Blown up or been blown up?

"Awesome," he said, carrying on down the road, his infected bodyguards twitching and aching to go at the wreckage. That probably meant there were still survivors inside. "No," he mentally chastised them, and he felt the tension in the chain go slack. That wasn't where he wanted to go—there was a much bigger prize in store.

He could feel them, thousands of them, and Owen changed his direction slightly and made his way to the main hotel outside Terminal 4. In the distance, he could see the occasional infected running, and he searched for the rest of them. Yes, here was where he would test the limit of his abilities. Controlling one or two was an achievement, but what if he could control them in large numbers? Wouldn't that be something? Wouldn't that make him something more than a man?

Owen stopped on the road and stilled himself. He had found that by concentrating, he could tune into the infected, could tell where they were, what they were doing. And the more he practiced, the more distance didn't seem to be an issue.

"Where are you?" he said softly. Images came to him, and within seconds, he knew where the thousands of infected were, saw what they saw, felt the hunger that they felt. Owen staggered, the impact of the thousands of hungry, ravenous minds almost overwhelming, and he cut himself off before the feelings overtook him. He felt it, felt their need, felt it become part of him for a brief second, and he was almost swept away with it. Fuck, he had to be careful. For a moment there, he almost became one of them. The feeling was intoxicating, almost seductive. He could just let go, let it wash over him. No more cares, no more worries, just the hunger and the need. This was going to take practice and patience.

"No," he shouted, slapping himself in the face. He was the controller here, not the controlled. Taking several deep breaths, he composed himself. He wouldn't make that mistake again.

The lobby of the hotel was a complete wreck, the glass revolving door shattered, and his shoes crunched across the broken glass. Claire made no complaints as she followed, and in the lobby, he turned to the three of them.

"Stay." They looked almost pained, like dogs who had been chastised. But of course they were less than dogs to Owen; he cared nothing for them. He had a plan, and it was painfully simple. All throughout the hotel, he could feel the infected clawing at hotel room doors, trying to get at the meat that was cowering within. Faced with the onslaught and no way out, hundreds of people had locked themselves away. There they cowered, behind barricaded doors, some crying, some glued to the still-working TV sets. Owen knew that if he got a master key card for the doors, he could give the infected access, but that would take hours. Perhaps there was a better way. Perhaps he could use mankind's fears against each other, and have immense fun in the bargain.

He encountered four infected by the elevators, and he ordered them to join Claire and her friends at the main entrance, his plan growing and shaping with every moment. The infected hesitated briefly, but then did as he bid, shedding their clothes as they left his presence. One of them was a male hotel employee, and Owen picked up his discarded corporate jacket. Only the king was worthy of garments in the new world, and this garment would come in very handy for what was to come next. Owen pressed the elevator button and waited. With nobody else using them, the lift arrived quickly, and he stepped inside the mirrored cage, ignoring the eyeless corpse that was propped up in one corner. The floor of the elevator was sticky with blood.

"Fuck me." Owen pressed the top floor, and the elevator began to rise. A brief thought about being stuck in the lift hit him, the power suddenly failing, his only companion the sightless decaying body behind him. A well of anxiety formed, but it quickly dissipated when the lift stopped and the door opened. Seven infected turned to look at him, one clawing the air menacingly.

"Kneel," Owen commanded, and within moments, they had all subserviently dropped to their knees, bowing their heads in supplication.

"Listen up, bitches," Owen broadcast in his mind. "This is what I want from you."

The party last night had been monumental. Winning a fifty-million-dollar business contract had resulted in an alcohol-fuelled indulgence that had ended with a night in the lap dancing club. He and his negotiating partner from the other side of the deal hadn't left 'til five in the morning, and he hadn't left alone. Waking up just after noon, he discovered a stripper in his bed and a hangover that could fell a rhino. It was then that he had switched on the TV to discover the end of the world had also arrived.

Right now, he was alone. On seeing the news, 'Candy' had dressed quickly and fled, saying something about her mother through tears that smeared already-smeared mascara. He was glad to see her gone, to be honest; the alcohol and the high of his success were making him do things that were normally against his moral code. Dressing himself, he had phoned down to reception, only to get no answer. He had a late check out because his flight wasn't 'til eight that evening, so at least he didn't have to worry about that. Kirk placed the phone back in its cradle and turned back to the TV. He flicked through the channels, finding some of the local channels unavailable.

"Shit, shit, shit!" he screamed. Yesterday had been the best day of his life, the culmination of five years' hard work and near bankruptcy. And he had made it. Fifty million fucking dollars, ten of that going straight away into his back pocket. But what use was money when fucking Revelations was unleashed upon the world? That was when he heard the first screams outside his window.

That had been hours ago. He had briefly gone down to the lobby, only to see panicked staff and panicked guests. Someone had been graced with the foresight to lock the main lobby doors, because seconds after Kirk had stepped out of the elevator, he had seen, across the expanse of marble and polished wood, the first of the infected hit the glass doors twenty metres across the hotel's main entrance. Kirk had stepped right back into the elevator just as the doors had closed, not holding them for the panicked woman who oh so nearly made it. He didn't witness what happened downstairs after that, but fled to his room where he locked what he hoped was a sturdy enough door.

It had been, and for the last several hours, they had been banging and clawing at it. Only once had he looked through the security peephole, and he had seen at least a dozen of them in the corridor outside, all trying to gain entry into the various rooms. Then one of them had looked at him, its blood-red eyes clearly seeing him, even though that should be impossible. The rhythm on his door increased as they attacked it with renewed excitement. He hadn't approached the door again, and he kept the volume on the TV subdued. Kirk had missed the live hacked broadcast by the terrorist group, but it had been replayed so many times on so many channels Kirk thought by now he had memorised the entire speech. Presently, there was a replay of a distant camera shot showing Parliament burning.

"Just to reiterate, we will be going live to the White House any moment where the president will be speaking to the nation," the voice on CNN said. Hours earlier, he had managed to phone his wife in Melbourne on the hotel's landline—his cell service had been out of action. She had been in hysterics, knowing where he was, knowing the danger he faced. Secretly, he also suspected her biggest fear was that she wouldn't be seeing any of the millions that she had been hanging on for. Perhaps he shouldn't think like that, but there was a certain reality one had to consider when you lived in a culture where two-thirds of marriages failed. Ironically, it was she who had insisted on the prenuptial, because when they had married, she had been the one from the relatively wealthy family, with a quite acceptable trust fund. The glint in her eyes when he had told her that his bid had been accepted had been hard for her to hide. He had just finished telling her that he loved her (did he?) for the seventh time when the phone went dead. He had tried since to re-dial, only to no avail. And now he was alone.

"We are going over live to the White House," the woman on CNN stated. The TV cut to the press briefing room, and a very well-dressed Damian Rodney walked out to stand behind the presidential seal emblazoned lectern.

"My fellow Americans, citizens of the Earth, it is with a heavy heart that it falls upon me to confirm to you the gravest of news. Earlier today, the United Kingdom was the victim of a biological terrorist attack that is, as we speak, decimating this once proud and great nation. We do not know much about the biological agent used. What we do know is that those infected become overtaken by an animal-like rage that causes them to perform acts of unspeakable aggression and brutality. But that is not all. Should those who are infected die, they come back to life to kill again." There was a loud murmuring in the background of the broadcast, dozens of reporters bursting to ask their president questions, but knowing they had to wait for the commander-in-chief to finish what needed to be said.

"As amazing as it sounds, the disease turns people into..." the president paused, as if trying to find the words, "into the undead. Zombies are real. They are here, on this planet. Our worst nightmares have become reality." The whole room erupted at that, and surprisingly, the president stood their calmly, letting the furore wash over him. After about half a minute, he raised a hand and calmed the crowd.

"But there is hope. Being an island, the natural boundaries of the United Kingdom should stop the spread of the disease at its borders. Whilst we must accept that the country is lost, we are hopeful of keeping the disease contained. The United Kingdom is now under a state of NATO quarantine. Nothing will be allowed in or out. And due to the unconfirmed threats that were aired across the Emergency Broadcast System, the use of nuclear weapons to deal with the contagion has not been authorised at this stage. I will shortly pass this press conference over to the Deputy Chief Commanding Officer of NATO, General Henderson. But before I do, I ask that you join me in a moment of prayer so that we may honour the memories of the millions that have died, to honour the greatness of a now fallen country. May God have mercy on our souls."

Prayer? What the fuck was prayer going to do? You are praying to the same God that was worshipped by the religious fuckers who released this plague, you arsehole. Kirk, enraged, threw the remote control across the room, where it impacted, the batteries flying out. The sound on the TV went mute, and Kirk sat on the bed, watching the scenes in silence. It was then that he realised something. He couldn't hear the infected at the door. That had been a constant background noise, their scraping and scratching and the occasional thump. But now he heard nothing.

"Can I have your attention," a voice said outside in the corridor. "We don't know why, but the infected have left the building." The voice got louder as the person walked along the corridor getting closer to Kirk's room. "It is safe to come out, and we have transportation to take you to a safe zone." Kirk jumped off the bed and ran over to the door. Looking through the peephole, he indeed saw no infected. Then a hotel employee walked into view, knocking on his door and the door opposite. Kirk heard further voices as people began to fill the corridor. He risked it.

Opening the door, the hotel employee continued along the corridor.

"Follow me, and I will lead you to the awaiting transportation. Do not take the elevators as there is a risk we will lose power." A half dozen people walked past Kirk's open door, and he ducked back inside to grab his overnight bag, seconds later joining the now two dozen people who were trusting their lives in somebody they didn't know.

"Where are the infected?" someone asked.

"Please, all your questions will be answered, but we need to move quickly in case the infected return." The majority of the rooms were emptying now, and Kirk felt himself swept along by the panic and the hope of escape. *I'm going to make it,* he thought to himself, *I'm getting out of here.* The hotel employee stopped by the emergency exit at the end of the corridor and opened the door. "Please make your way to the ground floor," the employee said, ushering people through the portal one at a time. Kirk was in the middle of the group, and thanked the guy as he passed through the door, one of the only people to do so.

"Just doing my job, sir," the hotel employee said, and then Kirk was heading down the staircase, the echoing of footsteps all around him.

Owen held the door open for the hotel guests until the last one was no longer in sight. There would still be a few left on this floor, but the majority were now heading towards the trap he had laid. He planned to do each floor one at a time, to savour the horrors he was going to inflict on these unwilling cunts. They were all his, they just didn't realise it yet, and one or two of the females had really caught his eye. The deception had been easier than he thought, much easier, and keeping his traumatised hand in his pocket had kept anyone from spotting the damage and asking questions. Owen needed compliance, not questions. To his left, a door opened and three infected stepped out. Together, they and Owen walked through the staircase door, which closed behind them. Owen descended, briefly leaving the infected behind to guard the barrier, out of sight of anyone on the lower levels. They soon followed, however, and would be the guardians of the doors once Owen stepped out into the ground floor lobby.

Kirk was the thirteenth person to exit the staircase. The lobby was silent, and the white marble was stained with blood in places. About a half dozen bodies littered the place, but none of them moved. He walked forward hesitantly with the others, doubt and fear making them cling together. Behind him, the last of the top-floor residents stepped through the door, followed by the hotel employee, who boldly walked past them to stand in the centre of the concourse. It was then that Kirk noticed the bandaged hand, and the fact that he was wearing jeans.

"Ladies and gentlemen, can I have your attention please," the employee said. In theatrical style, the man spun around to face them all raising his hands to his hips. "I have a confession to make."

"What's going on?" someone behind Kirk shouted, and another voice raised another question. The employee raised a finger to his lips and held it there for several seconds.

"Now is not the time for questions; now is the time for truth. I'm afraid I've not been completely honest with you." Kirk watched as the man took a step back, then another. The man looked around and he whistled, a smirk arriving on his face. Several scarred and mutilated heads raised themselves up from behind the hotel's reception desk. More bloodied bodies emerged from side doors and from within hidden alcoves. Within seconds, Kirk found himself looking at maybe three dozen infected, most with some form of visible bodily injuries. Some sported lacerations, others were missing limbs. All were naked, and that terrified Kirk more than anything.

"Folks, we are going to play a game. One of you gets to live today, the rest get to join my merry band," Owen said, sweeping his injured hand around at the assorted infected.

"What the fuck is this?" Kirk demanded. A young woman at the back of the group panicked and ran for the staircase, but the door opened before her, and an infected grabbed her arms in a vice-like grip. Kirk turned to look at her as she yelled, terror filling the air. He watched helpless as the infected who had seized her spun her round, now holding her by the throat and hair, stretching her neck, pulling her head right back.

"Please, please no," the woman begged. The infected turned his eyes towards its master.

"I didn't say anyone could leave," Owen said. As if receiving some sort of signal, the infected blood-red eyes lit up with pleasure and it quickly bit down into the woman's face. Kirk turned away; it was too much. Most of the group just stood in mortified fascination. One man fainted.

"Hey, hey, hey, eyes on me, people."

"How can you do this?" Kirk said, stepping forward. As if acting as bodyguards, two of the larger of the infected males moved towards Owen, who now stood with his arms folded. My God, could this maniac control them? Owen ignored the question.

"As I said, one of you gets to live, but only if you follow my rules. We are going to have a Battle Royal here today, folks. I'm going to stand here and watch you all beat the living shit out of each other. And the last man or woman standing gets to leave through those front doors." Owen pointed behind him. "So tell me, folks, who's it going to be? And who's going to throw the first punch?"

21.28PM GMT, 16th September 2015, The White House, Washington DC, USA

"Phillip, you can't be serious?" General Roberts, the Chairman of the Joint Chiefs of Staff, looked at the wall monitor with a collection of anger and bewilderment. "That would kill millions."

"I am aware of that, Rob," General Bradstone said. His image relayed by satellite showed him sat in his office in Brussels. "Our analysis shows it is the best move we have at this time. If it makes you feel any better, the British were the ones who originated the plan. They have always been cold sons of bitches when it came to this sort of thing."

"But how can we do that? How can we commit mass murder and survive it?"

"How can we not?" General Roberts turned to the person who had spoken, the voice grim and determined.

"Mr. President, you can't seriously be considering this plan? It would destroy your administration. Not to mention the very real threat made to what will happen should we use nuclear weapons. We cannot survive this contagion being released onto the streets of our cities."

"It is my job to consider all options presented to me. And, quite frankly, this is the only thing I've heard so far that seems to make any sense." Damian Rodney stared into the eyes of General Roberts. This plan had merit. This was the kind of thinking that was needed in times like this. "We are talking about the safety of the human race."

"But it's mass murder. If the press gets wind of it..." the general protested.

"Is it mass murder?" the president persisted. "Those people are dead no matter what we do. At the moment, they are locked in their homes, waiting for the inevitable horror that is going to descend upon them. It's only a matter of time, and by not taking action, we are talking millions more infected. And as it stands, it's inevitable that this virus will break through our quarantine. Great Britain may be an island, but let us not forget that these creatures can swim. And don't worry about the press. Once operation Clean Sweep is activated...well, you know what that means." Roberts did, had read in depth the way the federal government would take control of all media outlets. It wouldn't be too hard; most of them were owned by the big corporations who backed the government so long as they were looked after. Even the social media would be controlled, also owned and controlled by the same multinational conglomerates. For Clean Sweep to be successful, the majority of the population would need to be kept in the dark, whilst those who needed to be detained were rounded up. This would be one propaganda war they couldn't afford to lose.

"I'm not sure I can support this," General Roberts said, defeated. He ran a hand over his bald scalp, nausea threatening to envelop him. He had always wondered how he would react in such a situation. Now he knew. Could he be a party to this? Could he sit back and oversee the death of millions of women and children?

"You don't need to support it," the president said calmly. "You only need to obey the orders of your commander-in-chief. Can you do that, General? Can you do what your country needs of you?" Roberts looked at the man the Secret Service called POTUS. He saw the determination in the man's eyes, saw that he was both the best and the worst person to be in this position. The best because he was willing to make the decisions that needed to be made. The worst because, most likely, the man would go to sleep tonight without any problem whatsoever.

"Yes, Mr. President. If it's the opinion of the Heads of NATO and this administration that this plan of action is warranted, then I will do what needs to be done." The president didn't say anything, just looked at the man for several seconds then nodded.

"Very well. General Bradstone, I am authorising the use of nuclear weapons on the British mainland when the threat to our homeland has been neutralised, but not before. Please liaise with the other NATO members and get this done. If we can get the Brits to use their own nukes, then that would be an added bonus. Gentlemen, we will report back here at twenty hundred hours. Ben," the president said, turning to the White House chief of staff, "I want the head of FEMA here within the hour. Let's get this done, people." With that, POTUS stood and left the room. Nobody of note saw the look of satisfaction on the president's face as he left the room, except one secret service agent who knew when to ignore what he saw.

21.32PM, 16th September 2015, Heathrow Airport, London, UK

Kirk staggered out into the night's air, limping slightly from the pain in his foot. He didn't look back, afraid that the maniac would renege on his promise. Cradling his right arm, he almost tripped over his own feet, dizziness hitting him like a freight train. But he didn't fall, and managed to continue walking on legs that had little strength left, the adrenaline now deserting his system. He hadn't been in a fight for over fifteen years. That one he had lost because his heart hadn't really been in it. This one he had won, because when your life was on the line, you found resources you didn't even know you possessed.

When Owen had told them the rules, the assembled victims had looked at each other, perplexed as to what to do. That had changed to panic when a large Asian guy had lashed out at the woman next to him, sending her to the floor. She never got back up. Then all hell had broken loose. Kirk had stepped back, almost colliding with an infected, a strategy formulating in his mind. Wait it out, let the others weaken themselves. Had that thought really formed in his head? It didn't matter because the strategy had worked for all of two minutes before something had pushed him from behind, sending him sprawling right into the heart of the melee. By then, half the combatants were already on the ground.

He looked at the hand of his injured arm, saw the blood from where he had gouged out somebody's eye. He couldn't even watch a medical procedure on TV without feeling squeamish, and yet today, he had probably blinded someone. The hand hurt, bones probably broken from where he had punched someone, a woman. He probably had at least one broken toe as well. The shoes he wore were not ideal for kicking somebody in the head. The arm he had injured when someone had charged him, forcing him to the floor. He could move it, so he didn't think it was broken. But it hurt like hell. That had been the moment when he discovered he had the ability to stick his thumb into somebody's eye socket.

"We have a winner," Owen had said, as Kirk picked himself off the floor. He looked around at the carnage, disgusted with himself, enraged at the man who had caused all this. "You can go," the fucker had said. Kirk had just stared at him in disbelief. "I said you can go, arsehole. Or do you want to hang around whilst my children dine?" At that, Owen snapped his fingers and from all around, infected descended on the groaning mass of bodies. Kirk didn't stay around for that.

His attention was drawn to movement and he stopped in his tracks. An infected ran over to him, sniffing him, getting in close, almost touching him. But as soon as it had arrived, it ran off, somehow satisfied that he wasn't of interest. Kirk watched it go, his mouth open in awe at what he had just seen. That creature was what was left of Candy, her appearance changed but unmistakeable as the woman who had shared his bed last night. My God, what was he witness to here? And why weren't they attacking him?

22.14PM. 16th September 2015, Headland Hotel, Newquay, UK

Jack watched as the helicopter he had just disembarked from flew off into the distance. He stood, almost mesmerised for several seconds, and then turned to see his fellow passengers already making their way to the large hotel that had once been the heart of Newquay's tourist industry. It was called the headland because it stood on an outcrop that separated Fistral Bay from Newquay Bay. It wasn't a hotel anymore. Jack clutched his weapon and ran after the soldiers who had adopted him as one of their own. Well, technically, it had been Bull who had adopted him, but that was virtually the same thing. He had noticed that most of the men who interacted with Bull treated him with a respect that Jack had rarely seen. Even his now deceased boss, Clive, had only managed to create a kind of grudging compliance amongst his employees.

And Bull treated those around him with respect also. Jack himself was in awe of the man. Catching up to them, somewhat out of breath, they as a group headed to the front of the hotel where an officer waited.

"Gentlemen," a Royal Marine Captain greeted them.

"Sir," men around him saluted and stood to attention.

"At ease, men," the captain ordered. "Sergeant, a word." Jack watched as Bull stepped away from the men and walked over to the captain. He didn't hear what was said. When they finished, Bull saluted again and watched as the captain walked off. When he turned, there was a smile on his face.

"Right then, lads," said Bull, "it looks like we have easy duty." He looked at the dozen soldiers around him. Some he knew, some he didn't. In the chaos of the retreat, the normal structure of the armed forces had been mashed up. "We have billeting behind the hotel. Tents, I'm afraid, but beggars can't be choosers. You'll even have to put your own tents up because nobody's done it for you, so the sooner you get at it, the sooner you'll be able to get some hot food in you. See the quartermaster in the main kitchens on the first floor, and then meet me here tomorrow morning at 7 AM. Dismissed. Corporal," he said to one of the men, "you're with me." All but one of the men wandered off, and Bull made his way over to where Jack was standing.

"Don't tell me I have to share a tent with you again, Bull," the remaining soldier said jokingly. He turned to Jack. "The bastard snores like a fucking tornado."

"Thank your stars, Phil," Bull said to the corporal. "We have one of the remaining rooms in this glorious hotel." Phillip clapped Jack on the back and beamed with delight.

"Result."

"What about me, Bull?" Jack asked timidly.

"Why, I think we can find space for you. What do you say, Phil?"

"More's the merrier, Bull," Phil said. The three of them moved forward, Phil gently guiding the young man ahead of him. Just like Bull, he too had taken a shine to the teenager.

22.30PM, 16th September 2015, MI6 Building, London, UK

Victor Durand sat at the monitor, watching a close-up of the video feed of his test subject. Now this, this was science. The camera was zoomed right into Fabrice's face, and the man's head lolled from side to side, overcome with fever and delirium. Occasionally, an undecipherable mutter would escape the bound man's lips, and his head would thrash wildly, but then he would quiet and go back to his almost comatose state. This was not how they had documented the infection happening in others. This was taking too long. There was still no evidence of the conversion taking hold. It had been two hours; it should only have taken ten minutes. This was fascinating, and at the same time, infuriating because it represented an unknown variable.

By the side of the video feed, a second monitor relayed a host of the experiment's vital signs. That's what he was now in Durand's mind, an experiment. The man's heart rate and blood pressure were through the roof, as was the temperature. If he cared about the man, Durand would have been concerned about a stroke or even death, but the only thing Durand cared about was data, and the possibility that this was maybe something new, something unique, something wonderful. If this man was somehow immune, then could his body contain the cure? Davina's interrogation had already revealed that the man knew of no vaccine against the virus, and Durand doubted he could have been inoculated without his knowledge. How fortunate it would be if this killer of millions was naturally immune. Fortunate for Durand, that is. A cure would make him the saviour of the world. It would make him a worldwide celebrity. It would give him something he had always secretly craved.

He needed more test subjects. Durand needed more uninfected to do his experiments on, more fresh virgin souls for him to defile. Could he get away with it though? There were seven other individuals in the holding cells of the MI6 Building, two of them Fabrice's accomplices. Did he dare push this? Did he dare risk everything to get where he needed to be, against the wishes of those in charge? Of course he dared, it was who he was. He had taken risks all his life; some had paid off, others had almost ended his career, had almost brought him down into a realm of pain and infamy. But he was still here, his ability to pass the blame onto others almost as impressive as his understanding of genetics and microbiology. He was not only a genius, he was also a survivor.

Durand believed he was here for a reason, that all his life, all his experiences had added up to him being in this place at this time. He now knew that he was here to save the human race, to fight against the red tape and the prevailing moral decency, to take any measures needed to do what needed to be done. Whilst he wasn't in charge, he had just assumed enough power to do what others refused to do. He also had enough power to hang himself by his own actions too—that was something he needed to remember. So it was decided, Durand would have the others brought up from the cells to continue his experiments. And if he didn't get the results he needed from them, then he would start a careful selection of the non-essential refugees who had flooded the building in the initial stages, the consequences be damned. His problem wasn't even subject numbers. The problem was a lack of space to do the research in. He was sure he could think of a way around that though. Corpses wrapped in body bags didn't need much space after all.

Fabrice could hear them. In his delirium, his mind swam with the voices of the infected. He could only catch glimpses of what they were saying, but he felt them, felt their hunger, felt their confusion, felt their pain. He cried out something incoherent, reacting to the death of one outside the facility. He didn't know it, but he was undergoing the same transformation as Owen Paterson. Fabrice was infected, but for some reason, his body was stronger than the virus; it was using it, changing it. He felt it trying to burn its way through his mind, but instead of stripping him of his humanity, all it did was change him, improve him. The virus had become his puppet.

His body jerked in the chair, briefly seizing up, his muscles growing taught. In his semi-conscious state, he wasn't really coherent enough to witness what was happening to him, and he certainly wouldn't remember his body's fight with the contagion, except for brief flashes of distorted memory. But there was one thing his mind latched onto, one thing that consistently came to the front of his thoughts. Hate. Hatred for those godless heathens who held him, hate for humanity on the whole. And as the body processed the pathogen, as it mixed its DNA in with his own, his hate grew. And beneath the hate, something else. A yearning to connect with others like him. But for now, it was all masked by the fever and the ravishing of his transformation.

22.32PM, 16th September 2015, Heathrow Airport, London, UK

Owen sat on the slightly soiled leather sofa in the once-plush hotel, staring in awe at the mound of bodies in the centre of the hotel's lobby. There were at least twenty dead there, victims of his gladiatorial games. In all, he had let six people live and had instructed the infected in the locality not to kill them, to leave them alone completely. He left them for the zombies, the ever-growing threat that somehow had to be dealt with. His army had swelled in numbers, and even now, the majority of them were out hunting for unwilling souls to swell the ranks further. He wasn't alone though. He kept a hard core of twenty to defend him, his very own Praetorian guard, who took it in turns to patrol the perimeter. Occasionally, he would reward one of them by instructing them to feed on the corpses that had already amassed flies. The infected had cared not—they would happily feed off a bloated cadaver just as much as a live, thrashing and screaming victim. He would stay here tonight, but tomorrow he would move inwards, to the heart of London, and claim what was his by right. He would march at the head of his legion and devour anything and everything in his path.

There were four naked female infected curled up at his feet, each one spotless of grime and blood, having availed themselves of one of the hotel showers under his telepathic instruction. He didn't want these particular creatures bloodied anymore. He wanted them clean, pristine. Of course, Claire was one of them, and she would be until he grew weary of her. His good hand held a half empty bottle of wine, and he raised it to his lips, taking several mouthfuls. This was not the stuff he bought for five pounds in the corner off-licence. No, this he had found in the hotel bar, and it didn't burn his throat when it went down. Fuck, it actually tasted nice. This was how the other half used to live it seemed. Now it was how he lived.

He wasn't drunk though, that was the strange thing. Not even close. He should at least be feeling tipsy now, but all he felt was power coursing through him. He felt like a god, and lost in his own thoughts, he fantasied about his future. In his mind, he saw himself standing on a spectacular balcony, the sun setting behind the horizon, dark mountains silhouetted by the planet's star. Hundreds of meters below, through a drizzling rain, thousands of soldiers chanted his name, and their voices rose up and almost became the wind that buffeted the flags and banners that were on display everywhere. This was a future he had always dreamed of in the deepest recess of his mind, and now he had a chance to make it real. First, he would take London, and then he would take the country. And then? Then he would take the world, even if it meant him being the last human being alive on the planet.

22.37PM GMT, 16th September, Ramstein Air Base, Germany

The last of the four B-52 Stratofortresses settled into their designated slot off the runway and began shutdown. Their flight across the Atlantic now over, the maintenance crews rushed to them, ready to prepare them for the next stage of the many journeys they would undertake over the next few days. Group Superintendent Donald "Duck" Hales watched from the tarmac as the refuelling vehicles began their approach, ready to give aviation fuel to the flying harbingers of death. He did not envy the pilots of those craft, which would soon be loaded with almost 70,000 pounds of ground ordinance. He knew that two of the pilots were veterans from Gulf War 2, but he also knew even they would be unhappy with what they were about to be asked to do. Unhappy, hell, Duck wouldn't be surprised if one or more crews point blank refused. Whilst he didn't really expect that to happen, he couldn't really blame them if they did. Bombing armed enemy targets was one thing—it was what they were trained for, their mission in life. But bombing the cities and the streets of America's greatest ally was another thing entirely. In his heart, Hales wasn't too happy with it either, but those were the orders, and there was one thing Donald Hales never did, and that was disobey an order from a superior…especially when this order came from the commander-in-chief himself. And you just had to watch the news on CNN to know that there was a reason for those orders. The pending bombing was unpleasant, yes, but it was also essential. Because they weren't just going to be bombing civilians, they were going to be bombing potential soldiers in the deadliest army the world had ever seen.

And it wasn't even the worst job they might get asked to do, not in Duck's opinion. That was for the air-boys, the fighter bombers that would leave early tomorrow morning. They would get to see what they killed. But there was possibly an even worse job in all this. There was a very real chance that nuclear weapons would be used in the coming days, against a friendly nation. Hell, it would likely be the Brits' own nukes that were unleashed upon them, presently sat in the launch silos of the 4 Trident nuclear submarines presently dotted around the Atlantic. And the captains of those submarines would have to be the ones who ultimately unleashed nuclear death across a nation. The millions that would die would be horrific, and some would even make claims that this was a crime against humanity. But who was going to prosecute when the whole human race was at stake? Who was going to be critical when hundreds of thousands died in their beds and on the streets if it saved billions? This wasn't a war; it was a genocide against humanity, and there could only be one response against that. But the people who inserted the keys into the firing mechanisms, who ordered the missiles to fly, they would have to live with the task they would be asked to perform. How many of those men would kill themselves in the months and years that followed such an abomination?

22.47PM, 16th September 2016, Newquay Airport, Cornwall, UK

Savage needed sleep, but it eluded her. How was she supposed to process what had happened in the last twenty-four hours? It was perhaps fortunate, at this moment in time, that she didn't have any family, not really. Orphaned at birth, she went from foster home to foster home, never really finding the ultimate stability. Whereas others had retreated into drugs and violence, she retreated into books, and had managed to get a decent education despite the cards dealt to her. But still, she had craved stability, which is why she had let the military fund her university career. It had been the best decision of her life.

She had friends of course, many of them outside the forces. But they were either dead or facing death. Even worse, they might become part of the viral horde that would soon be sweeping across the country like locusts devouring crop after crop. Sat on the bed in her assigned quarters at the airport, she had wept tears of grief and frustration, knowing there was so much she wanted to do, but also knowing she was powerless to help anyone except those around her.

The tears were gone now, but the need to do something dominated her. So now she sat on the camping bed that had been provided for her, slowly picking through the thousands of files they had retrieved from the maniac who had started all this. All this had been sent to NATO headquarters, and there would be hundreds of eyes sorting through the data. But she had to make herself useful somehow. Then she uncovered the file called 'surprise'. When she opened it, she wasn't expecting a video file, its file name altered to hide any file designation. And she certainly wasn't expecting to be looking at the face of a man they had watched die several hours earlier.

"Okay," the voice of James Jones said. "If you are watching this, then my baby is hopefully sweeping its way across the country. I want to make it clear that I did this for my own reasons, not because I was part of some religious death cult. You need to understand that because it will help explain what I'm about to tell you. Believe me when I say, if I could have found another way, I would have. But I couldn't, so here we are." Jones was clearly agitated.

"What the maniacs who paid for my research don't realise is this. I despise them also. I have always despised religion, and the murder of my family only reinforced that belief. So if Abraham thinks I'm doing this purely for him, well he is sadly mistaken. I have done this for me, and me alone. And because of that, I have added a few little tweaks to my virus. Some of those tweaks will give you hope, others will give you despair. What you are seeing now is far from the end of it. The virus evolves, depending on the genetic code of the host. There are certain traits, very rare, that will create some interesting mutations. And some of those mutations will make your hair stand on end. So get ready for those, because they are going to make what you've seen so far look like a children's party." Jones was actually smiling now.

"But that's not the real surprise. The surprise is that all my research has been duplicated and was taken by one of Brother Abraham's henchmen days before the virus was released. What he intends to do with it I have no idea, but he will have spirited it away out of the country. But know that the man is absolutely insane, and is capable of anything. Anyone who gets on his knees and prays to an invisible friend with his level of dedication wouldn't think twice about releasing the virus on the rest of the world." The face on the video smiled broadly once again, although there was pain visible in the eyes. "So you have a nice day now." With that, the video ended. Savage sat there for several seconds, absorbing what she had just learnt. Unknown to her, a researcher in NATO headquarters had opened the same file thirty minutes before her, and the news was sending shockwaves through NATO strategic command.

Savage jumped up off the bed. She couldn't stay here, couldn't sit around doing nothing. She had to be at the heart of it, had to be where there was a chance of developing a cure. Still fully dressed, she stormed out of her room and walked the ten paces down the corridor. Part of her felt that this was a foolish move. Foolish? Hell, it was fucking stupid. She was reasonably safe here, as safe as could be expected in the circumstances. But how long was that going to last? How long before the horror of the virus breached the meagre defences being established? Days at most.

She knocked on the door, suddenly afraid she might wake up the occupant.

"Come in."

Savage entered and saw Croft lying on a bunk with his hands behind his head. His room was sparsely furnished just like hers. He lay there looking at her with an eyebrow raised. Naked from the waist up, she saw the scars on his body, saw the pain the man had been through in the past, understood another piece about the man who was still a mystery to her.

"You said they were holding out in the MI6 Building in London? You said that, right?" She stood in the doorway she had just opened, a hand clutching the door handle, the knuckles white.

"Yes," Croft replied. "The place is impenetrable. The general tells me they even have some scientists there, researching a cure."

"Then that's where I need to be. I'm useless here." Savage was almost pleading as she stared into his eyes. He looked back at her for several seconds, saw the fear and the confliction this decision was causing her, and knew there was only one choice for him to make.

"Okay then. Let's see if the good general will lend us a helicopter."

"Us?"

"Damn straight," Croft said standing. "I'm not staying here any longer than I have to, the food's fucking terrible." He walked over to Savage and took her gently by her arms. "I'm going to look after you, Lucy," he said, staring deep into her blue eyes.

"Why?" it was all she could think to say, her mind doing cartwheels. There was a connection between them, it was undeniable, and had been there since they had met at that briefing just a few short days ago. She had felt the spark, the way he had looked at her across the room, the way he had moved.

"Because it's what I do. And really, there's nothing else for me to do now." They didn't hear the shot that rang out across the other side of the airport.

Dr. Holden had volunteered to help with the refugees but had been told to go away and rest. One of her fellow doctors could see she was worn out, and had insisted she get a good night's sleep. She had only relented when Brian had given his opinion as well. They all needed sleep, because who knew what the coming days would bring. She had half-expected him to escort her to her tent on the edge of the airfield, but he had merely wished her goodnight. She found herself disappointed.

But, of course, she felt that she couldn't sleep. How could she? The events of the day were fresh in her mind, the images playing out in the carnival of her skull. She was used to death, saw it ever day near enough, but she had seen so many people killed in such a short space of time it was truly overwhelming. And she would see more before this was all done, a lot more. Of that, she was certain. The constant flood of humanity fleeing the infection would soon overwhelm this corner of the country if it was allowed, and she had heard rumours that the powers that be were only willing to try and save so many. Holden didn't know how valid those rumours were.

The images that stuck in her head the most were from the hospital where she had worked for the past ten years. The zombie with her chest opened for surgery, the intubation tube still dangling from her mouth. The infected police officer chasing after a terrified nurse. And the mother, overpowered by the virus, biting into the flesh of her own daughter. How could nightmares like this be real? How could any kind of God sit idly by whilst such torture was perpetrated on humanity? Lying on her bunk bed, still fully clothed, she gazed up at the tent canvas above her, the small camping light illuminating what she had been told was her temporary home. Tomorrow, they would move her and others to the local hospital where she would help run the triage unit.

She didn't expect sleep to come, but it did, sneaking up on her, seducing her mind into slumber. So deep did she crash that she didn't hear the gunshot two tents away, and wasn't woken by the commotion. She would only learn about the suicide the next morning, along with the seven others that had occurred that night. Not everyone had guns—others would resort to other means. Mostly hanging, although one woman threw herself off the nearby cliffs in utter despair. There were so many that saw the hopelessness of it all. Why carry on in a world that was only going to get worse?

22.58PM GMT, 16th September 2015, The White House, Washington DC, USA

Damien Rodney looked at the assorted faces on the monitors around him. He was no longer in the White House itself, but below it in the secure bunker that Hollywood had so often tried to recreate. Built in the Cold War, it was now obsolete for the original purpose, Russia's nuclear warheads now too destructive for it to have any hope of surviving a direct hit. Now, it was a command and control centre, connected to various other Washington strategic sites by a network of secure underground tunnels. Very shortly, he would be travelling to the Pentagon by underground monorail, but first, he had to give his authority to the next part of his plan. Martial law.

On the screens were eight men and two women. With the president in the room was his ever-present chief of staff and the Head of Homeland Security, Madeleine Cozens. The head of the FBI, Jason Tucker, stood watching the whole scene at the coffee dispenser, a sense of nervousness growing within him. Tucker felt that what he was watching was unprecedented, dangerous in the extreme. All his working life had been in law enforcement, and now at the age of sixty, he was in charge of the FBI. He had dedicated his life to upholding the Constitution of the United States, a dream he had nourished since seeing his father killed at the hands of white extremists. The colour of his skin hadn't stopped him. And through his meteoric rise through the ranks, he had resisted almost every attempt to twist or manipulate what was enshrined in that almost sacred manuscript.

At least that was the image he gave across. There had of course been occasions when the Constitution had been 'flexed' somewhat for his own personal prestige. But it was for the greater good, that being his ascension to the directorship. But he never thought he would live to see what he was witnessing here, the implementation of martial law in the United States of America. Was the president doing what was right for the country in a time of emergency, or was this an opportunity the POTUS had waited for all his life?

Tucker had never expected to keep the directorship under the Rodney Administration, and had been surprised when his position had been confirmed. But then Tucker was one of the most politically savvy players in Washington, and his successes in recent years in thwarting countless terrorist attacks had made him a darling of the media and Congress. It also helped that his brother was Republican majority leader of the Senate. His was a powerful family; some often said they could be the next Kennedys, despite them being black. Tucker didn't know about that. He had no desire to be president, but he suspected his brother might well have the Oval Office in his sights. Perhaps that's why the president kept him around, to keep a tight leash on him.

"The full list of executive orders the president will be implementing are before you," Cozens said to the people on the screens. She was a competent woman. Usually, the people who rose to such positions were political lapdogs, but this woman was nobody's fool. She was as feared as much as she was respected, and had reshaped and sharpened a broken organisation into an agency that could get the job done. And for someone in their early seventies, she had more passion and energy than someone half her age. "Let me reiterate, this is a temporary measure, designed to stabilise the country and get it ready for any potential outbreak of the likes seen in the UK. We will be implementing them as and when we deem the situations warrant, but will be starting with Executive Orders 10990, 10995, and 10997."

Tucker looked at his copy of the briefing paper.

Executive Order 10990 – The federalisation of all modes of transportation, including the control of highways and seaports

Executive Order 10995 – Allows the government to take control of all communication media

Executive Order 10997 – All electrical power, gas, petroleum and fuel supplies to be put under government control

The executive orders were just tools though for a plan that had been developed over decades for just such an eventuality, although perhaps the zombie apocalypse hadn't been the threat envisaged. They were all part of what was known as Operation Cable Splicer, the orderly takeover of state and local government. Designed to be temporary, they were used in cases of national emergency such as widespread national disasters. Here, it was being used as a preventive measure, for a disaster that hadn't even happened yet. What was more worrying to Tucker was Operation Garden Plot, which had never been rolled out across the whole nation. Already the National Guard and the regular military were being mobilised. That was why the ten people were here on video conference call. Garden Plot was the program to directly control the population, and was only supposed to be used in the direst of emergencies. Join them together and add martial law, and you had what was known to only a select few in the military and the administration. Operation Clean Sweep, the complete eradication of any and all dissenting voices in the USA. Tucker stood silently and watched developments with a growing sense of dread.

"The president will be meeting with the leaders of the Senate and Congress shortly to get their written approval, not that this is required. The attorney general has already clarified the legality of what is needed for the safety of the country," Cozens continued. That was the other thing about the head of Homeland Security. She was ruthlessly loyal to the president. "You will all be expected to implement Garden Plot over the next 48 hours. Your liaisons with Homeland Security, the FBI, and state governors will go through the list of people deemed a risk to the safety and the security of the nation. The lists are being collated by the Fusion centres in each of your FEMA regions." Fusion centres were information hubs that gathered all digital communications so it could be collected, stored, and inventoried. Big Brother was here, had been for years.

Tucker didn't say anything, because there was nothing he could say. Any objections he expressed would be listened to, but ultimately ignored. If he put up any kind of resistance, he knew another director of the FBI would quickly be found. This was not the time for protest. This was the time for calculated observation and meek obedience. The ten people on the screen were the regional directors for each of the ten FEMA regions that the county was to be split up into. His home state of Texas fell in FEMA region six. In those ten regions were over eight hundred detention camps ready to accept a steady flow of inmates. Originally set up under the Rex 84 program to deal with a possible massive influx of illegal immigration, each camp was fully manned and stocked and presently empty. Presently. The days that followed would see them fill up rapidly. Of course, to fill the camps up meant rounding people up and putting them on buses. Not an easy thing to do with an armed and paranoid population. That's where the National Guard and the FBI came in.

And it would likely be a disaster. Tucker knew that it would just take one incident, one person intent on defying the federal government to turn a peaceful containment operation into a war zone, especially in the states along the Bible belt. And it was his agency, the FBI, that would bear the brunt of it, he was sure of it. The military had no idea how to arrest people. Tucker knew that should anything go wrong, if innocents died at the hands of the FBI or on an operation overseen by the FBI, he as its head would be made scapegoat. He could see that plain as day. Was that why Rodney had kept him on? My God, had the man been planning for something like this all along, just hoping for the opportunity to claim the power presidents could only dream of? At this rate, would there even be an election next year?

23.57PM, 16th September 2015, Everywhere

They spread and they fed. Numbering in the millions now, the collective mind told them to scatter as far as possible, to cast themselves over as wide an area as they could. With so many people now infected, the contagion had become unstoppable, but deep down in their global consciousness, they had fleeting memories of things that threatened their existence. Now that they were legion, there was no longer safety in numbers. Now what guaranteed their survival was dispersal. Sooner or later, their prey would resort to its weapons of war, but such weapons would only be effective against large groupings. So they split up, forming smaller cells, sometimes as small as half a dozen. Each cell would swell its ranks from the humans it encountered, any resistance being met with the help of other nearby cells that would quickly rush to that location. But what resistance they did meet was minimal, the population unarmed and defenceless against a threat that was supposed to only exist in fiction. But this was not fiction, this was real life, and the suburbs of the country's major cities were swallowed up by the relentless push of the infected. They were coordinated, primal, and deadly.

The road networks were the quickest way for them to move between population centres, but they also used the rail lines, which cut through the cities and the countryside, allowing unhindered access to most of the country. With no need to sleep, and almost superhuman stamina, they moved out from the cities like the true plague they were. There was another reason for them to leave these areas though…fear. They did not fear man, even with his bombs and his guns. No, they feared the undead, whose numbers grew steadily. Many of those infected had suffered mortal wounds that even the enhanced healing powers allowed by the virus couldn't heal. Thousands dropped dead in the streets, only to return as a possibly much more deadly foe. The undead had no notion for strategy, for spreading or for protecting the collective. They cared only for the consumption of human flesh, be that human or infected, they cared not. Thousands of undead had risen again during the battle for London, and they massed together to form several great teeming masses that would slowly steamroll over anything and everything in their path. The infected, despite their greater numbers, quickly learnt to avoid them. So they spread, leaving the undead to pick off whatever was left behind.

But the infected also fed. As controlling as the collective mind was, the urge to eat sometimes became too powerful. As the day progressed, the hunger inside the infected grew, and they began to have their fill, satiating the gnawing in their very souls. They ate anything they could catch that wasn't human, the need to grow their numbers still strong.

Whole fields of cattle were attacked, the cows slaughtered, ripped apart by claw-like hands and teeth that weren't designed for such a use. Horses trapped in stables became easy pickings and the exotic creatures of the London Zoo were decimated in less than thirty minutes. Household pets died in the tens of thousands.

And then came the rats. Millions of them, lurking in the shadows, they fled from the noise and the fire as the humans tried to fend off the infected hordes. But when the guns were silenced and the bombs no longer fell on the street, the rats crawled out of their holes to feast on the rich pickings that littered the streets. Feasting on the discarded infected flesh, the virus quickly turned them, and their numbers quickly grew as infected rats brought the contagion to the nests, biting and clawing at their former kind. And they changed.

Projected spread of infection based on satellite and computer predictions

Day 2 of the Infection - 7.37 million infected

05.33AM, 17th September 2015, MI6 Building, London, UK

Fabrice opened his eyes and looked around tentatively. As incredible as it may sound, he felt amazing. Considering what he had been through the last twelve hours, his body felt strong, free of pain, free of anything but strength. He didn't know what that madman had done to him, but taking a deep breath in, Fabrice felt his body fill with power. The room around him was sterile and white, a metal table meant for human forms dominating one end, a large mirror the other. He was still sat in the wheelchair with which he had been brought to this room, and he tested the bonds that held him in the chair. They felt weak to him, and he flexed his neck, listening to the world around him.

He could hear nothing of the environment outside this room, and as far as he could tell, he was alone. But that didn't mean there weren't people watching him, various cameras scattered around the four corners. One camera sat blatantly in front of him on a tripod, a power cord extending from it. So if they were not watching him, they were at least recording, documenting what they thought was a torment. As the minutes passed, sat naked except for his own vomit, his thoughts began to gel, to stabilise. He had clarity, but there was something else. Looking around again, he thought he could hear voices after all, far-off, almost like whispers. The voices sounded pained, desperate, but also calculating and decisive. What were they saying? If only he could hear. It was as if someone was trying to talk to him.

"Who is that?" he called out, not out of fear, but more frustration. He needed to hear what was being said. Something inside him told him that the voices were important. Was this the voice of God? The thought just popped in there, and he knew it was ridiculous, and he felt almost ashamed at his arrogance. But what if?

Nobody was present to witness Fabrice's awakening; only electronics recorded the moment the man opened his eyes and looked around. Moments earlier, the machines monitoring his vitals had detected a massive spike in his brain's Delta waves as well as a dangerous but short-lived spike in his blood pressure. He had convulsed twice in the chair, and then had regained the stillness that had been the hallmark of the last two hours of his life. And whilst the blood pressure had come down to normal, the Delta waves had not, and they continued to spike until the very moment Fabrice opened his eyes. Then they had decreased to baseline, giving the illusion of normality. But as people were about to discover, Fabrice was now anything but normal.

06.34AM, 17th September 2016, Hayton Vale, Devon, UK

Gavin moaned from the pain in his head. In his head? Try his whole body. Slowly, he opened his eyes, amazed at how bright the world around him was. He was face down on the floor, and as he moved his head, it came away from the ground with a wet sound, cold vomit making an ineffective glue. The stench was incredible, and it took everything within him to not unleash more gastric deposits. Gingerly, he pushed himself up onto his hands and knees, feeling the vicious flu-like aches running through his system. On his first attempt, he cried out, pain shooting up his left arm. Jesus, that hurt, that really hurt. Gavin vaguely remembered smashing it on the toilet bowl when he fell. Probably broken knowing his luck of late. It took him a moment to steady himself, and with effort, and without the use of his useless arm, he moved his body so that he was now sat up with his back against the wall. Blackness swam through his vision, and he breathed as deeply as he could, the muscles of his rib cage protesting at their unexpected use. Briefly his vision shrank to nothing, only to return as he fought off the threatened unconsciousness.

There was another smell over the vomit, and there was a sound that was familiar but which he couldn't place. Using the wall, he carefully stood up, his legs almost giving way. Shivers ran through his frame, and although he felt cold, sweat poured from him. Was this the infection? Was this how he became one of the mindless killers? Turning back to the lavatory, he turned on the taps and washed his face in the cold running water one handed. He didn't look in the mirror, just used his hand to bathe the dirt and the vomit off of himself, finishing off the job with a hand towel by the sink. It wasn't white when he finished with it, and it dropped to the floor, no longer needed. If he was honest, he was afraid to see himself, afraid to see what would stare back at him from reflective glass. Turning off the tap, he steeled himself and lifted his head, eyes closed. Inhaling deeply, he opened his eyes and relief washed over him.

He didn't look any different. He looked dishevelled and ill, but he didn't look like a monster. There was no redness in his eyes like he had seen reported on the news, and although his mind swam in a sea of pain, he didn't feel anything but himself.

"Thank God," Gavin said softly. Cradling his arm, he stepped back from the sink and out of the lavatory. Moving towards the kitchen area, the sound grew louder, and the realisation of what was causing it came seconds before he saw the cause. Flies. Hundreds of them, feasting on the corpses of the dead dogs that had attacked him, said corpses presently splattered across the floor and cabinets.

"How the fuck am I going to clean this up with one arm?"

07.07AM, 17th September 2015, Shannon Airport, Ireland

Davina stood in the chill breeze watching the Cessna private jet come to a full stop. Normally used for transporting the rich and powerful, this particular plane carried someone fallen from grace.

"Use whatever means necessary. The only rule is you do not kill him." Those had been the words spoken to her by the head of MI6. How she shivered with delight when she was given the green light to truly practice her art. Terrorists, traitors, and criminals, it mattered not the crime. All that mattered was that once they were given to her, nobody stood in her way. She lived to bring true misery to those who pissed off the people in power.

"Here is his medical file." Davina turned to the man who had spoken and accepted the offered folder. "He has a mild prostate condition, but other than that, his last medical exam showed he was in good shape." Arnold Craver, head of a section of MI5 that no longer existed, watched Davina with a wary eye. He had never before met the woman, and had always thought the tales of her actions and her existence to be a fabrication, Chinese whispers within the organisations that thrived on secrecy. He watched as Davina opened the file, studying the contents. She absorbed the information, creating an image in her mind of the man she was about to interrogate. This was a big fish, a man used to respect and power and wealth. She would use that. She would use all of it, already knowing what she needed to do to break him, to extract the information people wanted her to acquire. Davina would do the job she was paid for, and as always, have immense fun in the process.

With the plane at a standstill, the side door opened and the ladder descended. There was movement and a man in a black suit appeared in the doorway. He looked around and, spotting those waiting nearby, began to walk purposefully down the steps. Then another man in black appeared, this time dragging a hooded man, handcuffed and dressed in a white jumpsuit. A shame, they had taken his clothes in favour of a jump suit. She always preferred such men to be fully attired when she started her sessions. Standing there, she would have the clothes ripped brutally from their bodies, leaving them naked, the prestige their fine tailoring brought them completely obliterated. It was the little things like that in the preparation that made her job so much easier. No matter. This man would still sing; he would sing his little heart out.

The trio from the plane made their way over to where Davina and Arnold stood, their captive not resisting. He was not a big man, a pen-pusher for sure, although no doubt skilled in self-defence and weapons. You didn't have to look like Schwarzenegger to be able to kill people. And you didn't get to work for one of the world's elite intelligence agencies if you were unable to handle yourself. This wasn't America; there were no political appointments here. Even now, in chains and blind to the world, Davina knew this was a dangerous man. She would use that against him too. She watched as Craver and two soldiers took charge of the prisoner, signing off on the paperwork one of the guards carried. How unfortunate that, even during the apocalypse, paperwork was still the rule. Davina waited till the formalities were over and stepped forward.

"Sir Michael," she said, respectfully. "It is an honour to finally meet you." She saw the head turn towards her, but the man under the hood said nothing. "We have never met, but I know you by reputation." She stepped forward so that she was inches away from him. "I'm looking forward to getting to know you better."

"Who are you?" a muffled voice said from under the hood.

"Oh, Sir Michael, you know who I am. And you know exactly what I am going to do to you. You have a chance now to tell these men what you know, to tell them your secrets."

"Go to hell, bitch." If not for the hood, she suspected the former head of MI5 would have spat at her. She nodded to one of the soldiers, and he punched the unsuspecting man hard in the stomach. He doubled over, obviously surprised by the hit. Arnold watched it all, uncomfortable with the prospect of what was going to happen, powerless to do anything about it. He knew this man, had dined with him on dozens of occasions. Had drunk with him, laughed with him. And yet here he was, guilty of the greatest of betrayals. He had forsaken the very country he had been tasked to defend, complicit in the death of millions.

"Oh, I have no doubt I'm going to hell," Davina said smiling. "And I intend to show you exactly where I will be heading. You're mine now, Sir Michael, all mine." She reached up and pulled the hood from his head, the eyes underneath squinting at the sudden brightness of the light. Watkins glared at her, defiant, resolute. Yes, there it was, that look she had seen so often before in men, especially the radicals. They think they can hold out, they think their piety and their beliefs are a match for her skills, for the terrors she could inflict with her hands. "I am so looking forward to breaking you."

07.10AM, 17th September 2015, Watford Islamic Mosque, Watford, UK

Rasheed awoke to pain and the stench of death. He opened his eyes to find the early morning light shining through the upper floor windows. It was almost spiritual, and his vision swam whilst the orchestra of agony played a symphony throughout his body. Everything hurt, and he moved his eyes, surveying as much as he could without moving his head. But then he found a new agony as his eyes settled on the slaughtered form of his father, whose dead eyes stared back at him, lower jaw missing from where it had been ripped from the skull. He moved then—he had no choice because to look at such carnage any longer would probably end him.

Rolling onto his back, he heard someone scream, and it was seconds before he realised he was the one screaming. Jolts of fire swept through his form, and he felt his neck spasm. How was he still alive? And why had he been spared this? Was he being punished? Left alive in a desecrated house of God, his friends and father taken from him, ripped apart by the demons...were they still here? Gingerly, he raised himself up onto his elbows, every muscle and tendon protesting. It felt like he was on fire, and he roared in despair. Outside on the street, something answered that roar. Were they still here?

Dragging himself across the floor on his backside, he propped himself up against the wall and tried to get control of his body. Breathing deeply helped, and he looked around the room, noticing only two bodies. One he recognised, the other he didn't, and memory told him it was probably one of the infected that he had shot. The last thing he remembered was being dragged down the stairs. He had no idea how he ended up back in this room. Looking at his watch, he saw that he had been out of it for almost half a day.

Insights came to him then, the fog lifting from his mind. He had soiled himself. The smell was unmistakeable even over the carrion call of the room, the cold dampness the least of his concerns. Rasheed's mouth was dry and tasted of stale vomit, and the whole olfactory assault was almost overwhelming. And there were more horrors. His father had been gutted, the entrails spread out around the body. Had they eaten him? By Allah, these were indeed the end times. But his father was a good Muslim—why had he been taken?

"*Feeeeeeeed!*"

Where did that come from? He couldn't pinpoint the direction of the voice. It seemed distant, almost like it was carried on the wind.

"*Feeeed. Spreeaaad.*"

With force of will, Rasheed pulled himself up to the window and looked out at the streets below. They were empty of life, but not of bodies. So if the voices were not outside, that meant they were downstairs. That meant he was still in danger. Abandoning the window, he crawled over to his rucksack, tears welling in his eyes at what he was having to endure. Grabbing it, he rummaged inside until his hand found what it was looking for: another clip of ammunition for his gun. The gun he had been planning to use this very afternoon.

It had become clear to him that his father's version of Islam was tainted and corrupted by Western Imperialism. Prayer and service were of no benefit to Islam when the Western powers bombed Muslim countries with impunity. Those who allowed their leaders to desecrate his brothers and sisters in the name of "peace" deserved no mercy. All were guilty in the eyes of the Prophet, and all needed to be brought to justice. Killing the infidel was a mercy, for the longer they remained in sin on Earth, the greater their torment in the afterlife. So this afternoon, he had planned to bring God's wrath down on the Crusaders, to show them that they were not safe in their self-imposed prison state. It was an act that would have shocked and sickened his father, but Rasheed believed the man would have understood given time. That was a false belief to defend Rasheed against the sickness of his own thinking.

Gripping the clip, Rasheed scanned the room for his gun and saw it lying at the top of the stairs. Managing to get to his knees this time, he shuffled over to it and sat on the top step of the staircase. The pain was easing slightly; his head no longer felt like there was a man with a baseball bat trying to get out. Perhaps the unwanted guest was now only using his fists. Reloading the gun, he looked down the stairs.

"Hello," he shouted, wincing at his own voice. There was no response from downstairs, and yet still he heard the faint voices. Where were they coming from? He turned and gave one last look at his father. The man had raised him, had loved him and had cared for him. Even though he was misguided in his beliefs, he deserved a proper burial. And that would come, but first, Rasheed needed to deal with the situation at hand. He descended the stairs on his backside, something he had not done since he was a small child.

07.27AM, 17th September 2015, Sheffield City Centre, UK

Kevin woke up to one of the worst hangovers of his life. He lay motionless for several seconds, trying to stop the world around him spinning. Now awake, closing his eyes only made the situation worse, and with effort, he brought a hand up to his head and groaned. He was still fully clothed, and the room around him stank of his sweat and other assorted body odours. So this was what the end looked like.

Carefully, he pulled himself upright. Swinging his legs over the bed, he let one dangle there for a minute as he composed himself, the other broken leg sticking out awkwardly. This was going to be a bad day, and despite what he was feeling now, he knew he would be drinking again before the morning was over. What else was there for him to do? The only problem with that was at some point, he knew he was going to run out of his precious beer. In the other room, he could hear the TV playing, whatever channel he had been watching still broadcasting. There were no other sounds really that came to him, which was both a good and a bad thing. The world outside sounded quiet, especially by last night's standards, and through an alcohol-induced fog, he vaguely remembered the rioting going on until the small hours of the morning. But even mindless thugs and desperation needed sleep. *How long before it all kicks off again?* he thought.

Grabbing the crutches which were propped up against the wall next to his bed, he slowly stood, fresh nausea hitting him. Standing there, he waited for the roulette wheel to stop, or at least slow down, knowing he had things to do and knowing now was the time to do it before the world woke back up. And anyway, he didn't know how much time he had left, and he was aware that the infected could arrive at any time. What would he do when that eventuality finally came true? What would he do when the streets below were filled, not by rioters, but by creatures from mankind's darkest nightmares? He honestly didn't know the answer to that.

It took ten minutes before he could even think about leaving his flat. Another fifteen to actually do so, his largest backpack on his back when he left. He locked the door behind him and used his crutches to hobble over to the lift. If he had to navigate the stairs, this might be a whole different ball game. But when he pressed the button, the lift began to ascend mercifully. When the doors opened, he hesitated briefly, suddenly fearful something would leap out at him. When nothing did, he used the lift and made his way to the ground floor. He expected to see devastation downstairs, but when the lift doors opened again, the lobby below was its usual pristine self. The only sign of the night's bedlam was an impact crater on the glass of the main door to the apartments, the double glazing in the small window crazed but still intact. There were no flats on the ground floor, and he had considered knocking on the doors of his neighbours before embarking on his epic voyage. But he didn't really know them. And what if they were the very people he had seen tearing the city apart the night before? No, for now, he had to get the job done alone and make sure that at least he himself was okay.

He left the safety of his apartment building, the reinforced door closing behind him as he hobbled out onto the deserted and littered street. To his right, a car still smouldered from where it had been overturned and set on fire in the middle of the road, and a cold breeze blew light debris past him. His city had been turned into a ghost town, fear and violence making it presently devoid of visible humanity. If the previous night was anything to go by, that would likely change very soon, so he needed to act quickly. Fortunately for him, his destination was the mini supermarket just next to the entrance to where he lived, and he found the security shutters ripped off and access available through the shattered entrance. The interior lights were still on, and careful of the broken glass that littered the pavement, he made his way inside.

The satellite did what satellites do, unseen by the millions who existed below its watchful eye. This one, a secret like so many others put up into orbit by its owners, was doing a different job from that which it was originally designed for. Previously, it spied on the comings and goings of allied nations, able to read a car licence plate and relay that information to the computers at the American NSA. Today, it had a different function: tracking and mapping the spread of the infection in the North of England. Presently, it was relaying live digital images of an infected horde that was beginning to swamp Sheffield, England's fourth largest city. The pack had used the M1 motorway to head south from Leeds, and had hardly deviated except to swallow up any humanity it came across. By the time it hit Sheffield, it was estimated to be a hundred thousand strong.

More detailed images were being transmitted by the Predator drone that was following the pack. It watched as the thousands split into groups to enter the city's northern suburbs. Being alone in the skies, it stayed with the largest sub pack, the one that followed the main highway into the heart of the city. There were no defences in the city against this mass, no way a disarmed population could hold back the ravaging viral surge. It was calculated that this pack would consume the city within the day, adding almost half a million people to the enemy's numbers. Those who had fled west across the Pennines had been hit by another pack that had detached from Manchester. The only way to escape the horror that fell upon the City of Steel was to hide and hope and perhaps pray. And those in the heart of the city who had chosen that route didn't even know that the infected didn't represent the greatest threat to their very lives. That threat came from man.

The supermarket was surprisingly well-stocked, despite the obvious looting that had taken place. Those from last night had obviously been intent purely on destruction, their actions keeping the hoarders like himself at bay. With no one around to stop him, he helped himself to as much as he could cram into his backpack. Alcohol, water, and tinned goods were his priority. The plan was to make several trips, to give himself as much of a chance as he possibly could. His present stocks of food were pretty sparse and wouldn't have lasted him more than a day or two.

That had been the plan, but that plan dissolved when he heard the scream. Urgency and panic hit him, and he struggled to get the backpack on due to its weight. It would have been a challenge with two good legs, but on crutches, he found it difficult to make any kind of speed. By the time he made it back out onto the street, he could hear the commotion in the distance. Looking up the road, he went as quick as his broken leg would allow, reaching his door just as he saw the first people of the crowd. They were well over a hundred metres away, but he saw by the way they were massed, by the way they moved, that these weren't rioters. The infected had arrived.

They were moving fast, swarming into buildings. Some were even climbing the buildings where they could, the ornate architecture acting as glorified climbing frames. Frantic, he took the keys out of his back pocket and unlocked the door, knowing that he had ten seconds at most. He didn't drop them. The key went into the lock in the first attempt, and he disappeared from the street into the relative safety of his apartment lobby. Safety? He wouldn't be safe until every one of those fuckers was dead and the streets were filled with soldiers.

Kevin reached the lift, and the door opened almost instantly as he hit the button. He entered and pressed his floor, hitting it several times, knowing that it wouldn't make the doors close any faster, but doing it anyway. Just as the doors slid closed, the first of the infected appeared outside on the street. Kevin wasn't witness to the way it and two of its comrades attacked the door. They didn't gain entry, and quickly abandoned their assault for easier targets. Even in the lift, Kevin could hear them, could hear their howls and the destruction they brought with them. The lift stopped, and he left the metal box, rushing as fast as he could to the safety of his flat. His leg ached from the exertion, his heart thumped in his chest, and his head throbbed with anxiety, but as the door to his flat closed behind him, he collapsed in a heap in the entry foyer to his flat, at least he was now safe. That was until his world was rocked by an explosion so violent every piece of furniture seemed to leap into the air, and the very air seemed to be forced out of his lungs. At the same time, the windows imploded, and his world went black as another explosive device hit the buildings across the street, the shockwave hitting him like a freight train. Kevin never regained consciousness, an incendiary bomb blowing the roof off his building seconds later, the thermite consuming everything in a fiery hell.

Seventy thousand pounds of explosive and incendiary ordnance. That was what the first B52 dropped on Sheffield's city centre. Whole streets were obliterated, the infected swarming in them either vaporised or ripped to pieces by the blast waves. At the same time, the incendiaries hit with such an impact that they created a firestorm that began to feed on the very buildings they hit. Within seconds, secondary explosions from ruptured gas lines and car petrol tanks added to the carnage. Thousands more infected and civilians were consumed by the firestorm as it burnt through the city's centre, and thousands more infected roared in fury at the decimation of their brethren. This, the satellite watched with robotic efficiency, measuring the spread of the fire and the destruction against the spread of the infected. The problem was that the bombers just didn't carry enough firepower; the population and the infected alike spread out over several square miles. In the official briefing about the attack, the results would be labelled "disappointing". In fact, over half the infected survived the attack, which outlined its utter futility. As the cries of the slaughtered infected died out, their kin quickly forgot the bloodbath and continued with the task at hand, spreading the infection to everyone they could find. By mid-day, the infected in Sheffield numbered one-quarter of a million. The army of the damned grew by the hour and humanity began to wither against the onslaught.

07.31AM, 17th September 2015, Hounslow, London, UK

Owen had not been able to sleep. He just wasn't tired, and he wasn't sure if that was a good thing or a bad thing. Eventually, he had given up trying, found himself a TV, and watched the world report what they saw as the end of the world. How could they be so wrong? This was anything but doomsday. This was a rebirth for the human race.

Bored of the hotel, now he moved, an army of several hundred following behind him, not so much marching on central London as meandering, the infected often disappearing off whenever they smelt fresh opportunities. Owen allowed this so long as they returned, fresh minds joining the faint murmur that existed at the edges of his awareness. And any stray viral carriers they encountered were quickly added to his legion.

He knew where he was going, had known it was the ultimate destination almost from the start. He was a king now, and kings needed the finer things in life. Although he knew the utilities would start failing over the coming days, that didn't faze him. He had a legion to do his every bidding, and very soon, he would have thick walls to defend him from the true threat. But he still had lingering concerns, doubts that prodded and teased at him, unwelcome thoughts that drifted into the front of his mind. The main one that had occurred to him last night was the lifespan of the infected. If those contaminated by the virus resurrected as the undead when their enhanced life left them, how long before his army turned against him? How long before his protectors came clawing for the flesh on his bones?

And there was another worry. Yesterday, he had almost lost control of his mind. He had let in the voices of the infected, and the hundreds of thousands of primitive minds across the city had very nearly overwhelmed him. Would that happen again? He knew he could block them most of the time, but what if his army grew larger? Would proximity affect his ability to keep them out? Or would he grow stronger, more disciplined in his thoughts? As good as this was, as excited as he was about his life right now, he saw the threats all around him. And deep down within him grew a small blossom of fear.

One of his elite guards ran past him, followed by two others. They had smelt something and took it upon themselves to disappear down a side alley. He looked behind him, saw Claire and the others, saw the throng that would kill for him and would die for him. Claire, no longer collared, did not react to his gaze, but carried on with that almost nervous head twitching that all infected seemed condemned with. And then she hissed, and Owen turned his head back round to see what she had seen.

At the end of the street, four zombies had appeared. They were about fifty metres out, clumped together as if they were holding hands. *And so it begins*, thought Owen. They moved slower than normal infected, with less coordination, but as he saw now, they could run, if in a shambolic fashion. Owen heard them moan as they clambered towards him. *Who is the prime target here?* thought Owen. Would they go for the mass before them, or would they aim themselves straight at him? That was a worrying thought.

"You, go," he ordered one of the front rank, willing him to run towards the walking cadavers, to see if they would be drawn off. All four of them ignored the infected and kept on coming, heading straight for him. "Shit," Owen said. Twenty-five metres now. Owen dropped his gun bag and pulled the machine gun from over his shoulder. Aiming was easy, hitting the target harder, the first three shots going wide. With plenty of ammunition, he had spent a good hour practicing with it in the hotel lobby earlier, but it would be a while before he was proficient with it. The fourth shot hit the first zombie centre mass, and it staggered backwards, only to surge forward again. Head shots, he reminded himself. You have to go for head shots. The pack behind him seemed to moan nervously, but he ignored them, knowing this was something he needed to do himself. The fifth shot hit one in the centre of the face, and it crumpled to the floor lifeless. It took another four shots before he destroyed the brain of another, and by that time, they were just too close.

"Rip them apart," Owen commanded, and the hundreds behind him surged forward, his body being buffeted by their charge. The two remaining zombies flailed valiantly, but in mere seconds, their limbs were flying through the air, their corpses decapitated by the sheer weight of infected power. And as the crowd parted to display the remains, it was then that Owen noticed something else. Deep in his mind, he could tell that not a single one of the infected had any desire to dine on the zombies' flesh. And every one of them feared the zombie presence. He needed walls, and he needed them quickly.

08.04AM, 17th September 2015, MI6 Building, London, UK

"So here we are again," Fabrice said to the man who stood before him. Clad again in his hazmat suit, accompanied by two other men similarly dressed, Durand stared at the test subject who should, at this moment in time, be a blood-crazed maniac. Only he wasn't, and he showed no signs of the infection whatsoever. Durand looked at the scientist next to him.

"I want a full blood workup done of this specimen. I want to know why he's different. I want to know why the virus didn't take hold." There was excitement in Durand's voice, Fabrice could hear it. The skeletal cretin was almost skipping around the room he was so delighted.

"So I'm a specimen now. How lovely." Durand looked at him.

"How do you feel?" the emaciated scientist asked.

"How do I feel? Fuck you, I'm not telling you a damned thing."

"Would you rather I send you back to your torture chamber?" Durand threatened. "We can start the pain again, start the agony. No? Then tell me how you feel."

"I feel great, is that what you want to hear, you fucking maniac?" Fabrice flexed the muscles of his arms, felt the power surging like never before. Great wasn't even close to how he was feeling—he felt incredible. It mattered not that he was sat strapped to a wheelchair in his own piss, naked in a room full of medical devices that could at any second be used on him. This was the best he had ever felt in his life, and he knew his day was only going to get better. Fabrice watched the men in front of him, saw everything about them. He saw the nervous bead of sweat on the brow on the scientist to his left. He heard the ragged breathing of the one on the right. And he could almost feel Durand's sense of self-importance and self-righteousness. It was as if he could look into their minds.

"I'm the maniac?" Durand was genuinely offended. He pointed a finger at the bound man. "May I remind you it was you that deliberately infected millions of people? I'm just trying to undo your dirty work."

"Ha. What I did I did in the name of The Lord Our God. What you do, you do for yourself, nothing more. I can see the egomaniac inside you. You don't care about those out there who have become God's vengeance. You care only for your own notoriety. Don't try and deny it. Even after all you've done to me, I pity you." One of Durand's fellow scientists stepped forward with a needle to draw blood. "You stick that in me, fucker, and I will rip your heart out."

"And how do you propose to do that?" Durand mocked. "You're helpless, strapped down. Very shortly, you will be secured onto that table there so I can examine you at length," Durand said, pointing to the autopsy table. "I regret to say my examinations will not be pleasant. We could sedate you, of course, make it painless. But that will all be dependent on how cooperative you are willing to be." The man with the needle stepped forward and grabbed hold of Fabrice's left arm, inserting the tip none too gently into a very visible vein in the crook of the elbow. Fabrice didn't flinch and watched the man's hands as they violated his skin. As the man holding him began to draw up blood, Fabrice flexed his right arm, the muscles growing taught, the veins on the whole arm becoming more prominent. Fabrice felt something shift inside him, as if something fundamental had changed. The very air around him felt different.

"What the hell? Victor, look at this," said the man with the needle, turning his head to the senior scientist. Victor never got to see what his colleague was trying to point out, didn't get to see the needle slowly being pushed from the experiment's flesh. That was because he never had a chance to do anything but panic. With inhuman strength, Fabrice suddenly broke the Velcro binding that held his right arm helpless. The left hand moved, grabbing hold of the hazmat suit of the man who suddenly realised he had gotten too close, his attention drawn back to what he thought was a placid experiment. Durand was already backing up when he saw all this happen, his own sense of personal preservation kicking in.

"What the…?" the man with the needle said, only for that needle to be snatched out of his hands. He tried to back away, but the grip on his suit prevented that.

"You want my blood, fucker? Well, you are welcome to it," Fabrice roared and jabbed the deadly weapon into the man's torso. On its own, the needle could do only minor damage, but it was what the needle was contaminated with that was the threat. Fabrice let go and the impaled man staggered backwards. Ripping free his other arm, Fabrice undid the Velcro on his legs and stood just as Durand and the third man exited the room, the heavy security door swinging shut behind them.

"Any time you want a piece of me, you know where I am," Fabrice said calmly. The man he had stabbed had fallen to the floor and was propelling himself away from his naked assailant as best he could. The doomed man collided with the wall beneath the large mirror, and Fabrice crouched down to look at him. "What do you think the chances of both of us being immune are?" Fabrice asked. "I guess we'll know in about, oooh, ten minutes."

He had thought his God had forsaken him, but now he believed he understood everything. The revelation came to him in a moment of complete clarity. The torture he had endured the previous day, the deliberate attempt to infect his body, that had all been a test of his loyalty and his faith, just as Job had been tested. The fact he was standing here now was proof that he had passed that test. Although he couldn't really remember what he had been thinking as Davina's devices had worked on him, it was evident that he had at no time denounced his God. And salvation was to be his reward. Not only that, but he had been given a gift, a strength he could not possibly imagine. He flexed the left bicep, seeing the muscle grow and flex before his eyes. He had always kept himself in shape, but never to this degree.

"Do you feel it working within you yet?" Fabrice asked. The man was panicking now, clawing at his hazmat suit to try and remove it. "Do you feel the Lord shaping you to be his instrument of death?"

"You're fucking crazy," the downed scientist said. He tried to get up, but Fabrice pushed him back down with a force that the man was unable to resist.

"Best you stay there for now. And best you keep this," he said indicating the yellow protective clothing, "on. That way when you start throwing up, you won't get it all over this nice clean floor." Fabrice looked up at the mirror, which he knew he was being watched through, and pointed. "The Lord is coming for you. I am his messenger. I am the harbinger of your death and your salvation. Repent your sins before God, because I'm coming, and Hell is coming with me." It felt good to say the words. When he stood, when he saw himself properly for the first time, he didn't recognise himself. Looking briefly at his arm where the needle had penetrated, he saw there wasn't a mark there.

Durand was already out of his hazmat suit and watching from the observation room on the other side of the one-way mirror. This was incredible. The subject was undergoing accelerated muscle growth. And something else, the colour of his skin was changing, getting darker in places, greyer. Then the normal flesh tones would return, the colour changes rippling across the man's body. This wasn't a pigmentation issue; if he had to guess, Durand would say the skin was getting thicker. There was a thud as Fabrice slammed his palm onto the mirror, the whole pane vibrating slightly.

"How strong is that window?" Durand demanded.

"Relax, its ballistic glass. Nothing's getting through it," someone behind him said.

"Don't you tell me to relax," he said loudly. "I need this specimen subdued and I need it done now. Can't you see the marvel he is becoming?"

"Screw that, I'm not going in there," someone else said. "You want him subdued, you do it yourself." Durand turned on the man.

"I'm the senior scientist here. You will do what I tell you to." The mismatch in size was quite telling. Durand, tall and thin, was raging at a man probably twice his weight.

"Go fuck yourself," the muscular scientist said calmly. "I'm done listening to you. You've been a nightmare since you arrived. Senior scientist my arse. You're a cunt, and you'll always be a cunt." Durand's eyes went wide with rage.

"How dare you, I'll not be spoken to like this. By God, I'll have you…" but before Durand could finish, the man just waved his hand at him dismissively.

"Oh fuck you." With that, the man left, leaving Durand to bluster after him. Such insubordination was intolerable. Durand was blissfully unaware how close he had come to getting his lights punched out.

His attention was drawn back to the window by another loud thud, and Durand turned to see Fabrice trying to smash the glass with a metal chair. Fortunately, he seemed to be doing more damage to the chair than the reinforced window.

"I want armed guards down here now. If he gets out, we've all had it."

08.07AM, 17th September 2015, Shannon Airport, Ireland

The room she entered was seven metres by seven, and only had three things in it to decorate the bare concrete walls and floor. In the centre was a gynaecological examination chair that had been borrowed from the local hospital. Next to it was a steel surgical table on wheels, its top covered by green surgical dressing. The other object in the room was Sir Michael Young, who stood at the far wall. This was his prison cell it seemed. Davina walked over to him.

"Do you know what I'm capable of, Sir Michael?" Davina asked standing next to her captive. "I'm sure you've read countless briefings about me during your time at MI5." Sir Michael Young said nothing, just stared at the woman defiantly. He was afraid, very afraid, but he wasn't going to show her that. This had to be a bluff—nobody would sanction this. "Why don't you tell me what I need to know, and then we can end this unpleasantness."

"Fuck you, whore of Babylon," Sir Michael spat. Davina took a step back and chuckled.

"That's the first time I've ever been called that. Well done, Sir Michael. But my offer still stands." She looked at her watch, a diamond-encrusted Rolex that she had bought on one of her many paid excursions to Dubai. Being a freelancer meant she could pick and choose the best-paid assignments, and with her reputation, the assorted secret security services and oppressive governments of the world were crying out for her skills. They paid her handsomely and upfront because she had never once failed to make a captive talk. "I will give you exactly one minute to tell me who the mastermind behind yesterday's little fun fair was. I want his name, nothing less will satisfy me. But you only have a minute, after that, well, you don't want to know what happens after that." Young struggled in his restraint. He was stood upright against a wall, his neck in a collar that was bolted firmly to the bare concrete, just a bit too high,

132

making him stand on tiptoes ever so slightly. He was fully covered still in his detention attire apart from a lack of shoes and socks. Whilst his arms and legs were free, there was no getting out of this imprisonment.

"Thirty seconds," Davina said, still looking at her watch.

"Go to Hell," came the response.

"Already been. Didn't like the weather." A door opened behind her and two men entered, both dressed in black overalls, their faces hidden behind ski masks. Big men, men who looked like they could handle themselves and handle others. They took alternate routes around the room's central contents so that they stood just behind Davina.

"Ten seconds, Sir Michael. This is your last chance." As so often happened, her captive spat at her, but the attempt was feeble, stifled by the restraint collar. Davina stopped looking at her watch and looked at the man she was about to torment. "I want you to remember this moment. I want you to get used to seeing things with two eyes. To hearing things with two ears. Because no matter what you now say, I will not stop for the next five hours." She stepped within reaching distance of him, unafraid that he might try and assault her. He was out of shape, his arms likely flabby and weak from sitting behind a desk all day. Oh, he'd been a field agent in his time, but that was decades ago, and time had taken its toll on his body. With a gun, he would be deadly, but here in this situation, he was nothing. If he tried to grab her or hit her, she could dislocate one of those arms easily. She took hold of his tie and undid it slightly, then gave him a playful pat on the cheek.

"You see what you don't realise is I know everything about you. I know what lurks down within your soul, the things that you're afraid of, and the things you deny yourself in the dead of night when sleep eludes." She stroked his cheek now with the back of her hand, the other hand unbuckling the belt of his trousers. "I know your desires better than you do, and I'm going to use all that against you." Davina stepped away slightly, allowing her to snake that hand into his underwear. He hadn't been expecting that, and he gasped in surprise, her skin as cold as her heart. Amazingly, he began to harden. "Oooh, you like my hand. See what I mean about your weaknesses? Here you are about to be tortured and yet your animal desires still win out." She worked her hand over him, his hardness swelling in her grasp. "I'll definitely be using that against you. But for now, I only have one question for you. Left or right?"

"What?" Sir Michael said. He had tensed himself up for an assault that hadn't come, his adrenaline making his body shake.

"It's a simple question, Sir Michael. Left or right?"

"I'm not playing your games, cunt."

"Perhaps I should have explained myself," her hand moved off his penis and grabbed both of his balls, which she squeezed tightly. Just as his hands came up, the two men who had entered stepped forward and each grabbed a wrist, pinning his arms against his body. Davina squeezed even harder. "I was talking about your testicles. Right or left? Which one do you want me to remove before the morning is out? Choose now, or I take them both."

"You can't be serious. You can't do this."

"I am and I can," she said releasing her grip. She pulled her hand out of his trousers and moved backwards, nodding to one of the men. On her previous instructions, they began to rip the clothes from his body. Despite his best efforts, he was no match for them, and within thirty seconds, he was naked. The bigger of the two men gave him a playful pat on his cheek and then smacked Sir Young on the arse.

"Sir Michael, this is Bob," indicating the larger man. "And this is Joe. Say hello boys."

"Hi, Mikey," they both said mockingly.

"They will be helping me today. You should know they both had family and friends who lived in London. The people closest to them are probably dead because of your actions. Isn't that right, boys?" Bob nodded solemnly and then struck Young square in the stomach. Not expecting the blow, he had been unable to prepare for it, and the impact ripped through him. He felt bile rise in his stomach, and the collar bit into his neck.

"I never do any of the rough stuff, Sir Michael. You should know that. My hands are too precious to be damaged like that. And these fine young men will take it in turns to hit you until you tell me right or left." That was the cue for Joe to hit the captive in the arm with a piece of rubber hose that he had extracted from behind his back. Young cried out.

"It's simply a matter of degree. Your best option is to tell me what I need to know, because at least then you get to live." Joe hit him again. "Did I tell you that Joe here is a homosexual?" Young looked at her, the statement not registering at first. Then the realisation dawned, and his eyes went wide in horror.

"No, you couldn't."

"Of course I could. Do you see anyone here who's going to stop me?" Davina looked around the room. "Because I don't. So what is it, right or left? Answer me right now and I won't let Joe here fuck you in the arse. What do you say, Sir Michael, do we have a deal? Are you ready to play now?" She looked into his eyes and saw what she always saw, the realisation that they were beaten. For some men, that look took days to arrive, for others mere minutes. How fortunate for her that Sir Michael fell into the latter category.

"Right," the deflated man said. "Take the right."

"Oh Sir, Michael," Davina said girlishly, clapping her hands together in front of her face. "You've made me so happy. An excellent choice, the right side of your body it is. I think we'll start with the ear."

"But you said…" Young blustered. He was close to losing it.

"Oh, don't worry, Sir Michael. I haven't forgotten. I will get to your precious testicle. But there is so much more of you to remove first."

08.10AM, 17th September 2015, Watford Islamic Mosque, Watford, UK

Rasheed was able to walk now. The after effects of whatever had happened to him had worn off quickly, but it had still taken a good fifteen minutes before he had felt able to stand up and walk around without much discomfort. He still felt fragile, but whatever had been wrong with him was rapidly fading away. His memory of the previous night had also returned in its entirety. He did not know what had happened to his friends. The entire mosque was empty except for himself and the three corpses. His father, the body of a man by the shattered front door, and the lifeless form of a baby that he found in the female toilets. It wasn't so much what he didn't find that troubled him. It was what he did find. A holy mosque that had been defiled, desecrated. Drying pools of blood and the occasional body parts soiled its interior. This was no longer a place of worship, not to him. He couldn't stay here. He had to move, and he knew exactly where to go.

He had his gun and had reloaded it with the fresh ammunition clip. Along with canned food and water, he took only what he thought he needed to survive from the mosque. This included a hefty steak knife from the kitchen. It was difficult for him. Although his body on the whole was feeling better, both hands hurt, as well as his left leg and right arm. His body was covered in multiple bite marks. Those on his legs had not penetrated the skin due to the protective thickness of his jeans, but there was a piece of skin missing from his left arm, and his right hand had deep teeth marks on the outer edge. He was lucky that part of his hand hadn't been ripped off. Rasheed had bandaged himself up as best as he could, but he knew the risk of infection was high. As extra protection for his hands, he had carefully donned some black leather gloves he found in the cloakroom. They were a little bit too small for him, and the pressure made his wounds throb. But he was willing to accept that.

Those who had bitten him could have given him anything, except it seems the infection itself. He had not seen the TV broadcasts, but had listened to the radio where the truth of this contagion was disseminated to the country and to the world. Those who were bitten turned within, on average, 10 minutes. But it had been hours. Why had he been so lucky?

Lucky? Was surviving in this world lucky? Or was it a curse? He didn't know, and knew that only time would tell. Wincing as he picked up the backpack, he took one last look at the mosque's interior and walked over to the ruined front entrance. That was when he discovered that the corpse wasn't a corpse, not in the traditional sense. As he approached the body, the head lolled sideways, the mouth opening as if in a silent scream. The rest of the body didn't move, and the jaws snapped shut, only to open again. The eyes, black as pitch, glared at him. It made no noise, the neck undoubtedly broken. But still it chomped at him. Rasheed knelt down before it, noticing the stench from the body. It was dead and yet it wasn't—how could that be? Stupid question, how could any of this be?

Taking the pack off his shoulder, he opened it and took out the knife from the side pocket. Casting the rucksack aside, he prodded the animated head with the tip of the blade. Could he do this? Of course he could. Yesterday, he had been willing to lay down his life for Allah, why should this be any greater a task? If anything, it was a mercy. This was not alive, that was clear. And yet it moved and reacted.

Grabbing the head by the hair, he plunged the steak knife into the left eye. He was thankful for the gloves in that moment. It was difficult, and the knife caught on the bone of the eye socket, the eyeball bursting, but with a push, he forced the blade further into the brain and tried to move the handle in a stirring motion. With effort, he withdrew the metal, careful not to cut himself, and he wiped it on the body's clothing. The head quivered, the jaw moving rapidly. If he didn't know better, he would have thought it was screaming. His attempts to kill the already dead were not a success, and now the beast just looked even more hideous with its one eye. He put the knife back in the rucksack and stood. Rasheed needed to get out of here. He needed to find people he could trust, the people he should have gone to in the first place. Coming here to help his father had been a mistake, his sense of duty overriding the practicality of what was really happening. Neither of his two friends had been happy about coming here, but he had persuaded them through the perverse logic that the mosque was a reinforced structure. And they had both paid the price for his foolishness. Rasheed stepped over the body and climbed out of the mosque through the wrecked van.

08.19AM, 17th September 2015, Somewhere over Devon, UK

Helicopters again. He hated the things—he always did and he always would—but in the new world, it was the only way to move around. Planes needed runways, which where they were going, were most likely overrun. They couldn't hover above the ground to allow someone to lay down covering fire either.

Croft had not been surprised when General Mansfield had given the okay to himself and Savage leaving for London. Croft suspected the general was glad to have the pair of them out of his hair, glad that the potential threat to his authority that Croft represented was gone. As much as he respected the general's reputation, Croft strongly suspected the man in charge of defending the UK safe zone was driven just as much by ego as he was by duty. One had to question if he was the right man for this particular job. Of course, with things like that, you never really knew until after the event.

Savage sat next to him in the helicopter, mesmerised by her precious computer tablet. She had shown him the confessional video of Jones last night, had told him why they needed to be in the heart of the infection. It was at that point that the wall she had built to protect herself against the previous day's event collapsed along with her. The tears had come, and she almost fell into his arms. Awkwardly at first, he had held her whilst the sobs wracked her body, only for their embrace to become natural. He had held her like that until she fell asleep in his arms. Waking up he found her gone, and a sudden sense of loss washed over him.

For a reason he couldn't quite understand, he had become very protective of her, an experience he hadn't felt for almost a decade. He looked at her, his eyes following the curve of her neck, the profile of her lips. Was it attraction that was causing this, or was there something more? They both felt the connection, both felt the pull when two souls started to melt together. Neither of them had acted on it yet, but it was only a matter of time. He suspected if he had made a move last night, they would now be lovers. But he hadn't, uncertainty and inexperience causing him to hesitate.

Was this the kind of world you could afford to hesitate in? The likelihood of either of them surviving into next week was grim. He could kill people in combat, make decisions that might see countless dead, and yet he was like a nervous teenager around Savage. For a decade, he had kept people out, and here she was, slipping right past his defences. Croft wondered if she even knew the effect she was having on him. She turned towards him, caught him staring and smiled briefly, her eyes skittering away, only to hone back in on his. She pushed a loose hair behind her ear, and he looked away, not sure what to say in the moment. Yeah, she knew.

But there was the other dilemma. Was this the world where you wanted to get close to someone? Was it wise to make emotional attachments to people when there was a zombie horde waiting to descend on you? Was it even worth it? Was the ultimate loss and the pain that would come with it worth those moments of happiness that would be all too fleeting? A smile rose to his lips and he settled on the answer. Of course it was worth it. What else left was there?

08.22AM, 17th September 2015, St Pancras Station, London, UK

Rachel shambled into the station, unaware of what the structures around her represented. She didn't know why, her thoughts nothing but random electrical impulses firing purely on instinct. The mass of undead with her had grown fivefold, and they all groaned with the one single driving force to their existence: human flesh.

Like a wave, they hit the ticket barriers to the underground, which held them for several seconds. Rachel was the first to scramble over the barrier, falling onto her face on the other side, the skin of her cheek tearing off under her non-existent eye. She felt nothing, all pain sensation lost to her. Valiantly, she tried to regain her feet, but she was pushed back down to the floor by a body that fell on top of her. She had shown them the way, and the hundreds with her slowly began to defeat the barrier. Some even tore through one of the baggage gates, its defences flimsy against the determined mass of undead. Again, she tried to stand, and this time managed it, her feet carrying her forwards towards the escalators which still ran. She didn't know why, but something had compelled her here, something primordial. If she could put words to it, she would say that she was seeking safety. But safety from what?

Approaching the escalators, she selected one going down, more out of pure chance than from awareness. Others were not so lucky. Stepping on the up escalators, they were propelled back into their fellow deceased, only to try again. Clumsily, Rachel stood on the steps, swaying as she descended towards the St. Pancras Underground level, like a confused zombie commuter. The zombie behind her lost its footing and fell past her, laying sprawled on the steps, wriggling as it tried to process what had just happened. It didn't get up, but just lay there flailing. As the escalator reached the bottom, Rachel got off, stepping over the fallen whose ripped jacket had been caught in the mechanism of the escalator steps. She walked away, dozens following her, crushing the trapped zombie underfoot. Behind her at ground level, dozens more undead took the same journey. Down in the underground station, the platforms and corridors teamed with more undead.

She suddenly stopped in her tracks, as if hitting an invisible wall. Her one good eye moved around in its socket, and she clawed at her own face, catching the strip of skin she had dislodged, tearing it away completely. Then her body rocked slightly, and a sensation was thumping into her head. Her body shook again, a tremor ripping through it, and around her the undead stopped, undergoing the same reactions. A feeling descended on them all, and although they no longer understood the words their food used, they understood the command that was broadcast to them. It was faint, but growing stronger, and its meaning was undeniable.

"Come to me, come to me, come to me."

Something clicked in Rachel's mind, and she turned full circle, suddenly conscious of the sights around her. Every zombie was stood stock still, and each was staring at her as if mesmerised. She looked at the skin she still held and let it drop from her fingers. The words in her mind, she had understood them.

08.33AM, 17th September 2015, M1 motorway, UK

Rasheed was driving now, in the van he had used to stock up his father's mosque. What a fool's errand that had been, and now he was alone, unsure of what he would find at his destination. But he couldn't have just abandoned his father, the man who loved him, the man who raised him and cherished him. The man had once been everything to him, and Rasheed owed him a debt he could never repay. Where was his father's faith now though? Rasheed had left the body untouched, and had left the mosque knowing that the man he had idolised as a child had been a banquet to the ever-growing mass of the infected. Rasheed still couldn't fathom how such a fate fell into the greater working of God's plan.

Strangely, Rasheed hadn't seen any of the infected since waking earlier. He had heard some, but their visual presence had eluded him. This had allowed him the luxury of getting fresh unsoiled clothes from a local charity shop. They fit but were more suited to someone three times his age. He wasn't bothered, pride and fashion even more meaningless now than it ever had been. He had considered going back to the mosque to wash up, but he felt that would be pushing his luck a bit too much. He had cleaned himself up as best he could using the kitchen in the back of the shop, but he had no illusions that, were he in polite society, people would comment about the smell from the young Asian man.

He encountered no infected on the motorway either. Most of his journey had been at a fairly rapid pace, slowing occasionally to avoid obstacles. And now he slowed the van again as the barriers came into view. The origin of the M1 motorway was blocked off by wire fences and military vehicles. Impassable. He would have to abandon his van, and most likely proceed into London on foot unless he could find something on two wheels. Although the southbound motorway carriage into the capital had been relatively clear, the roads it led to would likely be clogged by abandoned cars. Would he make it through? Or would he find himself surrounded by the blood-hungry monsters that humanity was now becoming? Would outer London be empty just like Watford, or would it be teeming with the unclean?

Rasheed stopped the van and turned the engine off. Sitting there for a moment, he let the quiet wash over him. Even in the darkest times, there were moments of beauty and of clarity. It was then that the pain hit him in the temples like a sledgehammer. Crying out at its intensity and suddenness, his vision went blank for a second, and he felt bile rise in his throat. Rasheed screamed again, and as he did so, the windshield of the van shattered outwards from some invisible force. He barely noticed, the pain so excruciating as to block out the reality around him. Almost blacking out, his head collapsed onto the steering wheel, the side windows of the van's cabin blowing out as well, the van rocking slightly as if in a strong wind. His hand flailed for the door handle, and he caught it, the door opening outwards. As it opened, the door bent slightly, a metallic groaning sound almost masked by his tortured cries.

Not wearing a seatbelt, he stumbled out onto the cold asphalt, collapsing to his knees, his head in his hands. Rasheed screamed again, and directly in front of him, a metal fence on the road's perimeter buckled, the support struts bending and contorting. Blood began to pour from his nose, from his ears, and lost in a world of pain, he still felt the ground shift below him as the tarmac cracked and caved downwards. An alarm started on an abandoned car several metres away, only for it to stop as the car seemed to get crushed in on itself as his gaze hit it. Everywhere around him, invisible destruction attacked humanity's creations. A huge dent appeared in the side panel of the van he had travelled in, and just before he lost consciousness, it crumpled in on itself. It occurred slowly, as if something immense was squeezing it.

Rasheed let out a final scream, the van lifting into the air and flying onto the next carriageway. Just as the world went totally black, he heard the voice deep inside his mind.

"Come to me, come to me, come to me."

08.35AM, 17th September 2015, Hounslow, London, UK

"How can you do this?" the man begged. He knelt before Owen, three infected holding him down, the saliva from one dripping onto the back of the man's neck. Another infected held the woman he was with in a bear hug, her limp form a testament to the absolute mind-numbing terror she was experiencing. Both were overweight, both black, both doomed. With all the excitement, Owen had almost forgotten how much he hated black people. He had considered using those he encountered merely as food, the elixir for his legion, but the infected weren't human anymore. Black, Asian, whites. All were now welcome in his beloved corps. This was a pure numbers game.

"Shut your mouth," Owen said dismissively. He looked around at his army and saw some make eye contact with him. Most, however, looked around for other prey, other threats. What should he do with these two though? They were already contaminated with the virus of course; the mere sweat from the bodies of the infected who held them was enough to pass the virus on. His warriors were hungry, they deserved the occasional treat. He could hear the chorus of their desires growing as the hours progressed, pressing on him, demanding that he let them satiate their craving. The infected were torn between two masters—Owen and the collective hive mind that constantly tried to pull them away from his influence. And sometimes he felt that hive mind pulling on him also.

"Feed," Owen said quietly and walked past the two captives as his minions descended on them. He let them feast, his attention drawn by a corporate chain sandwich shop, the anguish of those being eaten now an irritation to him. As a form of entertainment, it had already started to grow stale, and he knew he would need to find new things to keep boredom at bay.

The doors were wide open, and he stepped in, the cathedral of mediocre food willing to accept his blessing. He was getting hungry again. Damned if he didn't have the appetite of a goddamn horse. The refrigerated shelves still hummed and he picked up a packet of cheese sandwiches, his eager hands ripping open the container. The first went in two mouthfuls, and he'd barely swallowed it before he consumed its twin. Owen hardly tasted it. It was merely fuel. Dropping the now empty container to the floor, he picked another sandwich of the same flavour off the shelf, only for it to slip through his fingers as a pain seared its way into the front of his head.

"Fuck me," he cried, falling to one knee. A trio of infected scuttled in to the shop, drawn by his cry, their instructions to protect him etched into their minds. They watched helpless as their master fell to his other knee and a string of profanities hurled from his commanding lips. The three looked at each other nervously, twitching and gyrating as they tried to process what to do. Behind them, their potential meal was getting quickly depleted, both unfortunate victims now dead, their abdomens open and emptied, ears, digits and lips all gone.

Owen curled up into a ball, the pain in his skull increasing with every second. It felt like his head was going to split open, and at the same time felt as if it was being crushed. And then as quickly as the agony came, it was gone, and Owen blinked in surprise, trying to clear the stars from his vision. What the fuck was that? He felt wetness on his top lip, and raising a hand found blood flowing from his nose. Standing easily, he walked over to the service counter and plucked a wedge of paper towels to stuff under his leaking nostrils. Then he heard the voice.

"Come to me, come to me, come to me."

It wasn't like the subtle symphony that played endlessly in the background—this voice was strong, insistent. It seemed to be coming from the very centre of his consciousness.

"Who is this?" he said out loud but also he hoped telepathically.

"Don't question, come to me, come to me, come to me."

"Fuck off don't question. Nobody tells me what to do," Owen roared. He flicked his hand dismissing the three infected who left as quickly as they had entered. "I'm the one in charge here."

"No, not in charge, one of four. Come to me."

"You're persistent, I'll give you that," he said to the air. "You're coming in loud and clear. But you ain't fucking listening. You don't give the orders."

"COME TO ME," the voice demanded. Owen staggered backwards as if pushed. *Oh you want to play that game, do you?* thought Owen, and he pushed back with his own mind. He had already found he could pry into the limited thoughts of individual infected, and now he tried to use his growing skill on this new arrival.

"NOT FOR YOU," the voice screamed, and Owen felt the pain start again. He fell back against the counter, sweat now breaking out on his brow.

"Okay, you win, Jesus," Owen conceded, and the pain subsided.

"Come to me, come to me, come to me."

"Alright. Where do you want me to go?"
"*Follow my voice. Come to me.*"

08.36AM GMT, January 22nd, 2013, The White House, Washington DC, USA

Abraham had learnt early on that there was no such thing as Democracy in the United States of America. And he had used that knowledge to his ultimate advantage. The votes of the individual did not count for a hill of beans in a system rigged to support the elite, the bankers, and the military industrial complex. All that mattered was how much money you had and how many palms you were willing to grease. For himself, Abraham preferred to stay out of the limelight, to work in the shadows. Even his multibillion dollar corporation was a private entity. He had resisted the temptation to float it on the stock exchange, despite the extra billions in personal wealth that would have given him. He didn't need the money, he needed the power, and that power only came when he didn't have a board of directors and shareholders to answer to. The only thing he answered to was the Lord Our God. And besides, he had long ago been taught that the secret to wealth was not actually appearing to have any. His name certainly wouldn't appear in any gossip columns, or any rich lists. In fact, hardly anyone in the country would even know who he was, even though he employed nearly fifty thousand Americans. And yet within the day, he could amass enough capital to buy a small country, and had under his command whole platoons of elite mercenaries who would follow his orders without question.

His plan had taken years to grow from its tiny seed, and now here he was at the beginning of his life's goal. The scientist had been acquired, the virus already past the theoretical stage. The pieces were being moved into position, one piece in particular already firmly in place. He had spotted the fledgling politician early on, saw the truth behind the mask, saw the potential in the man. Without even a second thought, he had given over five million dollars for his campaign, something none of the incumbents could match. The fledgling had arrived on the scene like a locomotive. Young, energetic, handsome, and with a war record that made him look like the reincarnation of John Wayne. He was everything the Republicans wanted, and yet he ran as a Democrat, taking votes from both sides. With that money, he had amazingly won Texas, and with further financial support had held the state. Then it had been onto a host of committees steering laws and bills to favour Abraham's corporate interests, as well as pushing forward his own political career. Eventually, with the financial backing Abraham provided through trusts and corporate shell accounts, the fledgling matured, eventually becoming House majority leader at a time when the Democrats controlled both the House and the Senate. Now that was power, but not the power Abraham's protégé wanted. Abraham also demanded bigger things of him. So then the big one, the thing they had always aimed for. President. Twenty-five million dollars had spirited itself across the fibre-optic cables and satellite transmission to help fund that campaign, all from one man, a man who had seen the fledgling's potential, who had seen the desire and the ruthlessness the man possessed. Abraham knew he could use those traits to his advantage, and he did so mercilessly. The money spent returned itself a hundred times fold. Because there was something else that he liked about the fledgling…Abraham knew his darkest secret.

And now Abraham was here, for possibly the final time. The White House was quiet at this time of night. Three o'clock in the morning was perhaps a strange time to be having a meeting, but the fewer eyes and ears about the better. Abraham walked escorted by a single Secret Service agent, his credentials iron clad in this place. He was unofficial advisor to the President of the United States, what wasn't there to trust? Of course, there would be no record of his visit here, there never was, only a select few of the Secret Service even aware of his presence. That was how power worked. To the rest of the world, it was as if he didn't even exist.

The secretary wasn't in the outer office, and Abraham knocked on the door to the inner sanctum. There was a pause, and then a voice, a voice he had heard countless times.

"Come in." Abraham did as he was commanded, closing the door behind him, the Secret Service agent staying outside.

"Good of you to see me, Mr. President."

"You know I always have time for you, Conrad. And you know you can call me Damien, right?"

"Yes, Mr. President." The president smiled at the man's stubbornness. Abraham walked further into the room and sat on the sofa offered to him by the ruler of the free world. His face briefly displayed the pain his arthritic joints caused him as he made the manoeuvre. Damien sat down next to him, which was against convention, but this was his mentor, his co-conspirator.

"So it seemed your plan worked," the president said. "I will admit I had my doubts. But here I am, the most powerful man in the world."

"Doubts are the curse of the believer, and the tool of the powerful. I told you my money and my influence would get you the presidency."

Abraham had been asked to fly across the nation and come here in the dead of night. But why? Spirited in through some back entrance like some nasty family secret that some ruthless patriarch feared exposing.

"There is a problem, however. Your actions have been uncovered," the president said, matter-of-factly.

"How?" Abraham asked, sitting up in his chair.

"One of your inner circle. He isn't one of your true believers." The president picked up a folder from the table in front of him and handed it to Abraham. "The information in there doesn't name you directly, but the journalist involved is writing an expose on your companies. He's asking questions, following the money. It won't be long before he links you to my campaign." Abraham opened the folder, scanned the documents that had been printed off showing company details, cargo manifests and other details that should not be out in the open. Abraham's eyes grew wide with fury.

"How did you get these?" he demanded.

"My new friends at the NSA have been very helpful. They have apparently been tracking a hacker this journalist has been working with. Together, with the mole in your organisation...well, your business dealings are about to become an open book."

"He shouldn't have this information," Abraham said defensively.

"True. Which means people in your organisation have been sloppy." Abraham heard the accusation in the words.

"Can you contain this?"

"I think it would be prudent for you to clean up your own mess. You just need to make the threat disappear like you have so many others before him," the president said. "I could deal with it, of course, but that would cause questions to be asked by people I don't yet fully trust."

"I have true believers who will defend the cause."

"I think you underestimate your enemies in this regard. Your identity has now been compromised. If one person can uncover it, others can too. I can't have this coming out; I can't have the world knowing of our arrangement. You understand that, right?"

"Of course," Abraham said quietly. To succeed so triumphantly, only to be betrayed after the success. Abraham inhaled deeply, the truth beginning to dawn on him. "I see what this is now. This is my penance, the price I pay for my pride."

"I don't know anything about that," the president said absently. "I trust there is no record of you travelling here today."

"You need to ask me that?" Abraham said, visibly shocked. But then he looked down at the document again, saw his own failure bright as day. "Ah, perhaps you are right to. No, there is no record of me even leaving God's own state of Texas."

"Then I leave the matter in your hands."

"This is between me and my God. It will be dealt with," Abraham said. He reached out and gently grabbed his president's arm with a fatherly hand. "I had always hoped you would see the light of the One True God, Damien."

"And I think you knew that was never going to happen, Abraham. You knew from the start that I could never fall under that illusion. You used me just as much as I used you." Abraham let go of his arm.

"Thank you, Mr. President. I must be leaving now. I need to attend to this." Behind Abraham, the door to the Oval Office opened and the same member of the president's Secret Service detail entered.

"Goodbye Abraham. Keith here will see you get to your destination safely."

Abraham walked back the way he had come, the imposing presence of the Secret Service agent following him silently. Dealing with the journalist would be easy, and necessary. Whilst nothing was technically illegal in how he had funded the president's long-standing campaign, he couldn't have his involvement become public. Abraham needed to stay in the shadows, to lurk below the surface. The companies he ran weren't even officially linked, seemingly separate. Instead, they were a massive Hydra that wormed its way into huge aspects of American and international life. From pharmaceuticals to international arms trading, he made money where money could be made. This journalist needed to be stopped, with extreme prejudice. It would also be an embarrassment for the president who ran on a campaign of transparency and honesty to be seen as being bankrolled by a shadowy figure such as Abraham. This would not do. This would not do at all.

But what to do about the president? As far as Abraham knew, Damien was unaware of the secret file Abraham held on him, former youthful indiscretions that were supposedly buried by judges taking orders from a powerful family. At the age of 17, the man who now resided in the White House had drunkenly raped and almost killed a fellow classmate. A male classmate. The assault and the buggery had been so intense, so severe, that even to this day, the victim resided in a vegetative state in a hospital room somewhere. Being part of a rich dynasty living in small town America, the sheriff, a personal friend of Damien's father, had agreed to conspire with the judge to find another culprit, pinning the blame on a homeless black man who to this day still resided in prison. Corruption ran deep back in the days before the internet and mobile phones. And it still ran deep, only the nature of that corruption had changed.

But Abraham knew the truth, had signed death bed confessions from the judge and one of the sheriff's deputies. It would be enough to cause a firestorm in American politics, possibly enough to get the president impeached. Would he ever use it though? The president had not betrayed him and had always been upfront about his atheist beliefs. Of course, to the public he came across as God-fearing a politician as any in Washington. Abraham had used him to increase his own power base, to extend the reaches of his company's tentacles. No, he would not use it yet. So long as the president played his part, Abraham would keep the secret under wraps. Until the time came where it was time to make the big reveal. To rip the American political structure apart just at its biggest time of crisis.

08.32AM, September 17th, Hounslow, London, UK

Kirk woke from an exhausted sleep and looked at the surroundings around him. After escaping from the hotel, there had been multiple instances of the infected leaving him alone, whilst all around the streets were infested with the screams of those not so fortunate. Eventually, he had found himself a secure location, an empty house on a side street. The door had been opened and the building deserted. It had also possessed a well-stocked fridge and a cabinet filled with enough alcohol to kill a football team. Having eaten and drunken his fill, he had collapsed on the sofa, and for several hours, he was blessed with oblivion.

He hadn't even drunk that much, but his body was still recovering from the gargantuan drinking session the night before, combined with the trauma of having to fight for his life. He was sore, and he groaned whenever he moved. But move he did, and he picked up the TV remote control and tried to find a channel to watch. Most of the terrestrial channels were now dead, only the BBC was still broadcasting, and even that was just an information loop. One of the things that had drawn him to this particular building was the larger than normal satellite dish on its roof, and he quickly found he could access a host of foreign channels. All played the same news, that being the death of the UK. For the first time since the crisis hit, he finally realised he was never going to get home. He was stuck here, in a land he was unfamiliar with, away from friends and with no means of support.

"Fuck."

Sitting there watching Al Jazeera, he didn't hear the back door being opened, didn't hear the whispered voices and wasn't aware there were other people now in the house with him until a voice spoke angrily from behind him.

"You're not supposed to be here." Kirk spun his head to see three figures behind him. They had come in through the open plan layout where the kitchen joined the living room. The two black and one white man looked at him menacingly, and he stood, raising his hands up.

"I'm sorry, I thought this place was deserted," Kirk implored. He didn't like the look of these guys. The fact that they were all armed, one with a hammer, one with a baseball bat, and the white guy with a wicked-looking Rambo knife, did nothing to instil in him the confidence that they were not intent on violence.

"So you don't live here?" Hammer asked. "That means you're trespassing."

"Strangers don't get to be trespassing on our new turf," said Rambo. His dreadlocks were pulled back behind his head, and he waved the knife at Kirk menacingly. The dreadlocks were blond, and there was a single tear tattooed at the corner of his left eye.

"I'm sorry," Kirk said. "I'll leave. I'll leave right now."

"He'll leave," Baseball Bat replied mockingly. "You here that, boys? Well it ain't as fucking easy as that, is it?"

"No," said Rambo who took several steps towards Kirk. "It ain't that easy at all. Man got to pay the toll."

"You ready to pay the toll, bro?" Baseball Bat said. He brought the bat up and patted it against the palm of his hand.

"But I don't have anything." Kirk backed up even further, trying to edge his way towards the door that led to the corridor and freedom, but Rambo jumped in that direction, blocking off any retreat.

"You've got plenty," Hammer said, "and we're going to take it all."

"What the hell are you talking about?"

"This is the new world, asshole. We make the rules, and the rules say you've got to pay the toll." Hammer put his weapon down on the sideboard and stepped towards Kirk. "Now get on your knees."

"What?" Kirk couldn't believe what was happening and took a further step backwards, his back hitting the window, his hands finding the cold glass.

"I said get on your fucking knees," Hammer roared, storming up to Kirk and grabbing him by his shirt. "You will do what we tell you, motherfucker. Do you understand me?" Kirk just looked at him open-mouthed, the reality of the situation seeming to elude him. The slap across his face changed all that. "I said, do you understand?"

"No," Kirk almost begged. "I don't know what you want from me."

"Oh you know, because I bet you dream about it every night, you fucking little slut." Hammer grabbed Kirk by the throat and brought his face right in close. "Now get on your knees." Reality dawned on him. Oh God, not that.

"So wait, if I do this, you'll let me go, right?" There was laughter from behind Hammer.

"Maybe. But you better be good, slut, because otherwise, I will beat you 'til you bleed." Hammer took a step away from his newfound prey and nodded for Kirk to kneel down. At the same time, Hammer started to undo the belt of his jeans.

"Dude loves raping those white slut mouths," Rambo said, clearly amused by the whole scene. He turned to Baseball Bat. "You never been into that shit, have you, bro?"

"Nope," Baseball Bat said. Kirk looked at him briefly, but he could see there would be no help from that direction. The man would happily stand there and let his friend do whatever he wanted. Kirk did the only thing he felt he could do and got on his knees.

The seven infected heard the noise from a street over. Their hearing was so acute, the altercation between Kirk and his assailants was like a symphony to them, and they descended on the house silently so as to take their breakfast by surprise. Three went around the back, and four crept up to the front of the house. They would coordinate their attack and share the spoils. There was enough meat in there to satisfy them, at least temporarily, and they could smell the blood that they would drink and almost taste the sweat of the men. But there was something wrong. One of the humans had an aura around him, and the infected didn't know why, but they knew they couldn't touch him. Something about the feel of him told them he was out of bounds, almost taboo. But that was fine, there were still three others.

Hammer looked down at the kneeling man and dropped his trousers, which fell and collected around his ankles. He was already erect, probably not even from sexual arousal, more from the power he could now wield in a world without the police and the judiciary.

"Fucking hurry up, dude. We haven't got time for this," Baseball Bat said. Hammer laughed.

"That's up to him," Hammer said. "He knows what..." Hammer stopped mid-sentence and suddenly fell backwards. He had tried to walk, but had got tangled up in his own trousers. He impacted the carpet with a thud, his head saved by the softness of the sofa it fell against. Frantically, he started working to pull his trousers up.

"Dude, what the fuck are you doing?" Rambo asked.

"Infected," Hammer whispered, "there are fucking infected outside."

"Fuck." That was Baseball Bat. Kirk, now forgotten, watched as the man with the baseball bat ran over to the window and looked outside. The front garden was bordered by a stone wall and a gate, and baseball bat looked on in horror as three infected easily jumped the barrier.

"Out the back," Rambo screamed. Hammer, now on his feet, followed his friend the way they had entered the living room, Baseball Bat close behind. Kirk was left there kneeling, his heart beating with exaggerated ferocity. It felt like he was having a panic attack, and he tried to control his breathing. He almost jumped out of his skin when something slammed into the window pane behind him, his head jerking around to see the upper half of a woman who had slammed her blood-stained hands onto the glass. She looked at Kirk, almost quizzically, and then came the sound he knew would come.

"*Feeeeeeeed.*" The infected woman slammed the glass again, then head-butted it, but the double glazing held. Kirk tried to stand, but he couldn't, completely spent by the recent events. Instead, he just collapsed back so that he was sat beneath the window, now resigned to the fate life had determined for him. He couldn't deal with this anymore; there wasn't anything left of his spirit to even want to carry on.

There were screams from the back garden. Seconds later, Hammer came fleeing back in, a look of panic in his eyes. Kirk almost surprised himself when he started laughing, his would-be assailant staring at him in disbelief.

"Boy, did you choose the wrong house to invade," Kirk said, fresh laughter escaping him.

"Fuck you," Hammer said, retrieving the weapon he had hastily forgotten when he had fled. A fresh scream, this one tinged with agony, rolled through the house, and then an infected appeared. "Keep the fuck away from me," Hammer roared, but the infected just hissed and leapt at him. Swinging wildly, panic now his only real defence, the hammer struck the infected on the side of the jaw, sending it spinning backwards. It recovered quickly, almost oblivious to the fractured mandible it now owned, and came at Hammer again. His second swing was caught by the infected, who pushed the would-be rapist up against the wall.

"*Spreeeaaad,*" the infected screamed into hammer's face, spittle and blood splattering him. The hammer was ripped from his grasp and was flung across the room, smashing into the TV set, sending sparks and glass everywhere. Kirk, cowering from the eruption, didn't witness what happened next. With a useless jaw, the infected was now unable to bite, so instead it smashed its face into hammer's and rubbed infected blood all over him. Then it let the man go and watched, almost satisfied as the now contaminated man fell to the floor. Then it turned to look at Kirk.

"Well, come on then," Kirk said, absolutely exhausted. "What are you waiting for?" The infected took a step forward and was joined by a second blood-smeared and damaged creature. The first infected hissed and took another step closer. But then it stopped and looked at its companion. They stood like that, twitching for several seconds, and then left the living room, leaving Kirk with a man who, seconds later, started shrieking. Pulling himself to his feet, he looked out of the window and saw the other infected were also leaving.

"Fucking help me, man," Hammer implored as he tried to wipe the viral fluid off his face. Kirk didn't go anywhere near him. Instead, he escaped into the corridor and out through the front door, the curses from Hammer following in his wake.

08.36AM GMT, September 17th, 2015, The White House, Washington DC, USA

President Rodney sat behind his desk in the Oval Office. He had never felt more alive. This was his opportunity, this was his moment. This would see him through to the second term of his presidency, to kick through his true agenda. Now he had his chance, and he was going to take it. Until yesterday, he thought he had missed his destiny. But that was all changed now. Today, however, was going to be a difficult day.

He remembered the last time Abraham had been here almost two years ago. Rodney had only seen him once since then, briefly on a trip to Texas. The issue with the now dead journalist had sent the old man even deeper underground, and requests for presidential assistance on some policy or other had come only three times.

Abraham wasn't the only one who could find out other people's secrets. Rodney was well aware that Abraham knew of his little youthful indiscretion. That someone could uncover what was supposed to be hidden had annoyed Rodney, but at least he had put in place the mechanism that allowed for him to be warned that his secret had been uncovered. So the old man knew, so be it. Two can play at that game.

"You've been busy, my old friend," Rodney said, looking up at the glass in his hand. Vodka, neat. Not a very American drink, but one he indulged in occasionally. If Abraham really was behind this, if the cult of religious fanatics that the man had grown around him was the cause of the viral outbreak, it posed an issue that would need careful handling. That was when the phone rang. Not any of the official White House phones, but the encrypted burner phone in his desk drawer with the unregistered sim. It was amazing what you could get your hands on when you were president of the world's most advanced surveillance nation. He opened the drawer and picked up the phone.

"Yes?" the president said.

"Mr. President, it has been so long since we have spoken." The voice was distorted electronically. Rodney knew the identity of this deep throat though. His time on the intelligence select committee had earned him countless favours from the intelligence community.

"You have something for me?"

"Yes. Your mentor is responsible for the incident across the Atlantic. I'm sorry to bring you this bad news."

"I see. And the more pressing issue?"

"The threat to the homeland is false. He has no intention of releasing it here."

"You're sure about that?"

"Positive," the voice said. "This is the last time I will contact you."

"I understand." The call disconnected, and Rodney broke the phone in half. He would remove the sim card and put it through the microwave shortly. The kitchen staff were used to him appearing out of the blue to feed himself. One more visit wouldn't make any difference to them.

So Abraham was indeed the villain in all this. Rodney realised now how fortunate it had been for him to keep the old man at arm's length, ironically at Abraham's insistence. And even more fortunate that he had placed a spy deep in the fanatic's organisation. But now what to do with him? He couldn't be allowed to live, that was for certain, and really there was only one way to deal with the threat. There would be no court of law for Conrad Schmidt.

08.37AM, 17th September 2015, MI6 building, London, UK

Fabrice sat staring at one of the cameras in the corner of the room he was unable to escape from. In truth, he didn't even see the camera, his mind now elsewhere. He ignored the infected scientist that shared his prison, ignored its clawing and its groans as it tried to get out at the people it could smell outside. How did he know it could smell them? He had no idea, just as he had no idea why he could hear them, could feel the millions growing in the freedom of the outside world.

Fabrice had tried to break out at first, his fists slamming into the hardened glass that masqueraded as a mirror. But even with the strength he felt inside him, he had not been able to shatter his way out, and after several minutes, he had abandoned the attempt. He had been both angered and afraid. Angry at what these people were doing to him, afraid at the transformation in himself that he witnessed in that very mirror. As he had pounded on the silver surface, his skin had changed texture and colour, and his muscles had visibly grown. Sitting down, he had examined his hands, noticing the thickening of the skin where it had contacted solid matter. As he watched, the skin went greyer momentarily, visibly thickening, and then began to regain its normal pasty complexion. He looked at his reflection and saw his whole body had reverted to its original hue…but the muscles had remained. It was perhaps fortunate he was naked, because none of the clothes he had once worn would have fit him. He looked like a potential candidate for Mr. Universe, only bigger.

He had never been a sun person, his skin prone to Vitamin D deficiency. But it had changed. And he had a notion he knew why, knowledge that just seemed to appear into his consciousness. So he had tested his theory. Picking up an unused syringe off Durand's table of torment, he carefully jabbed it against his skin. There was no pain, and pressing harder, the needle actually bent, the denied entry point visibly changing. Having been through hell already, what he did next would have been a mild irritation if it had penetrated the flesh. Straightening the needle, he rammed it into his thigh. Only, again, it didn't penetrate the skin. His skin seemed to protect him against any trauma it encountered. Would it work against bullets? Fabrice suspected that at some point he would find out.

Sitting down on the floor after, he had resigned himself to the waiting game. By this time, the scientist he had infected was already become a distant memory, although he was momentarily distracted when the creature vomited inside its hazmat suit. That had made Fabrice smile, but the smile was ripped from his face as fresh torment had cracked his skull apart. It was so sudden it had taken his breath away. Then, as if from the very ether of reality, voices flooded in along with images of the outside world, of the carnage being wrought on London, on Leeds, on Manchester. It had overwhelmed him, and through gritted teeth, he had roared in fresh anguish. He thought he would be free of the pain, only for it to start again. His sanity stepped onto the edge of the abyss and he had felt himself being lost to the void. And then the pain stopped, and his mind had suddenly become crystal clear. Right there, he understood everything with a clarity that would even impress Brother Abraham. He knew why he was there, knew what his purpose was.

And then he saw them, saw the three. He felt the closeness he had with them, felt his mind beginning to merge with their thoughts. They were four, and together, they would be one. On pure instinct, he reached his mind out to them and connected with them one at a time. He witnessed the impact he had on them, and felt no guilt at the pain his actions inflicted. Of course, one of them no longer felt pain, the undead mind a void ready to be refilled. It became all so obvious to him. Four victims of the infection, each unique to the world, each with powers they hadn't even become close to mastering. They were four and they were one. Fabrice knew his Bible, knew the implication. Revelations. The Four Horsemen. It was true, all of it.

War
Famine
Evil
Death

His eyes broke with the camera, and he looked around. The skin of his body had thickened again, the stress of that last encounter taking its toll, sweat pouring off his body. That last one had been powerful, and was growing in strength by the hour. Although Fabrice had commanded him and the others to his side, he knew that this was not a ploy to try lightly in the future. He was not their leader; they were equals in their own right. And why had he felt obliged to bring them to him? Part of him knew, but it hid itself from him behind rumours and lies. Was he the player here, or was he being played? Had his faith met its ultimate reward? Was he now the channel of God? Was Fabrice now his voice in this infected world? And which of the four horsemen was he?

08.57AM, 17th September 2015, Shannon Airport, Ireland

"We have a name." Arnold Craver sat at a makeshift desk on the secure satellite phone. In the room next to him, he could hear Sir Michael Young begging for the torture to stop, the noise coming over the speaker even though Craver had turned the volume down. He didn't really want to hear what the torture was doing to him.

"Good," came the voice of General Marston. "The bastard gave us nothing. It looks like your advice to give him to this…what was her name again?"

"Davina."

"Yes, that's the name. Is she sure he's told her the truth?" It was a question Young had asked her himself. She had looked at him as if he had somehow insulted her.

"She is positive. She says she knows when men lie and when they try and pull the wool over her eyes."

"I'm meeting with the NATO chiefs in an hour. Can you have me a dossier in time for that? I don't want to tell the Americans anything until we have all the facts."

"Yes, I'll have whatever we can find for you," said Craver. "We are still setting up here, but Cyprus has all the backup records from Thames House. They are already putting things together." Craver paused before delivering the information. "The guy's name is Conrad Schmidt."

"Never heard of him," said Marston.

"Me neither. But apparently, he is a very big deal. Keeps a low profile, but has many friends in high places. Worth billions apparently."

"Thank you, Arnold. Keep me updated." The phone went dead. Craver looked at it and set it down at the desk he was sat at. He needed sleep, had been up all night trying to re-establish some kind of order to the chaos that had descended on Shannon Airport. MI5 personnel were in short supply, the agency effectively non-functional. MI6 had fared better, and he suspected it was a matter of days before the two agencies were merged together.

A fresh scream came over the intercom, and he turned it off completely. He did not like Davina's methods and did not approve that MI6 used her so frequently. But he had to admit that she got the job done, and in the new world, concepts such as morality and human rights had been thrown right out of the window. The concept of British fair play had been swallowed up and spat out by a virus only a madman would ever consider unleashing. So to catch the insane, one sometimes had to use distasteful methods. Besides, there wasn't a Britain anymore.

And would revealing the name come with fresh horrors? Craver knew what would happen if the man responsible was captured. If the threat that was broadcast to the world by these zealots was neutralised, then the gloves came off. The UK mainland was now a very real threat to the rest of the planet. If the infection started to threaten the European continent, there was no telling what carnage would be unleashed. But, at least for him, there was better news. In four hours, he would be getting on a flight to Washington DC, Ireland for now outside the quarantine zone. There, he would be the liaison between the Americans and what was left of the UK secret service, which still had bases and operatives in multiple countries. The Leer jet was fuelled and ready; they just had to wait on one of the other passengers. Davina. She had promised Sir Michael Young five hours of her expert attention, and Davina always followed through on a promise. That had been her price for getting the information out of the man…a flight to the United States of America.

09.00AM, 17th September 2016, Newquay Airport, Cornwall, UK

"What the fuck is that?" Brian stood next to Stan, pointing at a shape off in the distance. About a hundred metres away, the figure of a man hung down from a tall oak at the edge of the airfield. It was perhaps not a coincidence that the tree was right at the main entrance to the airport.

"Looter. Someone was caught trying to steal medical supplies from storage," said Stan, a steaming mug of coffee in his hand. Brian looked at him, dumbfounded.

"Are you serious?"

"People were talking about it at breakfast this morning. Told you skipping breakfast was bad for you." He looked at Brian and saw how serious his friend looked. "You were there for the briefing. They laid the law down straight."

"But we don't just go around executing people," Brian protested.

"We do now. I'm not happy about it, but it makes sense."

"What?" Brian said turning towards his friend. "You can't be serious. This…this is barbaric."

"Yes, it is, but it's also necessary. The only thing we've got going for us is discipline. If that breaks down, we haven't got a chance. And besides, it's not our call. The military are in charge here. It's not the first hanging, and it won't be the last." Stan put a hand on his friend's shoulder. "Come on, mate, we've got shit to do."

"Fuck."

They walked off to the main medical tent where several lorries were being loaded. Stan watched his friend and saw his frown lighten when he saw Holden step out of the tent, arms laden with boxes. Stan smiled. It was good to see his friend take an interest in the opposite sex again. Since Brian's childless divorce several years back, the guy had been a virtual eunuch. He hoped his friend would take the opportunity that was clearly before him. Stan liked Holden, saw that she was good people. She could be exactly what Brian needed. And he suspected that Brian was exactly what the good doctor needed as well.

Through a bit of crafty negotiation, Stan had managed to get them both assigned as security to the hospital that Holden would be stationed at. Why not keep the band together was his motto. They weren't soldiers; they weren't trained to be on the front line. And Stan certainly didn't want to be digging ditches and erecting fences. But guarding places, that they could do. Brian sped up and almost ran ahead of Stan.

"Need some help?" Brian asked. Holden smiled as she saw him, and nodded her head back to the tent.

"Plenty in there that needs shifting." Brian paused briefly and then made his way into the tent.

"Morning, Doc," Stan said, walking past her. She hadn't seen him grin so much since she'd met him.

"What?" Holden asked. She put the boxes she was carrying on the back of the nearest lorry.

"Have you heard? We'll be running security at your new hospital."

"Really?" Holden said. Stan could see a hint of excitement in her face.

"Yeah, so you'll be able to bring us coffee and make us snacks and stuff."

"I think I might be a bit too busy for that," Holden said. She knew he was joking.

"Of course, it also means we can keep an eye on you. You know, make sure you don't get up to any mischief." He winked at her, and then his eyes moved to the tent as Brian exited carrying a large brown box of surgical swabs. "I know Brian would like that," he said looking at his friend.

"I'd like that too," said Holden. She suddenly reacted as if she hadn't realised she'd said that out loud. She suddenly felt flustered.

"Blimey, Doc, you're blushing." Oh yes, thought Stan, this was definitely going places.

09.01AM, 17th September 2015, London Docklands, London

For the first time in seven months, Alexei did not go through with his normal morning routine. Although he was a creature of habit, he awoke late with the knowledge that none of it really mattered anymore. The money in his bedroom safe was now probably mostly worthless, and the entire property portfolio that he managed was likely about as valuable as the houses slowly rotting in Chernobyl. Lying there, staring up at the ceiling, he wondered if there had actually ever been any point to any of it. What had he actually gained in the big scheme of things? When all that faced you at the end was being buried in the ground and having dirt thrown in your face, why should anyone actually give a toss?

Ivan would say that there was never a point, but then Ivan wasn't a philosopher. He was merely an ageing gangster who had helped Alexei acclimatise to life in the UK, and who Alexei had subsequently looked after when his own rise to power had become meteoric. Alexei was loyal, and thus repaid loyalty shown to him. To cross him, however, well, that was possibly the worst thing anyone could do. The big Russian took particular exception to people who broke what for him was the cardinal rule. The last person to do so, an upstart who felt the world owed him a living, had suffered badly at Alexei's hands. His death had been unpleasant, Alexei choosing the tried and true method he had used so often. He had tied the man down across a table and put two irons on his body, held down tight with electrical cord. One on his chest and one between the man's legs—the latter was the one he had switched on first. It had been an hour before he had grown bored of the man's screams and had turned on the second iron, which slowly burnt its way into the man's chest, eventually killing him.

He still brushed his teeth though, and was reassured to see that the water still flowed freely. That was a situation that would not last forever of course, but Alexei was prepared. He did not live in your ordinary penthouse; it was also a survivalist's dream. The hardship of youth had instilled in him an assessment of risk that had led him to the belief that Western society was fragile, close to collapse, and a danger to the very people who lived within it. The previous day's events had shown how right he was in that regard, and he was ready. He had cupboards full of freeze-dried food. With a twenty-five-year shelf life, it was a much more sensible choice than cans. He also had ample stores of water, as well as vital equipment to survive when the lights went out. This was one of the reasons he had not attempted to flee the city. The time to do that would come, but it was not yet. First, he needed information, and where better than the internet.

He walked naked out of his bedroom along a short corridor that led to his office. The noise of Ivan snoring could be heard coming from the other room. They were the only two people in the apartment, the third man having left after midday yesterday to go to family where he felt he was needed. Alexei didn't stop him, and it wasn't out of any sense of respect. If he cared for other people to risk his life like that, then the man was weak and of no use to him. To survive in this world, you had to abandon the weak and the defenceless and align yourself with the strong.

The power was still on also, but the normal broadband was not. This was no concern to Alexei, for he had his own secure satellite-based system to use. Switching on his computer, he waited whilst it booted up and then logged into his encrypted email account and saw that there was a single message to read. He did not expect this. Surely, his bosses in Moscow would have nothing to say to him, their involvement in the UK technically over. Because there was no longer a UK to be involved in.

"Are you well, Alexei?" the message read. He hesitated briefly, almost touched by the concern. But then his brow furrowed, and he realised that it was unlikely anyone in Moscow was concerned with his wellbeing.

"I am well and secure," went his response. He didn't wait long for a reply.

"The Pakhan is disappointed in the way you handled business. Your investments in property have lost the family money. A lot of money." Alexei read the email stoically. Even with the world falling to hell, it was all about money for them. He did not respond for he had nothing to say. So despite the money he had made them in the past, which probably dwarfed this present loss, there was no forgiveness for something completely out of his control. The only way back into the life he had always known was to replace the losses, something that in his present situation was impossible.

"Shit," he said simply. There wasn't a man alive who had seen Alexei lose his temper or his composure. There were a few dead ones, but to most people, he was an emotionless rock. This development mattered because he didn't intend to sit and rot in his penthouse for more than a few days. He had planned to somehow make his way to the continent. But now any network he had there, any contact he could use were no longer of help. They were now the enemy and would actively work against him. He was effectively on his own. But then, perhaps it had always been that way.

09.03AM, 17th September 2015, M1 motorway, UK

Rasheed found himself lying on cold asphalt. The pain that had assaulted him was gone, as was the voice that whispered to him seductively. He easily lifted himself up off the ground, sitting in what was the middle lane of the southbound carriage, a feat unimaginable even one day ago. The air was crisp, untainted with human traffic, and a cold breeze rolled across him, his long black hair buffeted by it.

The van he had been driving was a wreck. Looking around, he didn't see any other vehicle he could use to get into London, so it looked like he was on foot, at least for now. It wasn't far, but even with that knowledge, he remained seated. What had just happened? Despite the almost mind-numbing agony he had been in, he remembered everything that had happened up to blacking out. The devastation around him and the fractured road beneath him was his doing. It was as if something deep inside him had been triggered, some unknown power of immense proportions that had simply been unleashed, like a dam unable to keep back the water that constantly pressed on it.

Looking down at the ground in front of him, he concentrated on a piece of rubble about the size of his fist. Nothing happened at first, and he realised that he had no idea how to unleash the power that was within him. Had it been him? Had it indeed been him that had flipped the van, shattered fences, and cracked the very earth beneath him?

"Move, God damn you."

The piece of rubble moved. Ever so slightly, it turned in the dirt. Rasheed felt something grow in him, felt a force shift in his sternum, and the rock lifted three inches into the air. Rasheed willed it to start spinning. After several seconds of simple levitation, the rock began to spin. Faster and faster until its movement was just a blur. Did he always have this power, or was this the result of last night? There was no denying he had been bitten—the teeth marks were all the evidence he needed. Bored of the rock, he wished it away, and it shot off down the road.

He had seen enough science fiction as a young boy to understand what was going on here. Instead of being infected, he had been granted a gift. Why, he did not know, but he knew that Allah in his mercy and his wisdom had a plan for him and that he as a faithful servant would not disappoint. Had that been the voice he had heard in his torment? The voice that said "*come to me*", had that been the word of God? Confused and still in shock from everything that had happened, Rasheed's mind latched on to the belief that he had been found worthy to be an agent of the Almighty. And in his mind, there formed an image, a place he had seen many times, a place he both hated and feared. That was where he needed to go, that was where the voice commanded him to go. Rasheed stood.

09.34AM, 17th September 2016, Hayton Vale, Devon, UK

Gavin's arm didn't feel any better, even after a handful of Ibuprofen. It was still definitely tender to touch, and he felt it was probably useless for most things. It also throbbed mercilessly. He knew it was broken, so he kept it in the hastily constructed sling, the urge to use it ever present. He still felt it needed looking at, another problem he'd never fully considered when he had taken up the survivalist lifestyle. At the end of the world, how did you access quality medical care? He had supplies and a secure bunker, but no way to fix a broken arm. He could try and splint it himself, but what if it was worse than he thought? He had a decision to make, and the answer to the question poised really was a no brainer. Alone and witness to the way his retreat had been so easily breached, and with the very real risk that he was the proud owner of a fractured bone, he'd taken the only decision that made sense. He headed west.

Well, not the only decision. There was always eating the shotgun, but for some reason, that had lost its appeal. Packing up his Land Rover with the essentials, he had awkwardly driven it off his farm and through the back country lanes of Hayton Vale. Of course, he had to drive slowly; trying to manoeuvre with one arm was challenging at the best of times. But it was quicker than walking. That was until he hit traffic. Within thirty minutes, the road had just clogged with abandoned cars. Although his car had the ability to off-road, that would definitely require two hands. So he'd had no choice. Several expletive-ridden minutes followed whilst he assembled anything he could into one bag, and then he had continued on foot.

Now he walked amongst other people. There were hundreds of them, all fleeing the same thing he was. The radio broadcast had said there was a safe zone in Cornwall, and this was obviously where everyone was heading. But how safe would it be? Gavin had first-hand experience of what the virus could create. How many others here had that first-hand knowledge? Most of them were fleeing merely from what they witnessed on their TVs, from what they heard on their radios. They had abandoned homes, businesses, possessions, even loved ones. The frail and the dying had no place in this exodus, left to fend for themselves in a world that could no longer support them. And there were many who could have joined the exodus who had seen the futility and the horror of it all and had simply ended their own lives, as Gavin had so nearly done yesterday. Last night, he had been all ready to blow the back of his skull out, but now he wanted to live. He didn't know why things looked different to him in the cold light of the new day, but suicide was now the last thing on his mind.

The air was cool, and he kept up the pace, overtaking some people, being overtaken by others. Nobody spoke, their focus on the road ahead, on making progress, on buying time. Because there was one thing that everybody knew—the infected were coming, and they would come in numbers likely so vast as to swallow up everything in their path. He shifted the rucksack on his shoulder as best he could and felt it digging in painfully. Gavin didn't have the luxury of swapping shoulders, so he stopped, letting it slip to the ground to give himself a much-needed break. That was when he heard the noise, building quickly, and within seconds two fighter jets flew directly over them, their engines shattering the relative peace of the Devon countryside. They disappeared off into the distance quickly, and he turned his head to follow them until they were out of sight. Reaching into his rucksack, he pulled out his water bottle and, after manipulating off the lid, he drank deeply from it. Just as he finished swallowing, the sound of an explosion in the distance reached him. Most people around him stopped moving and looked off into the distance. There was nothing for them to see.

She had not appreciated the call sign her fellow pilots had given her. But complaining about it would of course only make things worse, and at least it meant she had been accepted. As the only female pilot in her A10 squadron, she had been given the call sign Syndrome, after the fact that she was a woman and would, of course, suffer PMS. It wasn't even original, which probably made it even worse. But she was stuck with it, and at least it wasn't the most offensive she had heard. She knew of a pilot in another unit who had been assigned the call sign Fagmeister. When she had heard the story behind it, even she had cracked a smile.

She was accepted because she was good. She could outfly most of the jocks she found herself in the air with, and they all knew it. And they respected her for it. It also helped that she could drink any of them under the table, and was well versed at utterly humiliating anyone who tried to pull that sexist crap on her. And she loved to fly. It was in her blood. But she wasn't loving today's duty, not at all.

There squadron's morning mission was clear—blow the bridges, blow the roads, and destroy the tunnels. It wouldn't stop the infected, but it would cut off their main arteries of travel, causing them to go cross country, to swim the rivers. It would slow them down and buy the defenders the time they needed to at least try and form a defensive perimeter.

To be honest, her head was still spinning. Yesterday, she had woken up in her bed at the USAF base in Germany, and within hours, she was on combat alert. And now she was flying over a country she had always wanted to visit, but had never somehow had the chance. At no time in her career had she ever expected to be doing a bombing run on a friendly country to protect a military position against a possible wave of zombies and crazed infected that numbered in the millions. How was she supposed to get her head around that? But those were her orders, and now she found herself finally being involved in combat operations. Her target was a motorway bridge over the river Parrett. It wasn't a particularly wide river, and it was just one of many bridges that would be destroyed today in Operation Blockade. Her wingman had the follow-up run, and they were both armed with Mark 84 bombs.

"Coming up on target, over," Syndrome said.

"Roger, over." Her wingman, Vampire, so called because his parents were Romanian and also from the time when he threw up one night after a drunken bet to eat several raw cloves of garlic. She had been flying over the motorway for several minutes now, and coming in low, she could see it was packed with people. When she had been given her orders last night, sitting in the briefing room, her blood had run cold.

"The ultimate goal is thus twofold. Firstly, slow the ultimate spread of the infected. Secondly, to stop the flow of refugees before their numbers overwhelm the defender's ability to feed, clothe, and house them. Those are the orders from on high. Any questions?" That had been the end of the mission brief, and there hadn't been any questions. She had looked around at her fellow pilots and saw the look of horror in some faces, the excitement in others. They knew why they had to do it, understood the logic behind it, but that didn't change the fact that they were bombing civilians. But she would do it because this was war, against an enemy like no other.

The target came into view and she lined up for her bombing run. And then the bomb was away. Unguided, it hurtled down, two thousand pounds of explosive death. Her aim was true and, seconds later, it impacted on the southbound carriageway of the bridge. A second later, a second bomb hit the other carriageway. Concrete vaporised, and steel bent and tore, shrapnel and smoke rising into the air. They had made the bridge utterly impassable.

"How many people do you think were on that bridge, Vampire, over?"

"I'm trying not to think about it, over," came the response. Yeah, she would try not to think about it, but she knew that wouldn't work. And there would be many more incidents like this, more traumatic barbs to be lodged in her psyche. But that wasn't what she feared the most. Her biggest fear was one day waking up and not actually giving a fuck.

10.00AM, 17th September 2015, London Underground, London, UK

Her world was the stench of the dead and the sound of shuffling feet. By instinct, she and those like her knew to avoid the electrified third rail, and all around her the bodies massed, more joining them every minute. They filled up the tunnels, following her orders to leave the surface and come down here. They resisted, but she forced them anyway, the need for preservation overwhelming the need for food.

Why she felt the need to hide, she didn't know, but she did anyway. Sightless in the dark, she moaned slightly, shifting her position to give herself a better footing. Here, she would stay, and here they would gather until she felt the time was right to re-ascend to the surface, and then they would feed. Although she was dead, memories were returning to her now, and the voice spoke clearly to her. It wanted her to come, but she would not come yet because now was not the time.

"*Come to me,*" the voice said. She ignored it, her brain working in ways it had not since her death. Her whole body, numb from organ death and the demyelination of her nerves, had begun to feel again. Her skin tingled slightly, and she thought that perhaps she could feel.

"No," the word came to her lips. Did she know what the word meant?

"*Come to me, come to me.*"

"No." The word came again.

"*I command you.*"

"No." She would not come yet. She would come when she was ready, when her numbers were vast and when her mind understood. She would come, but first she would wait. Her name had been Rachel, she remembered that again. She remembered.

10.05AM 17th September, Swiss Cottage, London, UK

Rasheed had been lucky. Within minutes of leaving the M1, he had found a moped with the keys still in it. And although the roads were jammed, the pavements weren't. There were frequent obstacles, but nothing he couldn't bypass or go around. It was certainly quicker than walking. He felt the pull all the time now, but it did not control him. In fact, he followed its call merely out of curiosity now more than anything else. At least that was what he told himself. He had quickly come to the conclusion that this was not in fact the voice of Allah.

Ahead on the pavement, a Ford Escort blocked his path, and he slowed the scooter, the entire road now blocked by other cars. No matter, concentrating on the blockage, he willed it to move. The roof crumpled in, and it lifted on its end. Then it flipped into the air falling onto other wreckage, opening a path. Rasheed still thought he might be dreaming. To wake up to find you had superhuman powers was supposed to be science fiction, not reality. And yet here he was able to move things with his mind.

He looked behind him and saw a dozen shambolic figures following him. They had been drawn by the sound of his moped perhaps, and as they drew closer, he felt an itch in his mind. This was something he had been contending with since leaving the motorway. There were infected everywhere, and they always came after him. Until they got close that was. These were the same, the first reaching within ten metres of him. It was a woman, a slut with her short skirt and her tits out for the world to see. She stopped, her head tilting quizzically to one side. Rasheed saw it smell the air, and then it ran off to the left, now completely ignoring him. The others behind her quickly followed the same pattern. He was safe from the infected it seemed. But were they safe from him?

10.09AM, 17th September 2015, Osterley, London, UK

He stuck to the roads. Driving was impossible, but the bike he had found made the travel quicker, the horde he commanded running around him and behind, easily keeping up with his pace. Owen couldn't remember the last time he had ridden a bicycle, but he quickly found that it was true that you never forgot how to ride one.

It was hard work, exercise not something he was used to. The infected, though, they never tired, even running at full pelt. And they were everywhere now, numbering in their thousands, the mass spreading the virus wherever they could. Others were already collected, latching on to the growing swarm. There were so many that they now spread across multiple roads, taking a parallel course, all heading for the same spot. Some ran up ahead, scouting for danger, but strangely, they encountered only the occasional human out scavenging. Others they dragged from hiding places. But the undead, they saw none. Owen didn't know if that was a good thing or not. Like locusts, they swept across outer London heading for its heart.

He stopped the bike briefly, taking a moment to reach into his backpack and take a drink. Most of the infected carried on, but his own personal guard stopped, nervously rotating around him. And his harem, they stopped too, kneeling down before his feet as he had taught them. The urge to use one of them came and he swung himself off his bike.

"*Come to me, come to me,*" the voice insisted. It was there all the time now. Nudging, ordering.

"Fuck you, when I'm ready."

"*No now, COME NOW,*" roared the voice in his head. Owen fell, surprised again by the invisible force that commanded the voice. He landed on his backside, Claire jumping away so as not to get crushed.

"Motherfucker," he said under his breath. Sitting there, the voice pestering him, he closed his eyes and concentrated.

"Oh, I'm coming, bitch," Owen said in his mind. "You better believe it. But for now you SHUT THE FUCK UP." He roared the words telepathically and felt the world around him jerk slightly. Owen thought he felt the impact, felt the damage being done to the person in his mind. "I will get there when I am good and ready." Owen stood up and looked around. The infected had all stopped moving. They were looking at him, their eyes wide. Some of them took a step towards him. They had the look he had seen so often over the past twenty-four hours. They were looking at him as if he were prey. He felt a hand grab his leg, and he looked down to see Claire pawing at him. And then the hand withdrew. The infected around him turned away and resumed their quest. Shit, he had almost lost control then. Whoever this voice was, he needed to be dealt with. The voice was a dangerous distraction, and Owen couldn't resist it and control the infected around him at the same time. So yes, he would come, but whoever it was at the other end of the psychic telephone might not like what he brought with him.

10.10AM, 17th September 2015, NATO Headquarters, Brussels, Belgium

There were five people in the room, the meeting having been called by General Marston. General Marston, General Bradstone, General Phillippe Petain, the Chief of the French Defence staff, and Victor Frolov, the Russian Chief of the General Staff, along with his interpreter. They sat around an oval table, no objections being raised to the Russian smoking.

"My president has authorised the use of nukes, but only when the immediate threat to our national interests are contained. He believes it will be the only way to stop this," Bradstone stated. "Should that occur, we will, of course, inform all those concerned beforehand." The Russian sat back in his chair, allowing his aide to relay what was being said in his native Russian. He nodded gravely at the words that were being whispered to him.

"Whilst it pains me to say this, Her Majesty's Government has no objection to that. The country is lost, and as we saw this morning, conventional forces can't even make a dent in the infected numbers." Marston was now effectively Her Majesty's Government, having taken command after the death of most of the British Cabinet, killed by the assassin bullets at the very start of the crisis. He was about to say something else, but Bradstone interrupted to ask Petain a question. "What is the French view?"

"Whilst we are not overjoyed by the prospect of a radioactive cloud drifting over our northern border," Petain said in perfect English, "we like the prospect of the infected swimming the English Channel even less. We agree that nuclear weapons are now an inevitability."

"And the Russian view?" Bradstone said to Frolov. The Russian inhaled on his cigarette deeply, pausing a moment whilst the man behind him translated what had been said. Frolov spoke softly in Russian and the translator, a major in the Russian army, relayed the information that the Russians also had no objections. The major continued.

"We are threatened by this virus just like everyone else. However, the potential threat about the release of the virus in other countries has to be taken at face value."

"We know where the virus was developed and the name of the scientist who perfected it. We also know that it has been shipped to at least one other country," Bradstone said solemnly. "However, we now also know the name of the man ultimately responsible for this. The folder in front of you contains all the details." Each man opened the folder that had been provided for them, Frolov's and Petain's printed in their own language. Each sat there with the picture of Conrad Schmidt staring up at them. The Russian spoke first, stopping to let his translator relay his words.

"A double-edged sword that this man is an American. Both embarrassing for your government and fortunate that he is not in some difficult to reach hell hole."

"Not an American by birth. He was originally from Germany."

"Still," Frolov said through his interpreter, "it puts the United States in a very difficult—"

"Enough," Marston said loudly, slamming his hand on the table. Everyone looked at him. "General Frolov, can we please cut through this charade? I know very well you speak English."

"General, I can assure you—" the interpreter started, but his words were cut off by a raised hand from Frolov.

"You are correct of course, Nicholas," Frolov said, an amused grin on his face. "You will forgive the, how you call it, cloak and dagger. We Russians follow orders just like everyone else." The interpreter said something in Russian, but Frolov gave him a withering glance that dried the man's words in his throat.

"Well, then, let us get to the reason I called this meeting. Whilst the use of nukes is most likely inevitable, there is something else we can use in the meantime."

"Oh?" the Russian said.

"Yes, nerve agents. Unfortunately, the British Armed Forces no longer stockpile them due to our acceptance of the Chemical Weapons Convention."

"And as I am sure you are aware, the Russian Federation are also signatories to that convention." Frolov kept his placid exterior, but there was a hint of tension there.

"Oh, don't get me wrong, I am not saying for a moment that Russia would go against international law. Not intentionally at least." Marston reached down to his briefcase that rested at the side of his chair and withdrew a dossier. "Which is why I wanted to draw your government's attention to a rogue element in your military." Marston pushed the dossier across the table to Frolov. "I thought it best to give that to you in person. With the pending destruction of MI6, it's likely to be the only copy." Frolov accepted it graciously and opened it, concern etched on his face. Marston was well aware it was all an act and that he had to play his part carefully so as to allow the Russians to save face.

"If true, this is most distressing," the Russian said.

"Yes, the facility in the report had been infiltrated by MI6 two years ago. I think they planned to use it as leverage against your country's own security services, but well, now we let you have the information freely as a matter of good faith. It would be unfortunate for the actions of one unsanctioned project to damage Russia's relations with the west.

"Yes, yes, thank you, General. But what would the price of your generosity be?"

"Well, Russia, it now seems, is in possession of several tonnes of Novichok agent, in contravention of several treaties. Her Majesty's Government is willing to accept that this was not known about by yourself or your president. And we feel we have an ideal way to help you dispose of this unwanted ordinance."

"I will, of course, have to talk to my president first, and we will need to confirm these claims ourselves." The Russian picked up the dossier and handed it to his aide.

"Of course," Marston said, leaning back in his chair.

"This is outrageous," Bradstone roared. He had been quietly seething whilst the exchange between Marston and his Russian counterpart had been occurring. Now he erupted. "The American Government will not stand for this."

"General Bradstone, before you continue," Marston said reaching back into his briefcase, "I have a dossier for you too." He handed the folder to the Frenchman next to him, who passed it on to the head of NATO. The American's face blanched.

10.11AM, 17th September 2015, MI6 Building, London, UK

Fabrice picked himself up off the floor. When the voice had struck, he had been lifted off his feet and flung at the wall. There was a dent where he had impacted, his body hardening instantly to protect himself. The fourth was powerful, more powerful than Fabrice would ever be, but still Fabrice felt the urge to keep pushing, to keep cajoling. Owen, that was his name, Owen Patterson. He came with an army of thousands, soon to be millions.

They were all different, and they were all the same. They all came, but they all resisted. They were all joined, but they were all individuals, pieces of a puzzle yet to be unveiled. Fabrice had no idea what their purpose was, but he had faith in his God that the purpose was righteous.

Fabrice stood. He was still naked, which did not concern him. The other infected in the room he had killed because the creature's incessant pounding at the room's observation window had become an annoyance. The thing's head lay in the corner in a small pool of blood, the mirror painted with the arterial spray from the carotid arteries that had both been severed when Fabrice had ripped the infected head clean from his body and flung it across the room. He had been surprised by his own strength, and yet his efforts to break out of this room were still in vain. Was that why he felt compelled to call the three to him, to free him from this prison?

His reflection met with his approval. His muscle definition was superb, an improved version of his former self, but he did not let pride in appearance infest him. Pride was a sin and not a worthy emotion for God's agent on Earth. He thanked God every day for giving him the second chance. In his youth, he had veered down the road of darkness. He had sinned, had been lustful and a fornicator. But Brother Abraham had saved him from that. Brother Abraham had shown him the light and the way.

In his former life, he had gone by another name: Genji. He had been a player, a seducer of women, and had become addicted to the Game, as people called it. And he was good, rarely going home alone. He was very good, but it had consumed him, corrupted him. It became an addiction that had almost swallowed his soul.

He remembered the night well, the night it all changed, the night he had been saved. That had been five years ago. Standing in the shadows of the nightclub, he had watched the pulsating, animalistic throng like a predator. He had already selected five possible candidates, and he waited to see who would be selected and who would be rejected, knowing that his scrutiny was going unobserved, because right then he had just been another nobody in a cathedral of vanity. Over by the entrance to the nightclub's VIP section, around fifteen women had been flaunting themselves as the four men were led by their security detail to the relative safety of exclusivity. The women had been there for one reason only—to try and go home with and bed a famous movie star. The objects of the ladies' obsessions clearly knew what the score had been, and they played up to it. This was a meat market, and the A-listers were happy to partake in the copious offerings, even though at least two of them had been, according to the tabloids, happily married. Celebrity had its advantages it had seemed, but Fabrice knew that celebrity was of no interest to him. Women, now that was a different matter. And with his skills and his handsome features, women had been his sport.

Fabrice had watched the women with something that was a combination of pity and contempt. Their attempts at drawing the attention of the movie stars were a mixture of animalistic displays and ritualistic submissiveness. A breast thrust here, a hair flick there. Had they no originality? They certainly had no elegance, and no understanding of true attraction technology. Why they felt the need to try and justify their existence in this manner, by bringing significance into their lives by blowing some third rate actor, had always made him chuckle, and he had watched, a half-smile on his lips as at least half the women were rejected. He remembered the squeal of delight as a blonde with an almost non-existent red dress was chosen, and the superstars with their newly acquainted groupies slipped behind the barrier of nightclub security into the forbidden zone. Inside that zone, almost anything would be allowed, and there wouldn't even be any CCTV surveillance to spy on the lines of coke and the sexual acts that would be fuelled by never-ending supplies of free alcohol. These women were there to be used, and there was no pretence here that anything else was going to happen. All Fabrice then had to do was swoop in and mop up what was left over.

Good, two of his likely prospects had been turned down, and he made his choice, a blonde with visibly toned abdominal muscles and large, virtually naked, natural breasts. She walked on high heels that were more like stilts, and her golden dress would most likely be returned to the shop tomorrow afternoon. Fabrice watched her carefully, spotting the insecurity that dwelled deep within her, seeing the little girl that was so desperate to be loved but who was cowed by a determined and almost masculine ego. For some men, she was a dream woman; for Fabrice, she was broken, prey that he could manipulate without even trying. Fabrice could almost read her entire life's history; he had seen her type hundreds of times before.

She made her way to an unoccupied seating area against one of the nightclubs many mirrored walls, trying to hide her disappointment behind a brittle confident exterior. She wasn't having much luck at that, and Fabrice already knew that she didn't stand a chance. She just didn't know it yet. He waited several seconds and then casually made his way over to her seating area. Placing his drink on one of the free tables, he slumped himself with one seat space between himself and the woman he was about to seduce.

She gave him the briefest of glances, dismissing him almost instantly. Reaching into her small bag, she extracted the mandatory lip gloss which she applied to her collagen-enhanced lips. Fabrice leaned forward to pick up his drink.

"That must be disappointing, not being picked like that," he said without looking at her.

"Excuse me," the blonde shot back. She gave him a look that said she considered him less worthy than something she might find stuck to her shoe.

"Well, they had all those women to choose from, but they didn't pick you, which is something I can't understand. I mean, these guys have good taste—look at who two of them are presently married to. It's obvious they didn't see you properly." Fabrice slouched back into his seat and turned his head towards her. "Perhaps you need to try something different next time."

"Oh really?" the blonde said dismissively.

"Yeah, you need to try something to make you stand out. I mean, you're beautiful and everything, but for guys like that, mere beauty isn't enough. In a place like this," Fabrice threw his arm out in an arc to indicate the nightclub interior, "beauty is very common."

"Whatever." The blond made to turn away from him, but looked back over her shoulder and noticed that he wasn't even looking at her. Why wasn't he looking at her? Everyone looked at her.

"The problem with places like this is there is no elegance," said Fabrice. He swirled his drink, leaned forward so that his elbows were on his knees and looked down at her left shoe. He then turned his head up slightly and looked straight into her eyes. She rocked back and gave a little gasp of surprise as the power of his green eyes hit her. "That's where you have the upper hand on those other women and you don't even realise it. Deep down, you have the elegance of a movie star." Fabrice looked up at the ceiling and gave a look of frustration. "If only the light in here was good enough to show it."

"Who are you?" the blonde asked, shaking her head in mock exasperation.

"Come on, admit it. Why else weren't you picked tonight?"

"I'll have you know I've slept with dozens of stars," the blonde said proudly.

"Oh, I'm not disputing that," Fabrice turned sideways towards her so that he could place his chin on a clenched fist, "but tonight you weren't picked when clearly you were the best that was on offer."

"You're damn right I'm the best," she said almost defensively. Fabrice stared at her intently, his eyes gazing around a triangle made from the tip of her nose and her pupils.

"The thing is, I don't think you actually believe that." Two women sat down next to him. Evidently not as attractive as the scantily clad blonde, he still turned in his seat to look at them. The blonde tapped him on the shoulder.

"Hey, what do you mean I don't believe it?" The two women looked over to see who was talking and Fabrice rolled his eyes in exasperation for their entertainment. He placed his drink down and turned back to her.

"You say you have slept with dozens of film stars, but here you are alone talking to a complete stranger. If you are honest with yourself, I think you want more than one night stands. You want what those others can't have."

"Hmph, you don't know me."

"Really? So if I was to say what you really want is not just to walk out of this place with one of them on your arm. What you want is to wake up in the morning with the knowledge that that man wishes to spend time with you, wishes to desire you and cherish you." Fabrice snapped his fingers in her face. "That's what you want. And without an understanding of elegance, you're not going to get that." She was about to say something, but Fabrice looked away and turned to the other two women. With his bright, handsome smile, he introduced himself to them. "Hello, ladies, my name's Fabrice." One, two, three, and a hand fell on his shoulder turning him around. He noticed that she had shimmied right up to him and was holding her free hand out for him to shake.

"Hi, I'm Susan," the blonde said. Fabrice smiled.

But the seduction hadn't happened because a thought had fallen upon him in that very moment. Sat there, he had suddenly realised the futility of it. It was as if he had awoken from a dream. Looking around, Fabrice had suddenly felt uncomfortable, the loud noises and the flashing lights almost painful to him. What had actually happened was the late nights, the excessive alcohol and the drugs had suddenly hit him like a freight train. He hadn't understood it at the time, but he had started to suffer a panic attack and had fled the nightclub into pouring rain, the blonde's confused face watching him flee. For about an hour, he had stumbled down the streets of London, and exhausted, he had even collapsed in an alley where he awoke the next morning. To this day, he didn't understand why the crushing sensation had overwhelmed him that night, not understanding the damage he had been doing to his body and his mind. Sitting there, shivering, Fabrice had not realised that his body had simply rebelled from the abuse it had suffered at his hands. And so he searched for a meaning, and he found it in the face that appeared to him out of the hazy mist of his own near insanity.

"Do you need help, brother?" the sweet voice had said, and he had looked up at the figure standing over him. In his most vulnerable moment, fate had put him in the path of one of Abraham's missionaries. He still believed he had been saved that day, not understanding that he had merely fallen into the grips of a powerful cult.

10.19AM, 17th September 2015, Headland Hotel, Newquay, UK

"You're allowed to take a break you know," the voice said. Jack turned his head and saw the immense figure of Bull watching him. Jack smiled in return.

"It's all right. We'll finish these off and then take a breather."

"Good lad," Bull said and walked off without another word.

"That man scares the shit out of me," Jack's temporary partner said. He was a middle-aged man who had been partnered with Jack to fill sandbags. Jack, being younger and fitter, did the shovelling, the older man holding the bags for him to fill, the sand coming from a huge pile that had been dumped in the hotel carpark. They had filled about half the bags they had been allocated, and even with the gloves he had been given, Jack's hands were sore and blistered. He'd done most of the shovelling, the other man not seemingly able to do more than a half dozen at a time.

"He's alright," Jack said defensively.

"I don't think he likes me very much."

"I wouldn't worry," Jack said, collecting a fresh shovel full. "I don't think he likes anyone who isn't in uniform."

Truth was, Jack didn't want a break. The work was mindless, which was just what he needed right now. He had slept surprisingly well, but had woken up feeling numb and empty. Yesterday, he had lost what family he had left and had fled across a dying city, fuelled by adrenaline and fear and grief. Now he was alone amongst strangers, and although he had been welcomed by the likes of Bull, this all still felt alien to him. He shovelled harder and faster, the image of his sister lying dead in his arms still threatening to haunt him. No, he wouldn't think about that, couldn't, and he ignored the pain of the blisters on his hands.

"You need me to shovel yet, Jack?" the man holding the bag asked.

"No."

Bull marched towards where the hotel's defences were being erected. The wood from a local lumber yard lay strewn in great piles across the grass, ready to be inserted deep into the ground to create a thick wall. It would be several layers thick, and was effectively two walls with a space in between, with ramparts and watch towers to allow fields of fire to create killing zones. Bull had been put in charge of it all. His was a supervisory role though. He knew nothing about building walls or digging ditches. He was just there to make sure the men under his command did what the civilian civil engineer told them to. All the civilians had been allocated jobs based on skill set. Those like Jack who had no special skill made up the labour work force. Those too ill or too frail, well, a decision had yet to be made about what to do with them.

The wall being made would block off access to the hotel and would extend along the edges of the cliffs all around the grounds. There was no telling the capability of the infected, so they couldn't take the risk of them climbing the cliffs and getting around the barrier that way. Once it was completed, this would be the headquarters for the general. Well, of course it would be; the man would have the entire top floor of the hotel for himself and the most senior officers. The likes of Bull, the ones who actually worked for a living, had to resort to tents and the rooms on the lower hotel floors. But as a military man, he didn't expect anything else. This was the way it had always been.

There had been civilian complaints, of course—civilians liked to complain. It was what they did best. But when the military took control of all the food supplies and began centralising provisions in defendable positions, the complaints soon stopped. It was either work and eat or complain and starve. Looters and horders were warned they would either be hung or shot on site. And to date, a half dozen had been. Shooting was quicker, but it also wasted precious ammunition. The refugees and the local population, all unarmed and with no combat experience—most of them also still in shock from what had occurred the day before—on the whole acquiesced to the situation. Because as oppressive as the military seemed, the infected were the much greater threat, and everyone knew they were coming.

That was one of Bull's other jobs of course, to stifle dissent. His hulking figure and gruff manner quickly silenced the grumbling voices where he had encountered them, and he made sure he seemed to be everywhere on site. Walking over to where the civil engineer stood, he stood silently next to him, watching the mechanical digger tear up the earth in its mission to build a trench to allow the erection of the wooden wall. The engineer noted his presence after a moment. The guy was old, but he seemed to know what he was doing.

"Do you need anything?" Bull said eventually.

"No, I'm good, Bull," the engineer said. Bull had taken an instant liking to the man. Straight talking, no nonsense, he had apparently stood his ground when some of the officers had presented their grandiose plans. The engineer had calmly and confidently told them they were talking bullshit.

"Good," Bull said. He reached into his army fatigues and took out a walkie-talkie. "These just arrived. If you need me, I'm on channel seven." The old man took it with a nod and clipped it to his belt. Then he moved away from Bull to shout orders at someone who was obviously doing something he wasn't supposed to be doing.

10.29AM, September 17th, Westminster, London, UK

His master had called him Satan. Being a dog, he didn't understand that this was because his master was a dick who liked to use Satan to intimidate those who didn't see things the way master saw them. After all, he was a big dog, an Alsatian, and he liked to bark and growl at those who his master became angry at.

But he loved his master, and his master looked after him. He was not neglected or beaten. In fact, his master showed him nothing but love, and for that, Satan showed utter devotion. That was until master had been attacked by another human. Satan had tried to warn him, had smelt them, could feel that they weren't right. Satan had become agitated, pulling on his leash, barking loudly, and then beginning to whimper.

"What's wrong, boy?" his master had asked. Satan liked it when he was called boy. It was his other name, but he had ignored his master and looked off into the bushes in the place with the trees where they were walking. He had barked again, warning that the danger was here, but it was too late. Something had leapt out from behind a tree and collided with his master. Satan had wanted to intervene, to help his master, but fear overtook him. This thing, this attacker it hadn't smelt right. And after Satan watched in horror as his master was bitten, that smell transferred quickly onto a human that had raised him from birth. His loyalty died with that bite, and, already free of his leash, Satan ran away from the dozens of monsters he now smelt.

That had been yesterday, and he cowered in the doorway, cold and hungry. There had been opportunities to eat, bins to forage through, but the monsters were all around, and it was only his speed that stopped them from getting to him. He saw other dogs, wanted to join with them, but most of them were smaller than he was and ran away from him. Others smelt bad, like the monsters, and he had fled several times from them. The smell of them was everywhere now, like a blanket across the city, and he found it blocked out the smell of man.

He heard a noise, and his ears pricked up. Infected were coming, their smell rising above the background odour as they drew closer. Satan bolted from the safety of the doorway, catching three of them in a fleeting glance. They chased him, even though he was faster, and he turned the corner only for him to run into another pack of them, not human this time, but a combination of household pets. The wind had fooled him, and Satan quickly found himself surrounded, by men and animals alike. He tried to flee, but their hands were quick, and the other dogs and cats descended on him. He was big and powerful, and he hit, bit, and ripped at the throng that attacked on him. But it made no difference; he was powerless to save himself, and within seconds, he lay bleeding on the floor. But they did not kill. No, they honoured him and let him join their ranks.

11.36AM, 17th September 2015, Defensive position 5, Cornwall, UK

Captain Grainger surveyed the kill zone that was being created and knew that it wouldn't be enough. Off in the distance, past the ever-expanding wall, bulldozers that were scavenged from the local villages did their best to flatten the land, pulling up trees and ripping apart hedgerows. Several buildings were also being demolished. Nothing was to be left that could give the infected any kind of cover. This was not his operation. He was merely in charge of defending what was being created, and he stood in the erected watchtower to see if there was any chance that this position would hold. Maybe if they had a week or two. But they didn't. They would be lucky if they had another day. At least the bulldozers were nearly done out there.

The Air Force were reportedly doing their best to slow down what would be an anticipated tidal wave of infected, but blowing a few bridges would do little to stem the inevitable flow. It would come down to bullets and bombs and shells, and he didn't think he had enough of any of them. They needed artillery and tanks in the numbers that were present in the Great War. If he'd had the ability to lay down a barrage as had occurred in the Somme or Verdun, it might have been different. But he just didn't have the numbers of the equipment he needed, much of the army's artillery abandoned. They had salvaged the nineteenth and some of the hundred and third regiments of the Royal Artillery, as well as the whole of the twenty-ninth Commando Royal Artillery, but that was nowhere near enough, not for a front that spanned almost thirty miles. So it would come down to men with guns at relatively close range. And up against what could well be a million-plus infected who were notoriously hard to kill. The tanks, of which there were twenty, would help, presently lined up along a ridge behind their position. They were invulnerable to the infected, as were the assorted armoured cars positioned along the wall. But they also had a weakness, because they relied on fuel, and that was something that would run out very quickly because there wasn't any more of it being made, not in the UK. And even if it was, refilling the fuel tanks meant stepping out amongst the hordes that would most likely be surrounding the metal islands of safety. With no refineries and a naval blockade, the only way for resupply was by airdrop, and that would be of limited scope considering the level of demand that would be needed.

He was a student of history, had studied in depth the engagements of both world wars, where battles could see a hundred thousand dead in a single day. They had to try and recreate that kind of firepower here, in this place, and he wasn't confident he could do it, not for a sustained period. At the Battle of the Somme alone, the British used almost fifteen hundred artillery pieces, and fired almost a quarter of a million shells in one single exchange. That was what was required here, and he didn't have anything close to it. He took a sip from the mug of tea he held, thankful for small mercies, and tried to picture where and how the viral hordes would attack. The noise below him broke him from his thoughts, and he turned to see Vorne climbing up through the hatch in the floor.

"What do you think, Vorne? Can we hold this position?" Vorne pulled himself to his feet, stepped over to the edge of the watchtower, and put his hands on the wood that had once been someone's front door. It was all makeshift, rushed. Some would say rickety. But it was the best they could do with what they had. The flooring beneath him seemed sturdy enough though.

"All depends on how many come at us at once and how much air support we can rely on." Vorne looked at him. "I don't think it will hold though, sir, because when they hit us, they will likely be hitting the other positions at the same time."

"That's what I think. So what do we do to change that?"

"I can't think of anything. Normally, I'm not very impressed with Wedges, but this officer seems to know what he's doing." The captain of the Royal Engineers had decided to take a leaf out of ancient, pre-gunpowder defences. There was the double wall he was overseeing, which surrounded the defensive position and also extended north and south. It was already half a mile long, slightly curved inwards to the west so as to try and suck any infected assault into one spot. On the outer aspect of the wall was a layer of sharp wooden spikes facing outwards towards the attackers, with a deep trench that was only now being constructed.

Everything was designed to slow down the enemy, to keep them away from the wall and allow the snipers and machine gunners in the towers to rain death on them. They had considered putting spikes in the base of the trench, but that would become ineffective quickly, so that idea was abandoned. Also abandoned was the idea to fill the trench with gasoline, because they just didn't have enough.

Besides, they didn't have the time or the manpower or the equipment to do anything fancy. They didn't even have enough razor wire for every position, and it would be pretty ineffective anyway—the infected would just throw themselves on it. So it was reserved for what it was effective against, controlling the human populations that were now refugees in their own country. It was put further out so those working on the wall could build and dig unhindered. That wire would become the outer barrier if the order ever came down to close the position to refugees.

"The good news is that the general has given us another hundred men. They'll be here in the hour. I'll give them to the Wedges, let them help build the walls."

"Soldiers?" Grainger asked.

"No. A mixture of police and civilians. Not many will have fired a gun I'm afraid, sir."

"Shit."

13.41PM 17th September 2015, MI6 Building, London, UK

Owen looked at the imposing building from across the river, his hands pressing into the rough stone of the river wall he leaned against. He could hear the shots that emanated from the building, the infected around him flinching every time one of their own was gunned down. He didn't know how many infected he had gathered to his side now, their numbers swelling massively on hitting the heart of the city. But they were all under his control, waiting for his orders. Very soon, he would be unstoppable.

The river was calm, almost tempting, and the only sound was the moaning and breathing of the infected. The sky above was cloudless, the sun bright, almost positioned exactly between the two towers on top of the MI6 Building. Another shot rained out, and he felt a wave of fury flow through him. The emotion wasn't his; it belonged to the infected, and he felt the urge to go with it, to let it swallow and consume him. But he resisted because he knew where that road might lead. He had to keep control. He couldn't let them overwhelm him. He was the general, Goddamnit, and the sooner they learnt that, the better it would be for everyone.

"I am here," Owen said in his mind.

"*Wait, another comes,*" the voice responded. Owen looked around at the naked bodies surrounding him. What other?

"What the fuck do you mean another is coming? You never told me anything about that. Who else is coming?"

"*Two is coming.*" Two, who the fuck was Two? "*I am One, you are Four. Together, we are whole.*" Owen was about to answer, knowing the futility of it due to the cryptic nature of this mind invader, but then he heard it. Firstly, the noise from the sky, and secondly, the agitation from his pets. Their combined consciousness knew what that noise represented, and for the first time, he felt fear ripple through them. It was the sound of a helicopter, death from the sky.

Owen ignored the fear but allowed his minions to scatter. Turning towards the noise, he watched as the black shape appeared from above the buildings and flew over the river. It grew smaller in size and slowed to hover over the MI6 Building, slowly descending, eventually disappearing out of sight. *Why the hell am I here anyway?* Owen

179

thought. Why had the voice brought him to this spot? And who the fuck was Two?

13.42PM, 17th September 2015, Defensive position 7, Cornwall, UK

Gavin looked at the watchtowers that had been erected, saw the men inside. There were three towers visible from the road, and all around he heard the sound of bulldozers. He was amazed how quickly this had all been constructed. There were people surrounding him now, squeezed into one road, an array of fences and barbed wire funnelling them into one entry point. And they moved slowly, too slowly for anybody's comfort.

YOU ARE NOW UNDER MILITARY QUARANTINE
MOVE FORWARD FOR EXAMINATION

FAILURE TO COMPLY WITH MILITARY ORDERS MAY BE
MET WITH
LETHAL FORCE

That was the fourth time he had seen the sign. Hand written in black paint on a white wooden board, it was stuck to a tree on the side of the road. This was exactly what he had hoped to avoid when he had spirited himself away on the farm. He didn't want to be amongst the sheep when the shepherd needed them herded. He had always known that the end of the world would come, but even he couldn't predict something that not even a survivalist could escape from. He had hoped to avoid the soldiers, avoid the bread lines and the refugees, avoid the camps and the forced medical examinations. But what was it they said about the best laid plans of men?

Nobody spoke to people they didn't know, although some children cried. People were scared, terrified. Some from what was behind them, others from what was in front. Most of them had seen the hanging corpses, victims of the harsh regime that was now in force. Occasionally, they saw the soldiers, their eyes sunk in from lack of sleep and from the horrors that some of them had undoubtedly seen. Nobody here had any fight in them. They would comply with what the military said because it was the only chance they had.

Up ahead, he saw the gates that were allowing people past the watchtowers and the wall. The wall was far from complete and was being constructed in the fields to the left and right of him behind a long, coiled line of razor wire. The wire clearly wasn't for the infected. It was to deter the living, and far up the ridge, he thought he saw a human form lying motionless in the entanglement.

His group shuffled forward, a broken entity, its single goal the safety of the military enclave. It had one purpose: to get on the other side of the wire. About seventy metres to go in all and Gavin would be through. He suspected there wouldn't be that much more following after him, not with the explosions he had heard hours before. The Air Force were clearly blowing the bridges, destroying anything that might slow down the infected when they finally arrived.

Gavin looked at the sky when he heard the noise, as most people did. They had been doing a lot of that lately. Every thirty minutes or so, a large transport helicopter would travel slowly across them, those travelling west dangling huge loads below their bellies. Much of it looked like wood, trees chopped down from the forests of Devon most likely. He suspected that was the only reason they were letting people in at all. They needed able-bodied people to help build the defences. But Gavin had seen what the virus could create. Would he really be any safer on the other side of this man-made obstacle? Was coming here perhaps the biggest mistake he had ever made?

13.43PM, 17th September 2015, MI6 Building, London, UK

Croft looked out of the helicopter window as it travelled the last few feet to the landing platform below. He had witnessed thousands of infected across the river from where he now landed, had seen them scatter as the helicopter flew over them. The fact that they showed the ability to undergo self-preservation was not reassuring to him. These things could act together in a coordinated fashion, and that would make them more difficult to defend against.

Outside the window, there was only one man stood at the edge of the big H, one member of the welcome party to celebrate Croft's arrival into the very centre of Hell. He exhaled deeply as the wheels finally touched down, his buffeted flight finally over. Would there be a helicopter there to extract him should the need arise? General Mansfield had been unable to guarantee that, because General Mansfield couldn't even guarantee there would be anyone left to fly the bloody helicopters a week from now.

"You don't like helicopters, do you?" Savage said, removing her headphones. The noise of the engine was already dying.

"No, I do not," Croft said. He dragged his gaze from the man he had been looking at and found her smiling at him. "What?"

"It's good to see you're human just like the rest of us." He removed his headset also. "But I suppose it's understandable considering."

"You read my file, I see."

"Of course I did," Savage said. She was about to say something else, but motion outside the window distracted her. "Who's that?" she said, pointing out at the rooftop and also changing the subject.

"I have no idea. Let's find out." With little effort, he opened the side door and was hit by a stench that triggered memories he didn't want to remember. The air smelt of burning, not a great surprise considering the fires he had witnessed on the journey over the city. They had flown directly over Parliament, which still smouldered but appeared no longer to be on fire. The iconic tower that held Big Ben no longer stood, the damage to it causing it to collapse into the Parliament building. Croft stepped out onto the roof of the MI6 Building and Savage followed shortly after.

The man who waited for them had a face of stone.

"Afternoon, Major Croft," the man said, and Croft shook his hand. "We've been expecting you, Captain," he said, acknowledging Savage's presence.

"Who are you?" Savage asked.

"Snow," the man said. Snow's handshake had been firm, functional.

"If you've been expecting me, then I'll need to speak to whoever's in charge," Croft ordered. The three of them began to walk off the landing platform towards a metal door. It opened before they reached it, and two men came out and walked past them heading towards the helicopter.

"But that would be you, Major," Snow said. He caught the door before it fully closed and held it open for the two new arrivals. Croft stopped and looked at the man.

"I'm in charge?"

"Yes, Major. I thought you would have been told. General Marston's orders."

"Bloody marvellous," Croft said, without a hint of enthusiasm in his voice.

Snow led them into the heart of the building. Three flights of stairs and several corridors later, they emerged into a large room that was bustling with activity. Multiple large TV screens covered the walls, most of them showing scenes from across London.

"The surveillance network is still up, but there's no telling how long that will be for," Snow said, leading them into the room. "When the power does eventually go out, our backup generators should give us a couple of months' worth of electricity." Croft noticed that people were looking at him.

"Might as well get this over with," he said under his breath to Savage and then walked into what could be described as the centre of the room. About two dozen pairs of eyes watched him.

"Can I have your attention please?" Croft said forcefully. He knew how to project himself—it came with the job. When you were employed to make the tough decisions, to decide when men and women were to live and when they were to die, you learnt to make yourself heard and have your commands followed through without question. "I am Major Croft." He used the title because it still carried weight and brought almost instant authority. "By order of the Chief of the Defence Staff and NATO, I am taking command of this facility. Anybody has a problem with that, let's hear it now." He looked around the room, met people's stares. Saw fear in some eyes, resentment in others. In some, he even saw hope. "This is Captain Savage, formerly the head of research at Porton Down. She will be taking command of any and all research into the infected you are presently doing here."

"Frankenstein won't like that," a voice said from the back of the room.

"What was that?" Croft demanded. He couldn't see the speaker since there was a light blinding him, so he moved. A short, portly man with glasses came into view.

"Frankenstein is what people call one of the scientists here," Snow said. He was standing behind Croft.

"Why do they call him Frankenstein?" Savage asked.

"What?"

"They just arrived." The young scientist looked at Durand and thought he was going to burst a blood vessel.

"But I'm in charge here," Durand roared.

"Well, technically you're not…" the man said.

"Who the fuck is this Savage anyway?" Durand ordered. The door to his office, which was ajar, opened fully, and Savage walked in followed by Croft and Snow.

"That would be me," Savage said with a bemused look on her face. She walked over to Durand and held out her hand. "I don't believe we've met." Durand did not shake, but just stared at her, seething. Savage shrugged and turned to the other man in the room. "And you are?"

"Phillip Mackay." He did shake her hand. "I hear you're from Porton Down."

"Yes, and now I'm here. Who's going to fill me in on what you've been doing here?"

"This is intolerable," Durand stated through gritted teeth. Savage turned back to him.

"Oh, how so?"

"This is my research, and I will not have some usurper steal it."

"Your research?" Savage was genuinely taken aback at the man's tone.

"Yes, these are my breakthroughs. And I'll not have you or anyone else take them from me."

"Doctor Durand is very protective of his work," Mackay said almost mockingly, which got a harsh stare from Durand. Savage looked at Croft, who stood with just the hint of a grin on his face. She turned back to Durand.

"Doctor, like it or not, you work for the greater good, the greater good being NATO. And they have put Major Croft here in charge of the whole facility, what with the country now under martial law. And Major Croft, in his wisdom, has put me in charge of all infected related research. That means I work for the major, and you work for me. If it's prestige you want, then I can assure you all recognition for any discoveries will be suitably recorded." The man still seethed. "Of course, I've yet to see any evidence that you've actually made any discoveries."

"No evidence? I've made immense strides into how this virus functions."

"Really?" Savage said, genuinely surprised. She turned to Croft who just shrugged his shoulders. This was her show, and he was enjoying watching her slowly dominate the man. Savage looked back at Durand and caught him with a glare that could melt ice. "Strange how nobody at NATO High Command seems to know about your great strides." Durand became flustered.

"I was just about to inform them," Durand said defensively.

"Perhaps you should show the good doctor and myself what you have achieved," Croft demanded. Durand's skeletal features locked onto him.

"And who the fuck asked you? Who the hell are you anyway? You just waltz in and take over the place. How the blazes does that even happen?" Durand spat. There were veins pulsing on the man's forehead. Croft had met people like this before. In fact, some of the worst disasters he had cleaned up after in his job for the Centre for Protection of National Infrastructure had been caused by people just like this.

"Me?" Croft pointed to himself. "As far as you're concerned, from now on, I'm God. And if you don't calm yourself the fuck down right now, I will personally drag you to the roof and let gravity do what gravity does best." Durand's face went pale. "I'm in charge because people on high say I'm in charge. Do we understand each other? Because I really don't have the time to be nicey nice with arrogant dicks like you." The scientist nodded, all the wind taken out of his sails.

Rasheed heard the helicopter before he saw it, and then he only saw it fleetingly, the buildings around him obscuring most of the sky. But it was heading in the same direction as he was, the call of the voice guiding him to the spot in the capital he probably hated more than any other.

During his journey to the centre of London, his mind had hardened to the events he had experienced. The strength he felt inside him and the power that grew with every moment made him feel like a God. Of course, he knew he was not a God, but suspected he had been saved from the demons by Allah the Merciful himself. And now the voice called him. It was clear to him that this was perhaps an angel speaking to him, showing him the way to true atonement.

And still Iblis tried to stop him. Moments earlier, the undead had appeared in the street before him, dozens of them. This was the largest number he had encountered so far, and he stopped in surprise in the middle of the street as their bulk turned towards him. The fast and lively ones kept out of his way, but these lumbering beasts didn't seem to know any better. They seemed to sway and move together, and shuffling, they moved towards him, some with arms outstretched, some without arms. Rasheed had learnt hours before that the undead were not a threat to him, not now.

Rasheed watched them, considering his options. His power had grown incredibly during his exodus across London. At first, using it had brought on headaches and nausea, but that had quickly passed as he perfected the power's use. His nose still bled occasionally, and he sometimes got an annoying ringing in his ears, but his body seemed to be acclimatising. He didn't really understand how it worked—he just knew it did, and who was he to question the will of Allah? Just as he didn't really understand how his brain moved his arms and legs, he just knew that putting his concentration towards something would usually have the desired effect.

He did that now, intent on removing this new threat. With just a thought, he had willed them gone, watching as their shambolic approach suddenly stopped. The bodies of the undead had begun to jerk, some began to shake, the limbs moving spasmodically, some of them losing their balance and falling to the floor. Rasheed had felt that all too familiar feeling, what could almost be described as heat form around him, and then zombies had exploded in a mist of drying blood and decaying matter. So violent was the explosion that most of the windows in the street had imploded, and a decapitated head had actually landed at his feet. Kicking it aside almost casually, he had walked past where they had once stood, his feet sucking on the gore that now decorated the road tarmac.

"I'm going to need some new shoes," he said to himself absently.

"*Come, you must come. You are Two, I am One.*"

"I'm coming."

If someone had put Rachel in an MRI scan, they would have seen a miracle. The dead brain was reforming, neurons and neural pathways long since dead resurrecting and re-knitting. Stood in the dark, her senses began to return, and the utter stench of the undead grew around her. It was a comforting smell, because it was the smell of who she was. And as the brain repaired itself, words formed, and with words came meaning.

"I am Three," she said to herself. "I am Three and I wait." The walking corpses around her stirred at her voice, but they did not attack, for they were bound to her, part of her. They were hers to command, and with her growing consciousness, she began to realise the potential of it all. Why was she here? Why had she been stripped of her oblivion only to be given thought and will again?

She barely remembered coming down here, barely remembered her life before being infected, before being killed and reborn. Those memories were just fragments, but the fragments grew with every passing moment. Rachel briefly had an image of a small girl, felt an emotion she couldn't describe, a feeling that clawed inside her, threatening to rip her apart, and then it was gone, and all that remained was confusion and the ever-growing hunger. Because that had never left her, and she could feel the desires of the undead, demanding sustenance. But no, she would resist and she would wait. She was Three, and she had no idea what that actually meant.

Savage looked through the window astonished at what she saw. Fabrice sat naked on the surgical table, his legs crossed in the lotus position and his eyes closed. It looked like he was meditating. The room itself was a complete wreck, one of the halogen lights dangling from the ceiling giving an irregular strobe effect.

"Who sanctioned this?" Savage asked. She held a folder that detailed what had been done to the man.

"Well, it was Dr. Durand who gave the order to expose him to the virus," Mackay said defensively. Durand was not with them. He had decided to stay and sulk in his office.

"And this was the man who started the London outbreak?" Croft asked.

"Yes," Snow said. "He was locked up in one of the detention cells in the basement. Basically left to rot."

"Why hasn't he turned?" Savage asked.

"We don't know," was the only answer Mackay could come up with.

"What's his name?" Croft asked.

"Fabrice," Mackay said. He moved past her and sat down at a console. Tapping the keyboard, he brought up a host of medical data. "He was infected yesterday, but so far hasn't turned as we would have expected. He has however shown…unique abilities."

"Such as?" That was Croft. He was close to the window now, his nose almost touching the hardened glass.

"Increased strength. Invulnerability to damage."

"Invulnerability?" Croft looked away from the room. "Can he be killed?"

"We don't know," was the only answer Mackay could give. "Before he ripped off the tabs registering his brain waves, we did get some wild readings." Savage leaned down to read the data that was now being displayed on the monitor Mackay sat in front of.

"But if he's immune…" Savage let the thought trail off. "Have you been able to get a blood sample?" Mackay looked at her, then turned his head around and looked at Snow.

"Show her the video," Snow ordered. Mackay opened a file in the computer's video viewer. She watched from start to finish. Everything was over in less than a minute.

"That's not good," said Croft.

The video was time stamped 11:32 AM. Croft and Savage watched as two men in hazmat suits entered the room, the secure door closing behind them. One man carried a taser, the other a revolver.

"Get on the ground with your hands behind your back," the man with the taser said, pointing it at Fabrice. In the video, Fabrice was standing facing the far wall, and at first, he ignored both men. He rested his head to the side, and seemed to be talking to himself. Taser gave him the order again, and Fabrice shooed them away absently.

"Come back later, I'm busy," Fabrice said. He sounded tired.

"Final warning," Revolver said. Fabrice sighed and turned around.

"You shouldn't have come in here," the naked man said and he walked forward two steps. Taser fired, the twin prongs of his device shooting forwards. But they didn't do as they were designed. Instead of embedding themselves into human flesh, they just bounced off and landed on the floor. Shocked, Taser threw his now useless weapon to the floor and pulled a revolver out of the holster on his waist. The two men backed up. "But now that you're here," Fabrice said, taking another stride forward. Revolver altered his aim and pointed at the man's leg. There was a loud report as he fired, hitting Fabrice square in the leg.

"Fuck," Fabrice said, staggering. He stopped to look down, but there was no blood, the skin dark grey where the bullet had struck. "That hurt." Revolver fired again, this time at the man's chest. Again, Fabrice staggered backwards by the impact, but it did no damage.

"Get out of there," a voice said over the intercom. Croft recognised it to be Snow's voice. The two hazmat-attired men backed up towards the door, and that was when Fabrice moved with almost lightning speed. He wasn't a blur, but he definitely moved faster than a human should be able. Three more shots were fired, and Croft watched as both men were quickly disarmed and incapacitated. Fabrice let one fall to the floor, the other, Taser, he held by the neck, lifting him off the ground. Taser barely struggled, having received a blow that left him close to unconsciousness, and he dangled there as Fabrice slowly squeezed his neck. There was a crack, and the body fell limp, dangling like a discarded rag doll. He flung it away, the corpse smashing into the mirrored window before slumping to the floor. Fabrice bent down to the other man, pulling off the hazmat hood.

"I told you to leave me alone. I'm busy." With that, he grabbed Revolver's head with both hands and began to squeeze. Revolver, who had started to recover from the punch that had laid him flat, began to scream as the contents of his skull were compressed. There was a sickening sound as the bone of the skull broke, and then the man was still. Fabrice let go and walked over to the window, where he ran his blood-soaked hand over the glass. The dried blood was still visible there.

"And that," a voice said behind Croft, "is why they call the good Doctor Durand Frankenstein."

"Who the hell is this Durand anyway?" Croft asked.

"Some scientist I was ordered to bring here. He wasn't important enough for Noah, but they wanted him all the same," Snow said. "As soon as he arrived, he started organising things, setting up research on the infected. With no real hierarchy here, people just kind of went along with him because he seemed to know what he was doing. We never gave him operational control over the facility, but he just seemed to assume he was in charge of anything scientific. None of the other scientists seemed to want to say otherwise."

"So who was in charge before I turned up?"

"Some guy you never heard of. Guy blew his brains out last night. Anyone with any kind of authority bugged out yesterday whilst they still could, leaving grunts like me to pick up the pieces."

Durand sat in his makeshift office and seethed. How dare they…how fucking dare they. Nobody talked to him like that, absolutely nobody. He was a genius, Goddamnit. He demanded respect, he'd earnt that respect. He had been dragged here, away from his laboratory and been asked to help research the disease, and he had done so, without complaint. He had quickly realised that he was the only one here with the intelligence to get this research done, the only one with the will and the guts to make the hard decisions that needed to be taken. He thought he was in charge, thought he was the one calling the shots. And they had lied to him in that regard, obviously mocking him. And now that he thought about it, he could see that they were all pretty much laughing at him behind his back. That much was clear now.

Of course, what Durand didn't realise was that he was delusional. He had come in and thought he had taken over in a power vacuum. There were a handful of scientists here at best, refugees from the surrounding city, and those who had turned up too late to be shipped abroad in Operation Noah. Most of those with a scientific grounding weren't even in the right field for this kind of work, a collection of consultants and MI6 employees who had either been in the building or close enough to claim it as refuge. Durand had been the only one with the skills and the knowledge to study the virus. Until now.

"Fuck," he screamed. Sat at his desk, he swept everything off it with his right arm, papers and assorted stationary flying halfway across the room. He was about to be replaced, replaced by someone in authority who knew her shit. After she had left the room to go on her inspection, he had searched the online database on his laptop, had search for Doctor Savage's name in PubMed and the more secretive government research database, and had found over twenty-five research articles. She had been busy, and some of her research, mostly in biological weapons research, was ground-breaking stuff. What was even worse was the majority of those articles weren't how to create the weapons of war, but how to defeat them. Great Britain no longer researched the production of biological weapons, but it excelled at trying to counter their effects. She was going to come in here, she was going to take over, and he would be reduced to nothing but a lackey. He hadn't spent the last thirty years stepping over people and worming his way up the scientific hierarchy for him to have his greatest opportunity taken from him by a fucking woman. He wasn't willing to accept this. No, not at all. Something had to be done, and it had to be done quickly.

13.57PM GMT, 17th September 2015, FBI headquarters, Washington DC, USA

"Surely, you're kidding me." Special Supervisory Agent Fiona Carter had been sat in the briefing for less than 10 minutes before she had to speak out. She couldn't contain her growing dismay any longer. She had to do something, had to say something. This wasn't right.

"I'm sorry, Agent..." the man talking looked at her with an exasperated expression.

"Special Supervisory Agent, actually. Carter. And I say again, you can't be serious."

"Oh, I'm very serious, Agent Carter," said Brian Hannigan. The infamous Brian Hannigan, Under Secretary for the National Protection and Programs Directorate. A big cheese at the Department of Homeland Security for short. Carter had seen him when he had entered, knew the kind of man he was almost instantly. A bully, probably a sociopath, rising through the ranks by stepping on the backs and the hands of others, never being the one to blame for anything, but always being there to take the credit. The fact he took obvious delight in treating her like an underling spoke volumes, and although it wasn't blatant, there was just a hint of derision in his voice to let her know he felt he shouldn't be having to speak to her. "This order has come from the president himself, and has been passed to Homeland Security and FEMA by executive order."

"But you are talking about the indefinite detention of thousands of people," Carter said. "People, who as far as we know, aren't guilty of anything." That grew a murmur of support from the other assembled agents.

"Aren't guilty?" Hannigan said, almost incredulous at what he was hearing. "Let me remind you, most of these individuals are on the TSA no-fly list. Even more are on NSA watch lists, their entire lives an open book of disloyalty and radicalisation. In this state of emergency, we can't let such people roam free; they have to be contained. And for your knowledge, it's not thousands, it's hundreds of thousands. As I've already said, this is a coordinated action across the whole country."

"Christ," someone said at the back of the room.

"But what you are asking us to do is unconstitutional," Carter countered. She was getting exasperated now, but she kept that hidden under a professional demeanour. Don't let him get to you, don't let him rile you. That's what he wants, that's what half the men in this room want. They want you, the Ice Maiden, to lose your cool, to let the mask slip. That's what she knew some of them called her, behind her back of course, never to her face. The Ice Maiden, because she was strong, blonde, attractive, and not averse to busting balls when her fellow agents' performances were below par. And she also knew that, despite this being an age of equality and diversity, the fact that she was also of Jewish descent meant a great deal to the fevered imaginings of the minority of agents who still lived in a world of bigotry and prejudice. And she wasn't just talking about the men.

"The US Attorney General doesn't agree with you, Agent Carter. Neither do the Joint Chiefs of Staff or the president. And nobody's asking you to do anything. Ordering, yes, but not asking. I'm merely here to tell you what part FEMA will be playing in the whole scheme of things. So if you have a problem, you need to take it up with the president. I'm sure he'll be delighted to take your phone call." He stared her down, waiting for more objections. She shook her head and indicated for him to continue. "Thank you. Now as I was saying, each of your teams will be allocated a detention list. You will be working in coordination with State Police, FEMA, and the National Guard. During the round ups, normal policing will be maintained by the various sheriffs' departments. We want these people detained within twenty-four hours. The hope is that we can get the bulk of them before we get any runners. This will be a coordinated response across the nation."

Carter held back as the room emptied, Hannigan being the first to leave with his entourage. She watched the people filing out, saw the unease in some of their faces, the obvious delight in others. This wasn't how it was supposed to go down; this wasn't why she entered law enforcement. She was here to put away the bad guys, not to help fill up FEMA camps with people whose only crime was being guilty of being critical of the present administration on their blogs. Still seated, she noticed that someone else was lingering in the room, and when said individual was the second to last person present, she closed the door to the conference room and closed the blinds.

"Is there anything we can do to stop this?" Carter asked her superior.

"No," came the response.

"Shit, I can't believe it's come to this."

"The threat is too great for the politicians not to use it for their own ends. We've been heading towards this for decades. I just never thought it would play out so soon." Carter's superior, Wynona Cooke—the Assistant Director of the FBI Counterterrorism Division—pulled up a chair in front of Carter and sat down. Where Carter was tall with shoulder length blonde hair, Cooke was a short, overweight African American, who possessed a presence and formidable mind that made her physical characteristics unimportant. Thirty years ago, it would have been almost unheard of for two women to hold such ranks in the FBI, but here they were, witnessing the possible destruction of everything they believed in.

"I don't know if I can do this," Carter said, shaking her head in disgust.

"You have to." Cooke put a reassuring hand on her subordinate's knee and gave it a motherly squeeze. "You have to because you have to make sure it's done right. Your agents in the field are going to be faced with resistance and violence. The wrong person in charge gets people killed."

"I could resign. You know I've been considering it for a while now."

"You won't resign. You'll suck it up like you always do and do your job. You'll see to it that the doors are knocked on rather than kicked in. You'll see to it that the people are taken away in handcuffs, not body bags." Cooke sat back and her face almost sparkled. "Besides, if you walked out, I'd have to give your job to Henderson."

"The guy's a jerk," Carter said. She could tell when she was being played, but she couldn't hold it against this woman. She had too much respect for her.

"You weren't saying that a year ago." Cooke winked. Carter smiled, probably the first smile all day.

"Oh, that's low." Her relationship with Henderson had been brief and a complete disaster. No doubt much of the office gossip about her still came from his once-seductive lips. Carter had almost transferred out, but Cooke had expressly forbidden it, had pointed out that if she did that, the creep won. Thank God they hadn't slept together. That would have been a nightmare.

14.12PM GMT, 17th September 2015, Wall Street, New York City, USA

"Sir, I've just been told the FBI are in the lobby. They are on their way up."

"The FBI?" Harold Winchester looked at his secretary. "What are the FBI doing here?"

"I don't know, sir."

"Get my lawyer on the phone." The secretary nodded and left his office, closing the door behind her. What the hell was this? Why would the FBI be here? He was the owner of a multibillion-dollar hedge fund; he had protection. He didn't partake in insider trading, did everything by the book. Hell, he didn't even have any unpaid parking tickets. His landline rang, and he picked it up.

"Putting you through now, sir." There was a brief pause.

"This is Eric Wolfowitz," a voice said at the other end of the phone.

"Eric, it's Harold Winchester."

"Great to hear from you, Eric. How's the wife?"

"Oh you know, the usual. Always complaining." The voice at the other end laughed briefly. "Listen Eric, I might have a problem here. The FBI are here."

"Any idea what for?"

"No, but they will be here any minute."

"Okay, well so long as you haven't done anything wrong, I don't see it being a problem for you." There was a noise outside, and Harold could hear his secretary talking to someone.

"Hold on, Eric." He put his hand over the phone to try and hear what was being said. The door to his office opened.

"Please stay seated, miss," he heard said from outside, and then two men walked in. They were dressed in suits. So this is what the FBI looked like.

"They are here now..." Harold started to say.

"Put the phone down please, sir," one of the agents said.

"It's my lawyer," Harold said almost defensively. The second agent, the one who had yet to speak, stepped into the room and up to his desk. Forcefully, he ripped the phone from Harold's grasp and put the receiver back in its cradle. That done, he withdrew identification from his inside pocket. Thrusting his FBI credentials into Harold's face, he looked the man up and down.

"Harold Winchester?" the agent asked.

"Yes," Harold said hesitantly.

"Harold Winchester, under orders handed down from the President, I hereby detain you for the protection of the Homeland. Please come with me."

"What is all this about?" Harold said, starting to stand. He reached behind him for his jacket, the first Agent quickly drawing his pistol.

"HANDS WHERE WE CAN SEE THEM!" the agent screamed. Harold froze, never before having experienced anything like this. He was worth over a billion dollars, people didn't treat him like this. He had powerful connections. The second agent moved around the desk, grabbed his arms, and roughly yanked them behind his back. There was a pause and then he felt metal being slapped onto his wrists.

"But what have I done? You can't do this!" He saw the first agent re-holster his weapon. The second agent pushed him slightly, manoeuvring him away from behind the desk. He didn't resist, he didn't know how to resist. Even if he did, he was in his fifties, overweight, and had a heart condition. He was no match for two armed and trained FBI agents.

"All your questions will be answered shortly."

"But where are you taking me?"

"That's none of your concern" said agent one. Harold didn't know it, but he was being detained for one very specific reason. His name had appeared at the top of a political shit list, someone who had donated heavily to the other party at the last election. The president, it seemed, was making the most of the situation. He was using this as an opportunity to start cleaning house.

14.23PM GMT, 17th September 2015, Bird Rock, San Diego, USA

He had woken early to the sound of a house sleeping. His wife and kids were off visiting her parents, and he was due to fly out to join them in a day or two. But first, he had business to conduct, a story to break. And what a story it was, full of political intrigue and Washington corruption. It might even make him a household name, but if he was honest, he wasn't really bothered about that.

Climbing out of bed, he stepped naked onto the balcony that overlooked the Pacific Ocean and sat down on one of the sun loungers. He had no worries about being seen; the balcony was not overlooked, and he had complete privacy except for God and the few dozen seagulls that soared above him. The day wasn't too hot, perfect for him, and he lay down and let the growing warmth of the sun leach into his skin.

Where he was, he didn't hear the cars out on the street at the front of his property. He didn't hear the car doors open, didn't hear the half a dozen men exit the vehicles and make their way to the front of his building. He didn't hear the modified bus pull up thirty seconds later, didn't hear the frightened sobs of some of those on board.

He heard the sound of his front door caving in though.

"What the fuck?" The sound was familiar, and yet completely alien, and he stepped up from where he was lying, walked back into his bedroom, and put his bathrobe on. Now there was a new noise, that of people moving around inside his house, and a whole host of scenarios played out in his head. Surely not? Surely, the corruption hadn't grown to that degree. Standing there, he saw the shadows through the open bedroom door and started to back up. A figure appeared in the door, clad in green, armed to the teeth, a gun suddenly being pointed at his chest.

"FBI, DOWN ON THE GROUND, DOWN ON THE GROUND."

Minutes later, still in his bathrobe, he found himself sat on the cold metal seat of the bus with a dozen other people, his hands cuffed to the railing on the seat in front. As the bus pulled out, he looked around at his fellow prisoners, saw the bewilderment and the fear in their eyes. Up front, three National Guard stood looking over their charges, holding their machine guns menacingly. So it had finally come, he thought to himself. Secretly, deep down, he always knew it would. But even if he had seen this day arriving with absolute clarity, he wouldn't have changed anything. How could he? The pursuit of the truth was who he was; it was his very essence. Hopefully, this was some kind of temporary internment. Even with the powers the Federal Government had suddenly enacted, he really didn't see this as anything more than a power play. How very wrong he was.

14.32PM GMT, 17th September 2015, Hilton Head, South Carolina, USA

"Under Presidential Executive Order, you are being detained on national security grounds." The man on the floor was still groggy from the shock and awe of the home invasion. The air was thick with smoke, and the relentless screaming of the three-month-old child sliced into his brain. This time, the Feds hadn't come in suits. They had come in combat gear, armed with Kevlar armour and machine guns.

Duke Lee, an Iraq war veteran and former Marine, tried to shake the stars out of his eyes. But the knee on his neck and the fact his arms were pinned behind him meant he could barely move.

"My daughter," he tried to say.

"Stop resisting," a voice screamed in his ear, and he felt something slap the back of his head.

"I'm not resis…" He failed to get the words out because a hood was slipped over his head. Blinded, he felt himself being lifted up, his hands zip-tied behind him. Hands slipped up under his armpits, and he was dragged out of his bedroom and through the internal geography of his single floor house. He wasn't fully without vision—the sack allowed some light to get in—and as they dragged him outside, the bright morning sun did its best to show him the serene outside. Through the tiny hole in the material, he could see the three black SUVs with their lights flashing. Across the street two doors down, one of his neighbours was also being forcibly removed from his home. In the distance, he heard his wife screaming, and he craned his neck, trying to look behind him.

"Julie?" he cried, only to feel someone punch him in the kidneys.

"I said stop resisting." With no other option, he tried to use his legs to help propel himself forward, better that than be completely manhandled. Nobody had yet told him what this was all about, and it would be another seven hours before the light of his infractions was revealed to him. During the day, he ran a very successful landscaping business, but at night, he ran an online blog that complained about the corruption in the Federal Government. With over a hundred thousand followers, he was deemed a subversive risk worthy of detention. He was ripped from the bosom of his family by soulless men all because he had chosen to write words on a website critical of the government. It truly was dangerous to be right when your government was wrong.

14.43PM, 17th September 2015, MI6 Building, London, UK

Rasheed had spotted the crowd of infected and had detected that somehow these were different from the ones he had encountered on his journey here. Despite his power, he was still cautious, and curiosity drove him to seek information. Why were they here, right where the voice had told him to come? And why was this, the place of hate and pain that so many of his kind had been oppressed by, why was the MI6 Building his ultimate destination? Why did the voice bring him here?

Accessing the side building had been child's play, the door ripping itself off the hinges with invisible force. Four storeys up, he looked out of the window at the river bank, observing the thousands of infected that milled and swayed there. On the periphery, he saw several dozen coming and going, like ants exploring the outside of the nest. And then he saw it, a figure different from the others, separated by space and thought. Rasheed could almost feel the man, because that was what he was. This was no infected.

"*Come to me,*" the voice said.

"I am here," Rasheed said in his mind, "but I need information." He stepped back from the window, stopping in the apartment's kitchen briefly to hunt for food.

"*Come to me,*" the voice demanded.

"Not until you tell me why I am here. Not until you tell me what is going on." Opening the fridge, he found some cheese slices and used them to load the bread that he found still fresh in the bread bin on the kitchen counter. How long would the bread out there in the stores, in the homes last? A week, probably less. He made several sandwiches and walked back into the living room, where he sat down on a rather plush leather sofa. Western decadence, he thought to himself, how it fed upon itself.

"*You must come,*" the voice almost pleaded.

"And I will, but not until you tell me everything."

"*You are Two.*"

"Yes, I know, you said. But you haven't told me what that means."

"*I am One, I lead the way.*"

"You lead shit, mate," Rasheed laughed mockingly. "You are a voice in my head, for all I know a figment of my imagination. Perhaps you are the devil, here to tempt this soldier of Allah. Perhaps you are an angel. Who's to say I am not presently insane, and this is all make believe?"

"*Not insane, you are Two...you are Conquest.*" Rasheed paused mid-bite. He hadn't expected that.

"And the man on the riverbank? Do you know who he is? Why don't the infected attack him?"

"*He is Four....he is War. The infected are his to control.*" Memory sparked in Rasheed's brain. This was bullshit, remnants of the heretic Crusaders tales. He had always been taught that Christianity was a death cult, and here was the proof. Revelations, the Four Horsemen of the Apocalypse. But to be wrapped up in this sick and twisted theatre, how could this possibly be?

"You brought me here for this, to show me lies." Rasheed screamed this in his mind. There was a pause.

"*No,*" the voice said. It sounded pained. "*I brought you here to free me and to help me destroy this symbol of our oppression.*" Rasheed, his temples pumping with anger, heard the only words that would have calmed him down. Finally, the truth. He breathed deeply, noticing a pain behind his right eye that had started abruptly. He felt dizziness arrive suddenly, but it was fleeting, and he quickly regained his sea legs. Something was wrong though, the pain intense and sharp. Dropping what was left of the sandwich, he brought his hand up to his eye. The pain reached a peak and then died away almost as quickly as it had started. Bringing his hand away, he found his vision blurred in that eye.

"*Now will you come?*" Rasheed ignored the voice. Instead, he rushed from the bathroom and nervously examined himself in the mirror. There was still vision from his right eye, but it was blurred, distorted, perhaps a fifth of what it had been just seconds ago. He was no doctor; he didn't understand the intricacies of the human body, didn't appreciate the toll his powers were having on it. He didn't know he had burst a vessel in his brain. But he knew that whatever had happened, the power had caused it, knew that it was his rage that had caused the damage.

"Tell me everything," he said to the voice.

"*No, not until you come,*" came the response.

Croft was back in the control room. He looked at the monitors, looked at the image from the embankment across the river. "Who can get me what I need with these images?" A be-speckled man spoke up from across the room.

"I can, sir," the man said rushing over to him. "What do you need?"

"Your name for starters."

"Oh yes, sorry. It's Peter."

"Peter, can we zoom in on that scene across the river? I saw that crowd from the helicopter as we came in."

"Yeah, sure," Peter said, walking over to one of the work stations. It was abandoned so he sat down at it and began typing. The camera image zoomed in. "They've been there a while, but as they haven't crossed the bridge, we've kind of ignored them."

"That man in the centre, zoom in on him." From this angle, it was hard to see, but Croft from the air had seen what looked like a buffer around the man. The man stood still, staring intently into the camera, or at least that was the way it seemed. Croft noted many things about the man, but the thing that stood out the most was he was the only one not naked. "Have you noticed that he is the only one wearing clothes?"

"Now that you mention it," Peter said. "What do you think it means?"

"I think it means he's not infected. Look at the way he doesn't move like the others. Look how the infected around him have their heads bowed." Croft turned around and surveyed the room. The lights flickered briefly, then again.

"Power brownouts, micro ones due to nobody controlling the power generation. The lights will go out soon, I reckon." Peter looked at the man he had given the useful information to, but didn't expect the response.

"Take me to the roof that overlooks that, and get your best sniper up there too."

Something didn't feel right. There was a new presence that felt oppressive and powerful, it's influence descending like an all-consuming smog. It wasn't the voice, of that Owen was certain. It held more power than that. The voice he could control, even threaten. But this…No, this was something else, and it was getting closer. It made him feel nervous, agitated, and he was surprised to feel his heart fluttering, the rhythm beating strongly in his chest and throat. His hands started sweating, and he reached down to the bag on the floor and extracted a fully loaded machine gun. Something was coming, and he was afraid.

He hated to feel afraid, and it was an emotion he was well-versed in. Most of his life had been lived in fear. The fear was not of the physical. Stepping up to someone toe to toe was exhilarating, empowering. Even when he lost, those fights never repeated because the opponent knew that Owen was crazy enough to risk everything. That was not the adversary your random street thug wanted to face. No, Owen's fears were more spiritual than that. Until recently, he feared himself, feared what he would become on the path he had chosen. And now he was there. This is what the little whisper inside him warned he would become, the last vestiges of civilized humanity stripped from him. There was no turning back from this, no repentance that could save him from the madness that now enveloped his soul. And so he thought the fear had finally died. But it hadn't, it just hid inside him waiting for the moment to seep out and reap its vengeance.

A minute later, and he felt the murmur in the minds of the infected, felt them recoil from something just out of his sight. Was it the undead, had they arrived drawn by the opportunity for a feast? He didn't know why the infected feared their deceased cousins so much. They were strong enough and quick enough to protect themselves against the undead threat, but time and again, he had seen that they didn't do this of their own accord. Owen often had to be the one to order such actions, and he could always feel the infected resisting somewhat, pushing back against his influence. But this felt different to that, and he saw movement at the very edge of his vision. He jumped over to a wall and climbed up to give himself a better vantage point, the infected scurrying away before him. There was a man walking through his army, the naked soldiers parting before him as if he was a spear slicing through flesh.

"What the fuck is this?" he said to himself.

Croft walked out into the cold afternoon air, Peter somewhat timidly behind him, a black holdall clutched in his nervous hands. Peter wasn't an operative; he was a technician. He sat behind a computer for fuck's sake. And yet Croft treated him with a respect that he had rarely encountered from men like him.

A third man stood looking out at the city, a man Croft had met before.

"So you're the best sniper?" Croft asked, genuinely surprised, walking over to the individual who cradled a rifle in his arms.

"Yep," Snow responded. "What are we after?"

"North embankment, one o'clock. There's someone in that crowd of infected." Snow nodded and moved over to the edge of the roof. There was a wall waist high, and he balanced the rifle end on it. Snow looked through the scope, trying to find the target. Croft stood next to him, a pair of binoculars now up to his eyes. They both watched as the crowd parted, a man running through them to jump up on a wall. He was looking north, away from where Croft and Snow now watched. Somewhere else on the roof, a shot went off, one of the infected down below obviously getting too close to breaching the perimeter.

"He's not infected, doesn't have the look of them," Snow said.

"Or maybe he is and he's like our friend down in the basement." Snow cocked his head away from the scope so he could see the bigger picture. "That means he might be difficult to kill."

"Only one way to find out." Croft detected something else and moved his vision slightly. "Hold it, something else. To your right slightly." Snow took the scope off the target and moved around. Within five seconds, he spotted the other thing out of place. Another clothed man, walking through the infected as if they weren't even there.

"Yep, another guest to the party. Hang on." Snow lifted a radio out of his pocket and spoke into it, still looking through the scope of his rifle. "Control," he said into the radio, "this is Snow. Zoom in on the crowd at the Riverside Gardens. Have Mother run the two clothed individuals through her database." Mother was the supercomputer deep in the heart of the MI6 Building with full access to every file and every piece of data known to Britain's intelligence services.

"You know them?" Croft asked.

"Not them, him. The second guy. He looks familiar. Can't tell for sure though, not at this range. Mother will know."

The supercomputer took the image presented to it and ran the biometrics the high-definition cameras were able to record. It pulled in data from the street cameras directly surrounding the infected gathering, making billions of calculations within seconds. It didn't take long, partly because the huge computer wasn't being asked to do anything else.

"Mother has a match on both of them," the voice over the radio said. "The Caucasian is a little shit known to police. Lives in Hounslow.

Name's Owen Patterson. Low-level crime, although suspected of various other nasties."

"And the other?" Snow prompted.

"That's interesting. Rasheed Khan. Suspected Jihadist. The Watchers have been keeping an eye on him. There were plans to bring him in today as it happens. Intelligence had clocked him as a potential threat."

"Thanks," Snow said, disconnecting the radio. "Thought that face looked familiar. Had a memo about him a few weeks back."

"Peter," Croft said turning to his new willing helper, "give me that directional microphone, will you?" Peter extracted it from the bag he was carrying.

Owen watched as the newcomer walked up to him, a grim look on the Asian man's face. Owen held up his gun menacingly.

"That's far enough," Owen ordered, pointing the gun at the man's central mass. His hands were still slick with sweat, and his heart still pounded in his chest, so much that he could almost hear it. But he wasn't afraid of this Paki, refused to be. "Who the fuck are you?"

"I am Two. And, apparently, you are Four." Croft listened to the conversation over the headphones he had donned. What the fuck was this?

"How the fuck did you know that?" he heard Owen say.

"You hear the voice too, don't you? The voice that told you to come here."

"Oh, I hear the cunt alright. And nobody, NOBODY tells me what to do," Owen shouted angrily. "I came here because I wanted to."

"Yes," said Rasheed, "that's what I tell myself as well. You have quite the fan club here."

"They're mine. This whole city's mine." Owen sounded petulant, like a child almost.

"You're welcome to it. I'm just here for what's in there, and according to One, you're going to help me get in."

"Snow, radio." Croft threw a hand out and waited for the man to fumble the radio to him. Croft hoisted it to his lips. "Control, this is Croft. I want every sniper available to take aim on the north embankment. And contact NATO, see if they can give us any kind of air support." Lowering the radio, he turned his head to the sniper next to him. "Snow, take the shot."

Rasheed took a confident step towards Owen, only for something to suddenly hit him with force in the lower abdomen. Falling to the floor, the shock of the assault hitting him almost as badly as the bullet had, he was surprised when the infected swarmed him, covering him with their bodies, but not smothering or attacking him. His initial reaction was to lash out, but he quickly sensed that they were protecting him, forming a shield. His vision a mass of naked flesh, he felt strong hands grip him and his body was pulled along the gravel and then over grass. Over the howling of the infected, he could just hear more gunshots off in the distance, and he witnessed several infected get hit, some falling to the ground, some seeming to shrug off the wounds inflicted on them. In seconds, he was dragged behind a wall next to a cowering Owen. When the first shot had fired, the infected had swamped their leader as well and dragged him to this spot also, using themselves as a human barrier. Now the two were protected by a concrete wall no sniper's bullet could ever penetrate.

"Fuck me that hurts," said Rasheed, holding his stomach.

"You're bleeding, man," Owen said. "They shot you!" Rasheed noted there wasn't a hint of concern in Owen's voice.

"Bastards." Rasheed looked at his stomach and pulled the jacket away to examine the wound. A red stain was forming on his beige T-shirt, and he felt moisture running down the back of his pants. His crotch was damp he also realised. But Rasheed had been told that this would likely happen if he was shot. There was no shame in it; pissing oneself was the body's natural reaction to such a violent assault. He pulled the T-shirt out of his trousers and lifted it away to see the wound directly. The hole was red and angry, and blood oozed out of it. Gut shot, probably through the intestines, possibly a kidney gone as well. Without a hospital, he was as good as dead, and a very painful death at that. Even with a hospital, it would be touch and go…unless.

"Shit," Snow said. He had hoped to get a second shot on target. He hadn't expected the infected to react like that. "The infected are protecting them. What the fuck?" He fired a few more rounds off anyway, killing and injuring about half a dozen infected in the process. Seconds later, more shots rang out from across the MI6 Building's rooftops, and across the river, the infected began to scatter, taking cover where they could find it.

"I've got a theory about that," said Croft. "I have a feeling it has something to do with Mr. Indestructible down below in our basement. I don't know what he is, but it's time I had a chat to our guest." Croft took the headphones for the directional microphone off and left the device where it was positioned. Giving the binoculars to Peter, he stalked off to the roof's exit door. "Let me know as soon as they come across the bridge," he said, and then disappeared from sight.

He took the lift straight down. Exiting on the required level, Croft stormed down the corridor, several MI6 personnel stopping to watch him go past, alarmed by the intensity of the man. Some didn't even know who he was, but nobody stopped him. He just seemed to belong. Within minutes, he entered the observation room that was attached to Fabrice's makeshift prison cell and isolation chamber. Only Mackay was in the room, and Croft ignored him, which the amiable scientist was somewhat taken aback by. Instead, he walked straight up to the mirror and activated the intercom.

"Chevalier, you are going to talk to me." Fabrice didn't respond. Croft was surprised to see the man lying on the floor, and he seemed to be groaning with pain. "What happened?" he said, asking Mackay.

"I don't know. One second, he was sat on the table, the next, he just collapsed off it. He's been down there like that for several minutes. I didn't even see him fall. I was monitoring something else."

"Play the video back," Croft demanded. "I want to see the moment he fell." Mackay nodded and moved over to another computer, his wheeled chair squeaking across the linoleum flooring. As before, Croft watched history recorded, watched the man who had infected millions suddenly jerk his body, falling backwards and toppling head first off the table. Just before he fell, Croft got Mackay to stop the tape. Right there, plain as daylight, the man's stomach had turned deep grey, almost black.

"Chevalier," he roared, slamming his hand on the intercom, "I said you are going to talk to me." He turned to Mackay. "He can hear me, right?"

"He should be able to, yes." That was when he heard it. Laughter. Fabrice sat up off the ground his face looking at the mirror behind which Croft stood. The man was shaking with laughter.

"Oh, you've done it now," Fabrice said softly. "Now you've really pissed him off."

"Mackay," Croft said, releasing his hand from the intercom, "go and find me Captain Savage and bring her here." Mackay paused briefly and then nodded, standing awkwardly before leaving the room like an uncoordinated teenager. Croft, still in possession of the radio he had borrowed off Snow, spoke into it.

"Control, this is Croft. Get agent Snow down to room P436 ASAP. And tell him to go to the armoury first and bring everything he can carry." He pressed the intercom again. "Pissed who off?" Fabrice picked himself up off the floor and walked over to the window.

"The man you just shot. He really didn't enjoy that."

"So maybe we go up there and shoot him again. He clearly doesn't have your invulnerability."

"No," Fabrice said, "no, he doesn't." The man put his hands on the glass and stared out blankly, not knowing where Croft was standing. "But you won't get the chance again, and his wound is already healing. Within minutes, he will unleash upon this building." Fabrice tapped the glass several times and stepped back. He pointed wildly through into where Croft stood. "And you won't be able to stop him. He is Two, and Hell is coming with him."

"So why here? Why now?" Croft asked.

"Well, that's simple, isn't it…he's come for me."

Mackay found Savage in her office. She didn't need telling twice to follow, and Mackay led the way, knowing that the captain was likely still unfamiliar with the building's layout. She kept up with him easily; if anything, he slowed her down. The man even had to stop once to use his asthma inhaler. It always amazed her when people with brilliant minds let the body itself fester, his chubby form mildly displeasing to her. Turning a corner, she was surprised to see Durand walking towards them. She found this particular individual unnerving. By the man's reaction, he was somewhat shocked by the encounter as well.

"Victor, you should come with us. You might want to see this," Mackay advised. Durand slowed, but made no intention to change direction.

"I have things to do," Durand said, irritation etched over his voice. He totally avoided making eye contact with Savage, and with his defiance stated, he marched past the two of them. Savage turned to watch the man pass.

"Guy's a real piece of work, isn't he?" Savage said as Durand disappeared around the corner they had just come from. There really was something very wrong with that man.

"You don't know the half of it," Mackay replied, a smirk growing quickly across his chubby face. Durand had assumed command of the scientists in the MI6 Building because there really hadn't been anyone to match him in experience or intellect. That had all changed when Savage had arrived, and Mackay was secretly pleased to witness the man's obvious discomfort. After all, Durand was an utter prick.

Cunt. Bitch. Durand fumed to himself fingering the implement in his pocket. He had been on his way to see her, to deal with her, but had been taken unawares by the encounter in the corridor. With two of them there and the very real possibility of other armed witnesses appearing out of the blue, he had abandoned his plan, at least for now. No doubt she would shortly be with that maniac Croft, the man who felt he had the right to intimidate people. I am the one who intimidates, thought Durand, and he knew that he would have to resort to Plan B. Only he didn't have a Plan B, Plan A being a spur of the moment sort of thing, brought on by rage and passion and just a light seasoning of insanity. During his various tenures in his rise through the scientific ranks, he had never really noticed that people didn't actually like him. Whilst it was not unusual for scientists to be a little eccentric, if not a little weird, Durand was more than that. People detected something about him, something dark that they couldn't quite put their finger on, and so they did what they could to keep a distance from him. He was generally polite, generally well-spoken and well-mannered, but it had been noted that if he could use you for his own ends, he wouldn't think twice. They saw in him something that he only admitted to himself rarely. Durand was a sociopath, but a disadvantaged one in that he didn't possess the charm that many of his kind learnt to use early in life. It was only his intelligence and his ruthlessness that got him to where he was today. What made matters worse is he hadn't slept since he'd arrived, and had done his usual trick of staving off the sandman's attentions with high doses of caffeine and the amphetamine pills that he had taken to consuming regularly. His brain buzzed with the chemical infusion, hampering his logical thinking even more.

And now his blood boiled. He fingered the syringe, the contents of which he had mixed himself. But it was unlikely to be enough now, so his mind raced, trying to find a plan, trying to create a way for him to salvage what was being taken from him. And walking down the corridor he saw his chance, the sign for the armoury almost lighting up like a beacon. Was Croft armed? Would it matter if the man was taken by surprise?

Rasheed concentrated, his eyes closed, a tense grimace etched across his face. It hurt, hurt even more than being shot, the heat from the wound almost unbearable. Owen watched, transfixed, the bullet hole undulating, pulsating. He thought he was the only one who had been granted the gift, but here was someone who also had powers. No, Rasheed couldn't control the infected, but they didn't attack him either. And moments ago, hadn't they just rushed to protect this interloper? And now here he was, a mortal wound being healed by fuck knows what power. Owen seethed. The infected were his, Goddamnit.

"That's some real X-men shit right there, you know that?" Rasheed didn't respond, the blood draining from his face. Within seconds, the hole sealed itself shut, and almost seemed to glow white hot as the tissues knitted themselves together. Rifle shots continued to echo across the river, and Owen felt the cries of a half dozen infected who were caught out in the open. Owen wondered what would happen if he ordered the infected to attack the newcomer. A little voice inside his head told him that this would be a very foolish decision to make.

Rasheed opened his eyes and looked at Owen, the intensity in the man's eyes seeping fear down Owen's spine. But there was weakness there, Owen saw it. Close up, it was obvious there was something wrong with the man, one of his eyes pale and probably sightless. Rasheed moved, grimacing with the discomfort that his body threw at him.

"You need to rest, man," Owen said in all seriousness.

"Rest is for the weak. I am a soldier of Allah, peace be upon him. I am the spear tip; I am the fire to burn the infidels from their fortress." Rasheed pulled himself up into a full sitting position. He still felt bad, probably worse than he did this morning, but he had purpose now, resolve, and climbing to his feet, he staggered briefly, a wave of dizziness flowing through him. Owen stood also, wary of the interloper, but fearful now of the man's obvious power. If he could heal a bullet wound like that, what else could he do?

"We need to kill this thing." Croft stared intently at the figure behind the glass. But how do you kill something that was invulnerable? How do you kill something that could take a bullet point-blank range and barely flinch? Croft knew it was only a matter of time before Fabrice found a way out of his temporary prison, and when that happened, all bets were off.

"Normally, I would disagree with you," Savage said, "but I fear you might be right. But how?"

"You're the doctor," Croft answered. "Blunt trauma and penetration weapons don't work. What else might kill it?" Croft realised he was dehumanising the creature, but had no problem with that. This man had killed millions, and if it had been up to Croft, he would have been executed instantly the moment he had given up any useful information. Had he known about the torments Davina had inflicted, Croft might even have raised a glass and a quiet bravo. But those details had yet to be revealed to him. He turned to see Savage studying the ceiling of the room Fabrice occupied.

"There might be a way," she said, pointing up through the glass. "This building is fitted with halon fire suppression units in some of the rooms, that room being one of them. If we can set it off, we might be able to asphyxiate him."

"And you think that will work?" Croft asked.

"Ask me once we've tried it."

Snow rushed down the corridor, three machine guns draped over his soldier, and several boxes of ammunition in hand. He didn't see Durand turn into the corridor behind him, didn't see the scientist skulk towards the room Snow had looted moments before. Snow still couldn't get his head round what had happened earlier. He had shot a man, shot him with a killer shot. If the shock of the impact didn't do the job, the blood loss and trauma would easily finish him off. But Snow hadn't wanted to wait for that, had wanted to put a second shot centre mass where he had originally intended. Truth was, his aim had been off, and the second shot hadn't presented because the bloody infected had formed themselves into an inhuman shield. Had he done enough to deal with the threat? And more importantly, why had his shot been off? He never missed like that. That was his first mistake of the day. The second was leaving the armoury door unlocked.

14.45PM GMT, 17th September 2015, Washington DC, USA

Robert stepped out of the Starbucks he visited virtually every day. He spent nearly two hundred dollars a month of his boss's money in this place, and the staff there no longer had to ask for his name. One of the baristas there was even overtly flirtatious with him, had even tried to snag his number a few times. He didn't have the heart to tell her he was gay, and instead let her have her little fantasy.

Turning the corner towards the Capitol building, he was surprised to see the junction ahead of him full of vehicles with blue-and-red flashing lights. The traffic was backed up, and he wondered if there had been an accident. As he drew closer, he saw that wire fences were being erected, and a lorry was offloading large grey concrete slabs. He had seen their like before, many years ago in the days following 9/11. They had appeared all around government buildings as a defence against explosive-laden cars driven by suicide bombers. What the fuck was going on?

The cars on the road beside him weren't moving at all, and horns blared in obvious frustration. This was precisely why he cycled to work; you had to be completely mad to drive in this city. The politicians of any importance didn't care of course, because they all had armoured motorcades to move them from important point A to important point B that scythed through traffic as if it wasn't there. Some of them even had helicopters, and of course, there was the underground network that senior staff were allowed to use. At least his boss, the congressman, didn't go in for any of that shit. A true man of the people, he did his best to keep the tax payer's bill for his employment as low as possible. But then, he wasn't one of the important elite, just a fringe Republican from a state with very little power.

Robert saw that a checkpoint had been created, that cars were only being allowed through after inspection. Even those on foot were having to wait in line, and he merged with a growing crowd, all waiting to get past the barricade to the street beyond. He reached into his inside pocket and removed the Congressional ID that hung on its lanyard, and gently pushed his way through the massed gathering. Nobody really resisted him, although there was the odd shout of "watch it, buddy". Stepping to the front of the group, he saw that even the pavement was blocked off, and that a metal detector had been erected surrounded by wire fencing. Three heavily armed soldiers stood menacingly, and he stepped forward to pass through. Seeing the ID he held, one of the soldiers beckoned him forward.

"I'm secretary to Congressman Richards. What's going on?" The soldier examined his ID, looking Robert in the eyes several times.

"Homeland Security were notified of a threat to the Capitol building," the soldier said. "We've been ordered to secure the area." Robert looked around at the barrier that was being constructed, the noise of a truck loud against the background hum of the city as it unloaded another concrete block. "Okay, you can pass," the soldier said.

"Thanks," Robert said letting his ID fall as the soldier let go of it. It swayed slightly on its lanyard, and a realisation came on Robert. Perhaps being a government employee wasn't just beneficial for the pension. He knew exactly what this represented…martial law.

14.47GMT, 17th September 2015, FBI Headquarters, Washington DC, USA

"Listen up, people." The murmuring in the room stopped and all heads turned to look at Fiona Carter who stood at the head of the table in the conference room. There were twelve agents gathered.

"As you know, the president has, under executive orders, enacted Operation Garden Plot due to the potential national emergency the crisis in the UK might cause. We have been tasked with detaining the people outlined in your dossiers." Everyone was now sat down, and most of them opened the folders in front of them. There were some gasps of surprise and one muted exclamation.

"There's two congressmen here," one of the agents said.

"Everyone in the dossier has been flagged by Homeland Security as either a terrorist sympathiser or a potential subversive. And some of the names are surprising to me too."

"But I voted for this one," another agent said, pulling a photograph out of her folder.

"It's not our job to determine guilt," Carter said. She hated this, she hated how easy it was to ruin a Democracy. "It's our job to take these people in peacefully and without incident because every one of the people you are reading about is either rich, connected or, even worse, both." The agents looked at each other, most of them wary, some still shocked by what had happened earlier. One of their fellow agents had been sat at his desk, only to have his badge and his gun stripped from him by three Internal Affairs agents. The man, with a dazed and confused look on his face, had been taken away in handcuffs.

"Look, I'll be honest here," Carter said. "I don't like this. I suspect many of you here feel the same way. But we have our orders, and we need to follow through on those orders. Because this needs to be done right and by the numbers. Because if we don't do it, somebody else will, and they will probably fuck it up." That got nods of approval. "You have all been assigned your targets, so come on, people, let's get this done."

14.52PM, 17th September 2015, MI6 Building, London, UK

Fabrice looked up at the ceiling as the gas began to escape. There was no odour to it, but he saw the threat that it represented.

"*You must hurry,*" he said in his mind. "*They are trying to kill me.*" The gas quickly reached him, and he inhaled, feeling light-headed almost instantly. He felt his throat tighten, and black spots appeared before his eyes. For a moment, he felt himself slipping away, and part of him begged for the oblivion, the chance to be finally free of it all. But it was a small part, a weakness inside him that he cast aside and ignored for the imperfection it truly was. There was no place in him now for such doubt, he was better than that. He was the chosen one, for he had been moulded by God, and it was for God to decide if and when his life was to end. It was not up to the agents of Satan that kept him contained in this makeshift jail.

There was no point trying to hold his breath. This would either kill him or it wouldn't, and there was only one way to truly find out. Would God have given him this power only to allow it to be taken from him so easily? Would God's messenger be so vulnerable that he could not survive the removal of mere oxygen? Fabrice inhaled again, deeper this time, his vision now swimming, the world around him distorting and fading. But he didn't collapse, and he remained on his feet, a sick, satisfied grin forming on his lips as it became clear that the gas wouldn't be the end of him. The room now filled with its haze, and his visibility was reduced significantly. But he did not die. Quickly, the light-headedness passed away and clarity returned. The room around him stopped moving, and he no longer felt the need to steady himself. By all that was holy, he didn't even need oxygen, the virus somehow sustaining him against another threat that would kill a normal human being.

"Nice try, fuckers," Fabrice roared and launched himself at where he remembered the glass to be. The impact was loud, his hands slamming onto its reflective surface. The glass shook but didn't come any closer to breaking than in his original attempts. "You want me? Why don't you come in here and take me?"

Durand looked at the cold gun in his hand. He had never fired a pistol in his life, but how hard could it be? If the meatheads roaming the corridors of this facility could do it, then surely he could fathom out its intricacies. After several minutes of experimentation, he found out how to load a magazine clip into the gun, figured out how to load a bullet into the chamber. Looking at the side of the gun, he moved the switch from S to F. Durand held the gun, felt the weight and pointed it at the far wall of the armoury. One hand or two? Two would be more accurate surely, and he practiced doing just that. And he didn't even need to be that good a shot, because he intended to get close in. He wanted to be able to look them in the eyes when he pulled the trigger, to really make them feel the reason why he needed to kill them. How many would he need to kill? And would the element of surprise be enough to counter the training of the men he was up against? Of course it would. After all, he had a Ph.D. Genius always won out.

Durand contemplated firing a shot just to check, but he was worried that the noise would alert someone, give away the plan he had formulated in his diseased mind. Would the noise be loud enough to echo down the corridors to where Croft now stood? Would armed men come running to see what the noise was about? The answer to that fear was suddenly thrust upon him as he was encased in a bubble of terror. The floor underneath shifted slightly, and the whole world around him was swallowed up in the sound of grinding brick and tearing metal. Durand staggered slightly, the floor moving again, and he almost fell. Not being trained in firearms, he wasn't familiar with the most important rule. Only put your finger on the trigger when you intend to shoot. The resultant mistaken shot rang out, smacking his eardrums. He cringed, the gun jerking in his hand. He half-expected the bullet to ricochet around the room, but it didn't happen. As the ground stopped moving, Durand looked at the gun once more, satisfied that it now worked. He could do this; he could take back what was his. Making his way to the exit, Durand walked out into the corridor as another tremor hit the building. The roof of the armoury cracked, a fissure forming across it, and Durand rushed out into the corridor, suddenly afraid that the building would fall in on his head and ruin his chance for revenge.

Nothing happened at first. Staying out of sight in such a way that he could still watch the despised structure, Rasheed concentrated on what he wanted to do. Deep within him laid the desire to bring the whole edifice down on their unworthy, godless heads, but that might mean trapping One inside. And despite his better judgement, he felt he needed One to survive. No, he needed to be more careful than that, needed to bring down the outer perimeter walls and breach the defences, and at the same time, shatter the cell that contained the voice.

He concentrated harder, almost unaware that blood began to pour from his left nostril and his left ear. Owen saw it, saw the veins begin to stand out on the man's temples, saw the throbbing of the blood as the heart began to pump it harder around the body. The man's neck pulsed, his lips pulled back against the teeth in a deformed grimace. What Owen didn't see was the damage being done inside Rasheed, didn't see the tearing of the blood vessels, the overloading of the nerves. The power was growing, but the body was having difficulty adapting, unable to contain it as it grew. But still Rasheed persisted, ignoring the pain that now seared into his temples.

Very briefly the building across the river seemed to shift, only slightly. Then it shifted again, and the sounds of the building's foundations being put under strain hit them. Owen watched in wonder as one of the towers at the top of the building cracked away and fell into the structure beneath it, toppling down the front of the building's facade. The noise grew louder, and Owen was suddenly surprised to see Rasheed looking at him.

"Ready them," the Arab said, almost gasping for breath, his face bright red. Owen nodded and in his thoughts, he willed his infected forwards towards the bridge. He pictured them in their thousands storming forwards, scaling the walls, finding entrance through the holes and the breaches that were now being ripped into the MI6 Building by the psychic force. Owen, of course, would stay out here, where it was safe.

In their thousands, they charged. Emerging from behind walls and from within buildings, they now ignored the sniper's bullets, which were greatly diminished. In vast numbers, they coalesced into one huge entity and surged across the bridge that led to the other side of the Thames and their destination, the home of MI6. Some ignored the bridge and chose to swim the mighty river.

And they were angry. They had been controlled for too long, manipulated and abused by a mind they were powerless to ignore, but which they despised. Even when the mind allowed them to feed, they still felt the hatred for him, because he was mocking them, playing with them. But they could do nothing to resist the mind, so they vented their anger at the only thing they could: the humans in the building they now attacked. Dozens of them fell crossing the bridge, bullets ripping out and destroying vital organs. Some were killed outright, others resurrected and tried to attack the mass of infected, only to be overwhelmed by sheer weight of numbers. And then the steamroller hit the front of the building and forced its way through the fractures in the defensive perimeter. The infected were in. The supposedly impenetrable fortress had held out less than a day and a half.

The reinforced safety glass cracked due to the telekinetic assault. Snow saw it happen just as he entered and knew that it was now inevitable for the window to fail completely. Putting the ammunition cases on the table to the side, he dragged the guns off his shoulder and handed one each to Croft and Savage. Croft was surprised to see he had also acquired himself an LASM unguided rocket launcher. MacKay was not surprised that he didn't get a weapon. The three professionals loaded their guns as another tremor undulated through the floor beneath them, dust falling from the ceiling. One of the halogen bulbs above exploded, and MacKay was the only one who shouted in surprise.

"Time to go," Snow said to Croft.

"Is he causing this?" Savage demanded, pointing at the man who was now battering the inside of the glass with his fists.

"Kill you, I'm going to kill you all," Fabrice roared over the intercom.

"It doesn't matter," said Croft, ignoring the mass murderer. "Snow, how do we get out of here?" The situation had changed rapidly, and there really was only one viable option now left open to them.

"Easiest way is through the escape tunnels. There is one on this level that takes us under the river and from there we can take a boat. I just hope the whole building doesn't come down on us before we get to them." The building shook again, a second crack forming in what had been an impenetrable glass barrier. The monster inside abandoned his fists and started head butting the window at that spot.

"Free, let me free," Fabrice roared. Croft looked at Mackay.

"Can you shut him up?" MacKay seemed to jump out of a daze, and smacked some keys on the keyboard next to him. The voice of Fabrice was cut off. "Thanks," Croft said.

Durand had fallen twice, his thin frame and lack of athleticism no match for what was happening. The first time he had fallen due to the shaking under his feet, the second time due to a large piece of masonry hitting his shoulder as it fell from the damaged ceiling. It was a glancing blow, but Durand wasn't used to such assaults. He lay for a minute, stunned, clutching his shoulder that throbbed painfully. He didn't think anything was broken, and he pulled himself painfully to his feet.

"Attention, this is Croft," the voice boomed out over the tannoy system. "This facility is under attack by forces unknown. I am authorising evacuation. Avoid the streets wherever possible and head to your designated river escape routes. Good look, people."

"No, no, no, no," Durand muttered to himself. He couldn't let the bastard get away, couldn't let his moment to shine be extinguished. Someone ran up behind him and past him, and in frustration, Durand let off a shot, the bullet taking the woman in the small of the back. She fell with a scream, writhing on the floor, the blood spreading out beneath her. Durand stood open-mouthed for several seconds, amazed at what he had just done. There was no remorse, far from it. He was suddenly filled with a feeling of immense power, the pain in his shoulder almost forgotten. Stepping forward, he put another round into the woman, who he didn't even know. She stopped moving, and Durand stepped over the now dead body with no more concern than if he was stepping over a puddle. And in a sense, he was—only the puddle was made from blood rather than rain water.

He turned another corner and, briefly disorientated, he recognised the way he needed to go. If Croft had ordered the evacuation, that meant he too would be leaving, and that meant they were getting away. No, that couldn't be allowed to happen. He rushed back towards the experiment room, his mind now raging, heart beating almost into his throat. Through laboured breathing, he went in pursuit, his lungs starting to protest the unacceptable level of activity that was being asked of them.

Fabrice heard the shots. Were the infected here already? It didn't matter; he knew he would soon be out, free from this purgatory. Part of the ceiling collapsed in the room behind him, and Fabrice hit the window again where it had cracked. The crack grew, and spider web fractures spread outwards. Yes. He hit it again, and again, ignoring the pain in his hands and his forehead, knowing he was inflicting no damage upon himself. The Lord truly provided. But even saying that, he knew something wasn't right. He ignored the fuzziness in his head that had started to form, a feeling as if a mist was descending across his consciousness. He had to get out, and he slammed the window again. The glass finally gave way, a great chunk of it falling to the ground. Punching at the edges of the hole, he made his access bigger, until eventually, he knew he was able to escape.

Climbing through the window, he entered an empty room. Looking around briefly, he saw that this was where his tormentors had monitored and watched him. This was where they had plotted against him, where they had laughed and watched him perform for them. Well, no more, and Fabrice stalked out into the corridor outside. Ten metres to both sides, the corridor extended, and he saw someone disappear around a corner to his left. He turned to follow, eager to relish in his newfound freedom. He would subdue them and visit God's judgement upon them. But what then? Then he would free himself from this building and be with the others. Then he knew God would reveal.

Croft and those with him found themselves in a long corridor.

"It's this way," said Snow, and they ran after him, clouds of dust and debris falling from the tortured ceiling. Towards the end of the passageway, the foundations and walls vibrating and rocking around them, a voice cried out.

"Heathens." They all stopped and saw the naked form of Fabrice marching after them. A piece of concrete the size of a small suitcase cracked from the ceiling and smashed into the mutated man's head. He hardly even staggered, and kept coming towards them. Snow raised his weapon, but Croft put out an arm to make the man lower it. Bullets wouldn't do any good here.

"So you got out," Croft said. Fabrice slowed as he drew towards them.

"You would have left me in there to die."

"Of course," Croft said, "you are a threat. What do you expect when you kill millions of people? A knighthood and tea with the queen?"

"I did what my God commanded." Croft stepped towards the man, briefly turning to Snow and mouthing the word GO. Snow nodded and ushered Mackay and Savage to the end of the corridor. Fabrice ignored them, concentrating instead on Croft whose voice he recognised.

"You see, that's the thing I don't understand. If your God is so powerful, why does he need you to do his dirty work?"

"It is an act of faith, a test of my devotion." Fabrice stopped walking, ten metres away from Croft. He noticed that the three people with the man he was speaking to were already fleeing the scene, but he cared not.

"So the creator of the universe, the all-powerful and all-knowing needs people to bow down to him? I'm not buying it."

"I am not here to convert you to my cause," Fabrice said mockingly.

"Then what are you here for?"

"To bring down this corrupt society. To show the world how pitiful humanity really is."

"Well, I think you've probably succeeded in that." The corridor shook again, half the lights shorting out. Emergency lighting kicked in. "One question though."

"What?" Fabrice took two steps towards Croft, Croft stepping back in turn.

"As strong as you are, can you survive this whole building falling down on you?" Croft turned and ran. He saw Snow appear from around the bend, the rocket launcher coming up. Croft didn't look behind him, saw the flash as the launcher fired, felt the heat as the projectile soared past him. Am I far enough away?

15.02PM, 17th September, Newquay Hospital, Newquay, UK

A year ago, the whole hospital had spent a large sum of money to try and combat the ever-growing threat of antibiotic-resistant bacteria. The review by the hospital administrators had determined that hand-washing protocols and posters were not enough, because people were people, and some people, even medical staff, just did not wash their hands every time they needed to. And because of this, patients and visitors risked getting infections that could kill them, and that wasn't very good in the eyes of managers who weren't too chuffed about fending off the media, the lawyers, and the omnipotent Care Quality Commission. All because people were too ignorant and too bone idle to wash their bloody hands after having a shit.

Fortunately, technology helped combat this. New breakthroughs in nanotechnology had created a chemical that could be coated onto almost anything, a coating that killed most of the viruses and bacteria that threatened to swamp the medical profession in an age of growing antibiotic resistance. All the door handles, taps, and toilet flushes had been replaced with coated versions, which was why when Gavin opened the door to the lavatory, the virus expressing on his skin surface died instantly. It was why the virus didn't survive on the toilet handle when he flushed, or on the taps when he washed his hand.

Leaving the lavatory, he walked back through the crowded hospital corridor to the even more crowded reception area. There were no free chairs, so he stood with his good arm against the wall, rucksack on the floor, and waited for his name to be called, having already registered over two hours ago. It hadn't infected the X-ray machine when the radiograph of his arm had been taken, because the technician had followed good cross-infection protocols and had wiped down everything his patient had touched with chemical death. The virus didn't even penetrate his clothing to attach itself to the wall's surface, nor was it airborne, and he stood there completely oblivious to the fact that he was a walking Typhoid Mary with the power to wipe out humanity.

Truth be told, the virus had missed multiple opportunities to infect others. With only one good arm, Gavin had not helped up the old lady who had fallen in the road, and had actively stayed away from people in the crowds for fear of bumping his injury. On arrival at the refugee zone, the fact that his arm was in a sling had meant the soldier had filled out the registration form for him. The cup of tea he had been handed had been in a disposable cup which he had thrown into the trash, and being shy by nature, he had avoided starting any kind of conversation with anyone, the traumatic twists and turns his life had taken still causing his head to reel with the enormity of it all. Truth be told, he simply hadn't touched anything that could pass the virus on. But, of course, that was all going to change.

He was surprised moments later when he had heard his name called. He didn't know that having a potentially broken arm had moved him up the triage queue, past the sprained ankles, the lacerations and the blisters that most of those forced to march for their lives had presented with. The comfy Western lifestyle had made the majority unable to deal with the harsh realities of life after civilisation, and hundreds had died on the flight to Cornwall. Only the serious cases were bussed up to the small hospital, which would within days become the largest remaining medical facility in the country. As luck would have it for those on board, he hadn't even touched anything in the bus's interior that anyone else had touched, and had acquired a seat with no handrail to grab onto.

"Gavin Hemsworth!" Gavin looked over to where the voice had come from and saw the nurse who had spoken.

"That's me," he said, raising his one good arm. He quickly picked up his pack and wormed his way through the crowded room, spotting angry stares that he was getting seen before other worthier causes. He suspected that if it was not for the several machine gun-toting police officers in the room, the atmosphere would have been a lot more unpleasant, even violent. People had not yet realised that their sense of entitlement had actually died along with their country, and they mumbled under their combined breaths about how long it was all taking, how incompetent the medical staff were, and how they could obviously run things better if given the chance. Fortunately, the armed presence that controlled this small corner of England was very noticeable, and it negated the threat posed by tired, scared, and confused people who, only a day ago, were traumatised when they couldn't get a decent signal on their phones. He reached the nurse, who smiled tiredly.

"Follow me please." She turned and he fell in step behind her, through some double doors which he again didn't touch, and deposited him in a small curtained cubicle. "The doctor will be with you shortly," she said and then disappeared, closing the curtain behind her. Shortly turned out to be fifteen minutes, by which time Gavin was lying back on the bed with his eyes closed, the virus eager to infect whatever came near it. He was exhausted and was close to sleep, but he stirred as he heard someone enter.

"Hi, I'm Doctor Holden," the doctor said. She carried an A4 folder, and extracted from it an X-ray of his arm. He had had it taken when he had first arrived. "So the bad news," she said, sitting down next to his bed, "is you have a fracture. The good news it's incomplete, which means all you need is a cast and time for it to heal." She held up the X-ray for him to see and pointed at a particular spot. "If you look here, you can just see the break in the ulna bone, which is that one there. I assume you did this in a fall?" Gavin looked blankly at the X-ray, not seeing a damned thing.

"Yes," he said, "a fall." Gavin looked around the cubicle, then back at the doctor. "How long will I be in a cast?"

"Well, if any of us are still alive by then, six weeks." She noticed the look of shock on his face and realised the inappropriateness of what she had just said. Time to take a break, she thought. "Sorry, shouldn't have said that."

"That's okay, we've all been through a lot." Gavin reached out his good hand and Holden shook it. For the first time all day, she touched a patient without wearing gloves.

Stan stood in the hospital waiting area, watching over the throng of damaged humanity. They were traumatised people, many of them close to their breaking point, and the waiting was making several of them potentially dangerous. So he stood there, the imposing presence that he was, making eye contact with those he suspected were the most likely to snap. He made them know by his facial expressions that he was not going to have any bullshit on his watch. And if that meant subtly pointing the barrel of his fully loaded machine gun at them occasionally, then so be it. They would behave on his watch, because he was too tired and too past caring to have to deal with anybody's shit.

He caught the eye of one of his fellow officers, a man he didn't know well, and pointed to one of the side doors. Making a drinking gesture with his right hand, he waited for the other officer to nod his consent, and he wormed his way around the side of the seated masses, entering the restricted part of the hospital. He was dehydrated and was absolutely gasping for a cup of tea. Ten steps and one more door, and he was in the hospital's staff canteen, which was a small cramped affair in a room with no windows. Opening the door with a gloved hand, he found Holden in there, already pouring boiled water into a cup. The virus on the door handle had already withered.

"Make that two, eh, Doc?" Stan said.

"Hi, Stan," she said, smiling as he entered. Holden picked up another cup from the counter she stood against and plucked a tea bag out of a box at the side of the kettle. A minute quantity of skin oil and sweat transferred to the surface of the tea bag, but the virus thriving within it quickly died when she picked up the kettle and poured hot, liquid death onto it. The pathogen was not able to exist in such extremes of temperature, but without the heat, it could survive several minutes outside the host body. Waiting, just waiting. Everything Holden had touched in this room was now contaminated, and she picked up the mug by its handle, passing it over to Stan, microscopic death waiting to spread and infect. Before he could grab it, she pulled it back. "Sorry, forgot the milk." She put it back down on the counter and suddenly seemed to stagger slightly. Stan gave her the once over, a look of concern spread to his face.

"You alright, Doc? You look a bit peaky."

"Just this damned headache. It's been threatening all day, but it really hit about five minutes ago. Would you believe I'm in a hospital, and I can't find any bloody Ibuprofen anywhere?" Most of the lower level painkiller stores had been shipped to the refugee access points. The hospital was left with the harder stuff, but opiate-based narcotics were hardly the right thing for a mere headache, especially as she had to able to function for at least another few hours yet.

"As it happens," Stan said, reaching into one of the pouches on his utility belt, "I always carry some around with me." With his gloved hand, he lifted them out and threw them over. "Here, catch." They twirled through the air and she almost caught them. But just as her hands were about to make contact, her body shuddered and her arm spasmed. The small cardboard box landed on the floor and slid several inches, coming to a rest nearly under the room's only refrigerator. Something in Stan caused him to take a step back.

"Oooh, that hurts," Holden said clutching her side.

"Doc?"

"Stan, I'll be alright, just give me a moment." But she wasn't alright. Holden suddenly doubled over inhaling deeply. Her head began to pound now, every second bringing a thunderous beat to her temples. She felt her guts churn, and a knife suddenly twisted in the small of her back. She cried out, barely staying on her feet. "Stan? Oh my God."

"Shit," Stan said. He resisted the temptation to grab hold of her, because he had seen this before. One of the very first things he had been shown in his indoctrination was a video showing the first signs of the infection, the signs that Doctor Simone Holden was now displaying. With a gasp, she finally collapsed on the floor. "No, not this," she managed. As much as he hated himself, Stan fled the room and closed the door. It was the only thing he could think to do, self-preservation winning over him again.

"Code 99!" he shouted loudly. A nurse poked her head out of an office and looked at him. He didn't see her, too intent was he on grabbing the radio on his shoulder. "Dispatch, this is security at the hospital. Code 99, I repeat Code 99. Possible infected individual in room 10C in the hospital."

"Confirmed. Containment team has been dispatched," came the response in his ear piece. He let go of the radio. "I need fucking help here," he roared. Turning full circle, he saw nobody, so he picked up the whistle that had been handed to him at the end of the induction video. Dangling around a chord on his neck, he blew. If you see an infected, you blow to alert those around you. If you hear the whistle and you are armed, you run towards the sound. If you aren't armed, you run in the opposite direction.

15.03PM, 17th September 2015, MI6 Building, London, UK

"Target locked. Weapons free." Clarice Sterling brought the A10 in low, and as her thumb pressed down on the fire control, the GUA-8/A Avenger cannon began to unleash the thirty-millimetre calibre bullets into the crowd of infected. Nothing in the path of those bullets stood a chance, and within seconds, dozens of infected who were massing to cross the bridge were reduced to chewed-up flesh. Clarice, call sign Syndrome, banked up to go in for another pass.

"You are free to take out the bridge. I repeat, your primary target is now the bridge, over," came the voice over her headphones.

"Roger that, over." She pulled the plane up into the sky, bringing it round in a wide arc. She would lay one more pass into the fuckers and then her wingman could take out the bridge. She switched channels on her radio. "Bridge is all yours, Badger."

"Thank you very much," came the response. It was rumoured that Badger had a fetish for making things explode.

Rasheed watched the planes descend out of nowhere and witnessed the devastation they dropped onto the infected. The death of the infected didn't concern him in the slightest. He felt nothing for them. What concerned him was the bridge, he needed that. As powerful as he was, he had no intention of swimming across the fucking Thames. And whilst there were other bridges he could cross, he had even less desire to take a detour to get to his ultimate destination because who was to say they wouldn't be blown as well. He wanted across that river, and he was going to use this bridge to do it.

The vibration in the building stopped, and Rasheed staggered backwards almost in relief. The concentration and effort that he had needed to put into the destruction surprised him, and his head ached with an intensity that worried him. The vision in one eye was still blurred and his lower abdomen throbbed with a fire that suggested everything wasn't as healed as it should be. But no matter, this was God's work. Mere discomfort was irrelevant, the pain only proving that his fight was worthy. He had no illusion that he would be alive for much longer, and he could almost hear the bliss of the afterlife beckoning. Soon, he would join his brothers as the Prophet had promised, but first, he had work to do to earn that place.

But he needed the bridge, and so he turned his attention to the two specs in the sky. They were both turning now, coming back to attack again. He could tell instantly that they were too far away—even his power had limits—and he waited for the first plane to come into the range of his influence, feeling for it, testing his limitations. For a second, his entire vision blurred out, but then it quickly returned to the one good eye.

"There you are," he said to himself, and he concentrated on one of the wings, his mind examining the shape and changing it, distorting it, crumpling it. He didn't even realise he had brought his left hand up, his eyes now closed. He didn't see the fist clench, barely even felt the nails digging into his palm. The first plane bucked in the air, then swung violently to the right. It was done, and he quickly turned his attention to the second plane.

Clarice watched in horror as the plane of her wingman spun out of control. From where she was, she could see that one of the wings had crumpled in as if a huge invisible hand had reached out and squashed it. The whole thing had happened in seconds.

"Badger, come in. Badger, do you read me, Goddamnit?" There was no response, and she watched in horror as the other plane went into a spiral. Then her own plane began to vibrate, the controls suddenly becoming unresponsive. The plane dropped sharply, and her stomach felt like it was in her mouth. Cockpit alarms started to blare at her, and she knew she had only one chance to live. Whatever had happened had caused her plane to become dead weight, the flight stick completely unresponsive, so she did the only thing left to her. She reached in between her legs and pulled the lever to activate the explosive ejection.

Everything happened in a whirlwind. Clarice almost lost consciousness as the ejection ripped her out of the cockpit and into the air. She felt herself forced down into her seat, felt the dread that comes with knowing that this might not work, that the chute might not activate and that she might end up hurtling to her death a thousand feet below. But as the chair stopped its upward momentum, the drogue chute did engage, and she began to rapidly descend, the fall stabilising. Then the main chute opened and the chair fell away from her, now no longer needed. Clarice found herself floating in the air above the river, and with the limited time she had, she knew there was only one destination to aim for. The MI6 Building, the roof of which was quickly hurtling towards her. She didn't see her plane crash, but she heard it off in the distance. Shit, she loved that plane.

Croft had been thrown forwards off his feet by the force of the blast, and lay dazed face down as dust settled all around him. Fortunately, he had been far enough away to escape the brunt of the explosion, but it wasn't something he wanted to experience again in his lifetime if he could avoid it. He'd had too much of that shit in the past.

His head groggy and swimming, he felt hands grab him and almost reluctantly pushed himself up off the ground. It would have been so easy to just lie there, to just give up, to let the darkness come. But he was not the kind of person to give up like that. His ears still ringing, he cast a glance behind him and saw that the rocket had brought the whole ceiling down and blocked off the corridor. There was no sign of Fabrice.

"You alright, Major?" Snow asked.

"I'll live," Croft said, picking debris out of his hair. "Check me over, will you?" Snow looked over Croft's body, but was relieved to see he couldn't see any bleeding or wounds. Snow gave him the thumbs up. He'd be sore tomorrow though...hell, he was sore now.

"Captain Savage is round the corner. We need to leave." Croft nodded his agreement at Snow's advice and limped after him. Snow clearly knew the layout and he struck Croft as being a competent field agent. The major therefore had no hesitation in following his lead.

"Since when did MI6 stock bloody rocket launchers?" Croft asked, following the man who had probably just saved his life.

"Probably since the things were bloody invented."

"Fortunate for us, but not very James Bond though, is it?" Croft added.

Durand had heard the explosion, but was still surprised when he turned the corner and found the lights out and the way blocked. The air was filled with smoke that burnt his throat, and he retched briefly, retreating from the destructed corridor for a moment to consider his options. The ground around him still shook slightly, every ten seconds or so fresh tremors running through the building. A large crack appeared in the wall to his left.

"Shit." He had only been here a day, and he still wasn't fully in tune with the layout of the building. The place was like a maze, and his foe was nowhere to be seen.

He took a step forward, wondering if he could somehow climb over the mound in the middle of the corridor, just enough light filtering in from the undamaged corridors behind him. But then some of the rubble moved. Pieces fell down to the floor, followed by a metal support structure that had been balancing precariously. No climbing over that, it was too unstable, and he'd probably have to dig his way through. He was a scientist, not a damned labourer. Turning around, he made off in another direction, so he didn't see the hand that suddenly emerged, didn't see the pile swell as the force within it pushed outwards against the weight. Durand heard more concrete shift, but didn't see the head of Fabrice emerge unscathed from beneath the debris.

But Fabrice saw him, if only briefly, and even though the light was far from ideal, the Warrior of God recognised the scientist instantly.

"You!" Fabrice seethed through clenched teeth. By the time he had pushed his way free, however, the good doctor had a good minute's head start and was well out of sight. Fabrice considered going after the doctor so as to enact some sort of vengeance, but that could wait. He had more important things to do now. The three were coming and he had to be ready for them.

15.06PM, 17th September, Newquay Hospital, Newquay, UK

Brian had been stationed at the other side of the hospital, and he heard the Code 99 broadcast go out over his earpiece. He hadn't been expecting that, not here, not now. Then he heard the whistle, and he did what he had been instructed to do—he ran towards the sound. He navigated around the side of the small hospital and entered the A&E department through the main entrance. A frightened nurse saw him and pointed the way he needed to go. A minute later, he saw Stan and two other officers, weapons raised, outside a closed door. The door shook as something on the inside threw itself at it, the door having been locked by one of the other officers, the keys still in the door.

"Stan?" he said, coming up beside his mate. Stan didn't look at him at first.

"Brian, you don't need to be here. Let us handle this."

"I'm here now, I…"

"No," Stan said forcefully, giving him a look he had never seen before. "You can't be here. Go before the containment team arrives."

"Why?" Brian could sense the despair in his friend's voice and ice travelled down his spine. "It's not…" he couldn't finish the words.

"It's Simone. She's infected. That's why you can't be here." Stan flinched as the door was hit by another jolt, the wood cracking slightly. It would hold; it had to hold. He let go of his gun and grabbed his friend and began guiding him backwards. "Bri, seriously, get the fuck out of here." Stan could see his friend wanting to argue, but then there was the sound of running feet. Everyone turned to see five guys armed to the teeth charging down the corridor towards their position. Stan recognised one of them as possibly the man he had watched get off the helicopter yesterday. He couldn't tell for sure because they all wore black gas masks.

"How many?" Hudson asked, the police officers stepping back from the door.

"Just one," said Stan, "one of the doctors here. I saw her start to transform." He made a point of not looking at Brian when he said this.

"Good work, officer," Hudson said. Stan could tell his praise was genuine. The SAS captain turned to one of his men. "Carl, I want you to get the records of everyone this doctor has treated in the last hour. I want them contained, and I want them isolated. Take these officers with you." Hudson turned to Stan once again. "You up for that, lads?"

"But I know her," Brian said before Stan could answer. Hudson saw the look he had seen so many times, the evidence of someone's emotional core about to break. Hudson stepped over to Brian and put a hand on his shoulder.

"And I'm sorry. But now is the time for me to do what they trained me for. There's no other way."

The hospital waiting room was loud, dozens of people trying to talk over each other. They had heard the whistle, and they knew what it meant. Some of them had tried to leave, only to find their way blocked by armed police who pointed gleaming machine guns at them menacingly. One man sported a head wound from where he had tried to force his way past only to find himself clubbed in the forehead by an officer who seemed to be enjoying his power a little bit too much. This wasn't right. They had said to run if you heard the whistle.

"You're fucking lucky I didn't just shoot you," an enraged officer had almost screamed at the injured man. Carl walked into this and saw that the situation was very close to full-blown panic.

"You two stay here," he said to two of the officers with him. "You take your friend somewhere quiet." That had been aimed at Stan, who led Brian away from the growing madness.

"Can I have your attention please?" Carl said loudly to the assorted masses. Most of them ignored him. "Fucking civilians," he whispered under his breath. Stowing his machine gun, he withdrew his sidearm and held it up to the ceiling. He knew where to fire safely, and the report boomed across the room. That shut everyone up, and a nervous hush filled the room, terrified minds shocked into submission.

"I said can I have your attention?" Several dozen pairs of eyes looked towards him. "Thank you." His military fatigues told them all they needed to know.

"You need to let us out of here," a woman shouted from the middle of the room, murmurs of agreement rippling through those assembled.

"No," Carl said calmly, "no, I don't." He lowered his gun and re-holstered it. "What I need to do is shoot anyone who tries to leave before I say they can. And that is something I am more than prepared to do." He let that sink in.

"You can't do this," someone sobbed.

"Yes, I can, and I will. The situation is being contained. Stay quiet, stay put, and we will have you all out of here when it is safe to do so. The rules you have lived under no longer apply, and it's important you all start to realise that." He looked around the room. "Do we have an understanding here, people?" Most of the heads looking at him nodded in resignation. In the far corner, a child began to cry.

"Good. Nurse?" he said to a somewhat gobsmacked hospital employee. "A word, please." From behind where he stood, in the corridor he had just exited, multiple gunshots suddenly rang out. Carl didn't even seem to register the noise.

15.13PM, 17th September 2015, MI6 Building, London, UK

They had all gone through a thick security door which Snow closed behind them.

"If he couldn't get through the glass, he won't get through this," Snow informed them. He noticed they looked monumentally un-reassured.

"Are we under the river now?" Savage asked, slightly out of breath from the exertion. The corridor ahead of them went on for hundreds of metres. It was well lit and immaculate, the white tiles giving it an almost surgical cleanliness.

"Yes. Once we are through to the other end, we can get out to the surface and get a ride from the secure boathouse there." Snow had used this tunnel several times, and there would be similar tunnels that he hoped the other MI6 personnel were using to escape the collapsing building.

"And then what?" Mackay asked. This was not where he envisioned his life to be right now. He was a scientist, not a fucking secret agent. "Once we get onto the surface, even if we do get a boat, how long before the infected get us?"

"You let us worry about that. You just do what we tell you, okay?" said Croft. Mackay ceased walking and looked at his three companions with disbelief. All three of them stopped and looked back at him. Mackay was clearly upset.

"Don't fucking treat me like that. I didn't ask for this. I'm not trained like you."

"I'm not treating you like anything," said Croft. He had seen these reactions countless times before. Civilians, they were always more trouble than they were worth. "But be under no illusion, by your own admission, you are a liability. You either keep up and do as we say, or we leave you behind."

"But…" the man started to protest.

"Mackay, we don't have time for your bullshit." Croft raised his voice ever so slightly, just enough to get the message across. "You either do as we say when we say it, or I will more than happily abandon you to your fate. Your choice." Mackay looked like he had just been slapped, and there were almost tears in the man's eyes. Croft turned to see Savage looking at him with a disappointed look. He ignored it and marched off back down the tunnel. He wasn't here to make friends, and he didn't have to justify himself to anyone. He had only one priority now, survival, and anyone who got in the way of that be damned.

15.14PM, 17th September, Newquay Hospital, Newquay, UK

Brian sat in the corner of the room, his head in his hands. Stan stood looking at him, not really knowing what to say. He wasn't good with this sort of thing, had always left it to others to do the delivering bad news thing that the police were often called upon to do. Whenever emotional shit came off, Stan always tried to either ignore it or turn it into a joke, trying to deflect the discomfort it represented to him. It was one of the many reasons he wasn't married. And now his mate needed him, and he was at a loss about what to do.

"You know, it's funny," Brian said, the tears over with for now. "I kind of saw a future with her. I know I've only known her for a day, but there was something about her, you know?"

"I know mate, I saw it," Stan said. Even he had seen the connection that had formed between Simone and Brian. Being thrown together like that in such a traumatic situation could do that.

"But it's crazy, how could I even hope for that in this fucked-up world?"

"Hope's all we have, mate."

"And now she's gone."

"I know," Stan said again. He was still in a degree of shock himself. Simone had come so close to infecting him. He was about to say something more, only to be interrupted by a commotion outside.

"I will shoot you if you don't do as I say," a voice said outside the door.

"But I didn't do anything," a weaker voice argued.

"Stay here," Stan said to Brian, almost thankful for the interruption. No, there was no almost about it, he was glad for the relief.

Gavin hadn't left the hospital after being examined by Holden, because he had to wait for his arm to be put in a cast. So he had been sat in the cubicle when a demon of a man, armed to the teeth, had pulled the curtain aside and pointed a pistol right in his face. Gavin thought the man looked vaguely familiar, but the gas mask the man wore made it impossible to tell for sure. If anything, it was the uniform that was familiar.

"Put these on," the soldier had demanded, throwing a face mask and a face shield and a pair of nitrile gloves at him. So menacing was the soldier that Gavin did as he was ordered, and he had struggled with the gloves, every second expecting the soldier to shoot him in the head. But the guy didn't rush him, just stood there like a rock waiting for him to finish. Despite his protestations, Gavin had then been marched off at gunpoint by the soldier, three other people in a similar situation joining him in the corridor he was led along. He didn't see the police officer fall in behind the procession.

"In there," the soldier said to Gavin and the other three patients Holden had seen.

"But why?" Gavin implored. "What have we done?"

"Maybe nothing, but that's what we are going to find out." Gavin was the only man amongst the four, and he opened the door to enter a small consulting room. "Probably best if you lot don't touch each other."

"Why?" one of the women said almost in tears.

"We believe one of you might be infected." Oh shit, thought Gavin. It's me, it has to be me. Oh no, what have I done?

15.23PM, 17th September 2015, River Thames, London, UK

Croft let Snow drive the boat. It had a covered wheelhouse, and could probably hold a good dozen people, which was good because they were now heading back across the river towards an iconic building that was trembling on its foundations. Snow's radio had blared out that there were people trapped in the MI6 Building's river entrance, and Croft had made the decision to go back and get them. Whilst survival was his primary goal now, he still felt increasing their numbers was a viable plan. Snow agreed, especially as he knew two of the people trapped, both good men, both capable. As Snow had put it, "They are people you want on your side when the shit goes down."

It wasn't the plan Croft wanted, but it was the one he had. He had managed to get a call into NATO headquarters, and had tried to speak in person to General Marston. He wasn't surprised to hear that the Chief of the Defence staff was "indisposed". Typical, but not unsurprising. About as unsurprising as being told by the same lackey in Brussels that there were no assets, at present, to come and get Croft out of the shit hole he had been dropped in. The line had actually gone dead as the person on the other end had cut him off. Now that, he hadn't expected, but it confirmed what he had suspected. They were on their own, expendable. So whilst Snow had got the boat ready, Croft had sent an email off over the secure network using his smart phone.

To: General Marston
Sir
As you are no doubt aware, the last stronghold in London has fallen. Before it fell, I managed to establish that the virus is causing mutations in their human hosts. I was witness to one individual who had been made almost indestructible, able to take a bullet point-blank without any apparent ill effects.

I also suspect that there are other mutations. The MI6 was not attacked by any form of conventional weaponry, and Captain Savage and I theorise that some form of telekinetic power was used to destabilise the structure to the extent of allowing ingress of the infected. From my own observations, I believe the infected were being controlled somehow, perhaps by the same power that destroyed the MI6 Building.

We are going to rescue who we can and try and make our way out of London seeing as how we have been abandoned here to our fates. No hard feelings, General, I know how it is.

Looking at the device he now held, he turned it off and resisted the temptation to throw it into the river, putting it into an inner pocket instead. The boat suddenly rocked, buffeted by the waves, and Croft saw that they were mere minutes away from the building they had just escaped from. Mackay had initially started to express his extreme displeasure at the rescue mission. He soon shut up when Snow had threatened to throw him over the side of the boat or put a bullet in his leg and leave him for the infected to dine on. Now the scientist sat next to Savage, almost sulking like a frightened and petulant child at the back of the boat. Croft didn't give him a second thought; he was useless to them. Dead weight. Mackay would either do as he was ordered and have a chance to make it out of this, or he would do something stupid and end up getting himself killed. Either option was fine with Croft. In the world he lived in, you relied on yourself as much as those around you.

"You don't approve of the way I spoke to Mackay," Croft said to Savage almost absently.

"He's not used to having orders barked at him," she said, defending him. Croft looked at her; even with what had just happened, she still looked amazing to his eyes. It was a shame, if it hadn't been for all this, they could have had something together. He put that out of his mind now because really there was no hope for anything like that anymore.

"True, but I can't be babysitting. He's either on board or he's dead weight. You see that, right?"

"Yes," Savage said solemnly. "I think I'm finally coming to terms with how quickly everything has fallen apart. To be honest, I'm still trying to get my head around it."

"Aren't we all," said Croft. He turned back to look at the building just as a huge explosion ripped through the top third of the building.

"Wow," Snow said. "Glad I wasn't in there for that." The radio crackled.

"We need evac ASAP. Where we are is becoming unstable," a distressed voice implored. Snow increased power to the engines and forged the boat on towards its destination.

Owen sacrificed some of his army, safe in the knowledge that he could always get more. He didn't lead them into battle, but stayed well back, safe from the snipers whose shots began to diminish as the building began to slowly crumble in on itself. He also stayed away from Rasheed. Owen had taken an instant dislike to the man, for so many reasons. Firstly, he was a Paki, and he hated Paki's. Fucking Mussie as well—what was there to like about that? But those were just phantoms, excuses that he formed to hide the truth. The real reason he didn't like Rasheed he tried so hard to deny to himself. It was that Rasheed also had power. Which meant that Owen wasn't alone, wasn't as powerful as he thought he was, wasn't as unique. Which really meant that perhaps this city wasn't his after all. There could be dozens, maybe hundreds out there like him, which meant he might have a fight on his hands. Yeah, Owen could control the infected, but this guy, this guy could kill them in a heartbeat. This guy could take a shot to the abdomen and fucking heal it. He was a fucking threat, a danger that needed to be dealt with. And how many other threats were there lurking in this dying metropolis?

In his mind's eye, he saw his warriors storming across the bridge, saw them scaling the walls and the fences around the MI6 Building. Through doors and windows destroyed by Rasheed's power, they gained entry into one of the country's most secure buildings and unleashed mayhem. He saw them run through corridors, free to act at last against an enemy that had held out for too long. Dozens of them fell before bullets and knives, but hundreds more took their place. And whenever the path became blocked, that blockage was ripped apart by an invisible force. Owen reckoned he would have the building under his control within thirty minutes tops. He just hoped there would be a building left, because he really wanted to look inside, and the way Rasheed was going, there wouldn't be anything left but a huge pile of bricks and broken glass.

Snow pulled the boat up to the dock and noticed the half a dozen people waiting for them. Peter was with them, radio in hand, and Croft stepped to the edge of the boat and barked at them.

"If you're coming, move your combined arses." Seven people stepped off the dock onto his vessel, and he was disappointed to see only two of them had weapons.

"Thanks for coming back for us," Peter said to Croft as he stepped onto the boat. Croft was surprised to see the only woman in the group was wearing a flight suit, and raised an eyebrow at Peter. Where the hell had she come from?

"Who's this?" he asked. The woman, realising Croft was talking about her, stopped and flung him a salute.

"Captain Claire Stirling, United States Air Force." Croft flung her a half-arsed salute back, and saw a smile spread across the pilots' face. "Permission to come aboard, sir?"

"Granted," said Croft.

According to Peter, he had been on the roof when Stirling had fallen out of the sky by parachute like an avenging angel. She had very nearly overshot her landing, and it was probably more luck than skill that she hadn't toppled off the edge of the building. Peter had seen the aircraft fall from the sky, but she had descended from him out of his line of sight and had almost scared him half to death. Her landing had been hard, and Savage had seen the way Clarice was limping, favouring one leg, which was why Clarice was now sat at the back of the boat, having her ankle examined. But how the hell had she come to be here?

Snow pulled the boat away from the dock, disappointed that he had been unable to rescue any more survivors. Out on the Thames, several other boats moved away from their position, so it at least looked like some others had gotten away. But where would they all go? They had no refuge now, most government and military facilities in the city either abandoned or compromised. They needed somewhere that was accessible by water, somewhere that would give them a chance to rest, regroup, and plan. Then a thought came to him, and his eyes brightened. That might just work, assuming the person he was thinking of had survived this long. But of course he had survived. It would take more than a mere apocalypse to kill a man like Alexei. And even better was the fact that they could get to where Alexei lived directly from the river.

Durand sat at the front of the boat, his madness seething. He didn't talk to anyone, just viewed those around him with suspicious eyes. He had managed to escape Fabrice's clutches only to wind up here amongst a pack of wolves. Still wearing his white lab coat, now marred with dirt and grime, he fingered the hidden gun that he had planned to use to kill Savage and Croft and whoever else got in his way. But all his potential victims were armed now, and he knew this was not the time to take his vengeance. And was it even worth it? All his research was lost. The discovery he was so close to making was probably wandering around inside the MI6 Building, free to do whatever the fuck it wanted. Even though he had witnessed what Fabrice had become, no part of Victor Durand felt any kind of responsibility. All he felt was hate, and it seethed within him, his temples throbbing, any form of reason long since stripped from him. He had lived his life for significance, for recognition, and now he no longer had any of that. It had all been taken from him, and in his mind, there was only one person to blame...Savage.

Sat on this boat, he was nothing, worthless, and it burned him alive inside. For a second, he found himself staring at the back of Savage's head, the impulse to leap on her and commit violence strong. But he controlled himself, and, noticing that eyes were watching him just as he was watching Savage, he turned his head to find Croft drowning him in an intense glare.

"You okay there, Victor?" the major asked. There was steel in his voice, and Durand could tell it was not a question about his wellbeing. Durand didn't answer. He just turned to look out at the river, anxious palpitations suddenly striking him. He felt like everyone was looking at him, felt danger closing in, encircling him. Why were they all looking at him?

Croft watched the scientist carefully. There was something not right about the man, and he meant more than the obvious fact that Durand was a complete dick. No, despite the fact that he looked like a long streak of drink water, Croft could tell that the man was dangerous, something Croft had spotted almost instantly. Should he deal with him here and now? It wouldn't take much—two steps and he could grab him by the scruff of the neck and just hurl him overboard. Who was there to stop him? Croft was tempted, and he burned his eyes into his new foe. But no, as bad as things were, they weren't quite to that stage yet. Croft would keep a watchful eye on the scientist, and lose him at the first availability. All Durand's research was in a USB stick in Savage's pocket, so they didn't even need the man from a scientific viewpoint. But if he was honest, Croft suspected he might still have questions he needed answering from the man, and he would get answers one way or the other. Then, maybe Durand might suffer a tragic accident. Perhaps he even might fall victim to one of the infected he seemed to be so fascinated with. The world was now a dangerous and unpredictable place. But for now, he would watch and observe the viper amongst them. If he had evil intent, the serpent would show his hand soon enough.

15.28PM, 17th September 2015, MI6 Building, London, UK

Owen walked through the front doors, his minions gathered around him. He could feel them fighting their way throughout the now stabilised building, Rasheed no longer hell-bent on destroying the structure. That was because he too was here, and the man with the telekinetic power looked around in awe.

"I never thought I would ever walk in here willingly," Rasheed said. The man seemed dazed, not fully with it.

"What's your deal anyway, mate? Who the fuck are you?" Owen looked at the man, saw the toll his powers seemed to be having on him.

"I fight the Crusaders wherever I find them," Rasheed said absently. Some of the words sounded blurred.

"What the fuck is a Crusader?" Owen asked. Rasheed ignored him. Instead, he staggered off further into the complex, the infected moving away from him as he passed.

"Guy's a fucking fruit bat," Owen mumbled to himself. He watched as Rasheed wandered through an obvious metal detector, and followed him through, the machine blaring due to the arsenal he carried. Two days ago, he didn't even know this place fucking existed.

It wasn't Owen who felt the presence first. They were further into the building now, his infected reporting to him telepathically that virtually all resistance had been eliminated and were under the process of being converted. Owen was already bored, bored of the hunt, bored of the building, bored of the voice that had brought him here. This was not where he wanted to be, and he wanted to meet the fucker who thought he could tell Owen Patterson what to do and get whatever needed to be done or said over with. Owen objected to this individual being in his head, and he wanted to see just exactly what he was dealing with. Because nobody told Owen Patterson what to do, not now, not ever.

Rasheed was still ahead of him, and he could hear the guy mumbling to himself. Owen had seen an awesome film when he was younger about people with powers whose brains couldn't cope with the power the gifted individual's used. Was that how Rasheed was? Was the guy basically frying his brain every time he used his telekinetic abilities? And was that even what it was, telekinesis? Rasheed suddenly stumbled, falling against the wall, but he quickly righted himself. Fuck, at this rate, the cunt was becoming a liability.

Rasheed suddenly stopped walking, his head drifting about drunkenly. The dozen or so infected around Owen started to become agitated, and then Owen himself felt it, a presence that suddenly descended upon them. Two of the infected made to run off, but Owen reined them in quickly, the confusion in their minds palpable. He heard Rasheed say something in a language that he couldn't understand.

"What was that?" Owen said.

"I said he is here."

"Who's here?" Owen asked, although truth be told, he knew the answer.

"One. One is here."

Fabrice came to the top of a flight of steps, the sign saying he was now on the ground floor level. He wasn't out of breath in the slightest, another gift of the virus. Stamina, strength, and invulnerability, what more could he ask for? But the virus hadn't let him get his hands on the bastard who had done this to him, the scientist scuttling away like the coward he was. He had so much wanted to put his hands around the man's throat, to hold him whilst the infection took hold, to watch the man's eyes as they transformed and mutated into the red eyes of the damned.

Where is the doctor now? Fabrice wondered. Still in the facility or amongst those who had fled through a warren of tunnels that Fabrice couldn't even hope to decipher? And did it really matter? There was work to be done, and if it hadn't been for Durand, he'd still be down in the basement with the needles torturing his very essence. Hell, perhaps he even owed Durand his thanks. No, that was probably pushing it. Perhaps a quick death though, perhaps Fabrice owed him that.

Fabrice pulled the door open, the corridor full of the smell of cordite and death. The door handle crumpled in his hand, his newfound strength still unusual and unfamiliar to him. Three infected ran past, paying him no attention, and he looked at the four dead bodies that lay ruined on the floor. Three of them were naked, and all had gunshot wounds to their heads. The fourth, a man, lay with its neck twisted at an ungodly angle, great chunks of flesh missing from his face and his now bared arms. Fully clothed in military clothing, it represented the uselessness of humanity's resistance. All that weaponry, all that training, for nothing. Just as the Lord had planned, just as Abraham had envisaged. Stepping into the corridor, he let the door close behind him. For the first time since he was infected, Fabrice was suddenly wary of his nakedness. Was this really how he should meet the others? But no, the Lord made man in his image and sent him naked into the Garden of Eden. His naked form was exactly how he would stay if that was what the Lord wished.

Fabrice turned a corner and saw them before they saw him. Two and Four, here they were, the powerful voices that spoke to him, each with powers imparted to them by the virus, by the Lord. And infected, lots of infected, no doubt controlled by Four. Fabrice approved of their naked forms and saw the godliness in it. He didn't realise they were naked because Owen was a perverted and sadistic son of a bitch.

"The Lord be with you," Fabrice said loudly. Two sets of eyes turned to him, and neither of them looked particularly pleased by his presence.

"So you're the noisy fucker in my head?" Owen said angrily.

"I am he," Fabrice said, giving a humble little bow.

"Okay, well we're here now. So tell me, why have you dragged me halfway across the city? And more importantly, why haven't you got any fucking clothes on?"

"I was held captive by the servants of Satan. This is how they kept me." Fabrice raised his arms up to his sides. Rasheed said nothing, but just stared.

"So what's your name, mate? And none of this 'I am One' shit. What's your actual fucking name?" Owen asked. "I'm tired and I'm pissed off, so don't fucking test me." His hand drifted to the back of his trousers, and he fingered the gun there. He suddenly felt intimidated. The man looked chiselled like a Greek god, and his cock swayed impressively between his legs. None of the infected looked that impressive. Owen wasn't to know that it was the virus that had done this to him, sculpting the man as well as changing him.

"My name was Fabrice, but that name left me when the virus performed its miracle. Now I am One. Or if you prefer, I go by another name now, handed to me by God himself."

"Oh yeah, and what's that?" Owen inquired. He didn't like this guy either, he really didn't like him. Why was he suddenly surrounded by utter bastards? Fabrice? What kind of a name was that? And he spoke like a fucking Bishop or something. Well okay, Owen had never actually ever met a Bishop, but if there were any about they would undoubtedly sound like this guy.

"Death," Fabrice said with a smile. "I am Death." Rasheed seemed to recoil at that.

"Fuck you," Rasheed almost screamed.

"My child…" Fabrice started.

"Stop talking," Rasheed demanded. "You drag me here, you invade my mind, only to flaunt the beliefs of the heretic in front of me. No, I will not stand for it." He spat on the floor before him. "That is what I think of you and your Crusader infestation."

"Rasheed here has a thing about Crusaders," Owen said mockingly. "I've no idea what that's all about." Rasheed spared him the briefest of glances, and in that moment, Owen wished he'd kept his mouth shut. There was death in the man's eyes.

"There is no need for this…" Fabrice began, but then he felt the air around him swell, felt pressure building all around him.

"ENOUGH," Rasheed bellowed, the voice seeming to strike directly into Fabrice's brain. The man who now called himself Death staggered, struck by an invisible blow. "I came here to see what manner of being you were, and now I know." Fabrice fell to his knees, the pressure building. He felt something in his back crack, the force pushing in on him, crushing with a weight that grew by the second. "I see what you are, see the evil inside you. Demon, I will cast you out, and then I shall destroy everything you represent. Your lies will not infect me. By the will of Allah, I see the deception within you."

Fabrice tried to resist. He had survived when a whole ceiling collapsed on him, had been shot at point-blank range and hadn't so much picked up a scratch. But this was different. This was the Lord's power, and he almost wept at the irony of it all.

"Please," Fabrice managed to say. "Don't I…"

And then the shot rang out and the pressure released. Fabrice collapsed gasping to the floor, the pain in his back still present. His vision floated in and out of reality, and he lifted his eyes up to witness what had occurred. Rasheed laid a crumpled heap on the floor, the essence in his mind extinguished. Stood next to him, Owen stood with a gun still smoking, a satisfied smirk on his face.

"What…what have you done?" Fabrice almost begged. Despite being saved, Fabrice knew that this was not God's will. He tried to stand, managed it on the second attempt, pain shooting through his spine. Owen looked at him warily, but instead of pointing the gun, Fabrice saw the man lower it and tuck it back into his trousers.

"The man talked too much," Owen said, clearly pleased with himself. "Besides, I fucking hate Mussies." Owen pointed a finger forcefully at Fabrice. "And just for the record, I'm not too keen on you God squad nutters either. So keep your Bible bashing talk to yourself, okay?"

15.30AM, 17th September 2015, NATO Headquarters, Brussels, Belgium

"Good afternoon, General Frolov." Marston stood as the Russian was escorted into his office and came round the desk to shake his hand. The Russian smiled and shook his hand warmly in return. Marston indicated that Frolov was welcome to take a seat, and the Russian took it gladly. "Drink?"

"But of course," Frolov said, making himself comfortable. Marston had already poured the drinks several minutes before and now merely put ice in the scotch. Walking over, Marston handed one of the glasses over.

"Make the most of that, the world now has a limited supply."

"Truly unfortunate," the Russian said. He took a sip and savoured the taste. "Ah, the makers of this could almost be Russian." Marston sat opposite him. "I am afraid I have bad news for you, Nicholas." Marston didn't respond, just looked at Victor over the top of his glass as he slowly drank. "I put your proposal to my president, and he thanks you for informing him of the rogue element in our military. He has asked me to assure you that this has been dealt with."

"However…" Marston knew what was coming.

"However, my president feels that, with the threat posed by this virus, we need to store the nerve agents for our own defence. Should the virus ever get onto the European mainland, it may be our only way of stopping its spread into Russia."

"I see," Marston replied impassively. He wasn't surprised, not in the slightest. If he had been in the Russian president's position, he would have probably done the same.

"I hope you understand," Frolov said. The man almost looked genuinely embarrassed.

"Not to worry, Victor. And you are in good company—the Americans told me the same thing." That prompted a raised eyebrow from the Russian.

After the Russian had left, Marston sat in his office with instructions not to be disturbed. What was he even doing here? His country was dead, a large proportion of the soldiers he commanded doomed in what was surely to be a futile disaster. They called it Operation Hadrian, but who were they really kidding? The infected would sweep over the defensive positions like a Japanese tsunami, and he was already seeing that NATO was starting to distance itself from helping on the British mainland. There was already talk of reducing the aerial missions, and despite his protests, that talk was gaining traction. His army was a spent force, now dependent on resupply from foreign governments, and it was only a matter of time before those military units outside the UK were either disbanded or swallowed up by other countries.

And then there were the remaining overseas territories. They were going to be consumed by the world because there was no longer a United Kingdom to protect them. The Northern Ireland Parliament at Stormont was in emergency session, although large numbers of politicians had already fled that island nation. Great Britain no longer existed in any real sense, which meant Northern Ireland was on its own. Despite the protestations of the likes of the Ulster Unionists, reintegration with the rest of Ireland would now be an inevitability, although it might also be a bloody affair. The Spanish were already making demands to the United Nations that they should take back Gibraltar. And the Argentinians were going to make a play for the Falkland Islands—that was inevitable, although the five thousand UK troops recently stationed there might have something to say about the matter. Even the Americans, the UK's most trusted ally, had already insisted that they take over full control of Diego Garcia where they held a military base. It made sense, apparently. The Americans were also insisting they take control of the huge British Cyprus base so that they could protect the surveillance infrastructure there which was an essential part of their now damaged and depleted Echelon network. By the end of the week, Marston doubted he would even have a military to command.

A thousand years of history had amounted to nothing. An empire that had once been so vast that the sun never set on it was now in ruins. Not so much a laughing stock, but a pitiful remnant that needed to be euthanised so the distant relatives could pick over the bones. The vultures were circling, and there was absolutely nothing he could do save threaten countries with the UK's nuclear weapons, which were all at sea. But he wasn't foolish enough to make such a threat. It was pointless because it had a finite life. Sooner or later, those submarines had to come into dock. They couldn't remain at sea indefinitely. The United Kingdom was done. It was over. All that was left to do now was salvage what could be saved and contain the infection as best they could.

15.32PM, 17th September, Newquay Hospital, Newquay, UK

"You, take that mask off." The room had looked to see who had opened the door, and now they all looked at who the dangerous-looking soldier was pointing to. Nobody could see the soldier's face because, like with all of them, he was wearing the now mandatory gas mask. Gavin looked at the residents of the room all in turn and then nervously did as he was commanded. Because the soldier was pointing at him. He looked back at the soldier in the doorway and saw the SAS captain beckoning him. "I thought it was you. Come with me."

Gavin stood up and wormed his way through the assembled group. He ignored their glances, some sending him quizzical looks. Some of the faces accused him of atrocities not even Satan had committed. As Gavin approached the door, Hudson stepped back into the corridor, which was otherwise empty. "Stay at least three arm lengths away from me," Hudson commanded in a stern but calm voice. "If you approach me, I will shut that shit down in a heartbeat." The captain was holding something in his right hand, but Gavin couldn't see what it was.

"Please," Gavin begged, "I didn't..."

"Mouth shut," Hudson said menacingly. "Move that way, and don't take your time about it." Hudson pointed down the corridor with his right arm, and Gavin saw what he was holding. It was a taser. Gavin did the only thing he could do: he complied.

He walked down the corridor waiting for his next instruction. He didn't have long to wait. "Stop. Step into the room to your right." Gavin did as he was told, but almost fell backwards from surprise. Standing in the room were three other soldiers, similarly attired. Looking at them, he noticed they all had duct tape around their ankles and wrists so there was no gap between their gloves and their boots. Looking behind him, Gavin looked at Hudson.

"I wasn't bitten," he implored.

"I don't give a fuck," Hudson stated. "Move over to the radiator at the far side of the room." Gavin did as he was ordered, the three men parting to allow him entry, the room big enough so they could stay well away from him. Three paces from the radiator, Gavin noticed the set of handcuffs dangling from the metal pipe work. With all the soldiers now behind him, he turned.

"No, please, I haven't done anything."

"Then you don't have anything to worry about," one of the other soldiers said. He also held a taser. "But it's either the cuffs or several thousand volts through your fucking testicles." The man waved the weapon in front of him. "Your choice, but make it quick."

"Come on, cuff yourself to the bloody radiator already." Hudson watched as the man he had met the other day on the farm did as he was ordered, resigning himself to his new imprisonment. Gavin sat down on the floor, his back to the radiator, which had mercifully been turned off. He looked across at the death squad that had been assembled for his benefit.

"It wasn't my fault," Gavin began to cry. "I didn't know." He watched as Hudson removed the gas mask, now safely on the other side of the room, the face bringing recollection.

"Know what?" Hudson demanded.

"Fuck you," Gavin suddenly exploded, tears streaming from his eyes. "If I'm infected, then it's your doing, you cunt." The four soldiers exchanged glances.

"You'll have to explain that one to me," Hudson said calmly.

"You brought them to my farm," Gavin blustered. "You left me there to be...to be eaten by them?"

"Still need a little more detail there, son. And if I remember correctly, we offered you a ride out of there, which you very rudely declined. So what was it that tried to eat you?" Hudson asked the final question calmly, although he already suspected what was going to come next.

"The dogs, you bastard, you left me to the dogs."

15.41PM, 17th September, Newquay Airport, Newquay, UK

"That is an unfortunate development, Captain," General Mansfield said over the satellite radio. The room around the general was silent, everyone desperate to know if the infection had been contained.

"Yes sir," the captain said.

"Do you think the situation is contained?"

"Seems to be, sir. We are outside the quarantine window. Fortunately, Doctor Holden didn't have any interaction with anyone after treating the infected individual. It looks like we dodged a bullet." The captain's words sent a wave of relief through the room, and Mansfield heard someone say "thank fuck" under their breath.

"Good work, Captain," Mansfield said. "Of course, you know what I need from you now, right?"

"Yes, sir," Hudson responded calmly.

"And can I trust you to get that done?" There was a brief pause, but then the words that Mansfield needed to hear came across the radio.

"Yes, sir. I'll attend to that now, sir." The radio connection was silenced. Mansfield stood, looking around the room, his eyes finally settling on someone.

"Corporal, contact the defence teams. Shut it down. Nobody else gets past the wire. I don't care if the Queen herself is waiting in line to get in. Tell them they are authorised to use lethal force if necessary. And patch me through to NATO command. I need to talk to General Marston."

Hudson looked at the radio in his hand, and passed it to the gas-masked man to his side. Stood out in the corridor, he felt the acid burn into his stomach.

"Shit." They had no test for the virus, no means to see who was and wasn't infected before the infection took hold. So the hospital would stay in lockdown until someone said otherwise. Nobody in, nobody out, including Hudson and his men. And to think he had volunteered for this shit.

Gavin was a new development, one that hadn't been expected. Clearly, Gavin hadn't turned, and if he was infected, it represented a great opportunity. Within him might be the answer to defeating the virus. But he also represented a threat. If one person was immune, there would be others who might be free to spread the virus, to act as reservoirs of infection. And there was always the chance that Gavin wasn't the source, that it was merely coincidence, that he was indeed free of the virus. But Hudson didn't think so, not with what the farmer had told them about the dogs.

There was a commotion at the end of the corridor, and three men in hazmat suits walked through the set of double doors. Hudson, standing next to two police officers he didn't know, beckoned them over to him. His mask was still off. He knew what would come next. The new arrivals and others like them would turn the hospital into a laboratory. They now had a possible test subject, and hopefully a working example of the virus. With that and the equipment that was undoubtedly being shipped to this location, these men and women would soon create a test for the viral strain, and with luck, maybe even a vaccine. But they still had to deal with the immediate threat, and that meant keeping people calm. And he would do that by intimidation and force if he had to.

15.43PM, 17th September 2015, MI6 Building, London, UK

Bullets don't always kill, and sometimes even brain shots point-blank have been known to be non-fatal. Rasheed, however, was not that fortunate, the bullet entering his temple, and the shock wave and the projectile itself trashing both hemispheres of the brain. The electronic impulses and neural connections that made Rasheed who he was were irreparably damaged, and blackness came to the man who was already close to suffering a devastating stroke. Owen had effectively killed a man who was already dead.

But the bullet did not destroy the brainstem, the virus there changing, mutating as the tissues in the brain began to break down and decompose.

Lying alone, a hand twitched, the fingers stretching, clawing. Most of the infected who had died had done so from wounds to the torso or from loss of blood. Very few died from such severe head injuries, so with Rasheed, the resurrection was slower, but it still happened. Deep in the bowels of the MI6 Building, a low moan rolled through the deserted corridors, unheard by human ears. A few infected were still there to hear the sound, and they shivered in apprehension, for deep down they knew the power in that sound.

Another mind heard the sound. Not with her ears, but telepathically. Still deep within the underground system, Rachel cocked her head and sniffed. She smelt nothing but the undead around her, but she felt Rasheed within her, felt him changing, felt him becoming. And despite her human brain now being a dead husk, she understood, she knew what this new presence meant. Fabrice had wept at the death of Rasheed, not understanding that his death was inevitable. No human was meant to possess that kind of power, the physiology of the body just too weak to contain it. But now the virus was in control, shaping what nature had taken billions of years to create into a being of unfathomable power.

Rasheed pushed himself up off the floor. Coordination totally shot, it took several attempts for the corpse to become one of the walking variety. Uneasy on his feet, he circled several times, confusion rampant in the remnant of his neural matter. Only the reptilian part of the brain now thrived, the rest cast aside as useless matter. But still Rasheed understood the words that came to him, knew the source and stumbled off in search of the voice's owner.

"*Come to me, come to me,*" said the voice. Not Fabrice this time. No, this time, the voice belonged to Rachel.

12.09PM, 12th June 2004, British Embassy, Moscow, Russia

Snow sat in the smoke-filled room, the no-smoking rule that applied to most UK government buildings seemingly forgotten here. Snow wasn't the one smoking—that was reserved for the man sat across the metal table from him. The official name for this was a debriefing, but Snow was well aware that it would be more of an interrogation. Because the operation had gone wrong, badly wrong. The bandaged arm from where the bullet had passed through was part testament to that. If there was an American present, the word clusterfuck would undoubtedly have been used.

"Why don't you tell me again how the operation went to shit," the smoking man said impassively. The room was small, lit by a single bulb, and the interrogator took a long drag on his cancer stick. Being in Russia, they had to make do with the infrastructure the Russian Government gave them, and as much as they could freshen up the decor, there was a limit to what they could do to the historic building the British Embassy presently occupied. Of course, the first thing they had done was strip out all the listening devices that were embedded in the walls and almost every electrical appliance. You could never trust a Russian, that was Snow's motto.

It was almost ironic that the operation may well have even been one that the Russians would have approved of. With the collapse of the Soviet Union, the Russian Mob had flourished and had begun to flood the Black Market with Russian military armaments. Either sold by base commandants whose pay had become non-existent, or simply stolen from warehouses no longer guarded, it represented a dangerous destabilising influence on the world stage. Less readily admitted, it also cut into the profits of the Western military industrial complex, who made billions selling tools of death to regimes and warlords across the globe who really shouldn't have been allowed to handle anything more dangerous than a sharp stick.

The big threat, of course, was nuclear weapons. If they weren't poorly guarded, they were being left to rot. Through the Echelon global surveillance network, MI6 had uncovered a plan to steal and sell three suitcase nukes to Iran, and that just couldn't be allowed. Small and compact, the nukes could be easily transported and smuggled into any city in the world with devastating consequences. No Western power could allow a regime as rabid as Iran to get their hands on that kind of military might, and as he had spent thirteen months infiltrating the Russian gang in question, Snow was the obvious choice to find out when and where the weapons were being exchanged. It had been a last minute change to his undercover operation, and Snow had protested that there were too many unknowns. Turns out, he was right.

And now seven Russians, three Iranians, and one British operative were dead. Fortunately, Snow and his back-up team had managed to extricate themselves from that situation before Russian authorities had turned up, and there was even a slim chance his cover was still intact. What was more annoying than the operation being blown, however, was that the dead body on ice down in the embassy basement had not been killed by a Russian. The plan had been to witness and oversee the loading of the weapons cargo onto a ship, only for the ship to be intercepted by British warships at a later date. The freighter would be monitored by satellite, and Snow was there merely to confirm that the suspected cargo did actually exist. There were still some who had trouble believing that the technology actually existed to put nuclear weapons in a suitcase. Having seen the three metal cases lifted out of the back of an armoured limo, Snow had no doubts whatsoever. That was when the bullets started to fly.

"We didn't know Mossad also had an operation running. Apparently, they had been following the Iranians for over a year based on their own intel," Snow told the smoking man. "With everyone together to make the changeover, the Mossad assault team hit hard and it hit fast. The Mob guys didn't stand a chance."

"And you didn't suspect that this would happen?" smoking man said accusingly.

"Hey, don't try and pin this shit on me," Snow replied angrily. "I didn't set this operation up. I was just an asset on the ground that your department decided to acquire. My job was to confirm the package, not worry about other agencies fucking things up for us." And for the British, it had been a fuck up. For the Israelis, it was a huge success, the nukes undoubtedly now in their possession. Even mere hours after the firefight at the docks, the Mossad team were likely already halfway out of the country, the Russian borders made porous by low pay and the corrupting power of the US dollar.

"I note you saved two Mob guys from Israeli fire. Why was that?"

"They were my contacts inside the organisation. I was hoping to at least salvage something from this."

"You don't honestly expect to be allowed to continue with your op, do you?" The smoking man seemed genuinely surprised that this was even a consideration.

"I've spent nearly two years worming my way into the lives of these people. I'm close to getting the trust I need to get the information I went in there to get. Saving a few Russian lives seemed a good way of getting that trust. If anything, I should be the one outraged here." He had indeed saved two of the Russians, pushing them to the ground as the bullets started flying, which was where he had received his now patched-up injury. One of the Russians he saved was a man called Alexei.

15.47PM, 17th September 2015, Defensive position 5, Cornwall, UK

"I repeat, all borders are to be closed. Over." Grainger looked at the radio that had spewed out the words he hadn't wanted to hear.

"I still have a lot of civilians heading towards us, sir," Captain Grainger said into the radio handset. "It's going to get ugly if we have to turn them away. Over." He was in the command tent at the rear of his position. Five minutes ago, he had been up one of the observation towers and had seen the roads funnelling thousands of refugees to his position.

"I understand that, Captain," said the voice on the other end. "However, General Mansfield's orders are explicit. You will carry them out or you will be relieved of your command. Over." Grainger sighed heavily. The defensive perimeter he was now in charge of extended for several miles north and south of his position, and was more than adequate to keep out unarmed people. It was still being fortified, however, because the infected would wash over it in minutes.

"I understand the order and will follow it out. I want it on record that I think it is a mistake. The people we leave out there will only add to the army I'm going to have to face when the infected come. Over."

"Then you are free to take whatever measures you feel appropriate to eradicate that risk. Over." Grainger's blood turned to ice. He knew exactly what that meant. No, he would not fire on bloody unarmed civilians, not unless they resorted to violence. How could he order that?

"Yes, sir. Grainger out." The captain put down the radio hand piece and looked around the tent. Vorne stood next to him, his face as expressionless as ever, and their eyes met.

"You know what to do, Sergeant."

"Sir." Vorne knew this man, knew that he would never order the murder of innocents. But maybe the general was right. As abhorrent as it was, culling the herd was now the best way to limit the numbers they would eventually face. That's what the fly-boys had been doing all across the country after all, raining down explosive death on cities across the nation. But it was different when you were looking down the end of a rifle and shooting something you could see. Vorne knew his captain, and he knew his men, and there weren't many that could easily pull the trigger in those circumstances. But there were some, and he knew who they were, that he had always made a point of keeping an eye on them because they were usually trouble. But in this world, right now, they were everything that was needed and more. Grainger's strength of character was now a weakness, and Vorne was certain that the captain realised this. So if the unspeakable had to be done, Vorne would ensure the people who could do the unspeakable were where they needed to be. As he made his way to the main gate, he picked the radio off his belt and started the process of gathering those with an iron will and unhealthy mind.

15.51PM, 17th September 2015, Vauxhall Underground Station, London, UK

Rasheed almost fell down the escalator steps, instinct causing him to grip to the railings. The engineered steps still moved, and he swayed in place until they brought him to the bottom where the sound of the undead floated on an invisible mist. He still couldn't see them, but he could feel them, and he moaned softly to himself.

"*Come to me.*"

Yes, I come. Unlike Rachel who had died and slowly started to regain cognitive abilities, Rasheed still possessed much of his. He had lost the bulk of his identity, but he understood the basics of language and had a vague understanding of what had happened to him. All that he was though—his memories of past events, his beliefs, and his devotion to his religion—was gone, stripped from him by the assassin's bullet that was still lodged within his skull.

He still had awareness though. And he also knew that he still possessed his power, and he revelled to use it. Something inside him told him he no longer had to fear, because his mind was now freed from human constraints, the virus allowing its true potential to be unleashed.

"*Not yet, no not yet,*" the voice said. But it was so hard. Whilst he craved flesh, he craved the use of his power even more, and felt it building inside him.

"*Not safe use here. Wait.*"

Yes, he would wait, but he didn't know for how long he could do that. It was so hard, the urge and the desire so strong. And why were they down here anyway? He followed the feeling and stepped onto the underground platform. Still, none of the undead were visible, and he stumbled off the track, falling onto the rails on the track below. As he landed, his foot hit the live rail, and 630 volts coursed through him, causing his body to twitch and buck. The motion caused his foot to dislodge and the electricity stopped. If he hadn't been dead already, the voltage would have been a problem. Rasheed merely pulled himself up and, still smoking in parts, wandered off down the railway line into the blackness of the tunnel.

He didn't really need his eyes anymore; he just kind of sensed his way around, and it wasn't long before he came upon the first of his kind. But, of course, that wasn't quite right, because they were inferior to him. Rasheed could obliterate them all in a blink, could bring the whole tunnel crashing down upon them all. Was there ever any limit to what he could do? He didn't know, and for some reason didn't quite understand what the word limit meant.

15.51PM, 17th September, Newquay Hospital, Newquay, UK

Brian picked himself up off the floor. This was pointless. Sitting around moping wasn't going to bring her back, and it wasn't going to get him the answers he needed. And where the hell was Stan? He had been gone for a while now. Picking his machine gun up from the bed, he slung it over his head and walked out of the room he had been taken to grieve. He had nothing left in him now—all he had was anger.

"Brian, what you doing?" a voice said behind him. Stan appeared with two steaming cups. He handed one to his friend, but Brian didn't take it. When Brian persisted in his defiance, Stan put one of the cups on the floor by the wall.

"I need to know what happened," Brian said. Stan looked at him and realised he had never seen his friend like this before.

"You know what happened." There was frustration in Stan's voice. "Simone got infected, just like millions of other people."

"Simone wasn't other people," Brian said bitterly. He turned on his friend. "She was good people, she was decent. She didn't deserve this."

"Nobody did, mate."

"You know what I mean," Brian answered. He was speaking almost through gritted teeth. "I want to know why she got infected."

"Well, that's easy. One of the refugees they brought in is suspected of being a carrier. He carries the virus but doesn't present any symptoms." Stan took a sip of his coffee and instantly regretted it. It was from one of the hospital vending machines, and it tasted like dishwater.

"Where is he?" Brian demanded, grabbing Stan's wrist. Coffee spilt from the cup, soaking through Stan's glove, and dripped onto the floor.

"Jesus, Brian, you need to calm down." Brian let go of him and took a solid step back.

"Not until I have some fucking answers. I want to know…"

"You want to know what?" Stan interrupted. He needed to get through to his friend, because he could tell he was about to do something bloody stupid. He'd been a cop long enough to see the signs of a person close to tipping over the edge. "There's nothing you can learn that will help you through this. She's gone, Brian. There's no changing that."

"I refuse to accept that." With those words he turned and stormed off up the corridor.

"Shit," Stan said. Abandoning his coffee next to its discarded cousin, he went off after his friend.

"You, you're the one who came when Simone was infected." Hudson was standing talking to one of his men and he turned to see the officer storming towards him.

"You mean the doctor?"

"Her name was Simone," Brian insisted.

"Indeed it was. And you are?"

"We helped rescue her from London," Stan said, catching up to his friend. He tried to put a restraining hand on Brian, but he shook it off. Hudson let this all sink in, saw the fragile state the man was in, his fellow soldier stepping slightly to the side so as not to present a single target. Brian had his machine gun down at his side, but it wouldn't take much for him to swing it up.

"Then I'm sorry for your loss," Hudson said sympathetically.

"I don't want your pity, I want fucking answers."

"Well, what would you like to know?" Brian was almost taken aback by that.

"How did she get infected?" Brian asked. His hand moved away from the machine gun.

"We have a patient in quarantine who we believe is carrying the virus. We think he passed it on when she examined him."

"And where is this cunt?" Brian demanded, getting too close to Hudson. The SAS man stood his ground.

"Now that I'm not going to tell you. Now if you'll calm—"

"Don't you tell me to fucking calm down. That bastard killed my—" Stan was amazed by how quickly the man moved. One second, he was standing with Brian's finger pointed angrily in his face, the next, he had Brian struggling in a head lock. Brian fought back but the rear naked choke was expertly applied. Hudson looked at Stan.

"In several seconds, your friend will be out cold." Brian's struggles got limper and he quickly passed out. Hudson carefully let him fall to the floor. He looked back at Stan. "He will be disarmed, restrained, and taken to the edge of the hospital grounds under guard. I would advise you to go with him and take care of him until such time as he is his old self again." The soldier Hudson had been originally talking to plucked Brian's machine gun and sidearm off him. "Am I clear?"

"Yes," Stan said. "Yes, sir."

"Good man. When I know something, I will make sure you are informed, as a courtesy. Private, help the officer with his friend, would you?"

15.53PM, 17th September 2015, MI6 Building, London, UK

The four horsemen were not unique, but they were unique to London. There was one like them in Glasgow and two in Manchester, all still alive, all yet to uncover their gifts. Because they were out of range of Fabrice's psychic broadcast, even he didn't know about them. They would have to find their own way, and it was perhaps best for Fabrice not to know this because he still believed that they were sent by God, as foretold in Revelations. Knowing that there were more of those immune to the virus and made powerful by its mutation would have shaken his beliefs and caused him to doubt. And God's chosen should never doubt the intentions of the Almighty.

He had been in despair when Owen had put a bullet in Two's head, but now he could hear Evil in his mind again, could hear the faint chatter of his decaying thoughts and was witness to the power that was forming. And he saw that it was good. Fabrice was still displeased with Owen's actions, but perhaps they were all part of God's ultimate plan. Fabrice had been able to see the damage Rasheed had been doing to his human physiology, a constraint he was now freed of, and he could feel the power growing.

Now Fabrice sat on the banks of the river, a gentle breeze blowing smoke from the burning structures all around him so that ghosts danced in honour of a dead nation's past glories. He had gathered the four and he was free. Free from captivity, but not free from his duty to God. How ironic that God had chosen a follower of the heretic religion of Islam to be the face of Evil. But everyone had the right to make mistakes in life, so long as they repented and followed the one true path. Before he had seen the wisdom and the light, had Fabrice himself not been wicked and a fornicator? No worse than to believe in a false god, so long as you could see the truth and renounce that erroneous belief.

But what was his role now? He no longer had any power over them. Four had learnt to block him out, and even now was off somewhere up to God knew what. Two and Three he could hear, but they muttered amongst themselves, and Fabrice knew not why they were underground. What were they doing down there?

Three infected ran past him, and it was clear to him that they were fleeing from something. Seconds later, a group of about forty undead started wandering into view. Had they been called by Three, or were they just random, the new predator expanding its reach? Some of them wandered close to Fabrice as they passed, but they veered off and let him alone. Nor did they go after the infected, their decayed mission clearly to reach a set destination. More soulless warriors for Three then. At this rate, her army would be greater than the one controlled by Owen.

Owen watched the abomination that called himself One. Not through his own eyes, but through the eyes of the infected. How to deal with this fucker—that was the question that needed answering. How to remove the threat of someone who had the ability to reach into his mind? Owen had learnt quickly how to block him, but would that always work? What about when he was concentrating on controlling the infected? The more he controlled, the more it took from him, and the more he found himself swallowed up in their hive mind. During the assault on the MI6 Building, he had almost lost himself again.

This was not how it was supposed to be. He was in control here, him, not the infected, and not One. This was not what he had planned for himself. He wanted to take his slaves, his minions and his army and just camp out in the luxury of Buckingham Palace. That had been his plan, steadily growing a harem around him whilst his soldiers hunted and brought him food. But then the voice had started interfering with his mind and he'd had to divert from the plan, to adapt to deal with the interloper.

Perhaps now he was free he would just go on his way. But Owen didn't think so. No, he really doubted that was going to happen. The guy was going to cling to him and would keep prodding him to meet his agenda, not the one Owen wanted to follow. Perhaps he should have let Rasheed finish the job he had started, let one bastard kill the other. Yes, again he had perhaps been too impulsive when he had put a bullet in Rasheed's brain. But what was done was done. He would think of something, he was sure of it, and when he did, he would go back to the original plan. This was HIS city, HIS country, and he wasn't going to let anyone take that away from him.

16.01PM, 17th September 2015, River Thames, London, UK

Snow guided the boat down the centre of the river, wary of the bridges he passed under in case any infected decided to leap down from above. So far, they had been okay.

"His name's Alexie. He says he will help us because he knows in doing so we will help him," Snow said. "He was part of the Russian Mob I had infiltrated about ten years back. I was running an operation that went south in Moscow. The bloody Israelis fucked things up for us." Croft himself had never had any direct dealings with Mossad, but he knew they tended to be a bit of a law unto themselves. Despite being part of the Western alliance, they didn't have a tendency to be team players. Which was a shame because they were damned good at what they did.

They had to be; Israel was a tiny country surrounded by heavily armed enemies with the radical determination to wipe the Jewish nation off the face of the earth.

"And you saved his life?" Croft let Snow tell him the information that the MI6 man felt needed telling. His instincts were to trust Snow, so he didn't insult the man by asking pointless questions. Options were limited right now—you took what you could get.

"Yeah. Got a bit of shit for that and was moved back to London for a few years to ride a desk. But then the guy I saved turned up in London as a front man for the same Mob family, so I was borrowed by MI5 to help keep an eye on him and his activities."

"And you think he can help?"

"He's in charge of ferrying people and drugs around Europe. MI5 tolerate him because they know he will occasionally do them favours. The Russians are more than happy to sell out their own countrymen if it makes them even a modicum of profit. The Met have tried multiple times to pin something on him, but he's too smart for that." Croft looked at Snow and waited for the agent to answer his question. "He'll help if he determines it's in his best interest to."

"Good enough for me."

Alexie looked down at the ground below from his penthouse. So, Mr. Snow was still alive and had come to faithful Alexie for help. Alexei, as sociopathic as he was, had a moral code of sorts, and Snow had saved his life all those years ago in Mother Russia. And in recent years, they had used each other to further their own ends, the MI6 agent passing on certain information that helped Alexei impress his bosses. Alexei, of course, had returned the favour. For Alexei would happily sell out local mafia networks in competition to his own, and Snow would pass that information onto both MI5 and MI6, slowly redeeming himself for a failed operation that had tainted his service record. In fact, if he knew who she was, Alexei would sell out his own mother for similar advantage. Now the two men would use each other again, this time for mutual survival. Alexei had what Snow and his friends needed—a working, seaworthy yacht. Obviously, the yacht wouldn't get them to another country. The NATO blockade would see to that. But it would get them out of London, and from there, they could hug the coast to Cornwall. That suited him down to the ground.

Stepping away from the balcony's barrier, he walked back into his penthouse, unconcerned that this would be the last time he ever saw it. It was just a place to put his body when it was not involved in business, and except for the rare exceptions, he had no time for luxury. Luxury made you soft, and that was a death sentence in his line of work. He had risen from the gutter, and he was more than prepared to go back there. Poverty held no threat to him, for wealth really held no appeal. Despite the money he managed, despite the compensation he received from his bosses, it meant little to him. He ate the finest food more for the sake of his body than his own enjoyment, and this mentality would serve him well in the coming days and weeks. Hardship was his brother, and he was happy to embrace his blood.

"It is time to go, Ivan," Alexei called out. When the man didn't respond, he went in search of the old man and found him dozing in front of the TV. Alexei put a gentle hand on his shoulder, ignoring the body odour that escaped from someone who had been drinking too much and who had not utilised the penthouse's most adequate shower facilities. Ivan woke with a start, almost striking the bigger man. But seeing Alexei, he lowered his hand and smiled a drunken smile.

"It's time to go, old friend."

"Go? But where would I go?" Ivan quizzed.

"You will come with me and we will leave this decaying city." The old man laughed and shook his head.

"No, Alexei. I will stay here. This world has no place for an old man like me." Alexei took a step back and looked down at his friend sternly.

"You're sure?"

"I am an old man, and I can't walk more than two hundred metres without getting out of breath. No, I will stay here, and I will drink your wine and eat your food, and I will sit on your balcony and watch the city eat itself."

"You'll die," Alexie said, surprising himself by his own concern. "You realise that."

"I'm dead already." Ivan shrugged. "I never told you about my visit to the doctors, did I?"

"Doctors? No, no you didn't."

"They were very nice and very expensive, which I charged to you of course." Alexei couldn't help smiling at that. "But in the end, they gave me the news most people dread."

"I see. How long did they give you?"

"Six months at the most." Ivan stood, showing no sign of weakness that his age should have created. "Where will you go?"

"The British are trying to create a safe zone in Cornwall." Ivan gave him a puzzled look. "You went there once. You said you hated it."

"There's not much I like about this damned country. If only I could see Mother Russia once more." Ivan put a hand on his friend's shoulder. The younger Russian towered over him. "So this is goodbye then."

"Yes, my friend, I will not forget you." Alexei was caught by surprise as the older man hugged him. Despite his frailty, the hug was strong, and Alexei smiled and returned the gesture. He was going to miss this old fool.

16.07PM, 17th September 2015 Sizewell B Nuclear Power Plant, Suffolk, UK

"This is pointless," the corporal whispered to his friend. They had just finished reinforcing the north fence with sand bag machine gun emplacements. To the west, the sound of bulldozers could still be heard pulling down the rest of the trees that would act as cover for the infected when they finally arrived. "We're basically sat on one great big fucking nuclear bomb. You realise that, don't you?"

"I just follow orders," the private said. "As long as my wife and kid are here, I'll do what I'm told, when I'm told." The corporal was a known whinger, but good in a scrap, so people tended to tolerate him. But he wasn't the only one murmuring in the ranks, the disbelief with what had happened conflicting with the military duty that they felt compelled to comply with. There had been desertions, a few dozen men in all, but there were still close to four hundred soldiers ready to defend this facility, and like the private, many of them had been able to bring their families, most of whom were now camped out across the site. The military had arrived with a total of just over a thousand people, a minority of them actual military, nearly a whole battalion of the Welsh Cavalry.

Most of the staff of the power plant hadn't fled, but had kept on working their shifts. It was the general feeling that the safest place to be was surrounded by armed soldiers and Scimitar tanks. But there was a problem—you couldn't just turn off a nuclear power plant, and you couldn't just leave it abandoned to do its own thing. Because it needed constant monitoring and maintenance. Truth be told, nobody had ever envisaged this sort of thing happening, so nobody had a clue what to do.

"Yeah, but do you ever think that the people giving the orders don't have a fucking clue?" the corporal persisted. "I mean, look at how all this went down. The politicians didn't react properly. They should have left everything to the military."

"Whatever you say, Corporal."

"It's like when Foot and Mouth hit all those years ago. There were government inspectors running around panicking, wasting time whilst the disease ran through the cattle like wildfire." The private lifted up the last of the sandbags and heaved it into position. As he did, he saw the imposing figure walking up behind the corporal, who was still engaged in his rant. The newly arrived sergeant could clearly hear everything the corporal was saying.

"Corporal, are you flapping your lips again?" The corporal turned to see his bull-necked sergeant staring down at him.

"No, Sergeant, sorry, Sergeant."

"You bloody will be, my lad. Sling your hook, Private. There's a good lad." The private nodded, relieved to be spared any more of an ear bashing, and he quickly marched off. The sergeant waited until he had departed and then pointed at the corporal's arm. "Those stripes on your arm mean anything to you?"

"Yes, Sergeant."

"They mean you are in a position of authority. These boys who wear the uniform do so for Queen and country, and they don't need you undermining everything." The sergeant wasn't shouting, but kept his voice calm.

"No, Sergeant."

"So what's say you and me come to an understanding." The sergeant stepped in closer, allowing his bulk to intimidate his underling. "You stop talking shite, and I'll not have you digging latrines for the next two weeks. Do we have a deal?"

"Yes, Sergeant."

"Good. Now get your arse over to the supply tent. The quartermaster needs a hand." The sergeant watched the man leave. He didn't like being hard on the men, but he had to maintain discipline in the ranks, because that was all they had left. They had to hold this place until someone decided what the fuck to do with it. He couldn't have any kind of dissent, not now. Because even though they were surrounded by electrified reinforced wire fencing and claymore mines, the infected would penetrate that barrier. He had seen the videos from London, had seen what they were capable of. If they arrived in force, this place had to be ready. With the provisions they had brought and those that they had scavenged from the surrounding area, they had enough food and water for about a month. The problem was the sergeant suspected they would run out of ammunition long before then. The only hope they had was if the infected left them alone, and there was a real chance of that. Apart from Norwich to the north, there weren't any significant population centres close by. One could only hope, and hope was in somewhat short supply at the moment.

16.11PM, 17th September 2015, Defensive position 5, Cornwall, UK

"You are ordered to disperse," the voice over the megaphone boomed from above them. The voice was met with cries and wails and desperate pleading. Vorne looked down at the assembled masses and repeated the message again. They weren't going to listen to him, which was kind of inevitable really. These were frightened people, ripped from the normality of their lives by a situation even a battle-hardened Vorne was struggling with. But the sergeant had orders, and there was one thing he never did, and that was disobey an order.

"This is your final warning. Disperse and go back the way you came, or I will order you to be fired upon." The corporal stood next to him in the watchtower gave Vorne a nervous glance which Vorne ignored. He knew this week was going to be a shit stain when he woke up Monday morning.

"Corporal, let's give them an incentive. I want tear gas in that crowd." The corporal nodded, relief etched all over his face. Tear gas he could deal with, nobody died from that. Ten seconds later, four canisters sailed into the crowd below, bouncing several times as they scattered amongst the people, the gas escaping from the pressurised containers like white ghosts in the fading light. The people began to scatter, trampling over one another to escape the gas and get away from the wire—just another assault to break their will and flush from their lives the last vestiges of civilisation as they had known it. Looking down, Vorne showed no reaction, even as he saw a young girl get pushed to the ground. The frail figure disappeared amongst the throng, and only when the crowd had cleared that spot could her body be seen lying prone and unmoving on the ground, trampled by dozens of feet. He could hear the anguish and the anger of the crowd, and knew that it was now the only way.

One of the things that helped spread the infection so quickly was the fact that the British population was generally unarmed and unfit to face such horrors. In 1996, Thomas Hamilton killed sixteen children in one of the deadliest mass murders in UK history. As a result, the legal private ownership of handguns was severely restricted, and even shotguns became a luxury, requiring special vetting by the police before ownership was allowed. Unarmed and made unfit by the sugar-laden, exercise-deficient Western lifestyle, the people of Britain became easy prey, rich pickings for the infected that ran amongst them. There were guns about of course, criminals not caring too much about the law. The

Black Market for guns didn't so much flourish, but it wasn't hard to get a hold of an automatic pistol if you knew a man who knew a man and if you had the money and the guts to pay for it.

It was thus inevitable that some in the crowd would be armed. Sucked up by despair and the insanity of it all, someone took into upon themselves to fire several shots at the defensive wall. Nobody was hit, but as the sound of the shots echoed across the scene, the defenders on the wall did what they were trained to do. They opened fire. It only took one itchy trigger finger to set off what was a mixture of trained soldiers and semi-trained civilians. The shooting only went on for less than fifteen seconds, although it would have been longer but for Vorne shouting the ceasefire order over his megaphone. But fifteen seconds was enough to kill nearly a hundred men, women, and children who had come here for refuge. In a way, they got it, for they were relieved of the burden of living in a world now at war with itself. And as was the way with such things, nobody learnt who had fired the first shots into the crowd. The bodies they left outside the wire because the defensive line was closed, which meant nobody got in or out.

16.31PM, 17th September 2015, Docklands, London, UK

Alexei had left the penthouse with a rucksack on his back, warm clothing, thick steel-tipped boots, an automatic pistol, and an AR15 machine gun with enough ammunition to recreate the battle of Stalingrad. He did not take the lift, as inviting as it was, fearful that the power would finally fail and he would end up trapped in an unbreakable metal box.

Of course, the power didn't fail, and he exited the staircase into the deserted foyer of his apartment building. Some of the windows were smashed, but the concourse outside looked deserted. With the windows broken, he had no need to use the door, and he exited his home for the last time, machine gun raised, ready to fire at anything that moved. He didn't look back, the word sentimental not even in his dictionary.

This was the quietist he had even known the city. Normally bustling with life, even in the small hours, he was the only thing moving. Despite that, he hugged the walls and kept to the shadows where possible. Clouds had formed overhead, and the smell of burning was ever present in his nostrils. But it was nothing to the stench he would wake up to on the streets of Moscow, his own stench the least of his concerns. He ignored it and made his way to where he needed to go. Snow had been very clear in his instructions.

Alexei's yacht was seven minutes' walk from the front of his apartment building—he knew, he had timed it, and he knew he could run it in three. He left little to chance, and had run the route dozens of times so that it was ingrained into his head. And this was why. He had always known there was a chance he would need to flee, but he had always feared either a rival organisation or Scotland Yard causing his flight, not the infected and the undead. But that was the key to disaster preparedness; you never knew what the disaster was going to be.

Despite the temptation, he didn't run, because this required stealth. Running was foolish when the infected could run faster and with more stamina. And armed as he was, running blindly into a crowd of them would mean his death. Stopping at a corner, he sidled up to the marble façade and flicked his eyes around the bend. Nothing, nothing save a dog panting in the middle of the road. Alexei stepped out into what was a pedestrian throughway, and the dog looked at him, rising to its feet. It snarled at him, and from seven metres away, Alexei could tell there was something not right about it. The creature was visibly injured and foamed at the mouth. As rabies was not a threat on this island, there was only one other cause for this. The dog limped towards him, its movement hampered by the slaughter to one of its legs. From where he stood, Alexei could see his motor yacht, could almost taste it. But did he backtrack and go around or take the creature out? He stepped to the side and the dog countered with its own sideways movement.

"Fuck it," he said to himself and aimed the AR15 at the beast. The shot rang out and the dog fell with a startled yelp. He was already moving before the dog fell to the ground, and the shot echoed through the buildings around him. Seconds later, a response came, and in the distance, he heard what sounded like the roar of a crowd. He had time, he knew he had time, and now he did run, his destination fully in his sites. Up above him, he heard a feral scream, and then something solid collided with the pavement behind him. He didn't look back, knowing what had happened. By the time he reached the yacht, the cries were closer, but not close enough. Disengaging the mooring ropes, he made his way quickly to the wheel house, the infected surge closing in on him with every passing second.

16.33PM, 17th September 2015, Defensive position 5, Cornwall, UK

A single shot rang out, and Grainger watched from his elevated position as the young man running at the fence fell to the ground. Lowering his binoculars, he sighed at the enormity of the task he was now being asked to do, and the probable futility of it. All along the wire line, building work was still taking place with renewed effort, those working the machinery, swinging the axes and sawing the wood mindful that they were on the safe part of the wire. Another thief had been uncovered an hour ago trying to raid a medical tent, and this time, she hadn't been hanged. She had merely been shot and the body left to fall in a ditch. Military discipline was now absolute, and those not falling into line faced harsh penalties. Grainger objected to it, but those were the orders of his commanding officer. And there was another reason the civilians were mostly doing as they were told. They feared what was coming more than the oppressive regime they were now under. They were being fed and watered, and they had cover from the elements. Many of them were still in shock, stunned into submission. But how long would that last? How long before they started clamouring for "their rights" and would they accept the fact that, here and now, their rights had been suspended indefinitely?

There were worried murmurings about General Mansfield. He seemed to be relishing his command a bit too much, almost wallowing in the power. Grainger found the rumours hard to believe, the general having a good reputation with the troops…well, the male troops at least. He was a Gulf War Two veteran and had actually fought in battle. But this was a different kind of war; this was more akin to survival. There was no remorse or the possibility of surrender with this enemy. You either killed them all or you died, but could you actually kill an army that could resurrect, an army that likely numbered into the millions?

Raising the binoculars up again, he looked at the dead man that had just been shot. What the hell had he been trying to do? Was it desperation that caused him to rush at the gate like that? Was it madness? Surely, he wasn't infected, not this early on. They had at least another day left…didn't they? How quickly could the infected get here if they ran full pelt?

16.43PM, 17th September 2015, River Thames, London, UK

Alexei sat in the open top wheelhouse and watched as the smaller boat came towards him, the flare that had been fired to signal the newcomer's arrival now dead. The flare had been to confirm that this was Snow, and so Alexei had slowed the boat to allow them to catch up, but would the infected react to it? Or would they ignore the purple glow that shot into the air moments before? He kept the motor running, and the yacht was pulled along by the current. There was no way he was setting down anchor, not with the very real fact that the infected could swim. As wide as the river was at this point, there was no need for unnecessary risks. The binoculars he held to his eyes scanned not only the approaching boat but the waters surrounding him.

He had seen it himself. When he had pulled the yacht away from its birth, he had looked back to see dozens of figures rushing towards the dock's edge. They hadn't stopped, but had propelled themselves into the water like lemmings, intent on reaching him, swimming with a speed and determination that made Olympians look like novices. But there was no way they could catch up to the boat, and he quickly left them in his wake. The priority now was to get Snow and his friends on board, and get as far away from London as possible.

He watched as the small boat came up to the back of his yacht, which allowed the passengers to transfer. When the last of them was on board, he reengaged the power and the yacht smoothly surged forwards, leaving the smaller craft bobbing uselessly in the water. Alexei heard footsteps as people ascended to where he was. Snow and Croft appeared behind him, and he concentrated on steering the boat.

"Good to see you again, Alexei," Snow stated.

"Life keeps pushing us together, does it not, Agent Snow? Perhaps we should get married and adopt some children." There was no humour in the Russian's voice.

"This is Major David Croft," Snow said, and Alexei glanced back at the new arrival.

"You are Army?"

"Officially Military Police, but it's a long story," Croft said.

"Ah, so you have come to arrest the infected."

"Not quite." The boat veered to the side slightly as Alexei steered it around the river's bend. To the right, the Millennium Dome was visible in all its overpriced glory.

"Snow tells me I am to take you all to Newquay. Will there be a place for me there?"

"I'm sure we can find you something to do," Croft said.

"There are supplies in the lower cabins. I suggest you all make yourselves comfortable." With that, Alexei turned back to guiding the boat. Snow tugged on Croft's arm, and they both descended back down the same stairs.

"Bit of a strange one," Croft said so as not to be overheard.

"You don't know the half of it. I can't even say he's your typical Russian, because he's odd even for them. But he was the best option we had."

"Well then, let's get settled in."

Savage locked the door to the cabin she had chosen and sat down on the bed. All for nothing. She had left the relative safety of Cornwall to try and do what she did best, and she hadn't even had a chance to look down a microscope. She could easily accuse herself of having failed, but really, did she ever have a chance? They never really had a hope against the virus; to try and think otherwise was just delusional. The limited research she had collected may come in useful, and as much as she hated Dr. Durand's methods, he had given them valuable clues to the secrets of the virus.

Like Croft, she too had a smart phone connected to a secure government satellite network. Even though the government had fallen, the network was still up, and would persist long after the country's electricity failed. She knew that Croft had already been in communication with both General Marston and General Mansfield, so when she opened up her email account, she was not surprised to find she had been sent information about developments behind the defensive lines. She paid attention to one email in particular.

To Captain Savage,

A little bird tells me you are on your way back here. Let's hope there is still a here left when you arrive. We came across an old friend a few hours ago, that farmer bloke from where we landed the helicopter in Devon. Seems after he left, he got attacked by whatever was left of those "Demon Dogs" we encountered, and it appears he wound up getting infected. The strange thing is, he seems to be immune.
But he also seems to be a carrier. We had an outbreak in the hospital and those with more intelligence than me have pinpointed him as the cause based on his history. They say if he's immune, they may have a chance for a cure. So there you go, the good news I just know you were wanting to hear.
Say hello to Croft for me. I offered to come and fetch you myself, but the general was quite adamant that he wasn't able to spare me, my men or a helicopter...not to mention, I'm bloody stuck in this bloody hospital under quarantine. I'm guessing you and the good general don't get on ☺

See you soon,
Captain Hudson SAS

Savage saw that Croft had been Cc'd into the email, and she actually laughed. It was men like him and men like Croft that were the only chance they had. Determined, dedicated, and unwavering, and ready to do the shit that needed to be done. She said men because there just weren't that many women in the positions needed for it to make a blind bit of difference. She knew female officers and female soldiers that put their male counterparts to shame, but there were so few of them, and most of them were now either infected or dead. So Savage would hold it together and be ready when she was needed. If they had someone who was immune, that could change the whole game. If only they had the time to make something of it.

In the cabin next door, Durand knelt on the bed with his ear to the wall. He thought he could hear her breathing. Was that laughter? Was she laughing at him? Of course she was, the fucking bitch. When the time was right, he was going to kill her, and it wouldn't be a quick death. No, he had been thinking about this. He wanted to see the pain in her eyes as she saw who it was that killed her. For the past hour, his mind had raced with all the things he would do to her. There was nothing sexual in those fantasies, because he was by nature uninterested in that sort of thing. He felt dirty even thinking about it. Succumbing to such base emotions was unthinkable. Oh, it had happened in the past, and he had always felt disgusted that he could let his mind be overridden by such basic chemistry.

And most of his fantasies would never come to fruition, because he just wouldn't get the opportunity. But he would kill her, and Croft if he had the chance…and hell, anyone else who was there. He still had the gun, but for Savage, he wanted to use a knife, and had spirited one away from the ship's galley upon his arrival on the yacht. When the time was right, he would be there, and he would plunge the knife deep into her inner thigh, sever the femoral artery, and watch her frantic eyes as she started to bleed out. And then he would stab her again, and again, and again, each one an unfatal wound. He would torture her and show her the consequences of crossing him.

17.00PM GMT, 17th September 2015, Houston, Texas, USA

The broadcast went live to an average of five million people, and sometimes it went out three times a day. Thinking people, patriots, people who knew their government was lying to them, plotting against them. The broadcast went out on time, and went out strong. But today, it wouldn't last the designated three hours, and one of the country's most popular syndicated radio and live streaming internet shows would never be aired again.

"This is the Andrew James Show."

"Welcome back, ladies and gentlemen to this, the second hour in today's syndicated radio broadcast. It's as I feared. My sources inside the Pentagon have revealed to me, moments ago, that the government are implementing their power grab. In the third hour, we will have retired CIA operative Kevin O'Toole on to answer your questions, but right now, we need to talk about what's about to happen in this country. We need to lay down some knowledge on what the puppets in Washington intend to do to implement their master's globalist agenda."

"I've been saying this was going to happen for over twenty years. I've been saying that the command and control structures were being put in place to turn this country into an autocratic hell hole. And you know, people laughed in my face. Well, they're not laughing now. No, now people are listening, are seeing the truth that we have been shining a light on for decades. Let us be clear here. They will come for your guns, ladies and gentlemen, and if my sources are correct, they are already on their way. I have the documents in front of me right now, ladies and gentlemen, the executive orders they will use to lock you away and take away what little is left of your rights. Even now across the country, FEMA is coordinating with the FBI to take you and your children from your homes, to take you for your protection to processing facilities. That's what they always say though, isn't it? It's for your protection. Do it for the children, they will tell you—"

Andrew James was suddenly plunged into darkness, and his voice, the voice that had been shouting the message of conspiracy for several decades, disappeared from the airwaves.

"What the hell?" he shouted to his production team. Seconds later, the emergency lighting came on.

"We're off the air, boss," his editor said.

"Why hasn't the backup generator kicked in?" James asked. A sliver of icy fear wormed its way down his spine. Was this it? Was this how it went down? There was a muffled bang from somewhere in the building, followed by another. "Are you getting anything from the security feeds?" James asked, referring to the security cameras around the building.

"Shit," he heard someone say, their identity hidden by the gloom. He had a staff of over twenty people, all loyal to the cause. James stood up, frantic, and stormed over to the editing area in the room. Several monitors were black, except two showing video feeds. The surveillance system had its own redundant power supply, and because of that, he could see dozens of armed men storming the ground floor of his facility. This was indeed it.

"What do we do, boss?" someone asked.

"We make our peace with God," James said calmly. Finally, it was here, the day he always knew would arrive, and he knew he had mere seconds to make a decision. Did he get down on his knees and let them take him, or did he fight and take some of the fuckers with him? The latter wasn't an option, not here. The people who worked for him were devoted to the truth, but they didn't need to die. James took out his phone, saw that there was no service, and flung the now useless device across the room in frustration. James heard a pistol being cocked and saw Robert, his friend and longest serving employee, holding his Glock. "Put that away, son," James said. "It won't do you any good here." They could hear the sounds of their enemy working their way through the building. Situated on the third floor of the building they were in, there was no escape. From below them, he heard the muffled report of shotguns firing.

"I'm not going to let them take me," Robert spat.

"Yes, you will," James said. "Our job is done here. We've done all we can, and there's no point dying when there's no chance of changing anything. It's up to the people of this country now. It's up to them to decide whether they accept this New World Order, or stand up and fight for their freedoms. Put the gun down, lad. You have a family." Robert hesitated, and then he seemed to deflate, the gun almost dropping from his fingers to the table in front of him. Fortunate for him, because at that moment, something clattered onto the ground beside him. He looked down just as it exploded, the white light blinding, the sound destroying any thought of who he was. For seconds, all he knew was pain. He choked on the fumes, collapsing to his knees painfully, his vision pure white. He didn't see the multiple armed men burst into the studio.

"FBI, EVERYONE ON YOUR KNEES." James turned to the intruders, put his hands behind his head and did exactly as he was ordered.

"Entry in 5, 4, 3, 2, 1. Go, go, go," the voice said over his earpiece. Pushed up against the wall of the building, he watched as the steel-reinforced door to the building exploded, and as the debris settled, he followed his fellow SWAT team members into the building. Other explosions from other areas went off almost simultaneously. It was dark inside, and he flipped the night vision down from his helmet, the bold FBI letters on the Kevlar of the man in front of him shining brightly. He had done this hundreds of times, had stormed countless building, fired his weapon more times than he could remember, but he had never killed anyone. And there was something about this that didn't feel right. The people in this building hadn't broken any laws, at least none that he knew of. And yet those were his orders, plain as day. Take down the broadcast; the information the man possessed must not be aired to the public. The intel had come too late to seize those in question before they got to the broadcast centre, so they had to go with the next best thing.

"Ground floor clear," a voice said. And then the stairs, Mitch was going up, almost on autopilot, his training kicking in. He was good at what he did, one of the best. Soon, he would command his own squad. He knew he was first in line for promotion. Could he let his doubts jeopardise that? This is all he had ever wanted. To be here, doing this, with his buddies. But could he follow these orders blindly? Hell, he had listened to the guy's show himself, had seen the man's passion and his conviction. He held some extreme beliefs, but wasn't this supposed to be a Democracy? Didn't people have the right to those beliefs, no matter how objectionable, no matter how controversial?

"Bravo team, secure the first level. Alpha team, proceed to target." How many stairs had he ascended like this, the adrenalin pumping, the breath heavy in his lungs, forcing fire into his chest? This was the moment, this was living. But was he now living a lie? And could he accept that? The answer came to him almost instantly. Yes, he could. He didn't like it, but if this was the start of the new order, he wanted to be on the inside, be a part of it. For his family, for himself.

His ascent stopped, and there were multiple shotgun reports from the floor below, most likely breach rounds to force open locked doors. He heard a door kicked open and then the momentum began again.

"Move, move, move," the voice shouted to him over the ether. Up to the landing, through the door, secure the corridor, up to the broadcast room. Mitch threw the flashbang through the open door, the explosion and then the assault. They entered defensively, fanning out to confront what they knew would be armed civilians.

"FBI, EVERYONE ON YOUR KNEES." He heard people shout, heard himself shout. Through the smoke and the blackness, his enhanced vision saw confused, staggering forms. He turned to his left, saw someone reaching for a shotgun, felt his finger slip off the trigger guard as he stormed up the individual.

"Don't do it," his voice roared, but could the guy even hear him? The man looked in his direction, seemed to look through him, and the hand touched the weapon. And then the man's head shot back and the body flew to the floor as the bullet entered in the centre of his forehead. Mitch felt the pressure on his finger, the contraction enough to end a life.

"Studio clear," he heard his commander say. Mitch felt a hand on his shoulder.

"Clean take," a voice said in his ear. "Good job." It didn't feel like a good job. And in the background, someone was screaming. Mitch looked around, shock starting to set in at what he had felt forced to do. Hundreds of missions and he had never shot a man before. He'd taken down serial killers, drug barons, and white supremacists, and the first time he felt forced to use lethal force was some guy in a radio studio.

"Fuck," Mitch said under his breath.

Mitch sat on his own away from everyone. The sun was still hot, and he rested in the shade at the back of the building he had just raided. He held the phone, his hand shaking slightly. Pressing the on button, he made a call from the speed dial. The name that came up said simply one word: Sis.

"Hi, Mitch," the voice came from the other end after three rings. "How's Texas?"

"Fiona..." he suddenly found that he couldn't speak. Tears began to well in his eyes.

"Mitch, what's wrong?" came the concerned voice.

"I'm...I..."

"Talk to me, Mitch." The voice was calm, loving. That sweet voice he had heard so many times. He needed her, wanted to hold her, to just release the pressure that was building inside. For the first time since he was a child, he began to cry.

"He went for his gun," he said, the words almost gasping, full on crying now. He couldn't stop it, didn't know how. "I killed him." Over by one of the several ambulances parked outside the broadcast house, his friend saw him. From fifty metres away, he witnessed the pain, understood it, and began to walk over.

"You did what you had to do, Mitch," Fiona Carter said. Sat in her office in DC, all she could do was sit and listen to her brother's anguish.

"What am I going to do?" Mitch asked.

"You are going to do what you always do. You'll get through this. It's tough now, but that will go away. Trust me, I know." And she did know. The first time she'd killed a suspect, she'd been a wreck for several days. It had almost ended her career. And then she'd had to go through the investigations, the allegations that it was an unnecessary use of lethal force. The allegations of racism that came from the dead man's family. The fact the man she had shot had been holding a gun at his own daughter's head seemingly irrelevant. The fact that he had been high on PCP and had already shot his wife inconsequential. Of course, she had been exonerated, even receiving a commendation for saving a child's life. And the subsequent lawsuit from the man's family had disappeared when the media had finally begun to play the true story of what had happened.

"I didn't want to kill him, Sis," Mitch said, the tears drying now. Carter heard someone talking to him in the background.

"You did what you had to do, never forget that. We all do what we have to do."

18.11PM GMT, 17th September 2015, Resurrection Ranch, Texas, USA

Perhaps this was the final lesson God wanted to teach him. Abraham sat in the ornate office of his ranch, the mobile phone in his hand no longer receiving any kind of signal. The call had been cut off mid-sentence, which was troubling. Putting the mobile down, he picked up the landline and heard that there was no dial tone. So, that was that, they were coming for him. Abraham had expected as much. He was guilty of pride, of hubris and of arrogance—he saw that now. And now he was to suffer the Lord's ultimate judgement. Abraham dropped the phone receiver back into its cradle and stood on shaky legs. Time had not been kind to him, and he knew that he would very shortly be with his maker.

He had only been partially successful in his goal. He had underestimated the man he called president, the man who he had helped into the Oval Office, all with the ultimate plan of bringing the man down, and with him the high office of President of the United States. He had intended to humiliate the man and the office, to bring the government to its knees and show the people the false gods they elected to do whatever they could get away with. The president was supposedly immune to prosecution from anything done before being elected to the highest office of the land, but how would that constitutional rule play out against the president being accused of murder? But that wasn't going to happen now.

The betrayal by the man who had created the virus had been unexpected and disappointing. Abraham hadn't seen it coming, couldn't understand why the man had done what he had done. Because of that betrayal, his agent inside MI6 had been uncovered, and from that, Abraham's identity had been revealed to those with vengeance in their hearts. His hatred of the British had only been part of his master plan, a plan that was now thwarted. He had never intended to release the virus on the US mainland. The remaining samples had been sent to a much better place. Even now, they sat ready to be released at a predetermined time, to bring judgement to the godless and the heathens. How he had looked forward to seeing the heretics cower under the hammer of God. Well, he supposed he would now have to watch that from heaven.

The final samples of the virus were different from that released on the UK mainland. That attack had been a message, a warning and a threat to the world that God was watching and that God was vengeful. The new virus was for the purging, the removal of those who worshipped the false gods. It was a race-specific bio-weapon that would only infect someone with a specific genetic code. It would not infect those of the Caucasian race. But it would create an army of infected and undead that would see the world descend into the time of Revelations, as written by John the Apostle. The end times were here, and only the faithful would survive this ultimate test. Those who knew the word of God would be forced to rise up and fight the army of the damned, and in doing so, cleanse the world and remake it anew.

But he was undone. He had come so far only to be thwarted at the last step. His plan to release the devastating news that the President of the United States had assaulted and raped someone as a teenager would now never come out. Rodney had predicted this attack and had already countered it. With the country now under martial law, there was now no way the main stream media would break the news, not with Homeland Security rounding people up in their thousands. And even if it did, it would just be spun as conspiracy theory, and anyone with any sort of reach in that regard was probably already on a bus to the nearest FEMA camp.

His hope had been to throw the country into disarray so that true patriots could step up and make the country great again, one nation under God, not one nation under the almighty dollar and the corporate boot. And then, when the country was on its knees, threatened on all sides by its true enemies, God would strike again, turning the Middle East into an infected hell hole. That would still happen—the devices in Mecca and Medina were already primed. But now, his plan would be warped, tainted. It would be an emboldened president, unconcerned with public opinion, who would use the destruction of Islam for his own ends. For the first time in his life, Abraham realised he had been played by a mind greater than his own. Falling to his knees, he clasped his arthritic hands together and thanked his God for the final insight into his own flawed character. It was a lesson in humility and he welcomed it gladly.

He didn't hear the plane. He didn't hear the bomb that was released several thousand feet up by the Hercules transport, and as he prayed, the most powerful non-nuclear bomb in the US arsenal hurtled towards him. The FBI and the CIA had wanted to arrest him, to put him on trial, to show him to the world for the mass murderer that he was. But the president had overridden them. Why risk brave lives on taking an armoured compound when one bomb could do the work quickly and efficiently? Why give the monster a platform to vent his hate filled ideology? No. Better to send him to his God. And more importantly, better for him to die and take his secrets with him. And so the GBU-43/B fell from the sky, guided to the exact spot where it exploded, vaporising Resurrection Ranch and all those who dwelled within. Abraham died on his knees, and fifty others died with him. And no news channel ever reported the monumental explosion in the Texas backwater. In such an isolated location, the sound that reverberated around the canyons surrounding the ranch, and the miniature mushroom cloud that was visible for several minutes, was merely an interesting talking point for those few individuals who saw and heard the evidence of the explosion.

President Rodney thought that by killing his secret mentor, he would put an end to any threat. What he didn't realise was how this one action would speed up the old man's ultimate plan. Implanted under Abraham's skin was a small, yet powerful transmitter that went silent with his death. Far above the earth, the supposed weather satellite that one of his subsidiary companies had built and put in orbit registered the lack of signal, and the software on board waited the allotted time. When the signal was found to still be absent, it relayed that information to another computer back down on Mother Earth. And so began a series of fail safes and relays that when triggered resulted in Abraham's race-specific bio-weapon being unleashed onto a world that was already reeling from the previous day's events.

The hotel had over a thousand rooms and most of them were still full, even though the annual pilgrimage to Mecca was over. It had been built over five years ago, and everyone who visited was impressed by its splendour. What wasn't well known was who owned the hotel and who had ordered its construction. If a forensic accountant had been given enough time, he would have found that the corporation was just a subsidiary of a global business owned by a reportedly reclusive man whose heart had, minutes earlier, stopped beating.

The hotel had received recent upgrades to the fire suppressant sprinkler system, and that sprinkler system now kicked in, flooding the rooms and corridors with water. But, of course, there was no fire, and the guests scrambled from their rooms, cursing the drenching of their clothes and the annihilation of any electronic devices they possessed. They didn't know what the water contained, and as they gathered outside in the cold desert air, the staff of the hotel tried frantically to shut off the downpour. But it was too late. The water was laden with the latest version of the Chief Cleric's virus, another upgrade that wasn't in the official work logs, and over seven hundred people were infected. A similar scene was played out across the Middle East and North Africa. Two hotels in Cairo, one in Medina, one in Doha. The people, cold and wet, unable to go back into their hotels, drifted off to cafes and bars to try and dry out and stay warm. And they took the virus, still dormant, with them, spreading it throughout the communities surrounding and servicing the hotels. In all, over four thousand people were infected in the first wave, and as with London, the virus began its slow methodical mutation in its new hosts, taking the human DNA to improve and reproduce itself. But unlike in London, the virus was slower in its presentation, and it would take days before the infection finally kicked in, those infected becoming the perfect vessels to carry and transmit the plague. By then, the infection would be far and wide across the world, infecting only those with specific genetic markers, leaving the rest of the population untouched. In the days to come, Great Britain would be almost forgotten as the whole world went mad.

18.01PM, 17th September 2015, Somewhere in Devon, UK

They ran. In fact, they had been running flat out for the last seven hours. Despite the yearning inside them, they didn't stop, didn't rest, didn't deviate from the mission that was burned into their minds. Get west, infect and spread, attack the meat there, set the virus free in the so far untouched part of the country.

There were five of them in all, drenched in sweat, muscles burning from the relentless pounding. And yet they never quit, never rested, occasionally actually running through groups of refugees, never stopping, merely grabbing those they could as they passed, passing the virus on from the fluids coating their own bodies. But that had been hours ago, and with the military ever closer, they moved off the main roads into the back streets, the fields, even running along train lines. They begged to stop, to feed, to quench the thirst that tore them apart inside, but the collective mind drove them on, demanded their subservience, their sacrifice. The feeding would come later; now, they must serve the collective, submit to the greater good.

And they weren't alone. There were dozens of groups like them that had been tasked with sending the virus far and wide. The collective knew the dangers, knew there was still the threat of man's ultimate weapons. So they ran, and they left a viral infestation in their wake. But like so many of such advanced scouts, they would not succeed. They would fall to the weapons of the humans. Now ready, the prey waited, ready for what was the inevitable.

The shot rang out just after the head of the lead infected exploded. Stunned by the loss, surprised by the trauma, the group didn't have a chance to react even as the second of their number fell before the farmer's bullet. Caught out in the open, the remaining three scattered. Another was caught in the shoulder and managed to keep her feet despite the force of the impact. The second shot destroyed her right hip, shattering it as the bullet fragmented upon impact. She fell, now only able to crawl. Hidden by the undergrowth, she witnessed in primal horror as her remaining two brothers were jerked off their feet, their voices silenced in her mind. What to do, what to do?

She had failed, they had all failed, and in her mind, she wept. There was no response. The collective, registering her injuries, discarded her, knowing that even with her enhanced healing there was no surviving the trauma she had suffered. The virus tried, oh how it tried to repair the damage, but even the infected needed blood, which now drained from her through damaged arteries. And yet she continued to crawl, desperate to do what she had been programmed to. And then another bullet found her, somehow finding her in the long grass. Her jaw exploded, teeth and bone being flung in all directions. She died there, her mind withering as the last of her bled out into the fertile soil. And there she laid, an eerie silence falling over the green and pleasant field that had once been the epitome of leafy England. Now dead, the body waited for the field to reclaim her.

The field mouse found her minutes later. The body still warm, the rodent approached cautiously. It had encountered these beings before, knew them to be cruel and vicious. It had smelt them on the poisons and the traps in the big structures it sometimes tried to scavenge food from. It drew closer, sniffed. Then it scattered as the creature moved. From a safe distance, it watched as it stood up, staggering from some injury or other. Its nose twitched, the smell of something bad in the air. The mouse made to move away completely, and then it was stunned by the sound and sight of the huge monster's head exploding. It fell back down, now truly lifeless. Waiting, the mouse watched and waited. Eventually satisfied, it moved in and nibbled on the corpse before something bigger came along to scare it away from its prize.

Further north, more infected had spread, drawn by the large groups of hapless refugees camped out, trapped between a rock and a hard place. Many were stuck because their path was blocked by destroyed roads, collapsed bridges, and decimated tunnels. Others were trapped just by the geography of the land, and the huge numbers of humanity that was trying to pass through natural choke points. Thousands just sat at the side of the road or camped out in fields, completely at a loss as to what to do now that their one last hope for survival had been removed.

The infected, low in numbers, soon threatened to multiply as they ran riot through the packed in masses of humans who seemed to think staying together was a worthwhile plan. Had the military been there, the onslaught might have been stopped, but the scattered collection of handguns and shotguns amongst the hundreds of thousands of scared and frightened people did nothing to stop what would have been the creation of whole new infected divisions. The thing that stopped that, and which gave the defenders further west a few more precious hours, was the hell that rained down from the skies.

Satellite and aerial reconnaissance had spotted large numbers of survivors gathering. Clumped together, it was obvious that they were a threat that needed to be dealt with. So the bombers were diverted, and the same tactics that had been used on some of the nation's cities would now be attempted on a thin strip of land north to south just to the west of Dartmoor National Park. The B-52 came in waves, hitting the largest concentrations of people with high-level carpet bombing. The effect was devastating, and tens of thousands of people lost their lives to the bombs, hundreds more to the tortured fighter pilots who strafed the ground with tears in their eyes and their sanity in their throats. Bullets and napalm cut like a hot knife through the human population, and by hitting just as the infected arrived, it stemmed most of the infection.

The B-52s didn't just drop conventional bombs, however. They also dropped cluster munitions which littered the ground with anti-personnel mines which lay in wait in the long grass, beckoning forth human feet to trigger their glory. And even better than human feet would be the shambling, often naked feet of the infected. In all, 20 B-52s were used in that one bomb run, and the uncounted death toll hit over fifty thousand civilians, not to mention a few thousand infected.

The collective recoiled at the slaughter, but was not deterred. Within their combined mind was the knowledge of what had occurred and why, and they continued their advance towards the human stronghold, safe in the knowledge that it would be many hours before such an assault from the skies could be done again. So the flow of infected continued west, still in small groups, still with one objective—to breach the walls, to test the defences, to find the gaps and the holes and the voids that would let them in, let them surround and insert themselves into the heart of the humans. And then they would feed, like they had never fed before. And behind them, millions followed.

21.00PM GMT, 17th September 2015, The White House, Washington, USA

THIS IS AN EMERGENCY BROADCAST FROM THE PRESIDENT OF THE UNITED STATES. PLEASE STAND BY…

"My fellow Americans, I come to you tonight with a heavy heart. Our country faces the gravest of threats, and the duty to defend against those threats lies at my door. There are some who say I should not share this knowledge with you, that I should keep you in the dark. But that is not how Democracy works. You, the people, have the right to know the truth.

We, as a nation, are still mourning the loss of our friends across the Atlantic. A nation as proud and as noble as Great Britain has been destroyed by terrorists bent on mayhem and destruction. But, my fellow Americans, today I have learnt that such a fate was also meant for us, that agents of destruction within our own country had plans to unleash the virus here, on our very streets.

So as your president, and as commander-in-chief of our armed forces, I have today taken the most drastic measures to ensure our safety. It is with a heavy heart that I spoke to the governors of each and every state of the Union to inform them that, as of now, a state of martial law exists in this country. The FBI, working with Homeland Security, have already apprehended and detained many of those involved in this plot against the Homeland, but it will take weeks for the assassins and the terrorist threats amongst us to be rooted out.

So I ask you to be patient. As true patriotic citizens of this great nation, I know you will stand with me in this darkest of hours. The threat is real, but so is our resolve. We will not be cowed; we will not go meekly into the night. This is the United States of America, and we will stand tall and fight against those who would see our country destroyed. I would advise every God-loving American to pray for our British friends, and for the souls of those criminals that perpetrated these atrocities. And to you, my brave fellow Americans, I say this. Your government is in control, and with your help, we will defeat this deadliest of threats."

Projected spread of infection based on satellite and computer predictions

Coming soon…

NECROPOLIS

BOOK 3 OF THE NECROPOLIS TRILOGY
BY SEAN DEVILLE

"And the LORD will send a plague on all the nations that fought against Jerusalem. Their people will become like walking corpses, their flesh rotting away. Their eyes will rot in their sockets, and their tongues will rot in their mouths. On that day they will be terrified, stricken by the LORD with great panic. They will fight their neighbours hand to hand." - Zachariah 14:1

CHECK OUT OTHER GREAT
ZOMBIE NOVELS

900 MILES
by S. Johnathan Davis

John is a killer, but that wasn't his day job before the Apocalypse.

In a harrowing 900 mile race against time to get to his wife just as the dead begin to rise, John, a business man trapped in New York, soon learns that the zombies are the least of his worries, as he sees first-hand the horror of what man is capable of with no rules, no consequences and death at every turn.

Teaming up with an ex-army pilot named Kyle, they escape New York only to stumble across a man who says that he has the key to a rumored underground stronghold called Avalon..... Will they find safety? Will they make it to Johns wife before it's too late?

Get ready to follow John and Kyle in this fast paced thriller that mixes zombie horror with gladiator style arena action!

WHITE FLAG OF THE DEAD
by Joseph Talluto

Millions died when the Enillo Virus swept the earth. Millions more were lost when the victims of the plague refused to stay dead, instead rising to slaughter and feed on those left alive. For survivors like John Talon and his son Jake, they are faced with a choice: Do they submit to the dead, raising the white flag of surrender? Or do they find the will to fight, to try and hang on to the last shreds or humanity?

CHECK OUT OTHER GREAT ZOMBIE NOVELS

Z BURBIA
by Jake Bible

Whispering Pines is a classic, quiet, private American subdivision on the edge of Asheville, NC, set in the pristine Blue Ridge Mountains. Which is good since the zombie apocalypse has come to Western North Carolina and really put suburban living to the test!

Surrounded by a sea of the undead, the residents of Whispering Pines have adapted their bucolic life of block parties to scavenging parties, common area groundskeeping to immediate area warfare, neighborhood beautification to neighborhood fortification.

But, even in the best of times, suburban living has its ups and downs what with nosy neighbors, a strict Home Owners' Association, and a property management company that believes the words "strict interpretation" are holy words when applied to the HOA covenants. Now with the zombie apocalypse upon them even those innocuous, daily irritations quickly become dramatic struggles for personal identity, family security, and straight up survival.

ZOMBIE RULES
by David Achord

Zach Gunderson's life sucked and then the zombie apocalypse began.

Rick, an aging Vietnam veteran, alcoholic, and prepper, convinces Zach that the apocalypse is on the horizon. The two of them take refuge at a remote farm. As the zombie plague rages, they face a terrifying fight for survival.

They soon learn however that the walking dead are not the only monsters.

 **SEVERED**PRESS

CHECK OUT OTHER GREAT ZOMBIE NOVELS

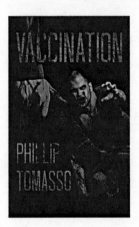

VACCINATION
by Phillip Tomasso

What if the H7N9 vaccination wasn't just a preventative measure against swine flu?

It seemed like the flu came out of nowhere and yet, in no time at all the government manufactured a vaccination. Were lab workers diligent, or could the virus itself have been man-made? Chase McKinney works as a dispatcher at 9-1-1. Taking emergency calls, it becomes immediately obvious that the entire city is infected with the walking dead. His first goal is to reach and save his two children.

Could the walls built by the U.S.A. to keep out illegal aliens, and the fact the Mexican government could not afford to vaccinate their citizens against the flu, make the southern border the only plausible destination for safety?

ZOMBIE, INC
by Chris Dougherty

"WELCOME! To Zombie, Inc. The United Five State Republic's leading manufacturer of zombie defense systems! In business since 2027, Zombie, Inc. puts YOU first. YOUR safety is our MAIN GOAL! Our many home defense options - from Ze Fence® to Ze Popper® to Ze Shed® - fit every need and every budget. Use Scan Code "TELL ME MORE!" for your FREE, in-home*, no obligation consultation! *Schedule your appointment with the confidence that you will NEVER HAVE TO LEAVE YOUR HOME! It isn't safe out there and we know it better than most! Our sales staff is FULLY TRAINED to handle any and all adversarial encounters with the living and the undead". Twenty-five years after the deadly plague, the United Five State Republic's most successful company, Zombie, Inc., is in trouble. Will a simple case of dwindling supply and lessening demand be the end of them or will Zombie, Inc. find a way, however unpalatable, to survive?

CPSIA information can be obtained
at www.ICGtesting.com
Printed in the USA
LVOW07s1630191117
556916LV00001B/71/P